SRI LANKA

Divisions and Destiny

SRI LANKA

Divisions and Destiny

Dr Mahen Tampoe

ATHENA PRESS
LONDON

SRI LANKA

Divisions and Destiny

ISBN 978 1 84748 365 2

First Published 2008 by
ATHENA PRESS
Queen's House, 2 Holly Road
Twickenham TW1 4EG
United Kingdom

Printed for Athena Press

To my parents, who gave me life and love

Acknowledgements

In the two and a half years taken to research and write this book, many people have helped me to find relevant sources, question my logic and temper my anger at those who have allowed personal ambition to blight the lives of the Sri Lankan people. I am indebted to all of them for their patience and encouragement. However, Judith, my wife, and Arun, my brother, deserve my very special thanks and gratitude. Judith for reading the proofs and making valuable suggestions, for tolerating the many lost hours when I was present in body but not in spirit, and for reviving my flagging spirits as I relived those years in which I experienced at first hand many of the situations I discuss in the book. Arun too needs special thanks for feeding me with valuable and current information, putting data in perspective, and patiently reading through two versions of the book. My friends Hugh, Roger and Jim, too, need to be thanked for reading early drafts of the book and giving valuable advice on content. Thanks are also due to the editor and the staff at Athena for guiding the manuscript through to its final appearance.

I am, however, responsible for what I have written and for the interpretations I have placed on the material of others. I have attempted to tell a human story. My judgments about those who managed Sri Lanka in the last fifty-seven years are made from the perspective of a management consultant and a student of leadership and motivation rather than a historian or political theorist. No, I have not borrowed their watches to tell them the time! Time is what the leaders of Sri Lanka have squandered and no watch can measure its passing.

Preface

This book narrates how the people of Sri Lanka have changed a dream into a nightmare. It describes how 2,500 years of civilisation has been betrayed and how the sweet scent of spices and frangipani have been changed into the stench of warfare and bigotry in a few decades.

When Ceylon attained independence in February 1948, a group of rich landowners, professionals and businessmen – drawn mainly from the Sinhalese community – took control of the island and legitimised their grip on it by holding elections that only they could win. They then systematically set about establishing the conditions that would enable them to keep a hold on power from then on. The result was a democracy in form but not in substance.

The country they inherited from the British was at peace; its coffers were full; it was a wonderful country to live in; and its future, as a respected member of the world community, was assured. But this happy state did not last long. By 1958 the ruling clique were presiding over a people who were killing each other in an orgy of hate. By 1968, the socialist policies had driven the economy into the ground.

Even the good things created problems. Improved healthcare and a disease-free environment had lengthened life expectancy, and a fertile population multiplied. The children born since independence, beneficiaries of a free education system, swelled the ranks of the educated unemployed. Their idle hands and minds were being manipulated by scheming politicians and troublemakers of all ethnic groups. The Buddhist clergy had been politicised; corruption had taken root in public life; a coup d'état was foiled and the Tamils had been alienated by laws that heightened ethnic diversity. By the end of the millennium another coup d'état had failed and the country had been ravaged by two insurrections and a civil war. Today it lives under the shadow of a shaky truce. But the ruling clique who govern it prosper. Everyone else, particularly the young, suffer.

The causes were more a part of the present than of the past. The problem has racial and religious overtones but they were and are a convenient excuse used by the conniving to channel idle hands for evil purposes. Although the Buddhist priests played – and still do play – a big part in the politics of the country, they do so as politicians rather than as representatives of their religion. The fuel that fed and feeds the fire of discontent was the deepening dissatisfaction of the Tamil and Sinhalese youth who found that they had been cut off from the little prosperity there was then and is now. They found that the brighter, better future they had been promised was only a mirage. The name change to Sri Lanka and the constitutional changes of 1972 and subsequent constitutional modifications did nothing to create an equitable society or entrench the equal right of every citizen to 'life, liberty and the pursuit of happiness'. The anti-terrorist laws imprisoned the people and gave dictatorial power to the ruling clique.

So the indiscriminate slaughter of innocents by suicide bombers and government-sponsored vigilante groups continued. The ruling clique could have staunched the flow of blood by engaging with the youth and addressing their alienation but they did not. They could also have reined in the troublemakers in their midst by withdrawing their power and subjecting them to due legal process but this they did not do. Instead they deployed more force, strengthened their terrorist laws, legitimised the lawbreakers in their midst and sought to legalise their acts of retribution. But this only served to increase the sense of injustice and alienation and to intensify the cycle of violence. Sadly, evil begat evil.

The way out of this awful cycle was to create a climate of peace rather than of oppression. It required that the brutality shown by all sides be roundly condemned and stopped. It required all those involved to accept that it was an act of extreme wickedness to take the battle to the highways and byways of the country so that the innocent were harmed. It required that the alienated youth of both races were reconnected with the wider society and that jobs were created for them so that their energy and creativity could be productively channelled. Above all, it required that a mass movement for peace, made up of all political parties and ethnic groups irrespective of their political ideologies, was initiated and allowed to blossom. It required that the consequences of continuing as now was spelt out clearly to the people by all those able to influence their minds and thoughts. The people needed to understand that the country would continue to bleed from its self-inflicted wounds unless the ceasefire became a permanent state of peace. Sadly, the leaders of all the people have failed to work collectively. Ever since the ceasefire every chance for peace has been lost in the bigotry and selfishness of small intractable groups in all communities.

The message of peace had to be accompanied by reconstruction and a rebalancing of power. The monopoly that the ruling clique had on power and prosperity had to give way to a more egalitarian society in which opportunity to prosper was considered the birthright of all the people of the island. This does not mean impoverishing the rich or emasculating the majority community, rather that their wealth should be invested in the country, creating opportunities for the poor and the fostering of an egalitarian society. It would require significant investment in creating new wealth through enterprise and productive endeavour whilst at the same time energising the many religions of peace and brotherhood that form the bedrock of the people's cultural values to defuse the animosity and hate prevalent in its society today. It would require the creation of rewarding and fulfilling jobs for the large number of unemployed youths so that the self-worth of a fruitful people would result in their counting their life dear and non-expendable. It will require that the country earn its keep so that it does not have to bend its policies to meet the demands of donors and their ideologies. In short, the country needs to be ruled for the benefit of all the people and to meet the needs of the people rather than the needs of ideologues.

The achievement of these aims requires a statesmanship of a kind not seen in the island for sixty years. Its leaders will have to create, through collective leadership and a cessation of party politics, a climate that will accelerate the regeneration of the economy and the productive involvement of the youth of all ethnic groups, before they seek to satisfy their personal aims for power and its rewards. Idealistic it may be, but it is the only choice they have today and the people have no choice other than to rise to the occasion, cast aside their crimson robes and don the white robes of peace and brotherhood.

Contents

Part Four

The New Imperialism

Part Five

Modern Sri Lanka

Part Six

Beyond Spices and Suicide Bombers

Part Seven

Discussion Papers

Introduction

The tsunami that struck the southern and eastern coastal belt of the island of Sri Lanka on Boxing Day 2004 left enormous tragedy in its wake. A million people were left homeless, an equal number lost their livelihoods and, by New Year's Day 2005, it was estimated that 28,000 people had lost their lives. The island, like the others affected by the quake – the epicentre of which was just off the coast of Sumatra – became the focus of the eyes, ears and hearts of the world and the recipient of its abundant sympathy and generosity. Few of those hearing the news and sympathising with this island people would have known that three decades of internecine strife, civil war and insurrection had created an almost equal loss of life, livelihood and property. The people of Sri Lanka, like the people living in the other countries affected by the tsunami, could do nothing to avert the natural disaster that caused them so much grief, but they could have prevented the pain and suffering of the thirty years that preceded it.

The Sinhalese and Tamil people have inhabited the island for more than 2,500 years. Although one group had subjugated the other at various times in the first 2,000 years of their history these short periods of conquest were not permanent. In the main, they were subjects of separate states and situated on different parts of the island. Their cultures, based as they were on different beliefs, were different. They spoke different languages and belonged to different racial groups. The Sinhalese civilisation on the island first lost its autonomy to the Portuguese, who arrived in 1505 in search of spices and found cinnamon in abundance. The Tamils lost their autonomy to the Portuguese in 1617. The wealth the Portuguese harvested attracted the Dutch, who displaced them, and who were in turn ousted by the British, who made the island a Crown Colony. When Sri Lanka gained its independence on 4 February 1948, the peaceful island of Ceylon was shared by the Ceylonese people made up of Sinhalese, Tamils, Muslims and Europeans. Since then, the desires of the Buddhist clergy and the personal ambitions of politicians have combined to force through policies that have created the conditions for racial disharmony and economic decline.

The unintended consequence of appeasing the Buddhist nationalists was the creation of injustices elsewhere and especially among the Tamil and Sinhalese youth. It is not easy to decide whether the racial discrimination the Tamils were subject to, or the economic and social isolation the rural Sinhalese youth were subject to, was the greater evil. What is clear though is that the ballot box did not help either group to gain redress for their grievances because the majority vote lay in the hands of their elders who, more often than not, voted in accordance with the wishes of the clergy in their midst. Frustrated, dispirited and disenfranchised, the youth of the country chose violence. At a crucial time in its history, the blood of those the country needed most – the young – was needlessly staining its earth, and the lives it needed to cherish most – those of their children – were being destroyed by the violence around them.

It is expedient to argue, like some, that if the Tamil and Sinhalese youth of Sri Lanka were gainfully employed in careers of their choosing rather than idling away their days, they would not have diverted their energies into insurgencies and pressure groups. But that is too glib an answer. An analysis of the country's recent history shows that the troubles of the island were the result of personal ambition and short-sighted and incompetent leadership, and that unless this changed nothing else would. In the early days it seemed as if succeeding governments ruled for the benefit of the Westernised elite (Sinhalese, Tamil, Muslim and Burgher) in Colombo because the members of this elite were their bedfellows.

After 1956 it seemed that succeeding governments ruled the country for the benefit of the Buddhist nationalists. The democratic process had elevated the Buddhist nationalists and a small group of racically minded clergy to kingmakers as they were able to help politicians win elections and stay in power. But the succeeding governments failed to do their duty to all the people. So the displeasure of the disadvantaged went from dissent in 1956 to discontent and eventually to discord. The Sinhalese youth formed the JVP (a party based on Marxist ideology) to fight their cause, and the Tamil Tigers emerged as champions to win parity for the Tamils. The Buddhist clergy continued as a pressure group and exercised so strong a hold on government policy that the CIA's *The World Factbook* acknowledges that the Buddhist clergy, like the Tamil Tigers, is an intense pressure group.

Whilst all this was going on, world events and poor economic management combined to adversely affect the country's economy. In the early 1960s, with less and less financial resources to go round, politicians sought scapegoats, and found them in the minority communities in Sri Lanka. The disaffected Sinhalese, helped by racist elements in their midst, attributed their problems to the Tamils and Muslims and encouraged race riots. In addition a succession of governments passed laws that blatantly discriminated against the Tamil-speaking community and justified their actions by claiming that it was the will of the majority in a democracy. The Tamils found that democracy did not work for them in a Sinhalese-dominated political system. Although the Tamils complied with the new laws they did not acquiesce. The political solutions that were on offer in the very earliest days were abandoned by both parties to the conflict. So, although politics was invented by humanity as a framework for dialogue and the peaceful resolution of disputes, and democracy became its shining star, the multi-ethnic democracy in Sri Lanka never shone.

In the gloom, resentment festered into dislike. Hatred spilled over into resistance, and the cycle of animosity that has bedevilled the island ever since was triggered with a ferocity and competence that the ruling clique did not anticipate.

The war that invariably followed created ghettoes of internally displaced and dispossessed people, and this in turn provided new breeding grounds for future violence. Each cycle of displacement and dispossession increased the desperation of the dispossessed who, when all else failed, resorted to force. And when they could not match the weapons of war ranged against them, like all partisan and guerrilla groups before them, they used the weapons and methods at their disposal; and when conventional means failed they used their bodies to disarm and destroy. Thus did suicide bombers become part of the tactics of war. In their desperation these 'freedom fighters' did not differentiate between those who created the conditions of their misery and those whose silent voices and votes kept their oppressors in power. To them, everyone who was not working with them to achieve equality of status in their homeland was an enemy and, as an enemy, was required to pay the price of their complicity. One of its early high-profile victims was Rajiv Gandhi.

By 2001 all sides in the conflict had found that the heartfelt grievances of a marginalised people could not be contained or redressed by force alone. Something else was needed. So, once again, a war-weary people resorted to politics. The hope for peace now rests with the Norwegian government that is acting as facilitator. However, a small and determined group are still pursuing – and being allowed to pursue – their bankrupting policies.

The religion and culture that created porcelain from rough clay has failed its children at this most crucial time of its rebirth as an independent state. In a world that, despite its troubles, is a place of promise and achievement, an island people with a long and illustrious heritage were allowing chauvinism to lead them down the dark abyss of destitution and despair. Peace – that fragile, beautiful, delicate and exquisite transformer of human clay into the humanity of a civilised people – has eluded the people of Sri Lanka for five decades.

The international community noted what was happening on the island. To them it was a fight between two reasonably well-matched opponents, and even though they were committing unmentionable atrocities to each other they were left alone, as no strategic interests were at stake. But the trouble with trouble is that in an interconnected world it spreads and infects the people of other nations too. So, although the international community chose not to intervene in the problems on this, to them, remote and faraway island, it could not prevent its problems from spilling over into their territories. Whilst the Sinhalese insurrection was contained within the island purely because they lacked the organising ability to draw on a wider populace, the conflict with the Tamil Tigers, which began around 1983, spread across the globe. It resulted in about 65,000 deaths and the displacement of nearly another one million people. The stream of refugees and asylum seekers transferred the problems of this remote island to large parts of the world. For many reasons, the people seeking refuge became a problem to their foster-countries. They placed a strain on diplomatic relations, as the host country was seen by one or both groups to be taking sides, and consequently ran the risk of being the target of hate. By being accorded refugee status, some brought with them the tactics of guerrilla fighting and terrorism – including suicide bombing – and legitimised them as acceptable tools of war. Finally, to gather funds to keep their cause alive, they undertook criminal activities and increased criminality in their host countries. The early recognition and correction of legitimate dissent might have saved years of bloodshed and saved the world a lot of grief.

The tsunami that hit the island on the 26 December 2004 has posed new challenges and opportunities. Despite its huge cost in life and property it may prove an emotional benefit if the world's generosity is shared fairly among all of the people of the island. Here at last is an opportunity for the Sinhalese majority to show that the Tamils are their kinsfolk. It offers them the chance to bury the past and to initiate a new era of shared grief and recovery that may eventually lead to mutual prosperity. If, instead, their tribal instincts were to dominate, and help be diverted first to the Sinhalese Buddhist areas of the country, and the crumbs be distributed to the Tamils in the east coast, the troubles will flare up again. Similarly the government would do well to ensure that the carpetbaggers who tend to follow are prevented from enriching themselves at the expense of the destitute and the starving. In this tragedy the government has been given the opportunity of a lifetime, provided it has the leadership skills to take it. The world will judge the Sri Lankan people by their own words and the actions of their officials. If the government fails, its partisan behaviour may unleash future atrocities and bring in a new period of bloodshed. For the sake of continuing with the current peace process and ensuring a lasting peace, the Norwegian government and other donor nations and international institutions not only need to ensure that their generosity is properly used, but that there is sufficient transparency in the way their gifts are applied to silence those who may wish to make political capital out of this disaster.

But there are many lessons that can be learnt from the sorry tale of this island people, and this book sets out to chart the course of the history of the island in an attempt to do just that. The last sixty years of misrule has resulted in the creation of a climate of distrust and hate. During this time the leaders of the country have:

- emphasised racial differences to gain political advantage;
- devalued the leaders of the minority groups and thereby played into the hands of the extremists, who could legitimately claim that the elected leaders were powerless to help the people they represented;
- ignored the legitimate concerns of the majority group who felt that in the early years of independence they were unfairly treated. As a result they were susceptible to the nationalist extremists in their midst who claimed that the minorities were benefiting most in the new country;
- politicised the religious leaders, compromised them and devalued their legitimacy as peacekeepers;

- ignored the legitimate needs of the young and impressionable and alienated them, thus making them willing recruits of racists and fundamentalists;
- failed to grow the economy so that the rising tide of people could be gainfully employed and enriched.

The failure of the leaders spilled over into the lives of the people. The present behaviour of the Sri Lankan people is not supported by their history. The culture of the Sinhalese, Tamils and Muslims has been moulded by centuries, sometimes millennia, of religious beliefs and customs that made it possible for them to coexist on the island. So what has changed?

To understand the reasons behind these problems, it is necessary to acknowledge and understand the island's past. Not to do so is akin to studying the leaves of a tree and ignoring its branches, trunk, roots and the ground it stands on. I have attempted to fill this wider canvas. I hope it shows that when, as in Sri Lanka, democracy is used to settle old scores, to establish tribal pre-eminence and to milk the system for personal advantage, it fails. I hope it shows that when the rightful needs of a legitimate minority are ignored, the majority suffer the ravages of the whirlwind. I hope it shows the majority communities in many new democratised states that democracy is not a zero-sum game in which the 'winners take all' or do as they please. Rather it is my hope that they will realise that to gain a lot they have to give a little, and that it is only then that democracy can work its magic and deliver a peaceful and prosperous nation in which all citizens feel that they have the opportunity to shine and contribute.

The book will show that, sadly, the majority community in Sri Lanka have failed to grasp this fundamental truth. In their greed for power they have sown the seeds of discontent and watched it blossom into dissent and mature into discord. In their hands, democracy has become a weapon of mass destruction, proving that when such a mature tool is placed in the hands of those lacking the maturity to use it, it can become a lethal weapon. In Sri Lanka, its misuse resulted in the creation of two nations out of one people, and inadvertently planted the seeds that made the victors of 1948 the vanquished of today. Those foreign governments and international institutions that advocate democracy owe a duty to the world to monitor and steer its application in newly formed democratic countries.

In the final analysis, the responsibility to create a peaceful and prosperous home rests with the people of the island. The rest of the world can help only if the island people have the will to change and call each other neighbour and friend. They need to realise that it is only by coming together to combine their skills and resources and willingly sharing the island they call home that all the ethnic groups who live on it can build a new future on the ashes of its lost hopes.

The book offers no suggestions on what should be done with the intense pressure groups such as the Tamil Tigers or the Buddhist clergy, because I believe that, like elsewhere, when the causes of disaffection are removed the engines of belligerence will fall into disuse and some 'warriors' will become statesmen. The book therefore proposes changes to the way the country is governed. It redefines the role of the Buddhist clergy and argues for a proactive populace, one that will judge their politicians on how they deliver peace, prosperity, social cohesion, health, safety, education and help for the disadvantaged and disabled.

This book is divided into seven parts, and a bibliography. Each part begins with a summary so that readers can get an overview of the part before they delve into the detail. Part One summarises the period of the island's history from 500 BC to AD 1505 when the major external influence on it was from the Indian subcontinent. Part Two covers the European period from 15 November 1505 to 1833. This shows the tendency of the kings and courtiers to play one against the other using the 'invaders' as allies. Part Three covers the period of British occupation and ends with the independence of 4 February 1948. Part Four charts the growth of a new ruling clique and attempts to show how race was used by them to hold on to power. Part Five assesses the consequences of post-colonial governance, and shows how the policies of the major political parties impacted on a range of political and economic issues and created the conditions for the current situation on the island. Part Six discusses the medicine it should, but may be unwilling to, take, because such medicine demands a radical shift in mindset – from one that is divisive to one that is collaborative on matters that are essential for the country's well-being. Part seven comprises two discussion papers. Discussion paper one documents the questions that arose during my writing of the book as regards the governance of a unitary multi-ethnic democratic state, particularly one that has a majority racial group to whom the democratic process delivers all the power. Discussion paper two asks 'Terrorism and Suicide Bombing – where do they come from?' In other words, are they a creation of bad governance or are terrorists just wicked people finding any excuse to pick a fight? I have tried to provide a mix of views so that the readers can think about the question and draw their own conclusions. The book also has an annotated bibliography, which, I hope, will help readers who wish to delve deeper.

A book that deals with current affairs is never finished. Events continue to change the nature and shape of the world day by day. For example, in mid-November 2005 Mahinda Rajapaksa was elected president. Whether he will control events or whether events will control him and make his presidency as sterile as those of his predecessors is the question on everyone's lips.

Part One

From Birth to Spice Island

Summary

Part One provides an overview of the period from 500 BC to AD 1505, when the Sinhalese kings ruled part of the island. It is my hope that time-travelling through over 1,500 years of history will help the reader gain a flavour of the way the people of the island lived prior to the arrival of the Europeans. The main points of interest are:

- The establishment and continuous use of Anuradhapura as a substantial religious, political and commercial capital of the Sinhalese people for close on 1,500 years until its decline from about AD 1000;
- the conversion of Devanampiya Tissa (247–207 BC) to buddhism and its establishment as the guiding principle and the basis of the values and culture of the Sinhalese kings and people from around 300 BC;
- the continuous threat to the Sinhalese kings and their kingdoms from marauding and conquering Southern Indian kings who invaded the island from time to time and stayed until they were thrown out;
- the six determined and militarily skilled Sinhalese kings, who, through their military strategy and defence capability, repelled the Dravidian invaders from Southern India;
- the engineering and construction skills of the Sinhalese who created large cities with palaces, pleasure gardens, Buddhist monasteries, statues, *dagobas*,[1] road systems, reservoirs and irrigation systems whose grandeur, even as ruins, qualify them to be classified as world heritage sites.
- The decline in the fortunes of the Sinhalese as is evidenced by the absence of substantial infrastructure and building work by Sinhalese kings until the construction of the Temple of the Tooth and the great lake in Kandy during the European occupation of the coastal belt;
- the fact that throughout the two thousand years preceding the European entry into the country, Sinhalese and Tamil societies and economies remained both feudal and agricultural;
- the existence of a Tamil community and a Tamil kingdom in the Jaffna peninsula that was separated by an area of no-man's land called the Vanni, which was occupied by a group called the Vanniyars;
- the division of the Sinhalese kingdom into principalities that were ruled

[1] Bell-shaped monuments that can be found in the ancient cities and elsewhere in Sri Lanka which the Buddhists use as shrines or reliquaries.

by different kings, although among the Sinhalese there was the concept of a 'greater' king who controlled the 'largest' territory;

- the islanders' willingness to allow Arab, Chinese and Indian merchants to act as middlemen carrying the natural produce of the island such as spices, gems, elephants, pearls and other commodities to European markets, rather than developing a maritime trading capability of their own.

Chapter 1

From Serendipity to Discord

The Romans called it 'Taprobane' and the Greeks called its inhabitants 'Palaeogoni'. The Arab traders called it 'Serendib'. The Portuguese who met the 'Singhalao' called it 'Ceilao'. The Dutch corrupted Ceilao to Ceylan and the British to Ceylon. But it was always known as 'Lanka' to the Sinhalese and 'Ilangai' or 'Eelam' to the Tamils. Until recently the modern world knew it as Ceylon. The island is still famous for Ceylon tea and in pre-British times it was famous for its spices, gems and elephants.

Sri Lanka lies off the tip of South India. It is separated from Tamil Nadu in India by twenty-two miles of warm tropical water that has an average annual sea temperature of 27° C. Its overall area of 25,325 square miles makes it roughly the same size as Ireland. You can leave its beautiful sandy beeches and its coral reefs and find yourself driving up country through the most stunning scenery until you reach Nuwara Eliya. There, at 6,000 feet above sea level you can enjoy a climate that averages a temperature of 16° C for most of the year. Today Sri Lanka is home to roughly 20 million people of whom 74 per cent are Sinhalese, 13 per cent are Sri Lankan Tamils, 7 per cent are Muslims, 5.5 per cent are hill country Tamils (whose ancestors were brought over from South India by the British to work on the tea plantations), and about 0.5 per cent fall into the category of 'others'. 69 per cent are Buddhists, 15.5 per cent are Hindus, 7.5 per cent are Muslims, 7 per cent are Christians, and 1 per cent belong to other faiths.

The island's history stretches back over 2,500 years. Its earliest inhabitants may well have been Nagas (hence the reference to the Nagadipa in the north of Lanka) or Yakkhas or hunter-gatherers. Over time they were displaced or absorbed by Aryan and Dravidian peoples from India. The Aryans, the forebears of the Sinhalese, established a Sinhalese kingdom in Anuradhapura in the north central region of the country. The Dravidians who came from South India were the forebears of the Tamils. They established their kingdom in the north east of the island. Both groups traded with the Indians, Chinese, Arab and Mediterranean peoples who came to their shores to buy gems, pearls, elephants and spices.

The earliest reference to the island is in the *Ramayana*, a Hindu epic committed to writing during a period ranging from about 100 BC to AD 100 but probably memorised and retold to countless generations for many centuries before then. It says that Ravana, the 'demon' king of Lanka, abducted Sita, the wife of Rama, and brought her to the island and held her captive in a beautiful city considered to be Sitawaka. The epic relates that her escape from captivity was achieved with the help of 'tree-men' whose leader was Hanuman, the monkey-god. Hanuman, it is claimed, built a bridge of stones that floated on water so that his army could cross over to Lanka. The invading army succeeded and Sita was returned to her husband Rama and, as is customary in these stories, they both lived happily ever after.

The detail in the story shows that the writer of the *Ramayana* must have had personal knowledge of the island, or known about it from others who had crossed the twenty-two miles of sea that divided it from India. (This crossing is also called 'Adam's Bridge' by Western commentators, implying that in prehistoric times the island was joined to India by a causeway.)

The Sinhalese civilisation on the island was known to the Mediterranean world. Megasthenes, the Greek Ambassador to the court of Chandragupta (321 BC–297 BC) knew it as the island of the people he called '*Palaeogoni*'. Pliny the Elder records that during the reign of Claudius (AD 41–54) a freedman of Annius Plocanus had been driven by the winds to the island and was the guest of the king for six months. Ptolemy (c. 100–c. 170) called the island '*Taprobane*' and included it in his map of the world. Some of the place names and their location on his map of Lanka are more or less the same as they are now, suggesting that his sources had an intimate knowledge of the island. The Chinese scholar Fa-Hsien (died c. 414) spent two years in Ceylon between 404 and 414. A Chinese Buddhist monk, he devoted his time on the island to studying Buddhist sutras written in Sanskrit before taking them back to China. In his book, *Spice,* Turner suggests that Byzantine traders reached as far as Sri Lanka. To illustrate and prove this point he recounts an incident, which is well worth repeating here.

> Cosmas Indicopleustes, a Greek-Egyptian monk who travelled to India sometime around 550, tells the tale of a Byzantine merchant who indulged in a little one-upmanship with a Persian trader at the court of a Ceylonese king, not long before Cosmas' own day. Thanks to the superior quality of his coinage, the Byzantine was able to convince the Ceylonese that he was the emissary of a king far greater than his Persian rival's.[2]

Money talked, even in those days. Trade was the prime attraction for those who visited the island. The position of the island made it a convenient stopping place for Arab, Indian and Chinese traders, who called regularly to replenish their cargoes of spices, gems, pearls and elephants which they carried to Europe, the Middle East and the Far East. Over the years they cemented their trading links by living among the people and establishing strong diplomatic and commercial relationships with its kings and nobles. Differences in language, religion, customs, race or ethnicity were subsumed by the commer-

[2] Jack Turner, *Spice: The History of a Temptation*, London, HarperCollins, 2004.

cial advantages that one group provided the other. Greek traders came during the second and early third centuries and again during the reign of the Emperor Constantine (AD 323–377). The Persians, specifically members of the Nestorian Sect, traded with the islanders from about the early Christian era up to the seventh century. Arab traders, too, called to buy gems, precious stones and spices to sell in Europe.

The Buddhist chronicles and archaeological findings of this rich period in the history of the island show that the Sinhalese kingdoms had achieved much and been on a par with the Europeans up to the time the Portuguese arrived. For example, Paul Wheatley is quoted in Renfrew and Bhan as pointing out that the cities of Sri Lanka, like those of some other countries, were designed with care and with an understanding of the world and its position in the wider universe.

> ...many great cities from China to Cambodia and from Sri Lanka to the Maya Lowlands and Peru are laid out on cosmological principles, allowing the ruler to ensure harmony between his subjects and the prevailing sacred and supernatural forces.[3]

Modern European and Sri Lankan historians have used the chronicles written by Buddhist monks, such as the *Mahavamsa* and the *Culavamsa*, and studied the ruined cities of Sri Lanka and the records of the Portuguese, Dutch, British and Indians to provide a more balanced view of the Sinhalese. Fernandez-Armesto, in his book *Civilizations*, points out that the Buddhist chronicles were biased towards the Sinhalese Buddhist kings and people. In his view:

> The Mahavamsa, chronicles of the long-lived 'Lion Kingdom' of Sri Lanka, are deceptive documents: in surviving versions, they were written down in the sixth century AD in a Buddhist environment, which dictated tendentious agendas: the sacralization of the Sinhala, the hallowing of their ground, the justification of their conquest ... It is hard to believe that they [the chroniclers] can be well informed about the period at which they begin, a thousand years before their narrative opens. Yet they inaugurate the history of the kingdom with a credible event: the colonization of this heavily forested tropical island by seafarers from the Gulf of Cambay in the sixth century.[4]

Despite the elaborations, the overwhelming impression is of an able people who had perfected many arts and sciences to ensure a comfortable life for themselves.

The Tamils also had a similarly developed economy and society based in the Jaffna peninsula; one that they had carried over with the highly developed

---

[3] Renfrew and Bahn, *Archaeology*, Thames & Hudson, 2001.

[4] Felipe Fernandez-Armesto, *Civilizations*, Macmillan, 2000, p.398.

Dravidian culture from southern India. Dravidian traders had trading posts in the north-eastern part of the island. It is likely that these trading posts predated the arrival of the Aryan ancestors of the Sinhalese and the likelihood is that it is from these trading settlements that the permanent Tamil presence on the island came about. The trading communities established a Tamil state on the north-eastern shores of the island and, having got a foothold, fought to keep it ever since. Ibn Batuta, an Arab traveller who visited the island in 1344 records that the north of the island, including Puttalam, was ruled by the king of Jaffna, a Tamil. Sadly the Sinhalese chronicles, when they mention the Tamils, present them as a people who challenged Sinhalese sovereignty over the island and endangered Buddhism. This is not wholly true. What is more accurate is that South Indian kings invaded and, sometimes, conquered territory and ruled the Sinhalese until they were ejected. And so for nearly two thousand years the island played host to both Tamil and Sinhalese states.

Except for very short periods in its history, the people of the island have not been subject to a single ruler. And, although they lived amicably, they had not shared responsibility for being 'their brother's keeper'. The bringing together of the different ethnic groups under a collective title called 'Ceylonese' and their governance by a single state was the work of the British. So, although the British, Portuguese and Dutch called the collection of Sinhalese, Tamils and Muslims on the island 'Ceylonese', they were not referring to a people who had mentally accepted the single identity conferred on them. These people continued to see themselves as a grouping of tribes, castes and creeds and reverted to their tribal groups after independence. This tendency to retain ethnic identity is referred to by Bernard Lewis in his book about the people and issues of the Middle East, *From Babel to Dragomans*. He points out that there, too, the concept of a single people and nationhood is fragile, if non-existent. He says:

> There is the imported, still not fully assimilated European notion of country and nation, and the idea of popular government deriving its legitimacy from the people over whom it rules and operating through some kind of legislative assembly elected by and responsible to the people. Against these, there is a very different tradition of identity defined not by country or nation, which are regarded as minor or insignificant, but by community, by religious belief and practice. In this tradition the individual owes his primary loyalty to the community and to the polity that is based on it.[5]

Lewis's point is that the collectivisation of various ethnic groups living in eastern lands as 'Asians' is a convenient shorthand devised by the European colonial powers to describe the brown and yellow skinned races they met on

[5] Bernard Lewis, *From Babel to Dragomans: Interpreting the Middle East*, London, Weidenfeld and Nicholson, 2004.

their conquests. The reality is so different. The only time in their history that the Sinhalese and the Tamils shared common cause was when an English-educated cabal collectively campaigned to recover the island from British rule. And the only time the different racial groups on the island were known as Ceylonese was during European occupation, which began when the Portuguese established trading posts in Sri Lanka, and went on to conquer the coastal regions. The Dutch took over from the Portuguese and the British from them. The British subjugated the peoples of the whole island and established more permanent links between the island and Europe.

The Sri Lankan people regained control of the island when the British handed it back to them on 4 February 1948. Creating a new nation out of this ethnic and cultural jumble was the challenge that faced the Western-oriented elist group on the island who became its new lords and masters (ruling clique). This was probably the first time in over two millennia that the islanders were able to live without threats from foreign powers. The island was theirs to deal with as they wished. Success or failure was in their hands. Unfortunately, the post-colonial history of the island shows that it is stained by the blood of inter- and intra-ethnic conflict. Peace has deserted it. Its present record is one of a meaningless power struggle, political expediency, racial disharmony and economic decline.

The European occupations did bring some benefits to the country. In 1948, the people inherited a thriving economy and an up-to-date infrastructure from the British. Some of the islanders had acquired European languages, religions, habits and customs, whilst the rest remained more or less true to the old traditions of their ethnic groups. This divide between the Western-educated elite of all races and the others on the island was much greater than the ethnic divide between the Sinhalese and the Tamils because it was only this small segment of the people – a ruling clique – who were able to compete in the post-Second World War years that followed. This caused resentment. The backlash took the form of Buddhist nationalism and anti-capitalism.

Consequently, the country the people inherited was systematically dismantled by succeeding governments, until by the late 1960s the economy was in tatters and the people had reverted to their ethnic roots. The people scrambled to grab what little spoils there were and sought advantage in their race rather than their ability. To this was added the demand by the Buddhist clergy for a pre-eminent place for Buddhism and the Sinhalese language. When vote-seeking politicians responded to their call, the ethnic differences that had lain dormant throughout the European period became an issue that the ruling clique used to justify their claim to a disproportionate share of a dwindling pot. Tamil anger, which had been simmering since 1956, erupted into full-scale war in 1983.

The conflict between the militant Tamils (LTTE) and the government has resulted in the island gaining notoriety for its suicide bombers, who, willingly or through peer pressure, sacrifice their lives and those of innocent bystanders to achieve political ends. In a interview with Tim Sebastian of the BBC in October 2001, President Chandrika Kumaratunga said that at that time:

> The largest number of suicide bombings in the world have been done by the Tamil Tigers, one third of the total number of the suicide bombings the world has known has been carried out by the Tamil Tigers.[6]

She was emphasising the intensity of the LTTE (Liberation Tigers of Tamil Eelam) campaign and the lengths people will go to gain fairer treatment in their homeland. What she failed to say was that the problems stem from the time her father, Mr S W R D Bandaranaike, promised exceptional treatment to the majority Sinhalese community in the island if they elected him prime minister. Never in the island's history has so much potential been squandered by its political elite in their squabble for votes.

The island bears the scars of the disunity that its founding politicians deliberately fuelled. Winning back those lost years is the challenge facing its present leaders. In recent years the representatives of the Sinhalese youth have been bought out by the establishment, and the Tamils are negotiating a peace treaty with the help of the Norwegians. Once peace between the Sinhalese and the Tamils is established will they both go after the Muslims? The jury is still out on this. History shows that trouble travels and lingers. One hopes that the government and people of Sri Lanka will have the good sense to pre-empt any further communal tensions and arrive at a formula for peaceful coexistence. Then and only then will they be able to harvest nature's rich bounty.

[6] *Hardtalk* interview: Tim Sebastian with the President Chandrika B Kumaratunga, BBC, 31 October 2001.

Chapter 2

Kings and Commoners

The feudal societies of pre-European Sri Lanka revolved around their kings. This was true for Tamils and Sinhalese. Broadly speaking, the hierarchy of governance divided into four main groups: the king and his court; a professional and commercial group in the city; the ruling clique at village level; and the villagers or peasant communities. The Buddhist and Hindu priests were not part of the chain of governance but they wielded significant influence over the whole population because their respective religions had permeated throughout their societies. Social stratification was based on caste, as was employment and occupation. People were categorised by the type of work they did, the families they belonged to and, to some extent, by their incomes. Social migration was almost unheard of, and jobs did not migrate between castes i.e. the son of a blacksmith did not aspire to be a court physician. But members of all castes could, if they were found worthy, become Buddhist monks. Buddhism, in theory, abhorred and discouraged the caste system, but the caste-based society of the pre-Buddhist Sinhalese community was absorbed by the emergent Buddhist culture. The living conditions of the people reflected their caste as well as their income, but income alone did not buy entry into a higher caste.

According to the chronicles, the first Sinhalese king, Vijaya, was a prince from an Indian state who arrived on the island in about 500 BC. The legend states that he and his closest friends were exiled by his father as punishment for their loose and lascivious lifestyle. Set adrift, they were carried by the tides and winds to Lanka. Here they met the original island dwellers, a race of dark-skinned people, they called *yakkhas* or demons. Kuveni, their queen, took a shine to the prince. She and the women in her community fed their appetites until they were bored with them and began to kill them by using, it is claimed, witchcraft. The prince and his group used their superior iron weapons to annihilate the community. Kuveni escaped with her two children but was slain by her kinsfolk. Kuveni's people are today represented by the few Veddahs left on the island. They retain their separate identity: a 'hidden' people, in that, in Sri Lanka, they fall outside the political system. Having made the island 'safe' from devils and witches, Vijaya and his followers decided to settle and sent a mission to India to invite women of 'noble' birth with whom they could create a new people who became the Sinhalese of today.

The DNA of this playboy prince and his companions are now part of the genetic structure of the Sinhalese people. These new settlers shared the island with the Dravidian people who lived to the north of them in their separate state. Fernandez-Armesto points out that "The Sinhalese – 'lion people' as they called themselves – spoke an Indo-European language and were:

> ...constructors on a stupendous scale and modifiers of the environment more resolute and startlingly imaginative than their counterparts in the Ganges, though their sages were less inventive and produced nothing to rival the logic, creative literature, mathematics and speculative science written down along the Ganges in the mid-fifth millennium BC.

The glory days of the Sinhalese kings were between about 247 BC – the time that Buddhism became the cornerstone of their social and value system – until a little after the end of the reign of Parakrama Bahu the Great in 1186. There were times during this period when internal war for territorial supremacy among the island princes and invasion from the Indian mainland by the Cholas, Pandyans and Keralans, disturbed the peace of the people. Despite these invasions by the kings of the three South Indian kingdoms the relationship between them and the Sinhalese kings tended towards mutual support as they acted also as allies when each was under threat from the other and cemented temporary alliances by marrying into each other's families.

These short interludes of South Indian occupation were followed by periods of unity and building, although it is not easy to discover where the skills and expertise for these came from. Fernandez-Armesto believes that they had no contact with the Harappan civilisation and that their ability to harness and use water to develop a thriving agricultural economy did not come from there. It is also unlikely that these Aryan settlers drew on Greek learning. It is more likely that they created their own civilisation by using the knowledge they gleaned from north and South India from their vision, the technology available to them and their good judgement and hard work. In time their settlement grew into a sovereign state and took its place in the community of nations in the Indian Ocean.

Their capital, Anuradhapura, was a thriving city, and large for the times. It was built using the science of the times, especially astronomy, engineering, metallurgy, pottery, building construction, irrigation and agriculture. Astrologers used their knowledge of the cosmos not only to produce horoscopes and to offer predictions of future events, (and identify auspicious days for carrying out a range of activities), but also to lay out their cities to ensure harmony between the people and the prevailing sacred and supernatural forces. The city and its surroundings were dotted with vast buildings that had stone foundations, walls of brick and wood and complex roofs. Their commitment to Buddhism was evident in the vast numbers of *dagobas* and religious buildings, the ruins of which still stand as a monument to their devotion to the teachings of the Buddha and their respect for the sangha. The kings also endowed the temples with their own sources of untaxed revenues. It is noteworthy that, except for Sigiriya and a few others, there are far fewer ruins of palaces than temples and buildings devoted to Buddhism to mark the period. A complex social structure developed that enabled the islanders to harness nature for their sustenance, especially the life-giving energy of water and the sun. Irrigation and agriculture were well developed. Water was collected in large man-made lakes that were provided with dams and sluice gates, and canals with scientifically graded slopes, to carry the water to the towns, villages and fields. Farmers produced enough food to meet their own needs and, for a short time it is claimed, to export rice to southern India. The principality governed by the king and his court was well administered. Revenues were raised by taxes in the form of a percentage of the produce of the villagers. Art – especially stone sculptures of the reclining and standing Buddha in Anuradhapura and Aukana, the stone statue of the sage in Polonnaruwa and the frescoes in Sigiriya – was of the finest. And they had a complex and sophisticated language and literature derived from their Aryan roots.

It is clear that the military capability of the kings of Lanka was similar to that in other countries at that time but seems far from adequate for a country that was at constant risk of invasion. The armies of the Sinhalese kings often had Tamil warriors and it would seem that they custom-built armies to help them repel invaders.

When challenged and overwhelmed, those kings who survived the attack took refuge by moving out of their capitals. When this happened, the people, presumably, were left to the mercy of the invaders. Charity demands that we treat these defensive tactics of the Sinhalese kings as the means to protect their kingdoms and not themselves. We must assume that, if they wished, it enabled them to regroup and relaunch an offensive response. The cynic may argue that they chose flight because they lacked the military capability and the moral courage to repel invaders. What is certain is that invasions occurred with some frequency.

Of the 171 Sinhalese kings, six were exceptional. These six created the military capability necessary to recapture the island from invading Indian kings and used their leadership skills and their personal qualities to unite the people so that, collectively, they could challenge and eject occupying forces. These were Duttugamani (161–137 BC) whose request to his father to allow him to expel the Tamils was refused, and who had to wait until his father's death to fulfil his ambition; Gajabahu (AD 113–135); Dhatusena (AD 463–479) who led his people from exile to reclaim their lands; Vijaya Bahu I (AD 1056–1111); Parakrama Bahu the Great (AD 1153–1186); and Parakrama Bahu VI (1412–1467). The military skills of Parakrama Bahu VI are acknowledged by Jeremy Black, in his book, *War and the World Military Power and the Fate of Continents 1450–2000*, who described the Kotte kingdom under Parakrama Bahu VI as one of a number of '...dynamic powers of note in the late fifteenth century'.

As the story of Dhatusena[7] illustrates, the evidence is that the successors of these kings did not build on what they inherited, and consequently the kingdoms fragmented, along with any sense of nationhood. Sometimes the ambition of a son or brother resulted in the premature death of a king or noble.

The capitals of these kingdoms, such as Kotte or Jaffna, would have been populated by people who were part of the circle of the court and professional and skilled workers. The quality of city life was vastly superior to that in the villages. The houses, the various public buildings and the palace and its surrounds were of brick, and the temples were richly adorned with golden images and various forms of gold ornamentation. The king and the aristocracy could relax and enjoy themselves in the beautiful parks with their large ponds and groves. The people of the court were dressed in rich clothes and wore jewellery and gold ornaments in keeping with their relative status. Their clothes said much about them. It helped differentiate them not only by wealth but also by status and caste. The lords and ladies of the court lived pampered lives. A large retinue of well-dressed and well-fed servants provided for their every need, even to the extent of walking behind them with parasols to shield them from the sun and rain. Transport in the capital would have been provided by bullock drawn carriages, palanquins and runabouts. Like their European counterparts. The lords and ladies were landowners and lived well on the produce from their lands. They also exercised considerable power over the villagers living in their lands and the territories over which they held sway.

The ruling classes of both Sinhalese and Tamil communities depended on people who could provide them with professional and commercial services. These 'professionals' learnt the different languages, commercial and legal conventions and processes of their trading partners such as the Arab, Chinese and Indian traders. They made themselves indispensable as intermediaries who were essential for the export of raw materials, animals and food. This group of intermediaries between the owners of the produce and the merchants formed an essential part of city life and grew rich by the sale of their knowledge and skill.

There is very little evidence that there was an industrious entrepreneurial middle class, like the one in Europe, which acted as the engine of innovation and development. And there is little evidence of a manufacturing or cottage industry in the island that manufactured goods for export. This contrasted with their Indian and Chinese counterparts, who wove and exported exquisite silk and cotton cloth, garments, carpets, tapestries and similar goods that were superior to anything made in Europe at that time.

The increasing demands of a growing population would have reduced the per capita income from agrisculture as the law of diminishing returns would have taken its toll on the productivity of the land. However, the export of

[7] See p.38, 'The Story of Sigiriya'.

cinnamon, a crop that grew wild, and other raw produce would have compensated for the diminishing returns from agriculture; but its profits had to be shared with the intermediaries. Without a class of people who could create new wealth the economy would have languished. And, without a significant contribution from manufactured goods the country would not have been able to support large-scale construction and infrastructure projects like those the earlier kings had built.

Village communities had their own microcultures, of the kind so excellently described by Leonard Woolf in *Village in the Jungle*. The landowners, whose fields the peasants cultivated and paid for with a levy on the produce, headed the caste list of local dignitaries. Other important personages included the village headman, the teacher, the local medicine man or woman, and the local witch or warlock. The Buddhist monks who served in the local temple wielded influence but they were not part of the governing elite of the village. The village was generally self-sufficient and the villagers who were not farmers provided a variety of services that an agricultural economy needed. The poor villagers lived in their one-roomed mud huts with roofs of woven coconut leaves and compacted mud floors. The richer villagers, like their city counterparts, had brick houses with tiled roofs and many rooms, and employed many servants to cater to their needs. It was a steeply hierarchical society in which relationships were bound by strong rules of caste-based social etiquette.

Villagers in Sri Lanka, because they were the source of the income of the Sinhalese and Tamil kings, were, like the villages in Europe at that time, the heart of their kingdoms. The poor seem to be always financing the rich, which probably explains why there are more of them and why they have to resort to revolt – as in France, China, Russia and Sri Lanka – to occasionally even out the disparities of money and power. A modern extension of this theme was expressed by an astute economist who claimed that foreign aid is the transfer of money from the 'poor in rich countries to the rich in poor countries'.[8]

The villagers lived in hamlets which where created by clearing the jungles. This made room for their homes and land for cultivation. One could imagine that during harvest time, vast acres of land would have given a Wordsworthian vista, not of daffodils, but of rice ripening in the hot tropical sun. The people living in these hamlets were made summarily homeless when these hamlets were razed to the ground by the British in the mid nineteenth century to open large tracts of jungle to plant coffee, tea, rubber and coconut. The price of progress was, to some extent, paid for by the villagers. But their descendants – the Ceylonese people – have benefited from the vast revenues that resulted.

Water for drinking, bathing, washing clothes and irrigating the fields came from the rivers, springs and wells. The monsoon rains refilled the rivers and dams and springs. The jungles that surrounded them were filled with an array of wildlife ranging from the dangerous – such as crocodiles, gavials, bears,

[8] Robert Guest, *The Shackled Continent – Africa's Past, Present and Future*, London, Macmillan, 2004.

leopards and poisonous snakes – to nuisances – such as monkeys, jackals, foxes – and the useful – such as elephants, cattle, goats and buffalo. The large and powerful water buffaloes were used for ploughing, irrigation and for threshing the paddy and for pulling carts. Elephants were tamed and used as beasts of strength and grandeur. At the command of the mahout they dragged logs, felled trees, cleared jungle tracts for cultivation, participated in processions called *peraheras*[9] and hunting expeditions, and provided safe and regal carriage for kings.

The forest had an abundance of birds. Among them peacocks, resplendent in hues of royal blue, would have roamed the royal parks and village greens. Their eerie cry would have disturbed the quiet of the dusk and dawn and their plucked fantail would, no doubt, have adorned headdresses of the king and others of his court and provided ornament for the palaces and the homes of rich people. The forest also had game birds, which were often caught by setting snares. A variety of spiders and red ants formed part of a wide range of insects. The mosquitoes that bred in the swamps were probably the most lethal as conveyors of malaria, yellow fever and similar deadly diseases. But there was also a whole range of beautiful butterflies and beetles. This great variety still exists. The Foreign and Commonwealth Office website says that:

> There are 400 species of birds (21 unique to Sri Lanka); 54 species of fish found in the waterways and marshlands, 40 species of frogs and toads; 2 species of crocodiles; 5 species of turtles; and 83 species of snakes of which 5 are poisonous. It also has sloth bears and leopards.[10]

Medicine in the village and the city was provided by the lay medicine men and Buddhist monks practicing homeopathy and Ayurvedic medicine. Some herbal remedies did, in fact, cure, because they contained chemicals that modern medical science has identified, extracted, purified, tested, validated and converted into medicines. But these herbal remedies were very much hit or miss affairs. In addition to these formal and 'approved' sources there would have been charlatans who offered untested remedies in an attempt to wield power over and exploit the unsuspecting villagers. These purveyors of 'snake oil' attributed their failure to the devil and advised people to submit themselves to various forms of witchcraft. The witches or warlocks would consult their supernatural informers and advisers and decide what form the ceremony of cleansing or exorcism should take. Illnesses were also ascribed to spells invoked and placed by those angry with the diseased, and a lucrative trade in casting and neutralising spells had also developed. The effect of this is that the poor villagers were constantly paying these various 'snake oil' purveyors and

---

[9] Sinhalese name for a carnival, which may have caparisoned elephants, drummers, players of wind instruments and dancers.

[10] *Country Profile: Sri Lanka*, Foreign and Commonwealth Office of the British government, www.fco.gov.uk, 25 November 2005.

the 'witch doctors' for cures of a wide range of ills, including those to do with finances and relationships. The poor villagers were, and still are, robbed by almost everyone they trust. Whilst these forms of medical and spiritual interventions may fail logical analysis, their use is so deeply ingrained in the psyche of the people that they still depend on them.

An offshoot of witchcraft was the development of the art form commonly associated with exorcism – devil dances. The masks used during these ceremonies took on the most violent and aggressive form as they represented caricatures of the different forms of human frailty, such as gluttony and greed of various types, envy and loathing. The music, with the strong rhythm of the drum and the cacophony and stridency of disharmonious wind instruments combined, we are told, to frighten the demons and to expel them. Of course the music of the temple and the *perahera*, although using the same instruments, provided music of a more sublime and pulse-quickening character.

Food and drink in the village and city came from natural sources. Thirst was quenched with the juice of the coconut and water drawn from wells. People drank the juice of squeezed limes and other citrus fruits. They, no doubt, enjoyed the strong taste of rice wine and *arrack* distilled from the flower of the coconut and palmyra palms. Ralph Fitch, in Hakluyt's collection of travellers' tales, recalls that:

> The tree is called the palmer, which is the profitablest tree in the world. It doth always bear fruit, and doth yield wine, oil, sugar, vinegar, cords [coir rope], coals; of the leaves are made thatch for the houses, sails for ships, mats to sit or lie on; of the branches they made their houses and brooms to sweep, of the tree wood for ships.[11]

The wine he refers to is called *arrack* or toddy and has a much higher alcoholic content than the red and white wines that we are generally accustomed to drinking today. Rice and milk products such as curd (a form of yogurt), vegetables, exotic fruits such as mango, pawpaw and pineapple, wild boar, venison, chicken and fish would have formed part of their diet. The flower of the kithul tree would have provided them with jaggery (a form of solidified honey) to sweeten their food. The low density of the population in those times would have made life for the villagers far more tolerable, if not enjoyable and satisfying in comparison to the life of their counterparts today.

Despite sporadic wars and, probably, famine and epidemics of malaria and other diseases the Sinhalese multiplied and basked in the sunlight for over 1,000 years. The Sinhalese civilisation began to wither and diminish but it is not known why this happened. It is likely that disease was a factor. The great inland seas and the irrigation systems connected to them could, if neglected, easily have been the breeding grounds of the malaria-carrying mosquito.

[11] Richard David, *Hakluyt's Voyages: A Selection*, Chatto & Windus, London, 1981.

Unable to contain a disease of epidemic proportions, the people may have abandoned the areas around these reservoirs and moved to the more fertile southern territories. Whatever the reasons, new blood and new ideas, new technologies, new values and customs were not introduced into society until the European nations came calling.

The Story of Sigiriya

The story of Sigiriya, the Lion Rock, epitomises the habits and attitudes of the Sinhalese kings. The story parallels the Hindu and Greek epics in its portrayal of human failings and majesty. It evokes contradictory feelings of beauty and treachery, courage and cowardice, reality and mythology, engineering excellence and folly. It provides a pen portrait of the jealousies and infighting that marked the reign of the Sinhalese kings.

The story of Dhatusena (AD 463–479) and his two sons, Moggallana and Kassapa illustrates an underlying weakness in both the infrastructure of governance and rules of succession that operated during the time of the kings of Lanka in that they were not able to overcome the natural human tendencies to greed and usurpation.

Dhatusena was of the royal Mauryan race. He was elected leader of the Sinhalese and charged with the mission of recovering Anuradhapura from the Pandyan king who was occupying it at the time. Having expelled the Indian invader, he established himself as the sole ruler of the island – a singular and rare achievement. His reign proved to be a 'golden period' in the island's history. Foreign influences had been expelled. The people were, again, able to enjoy the fecundity of the island thanks to their benevolent king who built a vast inland lake called the Kalavewa. The Kalavewa was a great engineering achievement. When full, the waters covered between 4,425 and 6,400 acres of land. The spill was made of hammered granite. A canal that was forty foot wide and fifty-four miles long carried water to Anuradhapura. In its first seventeen miles it meandered over country that permitted a gradient of no more than six inches per mile. The Kalavewa also fed another 180 square miles of irrigable land and over a hundred subsidiary village tanks.

Here was a man of formidable abilities: the imagination and courage to save his country from invaders, to then create a single sovereign state to rule over it and to harness water to ensure that his people could feed themselves. In doing all of this, it seems that he did not build a treasure trove for himself, and this last was to be his undoing.

Kassapa, one of his sons, asked his father where his wealth was hidden. His father took him to the banks of the Kalavewa and showed it to his son and told him that all his wealth was buried there. Kassapa was furious at what he thought was deception, and killed his father by walling him up, whilst still alive, in the embankment of the Kalavewa. How he managed such a feat can only be guessed at. Perhaps his father trusted his sons too much, or was too old to resist. It might even be that he had shared out the kingdom to his two sons and retired, and Kassapa had outfoxed his brother and taken it all. Kassapa obviously did not understand that a contented and productive people could generate wealth for him.

His brother, Moggallana, fled to India, not only to save himself but to also raise an army with which to defeat his brother and retake the crown. Kassapa acted to protect himself from his brother's wrath and moved his palace to Sigiriya, a huge impregnable rock that stood proudly above its surroundings and provided a panoramic view of the surrounding countryside. One side was protected by a large lake and the other by arable land and forest. Access to the top was by specially constructed flights of stairs. The top of the rock was four acres in size and housed the palace and the official buildings. Water was channelled under the floors of the building to cool it. A tank provided water for the king and his retinue. How the water was raised to the top of the rock fortress is not known, but it is likely that he used waterwheels or an aqueduct, although no evidence has been found for either theory. Both methods made the people on top vulnerable to a siege, so it must be assumed that he had devised a secure supply. At ground level he had built pleasure gardens and in the rock indentations he had frescoes of half-naked women painted. He lived in this pleasure palace for eighteen years until he was overthrown by his brother.

The battle that ended Kassapa's life was a debacle. Moggallana returned eighteen years after his exile with a contingent of troops from Malabar, which he supplemented with Sinhalese troops he gathered on his return, and vanquished his brother. His success was made easier by a misunderstanding. When Moggallana challenged him, Kassapa, without sending his general, decided that he would lead the fight against his brother. Kassapa's elephant strayed into a bog, and the king, in an attempt to get it out of the bog, turned the elephant back on its tracks with the intention of finding firmer ground before advancing. His troops saw him retrace his steps and thought he was retreating. They fled before him, leaving him to the mercy of his brother and his army.

Chapter 3

The Indian Connections

The physical and military shadow of India has hovered over Sri Lanka like the shadow of an eagle over a sparrow. Its people, culture, religion and philosophy came to the island many millennia ago and transmuted into the two major racial groups on the island – the Tamils and the Sinhalese.

The Tamils belonged to the Dravidian race and were from South India. The Dravidian people occupied a vast tract of India roughly demarcated by a triangle created by the Indian Ocean on two sides (Bay of Bengal and the Arabian Sea) and the Vindhya Mountain Range that cuts across the centre of India. Made up of low mountains, it extends from Varanasi in the east to Gujarat State in the west. It covers a distance of about 1,090 km (675 miles) and separates the drainage basin of the River Ganges on the north from the Deccan Plateau on the south. Elevations range from 455 to 910 m (1,500 to 3,000 ft) and reach a maximum of 1,113 m (3,651 ft). These physical barriers protected the Dravidians from invading forces from the north:

> Invaders never penetrated far to the south. After the Maurya break-up, the Deccan long remained separate and under its own Dravidian rulers. Its cultural distinction persists even today. Though Aryan influence was stronger there after the Maurya era and Hinduism and Buddhism were never to disappear, the south was not again truly integrated politically with the north until the coming of the British Raj.[12]

However, *The Rough Guide to South India* points out that 'some of the most defining cultural traits and traditions originated in the deep Dravidian south, from where they spread northwards'. It goes on to elaborate this claim by pointing out that:

> Dravidian culture of the deep south was being transformed by Sanskritic influences from the North. Nevertheless, they [a body of classical Tamil poetry known as the *Sangam*] vividly demonstrate that some of the most distinctive characteristics of Indian civilization – including yoga, tantra, the cult of the god Murugan and goddess worship – were almost certainly indigenous to the South, and widespread well before the Aryans came to dominate the region completely. The *Sangam* also records the stormy political relations between the three

[12] J. M. Roberts, *The Penguin History of the World*, third edition, Penguin Books, 1995.

> dynasties, (Cholas, Pandya and Cheras) who were frequently at war with each other, or with the rulers of neighbouring Sri Lanka.[13]

The Dravidian people were both militarily and culturally advanced, and no doubt posed a continuous threat to the Sinhalese. Some believe that the fear of Tamil domination is ingrained in the Sinhalese psyche. But, as we will see later in this chapter, history does not bear this out.

The Tamils referred to the island as 'Elam' or 'Elangai'. The likelihood is that, as soon as they were able, they crossed the twenty-two miles of water between India and Lanka and settled on the northern, north-western and north-eastern shores of the Jaffna peninsula and based their capital in Jaffna, more specifically in Nallur. They brought Hinduism, the Tamil language and the cultures and traditions of the Dravidian people with them. Places of Hindu worship and pilgrimage were well established in the north of the island from very early times and support the view that the Tamil presence on the island predates that of the Sinhalese. The Tamil settlements were probably trading communities established by Indian merchants, as most of them are located in natural harbours. The mountain ranges in the middle and the rivers and thick jungles beyond probably formed a natural barrier to southwards movement. These settled communities practiced their religion and their trade undisturbed by the indigenous communities. The peak of the power of the king of Jaffna was in the fourteenth century when he exacted tribute from the people of the south.

The Sinhalese were of Aryan descent and most likely came from the western and eastern coasts of India. They brought Aryan religions and languages, such as Sanskrit and Pali, and Aryan cultures with them. They and their families settled in the north central region of the island and, for the next millennia, ruled it from Anuradhapura, their capital city. Anuradhapura was a large city and proof of a vibrant and prosperous community. Here they grew a society that prayed to pagan or Hindu gods and spoke Sanskrit. It was not until much later that large-scale conversion to Buddhism took place. The ruined cities of Anuradhapura, Polonnaruwa and the surrounding towns and countryside are witness to the fact that they invested their money and time in erecting royal palaces, pleasure gardens, temples, statues of the Buddha, and monasteries to encourage the practice and spread of Buddhism in their domain.

The kings of India and Sri Lanka helped each other out when they were under threat from invading forces, but the Sinhalese kings saw the Tamils in the north and their ethnic compatriots in the south of India as constant threats to their independence and sovereignty. This perception was made reality from time to time by the fact that the South Indian kings, such as the Cholas, Pandyans and Keralas, often attempted and sometimes succeeded in annexing

[13] Abram, Sen, Edwards, Ford and Wooldridge, *The Rough Guide to South India,* Rough Guides, 2003.

the Sinhalese territories to their Indian states. However, there is little evidence to support a theory that the Tamils in the north were essential conduits through whom the South Indian kings channelled their challenge of the Sinhalese hegemony of the island. Neither is it clear that they had any long-term intentions of annexing Lanka to their kingdoms. As Fernandez-Armesto points out, any incursion of South Indian kings such as the Cholas:

> ...was probably just raiding, though there were footholds and garrisons in Sri Lanka and the Maldives and perhaps in Malaya. Its impact, however, was to cripple Srivijaya and enrich the temples of South India. Temples were the allies and support of the kings in managing the state, and the biggest beneficiaries of victories in war.

Their early invasions and occupations centred on Anuradhapura but subsequent incursions or disease drove the Sinhalese kings further south to Polonnaruwa, Gampola, Dambadeniya and, via a few others, eventually to Kotte. Kotte became the capital during the time of Vikrama Bahu III (c. 1357–1374). As de Silva points out in his guide to the Colombo Museum:

> The recorded history of Sri Lanka ... is divisible into: the Anuradhapura Period (437 BC–1017 AD), the Polonnaruva Period (1017–1235 AD), the Dambadeniya Period (1235–1341 AD), the Gampala Period (1341–1415 AD), the Kotte Period (1415–1597 AD) and the Kandy Period (1597–1815 AD). Yapavuva, Rayigama and Kurunegala were other places chosen by Sinhalese kings as their capitals during the period from 1235–1415 AD.[14]

From these capitals they attempted to re-establish sovereignty over the rest of the island, but failed. Thus, by long tradition, was established a division of the land between them, and it is therefore not surprising that the Sinhalese should view the Tamils with suspicion. To continue to do so, however, after the European occupation is political expediency.

It is likely that throughout history the Tamils spread throughout the island and intermingled with the Sinhalese, and that the Sinhalese did the same. The intermingling of the races also took place at the highest levels of society when, for strategic reasons, the Sinhalese kings married princesses or kept mistresses from the Indian subcontinent and some princes from the Indian subcontinent married Sinhalese princesses or kept Sinhalese mistresses. The idea of a pure Sinhalese or Tamil race on the island is not tenable. It would be stretching credulity to absurd limits to suggest that there still exists on the island people with blood that is not adulterated by that of the other races who have inhabited it through history. Despite this, it is quite clear that the two ethnic groups

[14] P. H. D. H. De Silva, *Illustrated Guide to the Colombo Museum. Part 1: Ground Floor Galleries*. National Museums of Sri Lanka 1976.

retained their cultural separateness, as they made no effort to merge their cultures or to become one nation under one sovereign.

The earliest memorable prince from the Indian subcontinent to subjugate the Sinhalese was Elara (205–161 BC). Elara had a reputation for being a just ruler. He ruled the country for forty-four years. He was defeated by Duttha Gamani who, out of respect for his defeated foe, ensured that he was given a proper burial and that the place where he was buried was marked by a monument. It is claimed that, on Duttha Gamani's orders, processions silenced their musical instruments when they passed the monument as a mark of respect to Elara. The second occupation of the island by Indian kings was during the reign of Vatta Gamani (104 BC) when five Pandyan kings expelled him in the fifth month of his reign and partitioned the country between them for fourteen years. However, Vatta Gamani recovered the country from them before he died. Six Malabar kings captured the country during the reign of Mitta Sena and ruled it for twenty-seven years (AD 436–463) when it was recaptured from them by Dhatusena. As told earlier, Dhatusena lost his life to his son, Kassapa.

After this episode, the island seems to have been ignored by the South Indian kings for nearly five hundred years. But it was invaded by the Chola Emperor, Rajaraja I, who captured the Sinhalese king Mahinda V, and exiled him to India in AD 1017, holding the island for thirty-eight years until it was retaken by Vijaya Bahu I in 1056. The *Lonely Planet Guide* to Sri Lanka claims that there still is an inscription in Tamil in an isolated complex of Buddhist temples near Trincomalee that bears the name of Rajaraja I, and that an image house on the same site was redecorated with Chola architectural styles during the reign of the Chola kings, including the use of Dravidian mouldings at the base. Vijaya Bahu married Lilavati, daughter of Jagatipala of Kanauj, and Tilokasundari of the Kalinga royal race. His sister Mitta married a Pandyan prince who was the grandfather of Parakrama Bahu the Great. These alliances ensured that Chola emperors did not return.

A strange action by Parakrama Bahu I rekindled Indian interest in the island. He brought Nissanka Malla, a Kalinga prince and probably a relative of his, to Lanka. Nissanka Malla ruled for nine years (AD 1187–1196). In AD 1215 Magha, a prince of the Kalinga race, invaded Lanka with an army of Kerala or Malabar soldiers and claimed the throne. His reign lasted twenty-one years. He was a bigoted Hindu and persecuted the Buddhist monks, desecrated the temples and appropriated the lands of the Sinhalese and gave it to his followers. The monks fled the country and took refuge in India and the sacred relics were hidden in Kotmale. Magha was no Elara.

Vijay Bahu III (c. AD 1220–1224) expelled Magha and re-established the Buddhist faith by recalling the monks. The king made Dambadeniya (a rock fortress) his base.

However, it seems that a Tamil king, Jaya Bahu, ruled in parallel in another part of the country for forty years. Parakrama Bahu II, a son of Vijay Bahu III, earned a reputation as an outstanding king, not only for his military ability in recovering lost territory, but also for his support of religious and literary activities.

In 1244–45 Lanka was invaded by a Javanese, Chandrabhanu, a sea robber who failed to secure a foothold. The Pandyan king Kulasekhara (AD 1268–1308) sent his minister Arya Chakravarti to attack and take Lanka. He did and probably held it for twenty years. During this time the Dalada was sent to the Pandyan king and remained with him until Parakrama Bahu III led a personal embassy to the Pandyan king and probably swore allegiance to him in exchange for the Dalada. It was at this time that Marco Polo visited Lanka. During the reign of Parakrama Bahu VI (AD 1412–1468), it is claimed that his son or adopted son, Sapumal Kumaraya, recaptured the Jaffna kingdom, suggesting that it had been in the hands of the Kalinga Magha dynasty for many decades until Jaffna and the territory ruled by the king of Jaffna was annexed to the Sinhalese throne in about 1449/50 or 1450/51, depending on whether his reign began in 1412 or 1415.

So what is apparent from this period is that the Tamils had occupied the north and east of the island and, except for a few years, continued to do so as an independent people during the reigns of the Sinhalese kings. Whilst the military exploits of Indian kings is of interest, their reigns did not have a lasting effect on the Sinhalese. But Buddhism, another Indian import, did, and still continues to have a powerful influence on Sri Lanka. It was probably the most powerful civilising influence the island had experienced and gradually became the bedrock on which Sinhalese civilisation was built.

Chapter 4
Buddhism in the Time of the Kings

The Lord Buddha lived and died at a time when the world enjoyed a period of enlightenment. As Strong points out in his book, *The Buddha,* 'the India of his [the Buddha's] day was caught up in a period of religious ferment and questioning, spawned by the rise of new urban centres and the breakdown of old political systems.'[15]

Although it was nearly five hundred years before Christ would preach his message of hope and forgiveness, and nearly a thousand years before Muhammad acted as the messenger of God, there was much going on in that other centre of civilisation – Greece. Greek civilisation, under Pericles, was at its zenith. Herodotus (c. 484–425 BC) invented the historical narrative by recording the history of the Greeks and their world. Pythagoras (c. 582–500 BC) developed aspects of mathematics. Socrates (c. 470–c. 399 BC), Plato (c. 437–c. 347 BC) and Aristotle (384–322 BC) laid the foundations of Western thought and culture, contributed to the development of political philosophy and gave birth to democracy. It was also the time when Greek military capability was first really tested by the invading Persian army at Thermopylae in 480 BC and although Leonidas I and his 1,000 men, 300 of whom were Spartans, were slain and his head displayed on a stake, the Greeks succeeded in routing the Persian army and navy and forced Xerxes I to flee to the safety of Asia.

Thousands of miles away in Lanka, the Sinhalese kingdom was beginning to take shape. The fledgling community that prince Vijaya had set up in Anuradhapura was now a thriving city. It was well on its way to nationhood and the messenger of King Asoka had found in its king a ready convert to Buddhism. King Asoka of the Mauryan Empire (268–231 BC) – a contemporary of Alexander the Great – had converted to Buddhism as a result of the remorse he suffered after his horrendous sacking of Kalinga. After his conversion, he used his influence and power to spread the message of the Buddha right across his empire and into Asia and Africa. He was to Buddhism what the Emperor Constantine was to Christianity.

According to tradition, Buddhism reached the island during the reign of Devanampiya Tissa (247–207 BC). Mahinda, the elder son of King Asoka, is credited with bringing its message to Lanka, and Mahinda's sister, Sanghamitta, with bringing the Bo Tree (*Ficus Riligiosa*) sapling that, 2,500 years later, is a giant among trees and is the oldest in recorded history.

---

[15] John S. Strong, *The Buddha: A Short Biography*, Oxford, OUP, 2001.

These accounts of how Buddhism reached Lanka are treated as myth and legend by some but others treat these stories as received truth and wisdom. Whether the events were true or legend both encounters certainly bore significant fruit. No sapling has ever produced such a large, old and venerated Bo tree.

The teachings of the Buddha were very advanced for the period. It would have required a sophisticated mind to appreciate its subtlety and respond so positively to it. Devanampiya Tissa had such a mind and, recognising the merits of the teachings, persuaded his court and his people to shed their earlier beliefs – Jainism, Hinduism or paganism – and embrace the new way of life that Buddhism demanded of them. He and succeeding kings invested large amounts of time, effort and money to establish Buddhism on the island. They provided monasteries for the monks and built *dagobas* and *viharas* to act as places of worship and as visible symbols of the new faith. And their efforts paid off.

Today, the memory of the Buddha continues to be reinforced by the constant reminders of him, such as the many shrines dedicated to him, the innumerable statues of him all across the country and the monks in saffron robes who walk among the people. However, a very special memorial to the Buddha is the tooth relic, (The Dalada[16]) which arrived on the island from Kalinga during the reign of Siri Megahavanna (Kit Siri Mevan) about AD 340. The importance of the relics of the Buddha to a Buddhist is illustrated by this episode recalled in Strong's book, *The Buddha*, where he quotes from Whilhelm Gieger's *The Mahavamsa or the Great Chronicles of Ceylon*.[17] It would appear that Mahinda was talking to Devanampiya Tissa about the Buddha and he complains:

> ...it has been a long time since he has seen the Buddha. The Sri Lankan king [Devanampiya Tissa] is astonished 'I thought you told me that Buddha had passed away into *parinirvana*' he says. And Mahinda quickly explains that he meant it had been a long time since he had been able to worship the relics of the Buddha, for 'when we behold the relics, we behold the Conqueror'.

Mahinda's words imply that when Buddhist pilgrims visit the Dalada it is as if they are paying a visit to the Buddha himself and receiving his personal blessing. The Dalada was kept in the capital city and was moved with the kings when they moved their capitals. In times of invasion or threat it was taken to a place of safe keeping until the threat was eliminated. The threat to the Dalada came from other Buddhist kingdoms. The desire of the Chinese for the Dalada began in the time of Kublai Khan (Yuan dynasty, AD 1280–1368) and lasted throughout the Ming dynasty (AD 1368–1644):

---

[16] The sacred tooth of the Buddha.

[17] *The Mahavamsa*, Chapter XVII, 'The Arrival of the Relics'. See www.lakdiva.org/mahavamsa.

> In AD 1405 the Chinese eunuch, Ching Ho, came to Ceylon at the request of the Emperor, Yung Ho, of the Ming dynasty (AD 1368–1644), to take away the *dalada*, and was treated badly by Vijayabahu VI. He came again in AD 1408, captured the king, the queen, and the officers, and took them to China.[18]

There was nothing the king could do. Chinese naval power was formidable. The sight of a fleet of Chinese warships anchoring off the shores of Sri Lanka, disgorging an army of Chinese warriors who then marched to Kotte to take the king and his court captive, must have been a frightening sight and a daunting and irresistible event. However, so deep was the king's faith and so strong his sense of obligation to the Dalada that he was willing to risk his life, and that of his court, to protect it. He could have hidden but he probably calculated that that would only be a temporary respite. When the Chinese attempt to use the Dalada as ransom for the king and his court failed, the Chinese released their captives anyway and extorted an annual tribute instead. But the biggest threat to Buddhism came, not from outsiders but from the Buddhist establishment and the kings had to protect Buddhism from the Buddhist monks too.

The Buddhist priests, as the guardians and proponents of the Buddhist way of life, were probably the intellectual elite of their time. They became, in time, a commonplace sight in the cities and villages. These 'sages' of Buddhism were respected and venerated by the people as they were the link between them and the teachings of the Buddha, which had to be read in their original Pali, understood, interpreted and taught to the people. As Horner points out in his chapter 'Buddhism, The Theravada':

> The Buddhists in Ceylon, Burma, Thailand, Cambodia and Laos regard the Pali *Tripitaka* as the source not only for a right and skilled method of conduct of life but of the 'religious' and spiritual aspirations that grow in degree and come near to fulfilment the more rightly and wisely they lead their lives.

And the Buddhist monk, as the primary means of guidance to leading their lives 'rightly', has tremendous influence over the thinking, attitudes and emotional drives of the lay Buddhist. Gradually, the Buddha became much more than a philosopher to the Sinhalese people and the Buddhist monks, like their counterparts in other religions, became the focal point for the spiritual, mental and physical health of the people. Renfrew and Bahn, in their book on archaeology point out that:

> The remains of an 11th century AD hospital attached to a Buddhist monastery outside the city of Polonnaruwa in Sri Lanka contained medical and surgical instruments, and glazed storage vessels, suggesting a sophisticated level of medical care.

[18] G. C. Mendis, *The Early History of Ceylon*, Asian Education Series, 1998.

They would undoubtedly also have been the sources of 'wisdom', justice and compassion for the king and his court. The Buddhist monk was also the source of education. Most temples had schools attached to them. Although their prime purpose was to train and induct novice monks, they served the wider purpose of teaching the children of the village the 'Buddhist way of life', and at the same time introducing them to other knowledge essential for their daily living.

But the Buddhist monks, being human, were subject to the temptations that assail us all – so they went astray from time to time and had to be renewed and purified. That task fell to the kings in ancient times. The ownership of temple lands and the wealth that they produced tempted some monks to enjoy their material blessings in a way unintended by the Buddha and certainly unwelcome to the kings. This pattern of lapsing, persecution and renewal had happened in the past and the kings ensured that Buddhism was not harmed. But the Buddhist monks, in turn, memorialised the history of the Sinhalese people and their links to Buddhism.

The *Mahavamsa* and other Buddhist chronicles have inexorably linked the island, the Sinhalese and Buddhism to each other by suggesting that the Buddha had prepared the island to receive his teaching long before Buddhism came to the island. According to legend, the Buddha visited the island 'in the ninth month, the fifth year, and the eight year after his enlightenment'.[19] In his very first trip the Buddha cleansed the island of demons, walked three times round it and cast a spell of protection on it. Having thus prepared it to receive his teachings he left for Uruvilva.

The linkage of the island and the Sinhalese people to Buddhism is made even stronger by the chroniclers (who were Buddhist monks) when they linked the Lord Buddha to Vijaya the first king of the Sinhalese. Ludowyk says that, according to legend, the Sinhalese Buddhists believe that Vijaya landed on the island 'on the very day on which the Buddha passed away between the *sal* trees in the grove at Kusinara',[20] and that, the Buddha, as he passed away, entrusted Vijaya to the care of the king of the gods because 'Lanka was going to be the home of Buddhism'[21] and Vijaya the founder of the people who would nurture it and protect it. The Buddha's precise words were, 'In Lanka, O lord of gods, will my religion be established, therefore carefully protect him [Vijaya] with his followers and Lanka'. The result of this request was that, 'The god Upulvan, disguised as a wandering ascetic, met Vijaya and his followers, and wound a charmed thread round their hands to ensure their safety'.[22] Although this story has chronological flaws in it – the date of Vijaya's arrival on the island (accepted as 543 BC) does not even come close to the

[19] Strong, *The Buddha*.

[20] *The Mahavamsa*, www.lakdiva.org/mahavamsa.

[21] Ibid.

[22] Ibid.

accepted date for the death of the Lord Buddha (483 BC) – the disparity is irrelevant in the context of the impact of Buddhism on the Sinhalese people. According to Strong, Buddhists:

> ...narrate many tales that have been remembered and revered, repeated and reformulated over the centuries, and whose episodes have been accepted as inspiring and worth recalling, whatever their grounding in history ... The narrations may contain 'fictions' about the Buddha – but these 'fictions' are in many ways 'truer,' or at least religiously more meaningful, than the 'facts'.

And that is the point. Irrespective of the authenticity of the chronicles, the Buddhists of Sri Lanka are part of the 'story' of the Buddha and take their role as the guardians of his teaching very seriously indeed. And, above all, they have willingly accepted the heavy burden that legend says the Buddha placed on them – to be the custodians and proselytisers of his teachings.

To keep the religion current and relevant, the kings often invited monks from other countries to make their home in Lanka. Around the fifth century AD, Buddhaghosa came to the island and rewrote the Sinhalese commentaries on the Buddhist Scriptures in the Pali language and composed the philosophical work *Visuddhimagga*. Similar attempts to kick-start the religion took place soon after the occupation of the capital by Tamil rulers, who presumably gave precedence to the Hindu religion and probably suppressed Buddhism. An example of this is the action of Vikrama Bahu (1111–1132) of the Kalinga dynasty, who, during his reign, persecuted the Buddhist monks and seized their lands. At other times the religion needed a shot in the arm to prevent the monks from losing their way or overindulging in the pleasures of this world.

The story of the Buddha preparing Lanka to be the home of his teaching, referred to earlier, had repercussions almost 2,500 years later when the Buddhist nationalist movement took root on the island. At least, subliminally, this act of branding non-followers as demons who needed to be excluded from the land of the Buddha is the first suggestion of exclusivity, which, in the mind of the fundamentalist or the immoderate could spark the flame of religious intolerance. Strong develops the theme in an attempt to explain the wider implications of the Buddha's act of cleansing the island of demons with fire. He says:

> In the case of the demons of Sri Lanka, we have ... an example of what I call the 'centrifugal Buddha.' Here the fire emanates out from the Buddha; refuge from it is not to be found in the center, but beyond the periphery. The solution is not to convert the demons and make Buddhists out of them [which he did in other instances], but to chase them away, send them into exile.

The chronicles do not record that the Buddhist community on the island showed any intolerance towards other religious beliefs during the time of the kings. In fact the Hindus, Muslims, and Buddhist shared many holy places, but the inroads that Christianity made on Sinhalese society sparked an intolerant response from the Buddhists. From about the mid-1800s a counter-Christian movement began to form. Its purpose was to help reinvigorate Buddhism on the island. But the movement bred a group of fundamentalists who sought exclusivity and preference.

These extreme elements of the Buddhist nationalist movement believed that it is legitimate to exclude or to accord inferior status to those who are not *born* Buddhists even to the extent that it is legitimate to exclude them from a Buddhist kingdom or state. To reinforce this argument they used the Sinhalese records to claim that the island belongs to the Sinhalese because it was gifted and purified by the Buddha for use by his followers. But the records do not support that claim. The records were kept more as Buddhist history in which the Sinhalese kings and people played a vital role and was a means by which the Buddhist establishment ensured its survival and prosperity. The claim of the chronicles that the Buddha cleansed the island so that Buddhism could thrive on it reinforces the linkage of the Sinhalese, the island and Buddhism but it does not licence the abuse of others of different beliefs.

Unfortunately for the Tamils there is no correspondingly famous Chronicle of the Tamil kings that shows how the Tamil kingdom on the island began, grew and matured during the corresponding period of Sinhalese history. The closest chronicle is the Yalpana Vaipava Malai compiled in Tamil by Mailvagana Pulavar of Madagal at the request of Jan Maccara the Dutch governor of Jaffna in 1736. So the impression left is that the Tamils were interlopers. This is also not true. So the Mahavamsa, whose purpose was to memorialise the links between Buddhism and the Sinhalese people and to ensure its survival through them, is being used for racist purposes today.

Part Two
From Spices to Imperial Ceylon

Summary

This part summarises the 450 years of European involvement. The Portuguese were the first to arrive. The years of Portuguese occupation are also noteworthy for:

- the active spread of Roman Catholicism by the Portuguese among the Buddhists and Hindus living in their jurisdiction;
- the conversion of the king of Kotte, Dharmapala;
- grants of temple lands to the Franciscans;
- the supplementing of the Franciscans by the Augustinians and the secular clergy;
- the infighting of the Sinhalese kings who were blinded by their dislike of each other and unable or unwilling to appreciate the strategic cost of their actions;
- the capture and execution of the king of Jaffna.

Unlike the Portuguese, Dutch involvement was via the Dutch East India Company whose focus was profit rather than conquest or conversion. But religion played an important part. The main themes of the Dutch period are:

- the slow erosion of the hold the Sinhalese kings and the Buddhist clergy had over the people;
- the acceptance by the Sinhalese kings that they had lost control of the coastal belt to the Portuguese and the Dutch, although they still held the interior, which they controlled from Kandy;
- the conversion of Buddhists to Christianity;
- the role of the Christian priests, who acted as buffers between these two secular powers, as defenders of the villagers from the kings and Dutch administrators, thus further strengthening the villagers' belief in their new God;
- the introduction of Roman-Dutch law, codification the laws of the Tamils into the *Thesavalamai*, introduction of schools, enforcement of school going, introduction of the concept of equality under the law, and continuation of the process, started by the Portuguese, of Christianising the country.

Dutch occupation of Lanka was brought to an end when the British took Trincomalee on 31 August 1795, following on to capture Batticaloa on 18 September and Jaffna on 28 September. Colombo was taken by the British on 15 February 1796. An agreement between the Dutch and British governments made in Europe in 1789 placed the 817,000 people living in Dutch territories in Lanka under British rule. The key issues from this period of the island's history were that:

- the coastal belt became a Crown Colony in 1802;
- the British took control of the whole island in 1815 by defeating the king of Kandy;
- the whole island became a single administrative entity in 1833 and held the Tamil-speaking Hindus and Sinhala-speaking Buddhists together by a smooth coating of administrative icing.

Chapter 5

The Europeans Arrive and Take Control

The modern history of Sri Lanka began on 15 November 1505 when Dom Lourenco de Almeida, the captain of a small fleet of Portuguese caravels, was blown off course by a storm and took shelter in Galle, a small harbour at the southern tip of the island. When the storm abated and he realised that providence had brought him to an island famed for its spices, gems and elephants, he cruised from Galle to Colombo in search of the capital and the king. A rock on which he carved the arms of Portugal, the indelible evidence of his arrival and determination to claim the island's riches for his country, was erected in what was later to be called Gordon Gardens in Colombo. The rock was also a permanent reminder that de Almeida had brought Europe to the shores of Sri Lanka and incorporated it into the larger global community of nations. Never again would the island's people be able to isolate themselves from the world beyond their shores. And they certainly would not be able to revert to their old state, as they had done when the Sinhalese kings had driven back the Indian invaders of the past.

Lourenco de Almeida would have noticed little social or spiritual disparity between himself and the people he met. As Bernard Waites points out in his book, *Europe and the Third World*:

> The states and societies they [the Portuguese] encountered were comparable to their own in every fundamental respect: monotheistic kingdoms, dominated by aristocratic warriors, served by literate clerisies and officials, and with economic structures and relations at roughly the same level of development. The intruders' sole technological advantage of any consequence was the gunned sailing ship, which could be used to terrorise harbour authorities and island principalities, though even the naval preponderance was not irreversible.[23]

To the islanders, de Almeida represented a people whose technological superiority was undisputed. They outclassed the island people in armament, navigation, shipbuilding and military organisation. Physically, too, they were different. Their fair skin, their strange clothing that included body armour of iron cuirasses and helmets, their greater energy and activity that contrasted strongly with the languid lifestyle of the island people, and their food, i.e. their tendency to eat 'stone' (bread) and drink 'blood' (red wine), set them apart

[23]Bernard Waites, *Europe and the Third World: From Colonisation to Decolonisation*, London, Macmillan, 1999.

from previous visitors to the island. Their religious differences, particularly the commemoration of the Holy Sacrament with its symbolic ingestion of the body and blood of Christ, may have stunned the sensibilities of the Buddhist laity and priests. Their wealth, too, would have impressed, as they paid for provisions with gold coin. But above all this the very loud noise of their cannons, with their ability to shoot iron balls long distances with such force that they destroyed battlements, would have been the most daunting and visible sign of their greater might. Their unfamiliarity and obvious abilities were both a threat and an opportunity.

It is useful to pause here and take a good look at the Portuguese. The Portuguese, like their Spanish neighbours, were accomplished seafarers and explorers. Hemmed in by the Atlantic Ocean and Spain, the Portuguese had no choice but to master and use the sea to explore and exploit the world beyond their home on the western edge of the Iberian Peninsula. Their wanderlust was fuelled by economic need. So, spurred on by tales of pirates' booty and the merchandise of European traders sold in Lisbon and other European cities, they went in search of the untold riches that earlier travellers such as Fa-Hsien (died c. 414) and Marco Polo (1256–1323) had written about.

Many skills had been passed down the generations from the time of Arab rule (from 756, until Afonso III completed a task that was begun almost a century before by expelling the last of the Moors from the Algarve in 1249). The scientific, technological and seafaring knowledge and skills of the Arabs was the most advanced in the then known world, as their scholars had not only learnt from the Greeks, Romans, Persians and Indians but had also converted this acquired knowledge to meet the needs of their times. The Portuguese drew heavily on this knowledge, especially Arab navigational aids and maps, such as *The Book of the Fixed Stars*, compiled in the tenth century by Abd-al-Rahman, to help them navigate the oceans.

> The typical European warship of that period had about four or five masts, high forecastle and poop decks, and two or more tiers of guns. These ships reached displacements of 900 tonnes or more and carried at least sixty guns. Later, armaments were increased, particularly in the British navy, so that ships of 100 guns were not uncommon.

The superior ships and armaments of the Portuguese demonstrated that they had improved on the navigational skills they had learnt from the Arabs. This was achieved because their shipbuilders, sailors and armourers received active royal patronage and support. The brother of the King of Portugal, Henry 'the Navigator' (1394–1460) established a school for sailors at Sagres by Cape St Vincent. King John II of Portugal, who ascended the throne in 1481, encouraged European craftsmen skilled in gunnery and shipbuilding to mount guns on Portuguese ships, thus making them lethal weapons with which to subjugate and control the trade routes. To ease the problems of provisioning the ships for long journeys, they built small ships that could be sailed by only a few crew members and did not need oarsmen. To reduce journey times they built ships that were able to use the wind to take them where they wanted to go.

The Portuguese used local navigators and translators when they ventured beyond the immediate boundaries of the seas that surrounded them and went in search of routes to south Asia. Their early explorers like Christopher Columbus (1451–1506), who died the year after de Almeida had landed on the shores of Lanka, had explored the New World. His ship, the *Santa Maria*, and the two caravels that made up his convoy sailed across the Atlantic Ocean, despite the handicap of not being able to accurately pinpoint their position when on the high seas. The *Santa Maria* was a decked ship about 115 ft long and the caravels about 50 ft long. All three ships had ninety men in all. A caravel had a cargo capacity of about 113 tonnes but could be larger or smaller. It had a broad bow, a high narrow poop deck and was rigged with three or four masts, of which one carried a square sail. These ships combined the advantages of both the European square-rigged ship with a single mainmast and the Arab ship with lateen sails.

In 1487, Bartholomew Diaz rounded the Cape of Good Hope. In 1498 Vasco da Gama weighed anchor in Calicut in South India and was warmly greeted by the Indian merchants who thought that the competition between the Portuguese and Arab traders would gain them higher prices for their goods. On this first trip, Vasco da Gama returned to Portugal with pepper, cinnamon, ginger, cloves and tin and he and his backers made a 6,000 per cent profit on the venture. Pedro Alvarez Cabral (c. 1467–1520) demonstrated the power of the Portuguese guns when his thirteen ships arrived in Calicut in 1500. They bombarded the town for two days to force the ruler to expel Muslim traders, and, although Cabral did not get his way, the pattern of future involvement was clear. Assured of rich pickings the Portuguese established a permanent base in Cochin in 1503.

The Portuguese broke into the eastern trading routes that the Arab, Indian and Chinese traders had monopolised until then. These earlier traders used the easier, cheaper and quicker sailing route to the Yemen and then took their goods overland using the established camel routes to Venice and the rest of Europe. The Chinese used the sea routes and the Silk Road, as they had done for centuries, to get their cheaper yet superior quality goods – such as cottons and silks – and other exotic goods – such as spices and gems – to European markets. The Arab and Chinese traders sailed in unarmed ships and in mixed convoys, believing that there was safety in numbers. As a group, they were better able to discourage or fight off pirates and weather the elements. As such, they did not pose any threat to the people with whom they traded, or to each other. They knew that trade carried out in a peaceful, cooperative and mutually self-supporting way was more profitable. The Portuguese, on the other hand, because the Arabian routes were blocked to them by the Ottoman rulers, sailed their trading ships right round the Cape. These far longer sea journeys made the goods they carried more expensive and of poorer quality because the cargo was often damaged by salt water; so to compete they used their naval strength to supplant trading skills, superior produce and peaceful coexistence of the others. In time, the Portuguese sold protection to the Arab, Chinese and Indian traders against Portuguese raiders such as Dom Lourenco de Almeida.

The Portuguese had one other advantage. The right to exploit the riches of the Near and Far East, Africa and parts of Brazil was granted them by Pope Alexander VI in the Treaty of Tordesillas. The treaty divided the world into two. It gave the Spanish the right to exploit most of the Americas and the Portuguese were 'given' Brazil and the rest of the world. The treaty enabled the Spanish and the Portuguese to expend their energy in exploiting these sea routes rather than fighting over them.

The king of Kotte, Parakrama Bahu VIII, may not have known all this when he first heard that Lourenco de Almeida had anchored in the harbour in Colombo. But the reputation of the Portuguese as a determined, ingenious and hard working people who would willingly use their strong naval and military capability and enterprise for financial gain would have preceded Dom Lourenco. So the king sent emissaries to Dom Lourenco and invited him to his palace. By this single act he made an ally of a potential enemy but he also set in train a chain of events that would eventually make the people of the island subject to foreign rule.

De Almeida jumped at the opportunity. He prepared a landing party of well-armed soldiers, advisers and translators and set off. To make sure that he kept in contact with his ship he ordered the ship's cannon be fired at every turn of the hourglass. The regular cannon fire helped him keep his bearings in relation to the ship and served as a reminder to his escorts that he had the superior weaponry.

The journey of five miles to the capital took three days because the king's emissaries, in an attempt to confuse and disorient the Portuguese, took them by a circuitous route to the Capital (Kotte). But the Portuguese knew better.

When the party arrived at Kotte, Dom Lourenco was able, for the first time, to assess the military competence and thinking of the people. As he entered the city he would have noticed the crocodiles in the lake surrounding the outer perimeter wall, and the barracks that housed well-armed soldiers, kept there to guard the four passes into the city and to defend it. He would also have noted that moats and battlements contributed to the defence of the inner city. He had reached the point of no return, but he must have judged that these defences were no match for Portuguese cannon or military competence. So he took his courage in both hands and entered the city in the hope of acquiring prized trading rights for Portugal.

He would have been greeted politely by the king and his courtiers and been introduced to the court. What Dom Lourenco made of them is unknown. But the information he gathered during the journey and again at court would have led him to the conclusion that the king needed the support of a powerful 'neighbour' and had chosen the Portuguese as that neighbour. He promised that the Portuguese would provide protection for the king and his people in exchange for the king's consent to the Portuguese establishing a trading community in Sri Lanka, and an agreement to an annual tribute of cinnamon, jewels set in rubies and ten elephants.

Lourenco's promise of protection was no vain promise. He could sail round the island in a few days. Travel overland though the jungles, marshlands and the mountain ranges in the centre would be difficult, but it could be done. The territory that mattered most to him was the cinnamon-growing areas, the gem pits and the pearl fisheries, and these he knew he could protect by using Portuguese ships and cannons to dominate the coastal towns and harbours, and protect not only their trading activities, but also the whole island from invasion. So, thanking Providence, he gratefully accepted the terms of the treaty. He left the island having established a fort, and within it a trading centre and a church for those whom he would leave behind. But exploiting the treaty would prove harder for the Portuguese who followed him.

The Sinhalese, too, would have difficulty accommodating Dom Lourenco's successors. Their comfortable life in a well-developed society with its well-established rituals, social, religious, legal, agricultural and commercial systems would all have to adjust to the new ways of these new people. They would still have taxes to pay, obligations to meet and the need to survive the whims and caprices not only of their feudal lords, kings and their village masters but of foreigners too. Behind the obvious and immediate threat to their security from the Portuguese was the far greater challenge of a continuously rolling sea of change that would drown them unless they learnt to use its force to their advantage.

They did not know then, but would soon learn that the European nations were on the march and were going out in search of the world's resources. Their naval and military superiority, combined with their undoubted political and administrative skills, ensured that the coming onslaught was unstoppable. In time, the peoples throughout the known world and the New World with whom they traded or conquered would be required to adopt their cultures, religions, laws, commercial methods, technological and scientific advances. And, in so doing risk losing their unique identity and all that they held dear in the cultures they had honed over succeeding millennia. De Almeida's arrival triggered a period of change unlike any their civilization had seen ever before.

Chapter 6

The Portuguese in Sri Lanka

Parakrama Bahu VIII (c. 1484–1518) began the process of handing power to his two sons, Dharma Parakrama Bahu IX and Vijaya Bahu VII in 1509, by making them co-regents with him. Parakrama Bahu IX (1509–1528) succeeded as senior king but he is rarely mentioned in the chronicles. Vijaya Bahu VII (1509–1521) inherited the kingdom of Kotte on his father's death in 1518, an event he is supposed to have expedited, and promptly acted to expel the Portuguese. The reasons for wishing to expel the Portuguese are obscure but it is assumed that the Moors, who wanted to regain their monopoly of the spice and gem trade, may have instigated his actions. However, despite help from the suzerain of Malabar, he lost the fight and the respect of his subjects. In 1521 he lost his throne and his life.

His kingdom was divided among his three sons – Bhuvanaika Bahu, Rayigam Bandara and Mayadunne. According to Muttukumaru, as Vijaya Bahu VII had not named a successor, the division of the kingdom 'was settled by a convention of nobles, supported by the King of Kandy' who stood to gain considerably by this new arrangement. Having split the kingdom of Kotte, the kings of Jaffna and Kandy reasserted their authority over their respective domains. Bhuvanaika Bahu VII (1521–1551), the senior king, was made King of Kotte and the seaports. Rayigam Bandara was made King of Galle and Kalutara. Mayadunne (1521–1581) was made King of Sitawaka. The island now had at least five kingdoms – Jaffna, Kandy, and those of the three new kings. The Portuguese were left with a treaty that now only applied to that part of the country ruled by Bhuvanaika Bahu VII. So they backed him. But he was the wrong horse, so to speak.

Mayadunne was ambitious and moved swiftly to annex the territory belonging to Rayigam Bandara, his brother. He then focused his attention on gaining the kingdom of Kotte, and, with the help of the Samorin of Calicut, challenged Bhuvanaika Bahu VII. Bhuvanaika Bahu VII invoked the treaty with Portugal, and with their help and an excellent general, his son-in-law Vidiye Bandara, he repulsed Mayadunne's attack. The aggressors sued for peace in 1539. The peace lasted until 1547. War erupted again in 1548 and this time the Portuguese sided with Mayadunne; but this was only a temporary alliance. They had not allowed for the wiles of Vidiye Bandara.

Vidiye Bandara was the son-in-law of Bhuvanaika Bahu VII and the father of Dharmapala, and was politically active from about 1535 to 1552. He was both a good general and an astute politician and would have made a good king, but not being of royal birth the ultimate prize was denied him. He and his wife embarked on a devious route to achieve control of Kotte. They persuaded her father Bhuvanaika Bahu VII to leave the kingdom to his grandson, Dharmapala. To ensure that this happened they sent an embassy in 1540, (immediately following the peace agreement with Mayadunne) to Lisbon with a golden image of their infant son as a gift to the King of Portugal and asked the King of Portugal to crown Dharmapala king in effigy on the death of his grandfather, Bhuvanaika Bahu VII. The King of Portugal, possibly unaware or dismissive of the succession rights of the Sinhala kings, agreed and made a proclamation to that effect. Mayadunne was furious and swore to avenge this treacherous and traitorous act, and although the Portuguese had befriended him in 1548 they now lost his support. He and his son would remain their enemies for the remainder of their lives. Bhuvanaika Bahu VII was assassinated in 1551. Vidiye Bandara had won round one. When Dharmapala (1551–1597) was crowned king, he was about eleven or twelve years old and his father was looking forward to many years as regent.

On Dharmapala's accession to the throne of his grandfather, Vidiye Bandara became the regent and de facto king. Vidiye Bandara's ploy had worked, and he had outwitted Mayadunne to the throne of Kotte. But it was a pyrrhic victory. In 1552, the Portuguese Viceroy, no paragon of virtue himself, sensed that Vidiye Bandara intended to supplant his son and declare himself king, so he had him kidnapped. Vidiye Bandara escaped with various valuables, including the Buddha's tooth, the Dalada, a priceless relic, and joined Mayadunne, marrying Mayadunne's daughter. Mayadunne's action in taking Vidiye Bandara under his roof is hard to explain. It may have been a defensive manoeuvre, as it stopped other would-be kings from laying hands on so rich a strategic talent, and provided him with valuable information about the Portuguese and the situation in Kotte. Mayadunne's son, the eleven-year-old Rajasinha, saw Vidiye Bandara as a threat and acted to prevent Vidiye Bandara stealing his kingdom. Thus Vidiye Bandara found that Rajasinha and the Portuguese were both pursuing him. Attacked on both sides, he sought refuge with another ruler and, whilst still a guest, killed his host and usurped his dominion. However, Rajasinha and the Portuguese continued to pursue him and forced him to take refuge in Jaffna, where he was eventually killed in a personal vendetta.

Dharmapala was now without his father and mentor, and, because of the threat from Mayadunne, at risk of losing his kingdom. For this reason, to consolidate his position with the Portuguese or through genuine conviction, Dharmapala, who had been educated by the Franciscans, converted to Christianity and was baptised Dom John Dharmapala in 1557. But this displeased his subjects who were Buddhists and he lost their support. Dharmapala also angered the Buddhist clergy because he distanced them from the court and diminished their political authority. By donating the temple lands to the Franciscan Friars who had educated him and converted him to Catholicism,

Dharmapala deprived the Buddhist clergy of income. So the people, urged on by the Buddhist clergy, defected to Mayadunne, weakening Dharmapala even more.

To protect their trading interests and to provide guidance to Dharmapala, the Portuguese sent the Viceroy of Goa to Lanka. Instead of helping Dharmapala, the Viceroy robbed him and plundered the city. The King of Portugal ordered restitution but the delay in communications made this order of little material value. However, as they were locked in a situation of mutual self-interest, the Viceroy joined Dharmapala and together they acted to successfully repulse Mayadunne's attack. However, the Viceroy decided not to capture Mayadunne but to leave him in place, probably to ensure Dharmapala's dependence on the Portuguese. This realignment of the balance of power ensured that Kotte and its environs remained in Portuguese-friendly hands and ensured their supply of cinnamon and other spices, and their access to the ports of Colombo and Galle. Thus Mayadunne's attempt to gain sovereignty over most of the island was thwarted.

Mayadunne's battle for the island was continued by his son, Rajasinha (1554–1593), who at the tender age of eleven showed astuteness and military prowess by eliminating Vidiye Bandara as a potential rival for his father's throne.

Rajasinha, continuing the vendetta started by his father against Dharmapala's grandfather, took chunks of the kingdom of Kotte from his cousin and also took the Kandyan kingdom. By these manoeuvres he completely surrounded the kingdom of Kotte and made his cousin a virtual prisoner. The Portuguese, unable to protect Dharmapala in Kotte and to prevent Rajasinha from establishing his court there, razed it to the ground and took Dharmapala to the Portuguese fort in Colombo. Rajasinha then decided to attack this fort in an effort to dislodge the Portuguese as a first step in removing them from the island altogether. But his efforts were unsuccessful due to other battles against his nemesis, Vimala Dharma Suriya I, whom we will meet later on in this chapter. Rajasinha died of blood poisoning in early 1593.

With the help of Rajasinha's favourite general, Manamperi, the Portuguese recovered Kotte in 1594 and Dom John Dharmapala, their nominee, was now back in charge. In that year they also decided to capture the King of Kandy and take control of the whole island. But this attempt failed. This left the country with a king in Kandy who rejected any control by the Portuguese and one in Kotte, Dharmapala, who was a puppet of the Portuguese. When Dharmapala died in 1597 he donated his kingdom and its management to Philip I of Portugal and Philip II of Spain, as Portugal had by then been annexed by Spain. For the next ten years there were a variety of uprisings and rebellions. Some were spontaneous and others were instigated by the king of Kandy.

In the early years the Portuguese had left Jaffna alone. However, in 1544 the king of Jaffna, in an attempt to stem the conversion of the people of Mannar, who were Hindus, to Catholicism, massacred the converts living there. The Portuguese were too busy protecting their southern possessions to do anything about it. They took their revenge in 1560 when they attacked Jaffna. The king of Jaffna took refuge in India but returned to retake Jaffna. It was only in 1591, when the king of Jaffna attacked Mannar again, that they conquered him and took permanent control of Jaffna.

By the early seventeenth century, the Portuguese had established a strong foothold on the island. They had built forts in Colombo and Galle and other strategic ports along the south-western coastline. These fortified cities gave them security. The Sinhalese kings did not have the armament or the naval capability necessary to breach their defences. These forts enabled the Portuguese to keep open their vital trading links and their supply lines for food and reinforcements from Goa when Sinhalese land forces besieged them. In this way they were able to thwart several attempts by Rajasinha's troops to starve them into submission. When, in addition, they inherited the kingdom of Kotte from Dharmapala, they had most of the land they needed to meet their commercial objectives. When their arch-enemy, Rajasinha, died in 1593 the only part of the island that was not under their control was the Kandyan kingdom that Vimala Dharma Suriya I had craftily wrested from them.

Vimala Dharma Suriya I was as crafty as Vidiye Bandara. He used the Portuguese to help him realise his ambition to be king of Kandy. We first meet him as Konappu Bandara. The Portuguese knew him as 'Dom John'. His change of name probably denoted his conversion to Catholicism – motivated, one presumes, not from conviction but out of political expediency. In 1590 when Rajasinha was again laying siege to Colombo he, with the blessing of the Portuguese, started a second offensive in Kandy, forcing Rajasinha to fight on two fronts. His strategy worked and he succeeded in ousting Rajasinha from Kandy. The Portuguese installed a man called Dom Philip as king of Kandy believing, probably rightly, that in him they had found another Dharmapala. Dom Philip was the first cousin of the rightful king of Kandy, whom Rajasinha deposed in 1580 and who had died of smallpox whilst in exile.

The rightful king of Kandy had placed his infant daughter, Doña Catharina, in Dom Philip's care before he died and designated Dom Philip as his successor to the Kandyan throne. The understanding was that his tenure as king was for a limited time and applied only until Doña Catharina came of an age to act in her own right. Fortunately or by design, soon after regaining the Kandyan throne, as its custodian for the Portuguese, Dom Philip died and Konappu Bandara turned on his sponsors, the Portuguese. He defeated them, and took the Kandyan kingdom from them. He married Doña Catharina to legitimise his claim to be king. To gain the acceptance of his subjects he changed his name to Vimala Dharma Suriya I, which implied a conversion back to the Buddhist faith. It was in this guise that the Dutch first met him. This pattern of changing faiths to gain power and political advantage recurred throughout the next 200 years or more.

These upheavals and the lack of a single Sinhalese king who could rally the country behind him meant that the Sinhalese civilisation was unable to progress like its counterparts in Europe, India, Persia, Russia, Japan and China. The Sinhala kings not only fought each other, they allowed the Portuguese, under the guise of helping them, to exploit their people and to force Catholicism on them – often at the point of the sword, if persuasion failed. Consequently the people were disorientated and their loyalties were constantly shifting from one local ruler to another. Buddhism, too, would have suffered from the attempts of the Portuguese to convert the Buddhists living in the coastal regions to Roman Catholicism. They would have persecuted the monks and the people, and some would have sought refuge in the Kandyan territories or overseas. Judging by contemporary records, once the Portuguese had taken control of the country – using Dharmapala's bequest as an excuse – they adopted a brutal and arbitrary approach to their governance of it.

The role of the Buddhist clergy is not stated in the chronicles but it is a fair bet that they were instrumental in the wars between the brothers (Bhuvanaika Bahu VII, Mayadunne and Rayigam Bandara). It is likely that they backed both sides so that they always won. Similarly, it is hard to fathom why the king of Jaffna drew the attention of the Portuguese and forced them to act against him unless he had been enticed into doing so by those with most to lose – the Hindu clergy.

Both groups would have been concerned that Christianity was taking hold on the island and drawing converts from the Buddhist and Hindu faiths. There is no doubt that they would have fought hard to stop the drift. So it is easy to see that the Buddhist and Hindu clergy would have built up Mayadunne and his son, Rajasinha, as defenders of their respective faiths, and justified their ongoing fight with Bhuvanaika Bahu VII and his grandson Dharmapala. The latter, because of his dependence on the Portuguese and because of his conversion to Catholicism, would have been seen by the Buddhist clergy as an enemy of Buddhism. In addition, the brutality associated with the Portuguese in their attempt to make converts for Christ, and when they broke faith with Dharmapala and sacked Kotte, would have made the islanders wonder what 'devil' their king had introduced and was now succouring, and this would have justified any action aimed at ridding the island of them.

So when the Dutch arrived, the islanders were happy to collaborate with them to rid themselves of Portuguese domination. This was a Faustian bargain. A new and more powerful organisation called the Dutch East India Company, whose main purpose was profit, had taken the place of the Portuguese. The people living in the coastal areas had jumped out of the frying pan into the fire.

Chapter 7

The Dutch in Sri Lanka

On 12 May 1656, the Portuguese garrison in Colombo surrendered to the Dutch. They had heroically resisted a Dutch siege that had lasted six months and twenty-seven days and that had reduced them to a state of famine. The coup de grace was their surrender of Jaffna to the Dutch on 24 June 1658. The Dutch, represented by the Dutch East India Company, became the new masters of the coastal regions of the island. A new era in the history of the island had begun.

Dutch involvement in Lanka was always through the Dutch East India Company, one of the great inventions of the Europeans. It was created in 1602 and went into liquidation in 1799. From 1619 it had its headquarters in Batavia (Jakarta in Indonesia). The company was a powerful force and the Board of Governors had great powers; their powers exceeded those of the board of directors of a global company today. The company got its authority to act from the government of the Netherlands under a charter that was renewed every twenty years in exchange for financial considerations. The charter permitted it to acquire and administer any territory it judged it needed to fulfil its objectives. In the acquired territories it functioned as a government, and the people of that territory were treated as subjects of the company and were bound by its decisions and its actions. In these territories the company had the right to pass laws, issue currency, negotiate treaties, wage wars, administer justice, levy taxes and exploit natural resources and the people. However, it did not tolerate acts of tyranny or physical abuse by its officers upon the natives. It is not clear whether this code of conduct was prompted by strong Christian beliefs, or for the pragmatic reason that it was costly to suppress revolts. At least one Dutch Governor, Vuyst (1726–1729), was arrested, tried and executed for his excesses by his own masters. The company's main aim was to generate revenue and profit from trade with the East. In its early years it was phenomenally successful and between 1602 and 1696 paid annual dividends of no less than 12 per cent and sometimes as high as 63 per cent. In 1669 the company had forty warships, 150 merchant ships, and 10,000 soldiers.

The company's involvement with the island began when Joris van Spillbergen, the admiral of the Dutch fleet, set foot on the island in 1602 at Batticaloa and attempted to negotiate a trading agreement with Vimala Dharma Suriya I. Admiral Sebald de Weert, who arrived later in the year, attempted to win over the king of Kandy but failed. Exasperated and much the worse for liquor, he insulted the king and he and the other Dutchmen with him were killed for their insolence. Thus, by 1603 relations between the king and the Dutch had soured. Understandably, the Dutch were reluctant to make an alliance with such a capricious king and it was almost ten years later that fresh approaches were made to the new king of Kandy, Senarat (1604–1635). He had inherited the Kandyan throne in 1604 from his first cousin, Vimala Dharma Suriya I. Senarat was a Buddhist monk who readily discarded his robes to accept the throne. His accession was challenged by another aspirant, Mayadunne of Uva, but the challenge failed. Senarat consolidated his position by marrying his predecessor's wife, Doña Catharina. For the second time in her life she had become a pawn in a power game.

On 8 March 1612, Marcellus de Boschouwer arrived on the island, and spent the next three years trying to get the king to sign an agreement with the company, but de Boschouwer failed. He promised the king that, in exchange for giving the company trading rights, he could persuade the Dutch based in Batavia to help him expel the Portuguese. He stayed in Lanka until 1615, and having failed, sailed to Holland to persuade officials there; but, failed there as well. So he went to Denmark in 1617 and persuaded the Danes of the value of establishing links with the king of Kandy. The Danes sent an expedition to Ceylon which arrived in 1620, found that Boschouwer's claim that he was representing the King of Kandy was untrue and that their journey had been in vain. They were allowed to build a fort in Trincomalee, but the Portuguese, who were still masters of the Maritime Provinces repulsed them. The Danes never tried again.

Senarat had divided his kingdom between his own son, Rajasinha – to whom he gave the Kandyan district – and the two sons of Doña Catharina, Kumarasinha and Vijayapala, to whom he gave Uva and Matale respectively. Rajasinha poisoned his stepbrother, Kumarasinha, and annexed his territory and restyled himself as Rajasinha II (1635–1687), King of Kandy. His other brother, Vijayapala, retained his third share of the kingdom. In 1636, Rajasinha II approached the Dutch and asked for their help to expel the Portuguese. The Dutch agreed and entered into an agreement with him. The agreement was converted into a formal treaty on 18 May 1638. In exchange for helping Rajasinha II rid the island of the Portuguese, he gave the Dutch monopoly rights to the export trade, allowed them to establish forts in Kottiyar and Batticaloa on the eastern side of the island and promised to meet the costs of the fleet. In doing this he had reneged on a deal with the Portuguese who had no choice but to ally themselves with Vijayapala, the king of Matale, and attack Rajasinha II. Their attempt to dislodge him failed and they withdrew to their fort.

The Dutch had not got a bargain. They found that Rajasinha II was an unreliable and duplicitous ally. It is reported that he was a despot and a tyrant. He was capricious and suspicious and kept his chiefs hostage in his court to prevent them from conspiring against him. He was disliked by his own people who showed their displeasure by staging the occasional revolt. As Robert Knox recounted in his book on Ceylon, written after his escape from imprisonment by Rajasinha II, he and his father found that he treated any Europeans who strayed into his court as trophies.[24] He ignored the diplomatic niceties that facilitated the global interaction of nations and created and broke treaties as he willed, thus making it difficult for the Dutch to work with him. He seemed always to arrive at battles after they had been won by the Dutch. He refused to meet his financial commitments and rowed with the Dutch about the retention of the Portuguese forts they had captured. He wanted them destroyed, but the Dutch decided not only to keep them but to reinforce them. Much to the annoyance of Rajasinha II, the Dutch and the Portuguese carved up the island between them when their respective kings in faraway Europe entered into a peace treaty. However, he continued to play with the Dutch. In 1671 he entered into negotiations with the French and encouraged them to occupy Trincomalee, which they did. However, the Dutch drove them off in 1672. Rajasinha II died on 25 November 1687. It is clear that he saw the Dutch as his mercenaries who had served their purpose once they expelled the Portuguese from the island. His desire to have the Portuguese forts destroyed was his way of preventing the Dutch from settling in for a long stay.

It would seem that both sides misread the other's intentions. Writing about this, Ludowyk says that Rajasinha was not the only one who played fast and loose with the treaty terms; the Dutch also reneged on their treaty commitments. But, they, in accordance with European conventions on keeping treaty obligations with non-Christians, felt that they had no moral duty to uphold their end of the treaty terms:

> It had long been a principle of European nations that treaties entered into with Oriental and African potentates could not bind them as treaties between Christians might. From the operations of law and morality which were supposed to regulate the conduct of Christians, Moors, and Gentiles were expressly excluded 'because if the principal part of (man, namely) the soul is condemned, the part which it animates cannot be privileged (to have) the benefit of our laws as they are not members of the Church'.[25]

When Rajasinha's son, Vimala Dharma Suriya II (1687–1707), inherited the Kandyan kingdom from his father he set out to re-establish relations with the Dutch, as he thought that, for practical reasons, continuing his father's feud was counter-productive. The practical reason was that, even if only for a short time, they had complete control of the coastline and the ports and were therefore able to isolate the kingdom from the outside world. Having re-established relationships with the Dutch he decided to focus on re-invigorating the Buddhist priesthood, which he believed needed reform. There may have

[24] Knox, Robert, *An Historical Relation of the Island of Ceylon*..., Tisara Prakasakayo, 1966.

[25] Ludowyk, *The Story of Ceylon*.

been a few reasons for this. Although not explicitly stated, there seems to have been a concern that the monks were enjoying nirvana on earth by expropriating the temple lands and treating the lands and the income they produced as theirs and their families' hereditary possessions. Another factor may have been the pressure by the Portuguese on the Buddhist community, which may have decimated the Buddhist priesthood. The third reason may have been an excuse to seek foreign assistance to rid him of the Dutch. The fourth may have been that the pure traditions of the priesthood had been diluted and needed renewal. The fifth, and most likely cause was that the Buddhist establishment was putting pressure on him to save Buddhism from Christianity, which was fast becoming the religion of state in the coastal regions and could well infiltrate the Kandyan kingdom. The king acquiesced because he needed the help of the monks to control the people in his domain, and if the people had converted to Christianity his and the Buddhist monks' influence over them would cease. To rectify the situation he sent an embassy to Aracan to get a new group of priests. He also built the Temple of the Tooth in Kandy.

Vimala Dharma Suriya II died in 1707. He was succeeded by Narendra Sinha (1707–1739), who built the Kandy Maha Dewale in 1731. When Narendra Sinha died on 13 May 1739, the dynasty of Sinhalese kings died with him. He was succeeded by his queen's brother, Sri Vijaya Rajasinha (1739–1747), a Dravidian who belonged to the Nayakkar dynasty of Madura. Codrington says, 'A new spirit characterised the kings of the Madura dynasty, and in 1743 Sri Vijaya Rajasinha destroyed the churches and initiated a persecution which continued under Kirti Sri.' The Dutch, for purely commercial reasons, showed considerable tolerance towards this persecution, but found that the more tolerant they were, the more demanding the court became.

When Sri Vijaya Rajasinha died he was succeeded by his brother-in-law, Kirti Sri (1747–1782), a devout Buddhist who imported priests from Siam in an effort to revive Buddhism. He also persecuted those of other religious beliefs who had taken refuge in the Kandyan kingdom, such as the Muslims and the Catholics. He made sporadic forays into Dutch territory and at other times incited the people against the Dutch in an attempt to dislocate their trading and religious activities by impeding the shipment of cinnamon as well as the building of a church and a school. The king seemed to treat the Dutch as both enemy and servant; but it could be argued that he was playing a subtle game, one that is consistent with someone who holds a weak hand.

The Dutch played into the kings' hands. The kings held to the view that in their domain only they had the right to govern the people. So, in the areas they ruled, the kings acted as the supreme authority and punished chieftains and others who exceeded their delegated powers. The Dutch focused more on profit rather than governance and delegated the welfare and management of the people to local overlords. In time-honoured fashion, these local dignitaries abused their status and often implemented policies in ways that imposed heavier burdens on the villagers and impoverished them more than their Dutch masters had intended, or than the problems they had suffered under the Portuguese.

The people revolted against the Dutch on a regular basis in protest at their imposition of measures that caused them hardship in the hope that they would moderate the overlords. These grievances ranged from anger at being fined if children failed to attend school to the appropriation of land for cinnamon growing that the villagers had cleared from the jungle for growing their food. These embers of discontent were fanned into flames of revolt by the kings, who used it to harm Dutch revenue streams. It was easy for them to do this, as the cinnamon fields were in the territories they ruled and the cinnamon peelers were their subjects. They had two weapons: they could harvest the cinnamon and export it through other ports; and they could incite the cinnamon peelers to stop work until their grievances – usually concerning money – were redressed.

The Dutch found the use of the cinnamon peelers as political agitators unacceptable and sometimes responded harshly by using excessive force. When they did, they had to be reined in by their superiors in Batavia. But they also took practical steps to safeguard themselves from these acts of sabotage by introducing new crops such as coffee in 1720 and pepper in 1753, and by successfully growing cinnamon much closer to Colombo and within areas under their direct control.

The scent of the cinnamon grown in these fields would waft up to seventeen miles out to sea and alert ships on the Indian Ocean that they were nearing the island. Centuries later, these cinnamon fields would became the most expensive real estate in Lanka, with the enchanting name of Cinnamon Gardens, and its streets and parks would bear the names of successive British Governors. The Dutch also cultivated new crops in the northern peninsula. De Silva says:

> Ryckloff van Goens [who had captured the fort of Mannar from the Portuguese] arranged the cultivation of tobacco in the Jaffna Peninsula and rice throughout the Dutch territories. He attempted to culture silk worms and started the dying of cloth in Jaffna, bringing to Jaffna skilled workmen from South India.

In February 1765 the Dutch captured Kandy, and the king, although willing to make considerable sacrifices, abandoned his capital rather than submit to being a vassal of the company. The Dutch were unable to hold the kingdom and it returned to the Kandyans by April of that year. Peace was re-established in 1766 after the king had ceded all the coastal territories he ruled, which meant that the Dutch controlled all districts bordering on the sea, making the Kandyan territories landlocked. But this was a temporary respite, and he probably agreed to this purely to get the Dutch off his back. Once things had settled down again, the king began to demand some of his territory back, especially access to the pearl fisheries. He also attempted to reach an agreement with either France or Britain to help him rid the island of the Dutch.

As often happens, there was a Judas waiting in the wings. The king's chief minister, Adigar Pilima Talauva, allowed his personal ambition to get the better of his duty to his king and his country. He decided to dethrone the king and take his place. Like Vidiye Bandara and Konappu Bandara before him, he sought the help of a foreign power in the country. To win their confidence, he supplied the Dutch with information that led to them intercepting correspondence between the king and the French. This action by Pilima Talauva ensured that the French did not come to the help of the king and forced the king to comply with the treaty terms. Despite the Dutch gaining the upper hand, their power began to ebb, and with it Pilima Talauva's ambitions. There were many causes for this, among which were the unsettled relationships with the Kandyan kings, regular uprising of the people against harsh financial impositions, the company's declining fortunes, the rising military cost of holding on to their possession, and the increased pressure by the English, who were now active in India and taking territory from the Dutch. Significantly, they took Nagapatam in 1781 and forced the Dutch East India Company to move its mint to Colombo.

The future direction of the country and its people was now in the hands of the European powers. The island had become a pawn in a European power game and the policies regarding the island were increasingly being taken out of the hands of the Sinhalese kings and the representatives of these foreign powers. Events such as the American Revolution and the emergent American nation, the shifting power balance between the English, the Dutch, the French, the Spanish and the Portuguese were all beginning to affect this small island. The Portuguese had certainly had a small impact on the territories they'd held in the island, but in many ways, real changes to the way of life of the Sri Lankan people began with the Dutch 'occupation'.

The Dutch codified the laws of Jaffna called *Thesawalamai*, and they introduced Roman-Dutch law. They also introduced systems of justice, which governed the adjudication of criminal and civil disputes particularly between the islanders and the Dutch. The Dutch Reformed Church was active and had headquarters in Colombo, Jaffna and Galle. The Church established schools where, in addition to the catechism and prayers, the children were taught to read and write in their own language. In 1788 there were fifty-five schools in a small region in the Galle district, seventeen elementary schools for Dutch children and schools to educate the clergy, school teachers and catechists. They translated the New Testament and a large part of the Old Testament into the vernacular. In keeping with their tradition, they built canals and waterways in the plains close to their forts. In this way they drained mash lands and probably also reduced malaria. They made slight modifications to the old systems of governance by merging certain village positions to remove discord among the village leaders. However, they made little or no change to the age-old ways of the kings of Lanka.

Their most lasting action was to open up European education and knowledge to those who had converted to Christianity. Through their schools and the work of the Christian clergy, these converts got the chance to keep abreast of the giant strides being made in the West. Unfortunately for the Sinhalese Buddhists of the interior, this opportunity was lost and with it their ability to compete in the more demanding periods ahead. By remaining within the jurisdiction of the Sinhalese kings, the Sinhalese Buddhist villagers in the Kandyan kingdom were still subject to the arbitrary justice of their king and noblemen whilst their coastal cousins were beginning to benefit from the greater equality of Roman-Dutch law and a system of courts. Their children were being educated so that they could support Dutch administrators. They were no doubt benefiting from new technologies in agriculture and benefiting from the job opportunities the new but limited plantation sector offered. To some groups of Sri Lankans, living under Dutch and Christian rule was proving better than living under Sinhalese Buddhist rule. And this situation, from the viewpoint of the Sinhalese Buddhists, would get worse under the British. However, it is during the Dutch period that the Sinhalese kings, at long last, began to focus on managing the foreign powers in their midst and harnessing popular resistance against them. They did not have the military skill and armament to expel them completely. But, unlike the Sinhalese kings during the first hundred years of the Portuguese occupation who were diverted by their family squabbles, these kings – perhaps because there were no other Sinhalese kings to fight with – focused more on harassing the European invaders. But by now it was far too late to avoid the inevitable. The British displaced the Dutch and changed the island for ever.

Chapter 8

Joining the British Empire

Ralph Fitch was the first Englishman to visit the island in 1589 (see box on p.76 for his impressions). James Lancaster visited in 1592. Andrew, a Franciscan friar, was the first Englishman to visit and stay in Lanka. He worked in the north and was killed by the Hindus in around 1627/28. The master gunner in the service of the Kandyan king was killed at 'the Great Stockade' in 1632. Robert Knox was shipwrecked on the island and taken prisoner by the king of Kandy in 1659. But as Ludowyk relates, Knox, a Londoner born in Tower Hill on 8 February 1641:

> ...was never in a prison in the Kandyan kingdom; his father, himself and some of the members of an English ship were captured by the king's men when they had gone ashore in the Bay of Kottiyar. They were taken to the Kandyan hills, and were moved from village to village, where as the king's 'captives' they were looked after by the villagers.

He managed to escape in 1679. Once back in England he wrote a book about his stay on the island. His book provides valuable information about the life of the villagers and also of the court. The king who held him captive was Raja Sinha II. According to de Silva:

> Although Raja Simha was by name the Emperor of Sri Lanka he only ruled Udarata and the parts that the Dutch company could not asset some claim. Numerous attempts were made on his life and finally he left Kandy for Nilambe, to the south of Kandy and thence to Galauda, Medamahanuvara where he remained until his death in 1687.

Formal contact between the British and the king of Kandy took place in 1762 when a mission led by Pybus was sent from the English East India Company Headquarters in Madras. The mission failed, but contact had been made and would lead to more talks. In January 1782, whilst the War of American Independence was raging, the British admiral, Sir Edward Hughes, captured Trincomalee from the French and sent an ambassador to Kandy. Unfortunately, Kirti Sri had died on 2 January and the new king, his brother, Rajadhirajasinha (1782–1798) refused to see the messenger because he was not authorised by King George III. Although the French, led by Suffren, recaptured Trincomalee, it was returned by them to the English East India Company in 1784.

Negotiations continued. Robert Andrews, a civilian in the Madras service was sent as ambassador to Kandy in an attempt to agree a treaty with the king. He returned with a delegation from the king led by Migastenne Disawa, and they agreed the terms of a treaty in February 1796 which gave the king of Kandy access to a port to ensure his people their supply of salt and fish. He was also allowed the use of ten sea-going vessels free from inspection. Unfortunately, when Andrews returned to ratify the treaty and get the king's signature, he rejected it. The British realised that they did not need it. The offer lapsed and it was decades before it was re-offered and accepted.

At first, the British settlements were managed by the British East India Company from Madras through military governors. The Sri Lankans living in the British territories were subject to administrators brought in from Madras. This proved a failure, as the people disapproved of being managed by Indians (Madrasis and Tamils) who seemed to focus their efforts on farming the revenues. They also protested at the discontinuance of certain age-old traditions as regards service-tenure of paddy crops.

On 1 January 1802, the British settlements in the island were made a Crown Colony with a council made up of the chief justice, the commander-in-chief and the chief secretary, and a new civil service – the first to be established in the East under the Crown. This administrative arrangement remained in force until 1833. The chief sources of revenue at that time were the pearl fisheries, cinnamon, *arrack* – which sold well in India – and duty on areca nut, salt, tobacco and a tax on the Moors in lieu of personal labour. There were 170 schools in 1801; schoolmasters were also notaries and registrars. An academy was opened in Colombo with three preparatory schools. The first Governor of Ceylon was the Hon. Frederick North, later Earl of Guildford. He took steps to correct some of the causes of the riots that had preceded his arrival but his management of his relationship with the Kandyan court led to costly mistakes. He lost his nerve; the stress resulted in his developing neurasthenia and a request by him to be relieved of his duties on the island. North left in 1805.

On 26 July 1798, Rajadhirajasinha, the king of Kandy, died. Adigar Pilima Talauva used his influence to ensure that a young relative of Rajadhirajasinha ascended the throne. The new king, who called himself Sri Vikrama Rajasinha (1798–1815), was from the Nayakkar dynasty of Madura. Pilima Talauva, acting as regent, sought a meeting with Governor North to assess the Governor's response to Pilima Talauva's suggestion that he depose or kill the king and take the throne for himself. He tried on various other occasions to gain the support of the Governor, but when he failed, he set out to create an incident that would force the British into launching a military campaign against the king.

Realising that the British took their responsibility for the lives of people living in their territory seriously, Pilima Talauva arranged for Moors from Puttalam to be attacked, ill-treated and robbed. The Governor probably suspected that the attack was inspired by Pilima Talauva, but he responded by sending a force on 31 January 1803 to avenge the injustice. Pilima Talauva had trapped him into acting prematurely. The force occupied Kandy on 21 February of that year and Sri Vikrama Rajasinha fled the capital but remained at large. Much to Pilima Talauva's chagrin, instead of appointing him, the British appointed Prince Muttuswami, the rival claimant to the throne, who had fled to Jaffna and British protection when Sri Vikrama Rajasinha became king. Pilima Talauva, not to be outdone, proposed that as Muttuswami had no following in the Kandyan kingdom it would be safer if he was appointed the supreme authority for the Kandyan kingdom whilst Muttuswami could reign as king in absentia from a secure base in Jaffna. In recognition of Muttuswami's sovereignty over the Kandyan kingdom Pilima Talauva would pay him an annual tribute.

Unfortunately this plan failed. The king, Sri Vikrama Rajasinha, reasserted himself. He attacked the now depleted[26] British garrison in Kandy on 24 June 1803 and was repulsed. The garrison commander, Major Davie, and his men, realising that they could not hold Kandy, sought to retire to Trincomalee. Unfortunately, the Mahaveli Ganga (a major river) was in flood and cut off their retreat. The king had them at his mercy, but no mercy was shown. He killed Muttuswami and ordered the unarmed British soldiers return to Kandy where they were massacred on 26 June 1803 at a place called 'Davie's Tree'. But Pilima Talauva had won in his intent. The king, emboldened by his recent success, attacked the British with the support of his own people and those in the occupied territories and reached within fifteen miles of Colombo. However, his six-pounder guns were no match for British armaments and the British military machine, and he was chased all the way back to Kandy. Peace reigned for the next seven years. The king was now an enemy of the British and would be eventually required to pay for his actions.

Sir Thomas Maitland, who replaced North on the 19 July 1805, focused on building a sound administrative system for the island and ignored the Kandyans. He changed the basis of taxation to one that the people found more acceptable, limited grants of land to Europeans to Colombo and its districts, introduced trial by jury to apply to all British subjects, Ceylon's Catholics were relieved from the disabilities imposed on them by the Dutch, and he appointed village headmen and entrusted them with policing duties.

The King of Kandy, Sri Vikrama Rajasinha, in the meantime, continued to believe in Pilima Talauva, despite his various machinations, until 1811 when he had him beheaded for his treachery. Pilima Talauva was replaced by Ehelepola who was made chief minister. But the king took steps to prevent his minister plotting with the British to overthrow him. He divided his kingdom into smaller bailiwicks to prevent his chiefs from acquiring the power to unseat him. He also curbed their powers, which displeased them. All of them made

[26] 'Europeans were dying at the rate of six a day', Codrington.

contact with the British, primarily through a civil servant called D'Oyly, who was proficient in Sinhalese, and through him sought British help to unseat the king. But the British knew better than to fall for this trick a second time.

Maitland was succeeded by Sir Robert Brownrigg (1812–1820), who focused on sorting out the Kandyan issue. In 1814 Brownrigg got the chance to capture Kandy. The king suspected that Ehelepola was plotting against him and ordered him back to Kandy. But Ehelepola, fearing for his life, refused to obey and rebelled. Molligoda, the head of the other province, quelled the uprising and became chief minister. Ehelepola took refuge with the British. Ludowyk says that Ehelepola 'left his wife and family in Kandyan country and Sri Vikrama Rajasinha proceeded against them with the utmost rigour of the Kandyan law'. Ludowyk, however, dismisses the claim that the king took revenge on Ehelepola by getting his wife to pound her children's heads in a mortar before she was killed. He thinks that 'its gory trimmings are more likely to have been corroborative detail familiar in folk belief about the activities of *yakkhas* than the sadism of any human being'. What is certain, though, is that Ehelepola now knew that his life depended on deposing the king. So, with this thought in mind, he agreed to provide the British with valuable help and to draw on the help of his contacts in the Kandyan court as well. Besides, the king, being a Tamil, was 'not one of us' and was considered fair game in Ehelepola's and his associates' attempt to wrest back the Kandyan kingdom for the Kandyan people – that is, themselves. The British realised that, provided they could get the help of Molligoda and the other chiefs, they could defeat the king and capture the Kandyan kingdom. To do this they promised Molligoda's party that they would retain all their privileges and rights under British rule. Having prepared the ground, they used the atrocity perpetrated on ten British subjects, the continued animosity of the king to the British and his unwillingness to enter into a treaty with them, as a reason for declaring war.

Molligoda surrendered his province after a mock defence, and an unopposed British army marched into Kandy and took it on 14 February 1815 and captured the king four days later. The king died in exile in India on 30 January 1832. His only son died childless in 1843, thus permanently ridding the island of hereditary kings. On 2 March 1815 a convention was held in Kandy between the governor and the Kandyan chiefs, at which control and administration of the Kandyan kingdom was ceded to the British, who decided to run it using a Board of Governors rather than appointing a new chief. Ehelepola was disappointed.

The British now had control of the whole island and continued to rule it for 128 years until it ceded control to the island people on the 4 February 1948. During that time they built a nation and an economy and left both behind for the indigenous people to enjoy and build on.

Ralph Fitch, an English visitor to the island in 1589 says of Rajasinha and his people:

> This Ceylon is a brave island, very fruitful and fair, but by reason of continued wars with the King [Rajasinha] thereof all things are very dear, for he will not suffer anything to be brought to the castle where the Portugal be, wherefore oftentimes they have great want of victuals. Their provision of victuals cometh out of Bengala every year. The King is called Raja, and is of great force; for he cometh to Colombo, which is the place where the Portugals have their fort, with a hundred thousand men and many elephants. But they be naked people all of them, yet many of them be good with their pieces, which be muskets. When the King talketh with any man, he standeth upon one leg and setteth the other foot upon his knee, with his sword in his hand. It is not their order for the king to sit, but to stand. His apparel is a fine painted cloth made of cotton-wool about his middle. His hair is long and bound up with a little fine cloth about his head. All the rest of his body is naked. His guard are a thousand men, which stand round about him, and he in the middle; and when he marcheth many of them go before him and the rest come after him. They are of the race of the Cingalese, which they say are the best kind of all Malabars. Their ears are very large, for the greater they are the more honourable they are accounted. Some of them are a span long. The wood which they burn is cinnamon wood, and it smelleth very sweet. There is great store of rubies, sapphires, and spinels in this island. The best of all be here, but the King will not suffer the inhabitants to dig for them lest his enemies should know of them, and make wars against him, and so drive him out of his country for them. They have no horses in all the country. The elephants be not so great as those of Pegu, which be monstrous huge; but they say all other elephants do fear them, and none dare fight with them though they be very small. Their women have a cloth bound about them from their middle to their knee, and all the rest is bare. All of them be black and but little, both men and women. Their houses are very little, made of branches of the palmer or coco-tree [coconut tree], and covered with the leaves of the same tree. The eleventh of March we sailed from Ceylon and so doubled the Cape of Comorin. Not far from thence, between Ceylon and the mainland of Nagapatam, they fish for pearls, and there is fished every year much which doth serve India, Cambaia and Bengal.[27]

[27] Richard David, *Hakluyt's Voyages: A Selection*.

Part Three

Ceylon, the Country the British Built

Summary

This part discusses how the British converted a feudal, agricultural people into a modern democracy based on the rule of law and a plantation economy.

When Dom Lourenco de Almeida arrived on the shores of Lanka he had found a country living off its ancestral wealth. The great cities of Anuradhapura and Polonnaruwa, with their giant inland seas, wonderful and costly buildings, and the fortress capital of Sigiriya, a feat of considerable engineering genius and artistic beauty, were ruined cities and lost to the jungle. Today they are World Heritage sites and tourist attractions. The last Sinhalese king of note was Parakrama Bahu VI who '...raised the nation to a height never attained since the days of Parakrama Bahu II, and never afterwards rivalled.'[28] The grandeur and splendour of Sinhalese civilisation died with him.

The Portuguese had earned much from the export of cinnamon. But they also had to contend with the Sinhalese kings who seemed to be continuously at war with each other and with them. Dutch interests were mainly commercial, but they had established a social, political and economic superstructure to help them administer the Maritime Provinces under their control. So when they transferred control of the island to the British in 1796 the foundations of British rule had been set in place. The Madras government of the East India Company administered the Maritime Provinces until the island was declared a Crown Colony in 1802. From then on, the island was ruled by a governor who was appointed by the Crown. The governor was answerable to the Secretary of State and through him to the Imperial Government and to Parliament in Westminster.

Early attempts to bring the whole country under British rule by capturing the Kandyan kingdom failed, but it eventually succumbed in 1815. From 1815 to 1833 the British administered the Kandyan kingdom and the Maritime Provinces as separate administrative units. On 28 September 1833, on the recommendation of the Colebrooke–Cameron Commission, the old constitution was revised. Executive and legislative councils were established, the separate administration of the Kandyan kingdom was abolished, and the whole island was, for the first time, treated as a single entity, but divided into provinces for administrative convenience. English became the commercial and official language of the island. The British had set the stage to reap the benefits, and they did.

In addition to these political changes the British administration in Ceylon encouraged the development of a commercial plantation sector. In the course of creating large coffee and tea plantations, many village communities were

[28] Codrington, *A Short History of Ceylon*.

moved from their traditional homes and Indian labour was imported to work the plantations. Their working conditions were far from perfect, but there is a tendency to portray the colonial period as one in which the people of the island suffered at the hands of an uncaring colonial master. Whatever hardships the people may have suffered during this time it is important to view it against the backdrop of a period in British history, which saw it transform from an agricultural economy into the most powerful industrial power in the world. In that process of change, British men and women and children in industrial cities such as Manchester, Liverpool and Birmingham suffered similar hardships to those experienced in the colonies. This does not excuse what may have happened but it must not be construed that the overseas subjects of Queen Victoria and those of her immediately preceding and succeeding monarchs were treated more unfairly than those in Britain.

It was a time when Britain's men and women of science and literature were of the highest calibre, her naval and military might was at its peak and her industrialists were producing goods that the whole world desired. The bad news was that the rapid changes that the country faced during this time meant that in many areas its social structures were found wanting. Prompted by reformers such as Wilberforce and Wesley and many others, legislation was passed to improve working conditions and protect the workers from exploitation. This moral crusade also bore fruit in the colonies, but to a lesser extent.

Working conditions in some places such as Manchester were bad enough to inspire Engels to write *The Condition of the Working Class in England*, and to feed Marx with fuel for his own views on the evils of capitalism. The factories of Victorian Britain were not the most salubrious places. The men, women and children who worked in the mills and factories were exposed to long hours, dangerous machinery, dark and humid conditions and the caprices of overseers and owners. It was not until the 1860s that Factory and Workshop Acts provided women and children with some protection. But the enterprising found great scope to create profitable businesses. During this period democracy matured in Britain. Universal suffrage became a reality when women over twenty-one years of age were given the right to vote in 1929. In the very early years of its occupation of Ceylon Wellington had decisively beaten Napoleon at Waterloo. Towards the end of its occupation Britain had, for the second time in a short space of thirty or so years ended two long wars that had sapped her of her young men and much of her capital – a price paid also by her colonies. She emerged from the Second World War with many of her major towns severely damaged by German bombs and owing large sums to the United States, a debt that has only been paid off recently. She rapidly lost her colonies and with them her captive markets. Today, she is the fourth largest economic power in the world. When the British left Ceylon in 1948, they left behind an economy, a political system, an infrastructure and a system of administration that if used by a united people would have also projected them into the ranks of a role model for emergent democracies.

Not all the Europeans who spent time in Ceylon saw it as a money machine. Some loved it dearly and gave much in return. It seems right to end this summary with 'Hymn For Ceylon', a poem by Walter Stanley Senior to his 'Foster-Mother'.

Hymn for Ceylon

Jehovah, thou hast promised
The isle shall wait for thee;
The joyous isles of oceans,
The jewels of the sea,
Lo! we, this island's watchmen,
Would give and take no rest,
(For thus as Thou commanded)
Till our dear land be blessed.

Then bless her, mighty Father,
With blessings needed most,
In every verdant village,
By every palmy coast;
On every soaring mountain,
O'er every spreading plain,
May all her sons and daughters
Thy righteousness attain.

Give peace within her borders,
'Twixt man and man goodwill,
The love all unsuspicious,
The love that works no ill;
In loyal, lowly service
Let each from other learn,
The guardian and the guarded,
Till Christ himself return.

To Him our land shall listen,
To Him our land shall kneel,
All rule be on its shoulders,
All wrong beneath its heel;
O consummation glorious
Which now by faith we sing!
Come cast we up the highway
That brings us back our king.

Rev. Walter Stanley Senior, 1876–1938

In many ways, Stanley's attitude epitomises that of many British people who lived and worked in Sri Lanka during the 150 years or so of British occupation. It could not be said of him or others like him that they exploited the country. In the Foreword to his book *Call of Lanka – Ceylon in Prose and Verse,* which was compiled and published by two of his pupils in 1960, Canon R S de Saram, the Principal of my alma mater, St Thomas' College, Mount Lavinia, says this:

> Here is some of the work of a man who lived in Ceylon for twenty years and regarded them as the best years of his life. He loved Ceylon with all his heart. 'Foster-Mother' he calls her, and himself, humbly, 'child of an alien isle.' Would that all we who were born here and call this lovely land our own, loved her as truly and had as high an ideal for her.[29]

By the end of the Second World War, Ceylon was also able to benefit from the world's hunger for rubber. So healthy was the economy of the country at independence that it could afford to initiate a welfare state that subsidised the cost of essential foods and provided free health and education to its people. So, by any standards, the country had been converted by the Europeans – and especially by the British – into a modern democratic state with a sound economic base. All the Ceylonese had to do was build on their inheritance.

---

[29] Canon R. S. de Saram, 'Foreword', in Walter Stanley Senior, *The Call of Lanka: Ceylon in Prose and Verse*, Kandy, Trinity College Press, 1960.

Chapter 9

The Political Development of the Island

The Sri Lankan people, like many peoples of earlier ages, lived for over 2,000 years in a feudal society. They were subject to the whims and caprices of their immediate overlords and the king. The clergy – in their case, Buddhist monks and Hindu priests – also influenced their lives and made demands on them. The caste system imposed rigid constraints on their freedoms, reinforced the social divide and limited their expectations. People knew their place and were kept in it by custom and convention.

There was no involvement by the people in the way they were governed. The king and his nobles lived off them. It is not even certain that they did much to protect them from invaders. The people did revolt from time to time but they did not have the resources to change the way they were governed. Besides, fatalism – preached by Hindu and Buddhist clergy – tended to limit people's aspirations.

The arrival of the Portuguese in 1505 did little to change this. Dutch rule was brutal, too. But they introduced Roman-Dutch Law to the country and also put in place a system of administration and social reform that were of immense benefit to the British.

At the beginning of British rule, the Madras government of the East India Company administered the Maritime Provinces that the Dutch had ceded to the British in 1796. The Sinhalese in the central provinces were still ruled by the king of Kandy. 'The Madras administration proved a failure'.[30] In 1797 the Sinhalese revolted forcing the British to collect revenues, according to Codrington 'at the point of the bayonet.' So, in 1798, Frederic North was appointed Civil Governor by the King and on 1 January 1802 the Maritime Provinces became a Crown Colony ruled by a governor answerable to the British Crown.

After the British defeated the Kandyan king in 1815 they ran the Maritime Provinces and the Kandyan territories as two different administrative entities. Following the Colebrooke–Cameron report in 1833 they treated the island as a single political entity. British rule was administered by the governor who was the island's chief executive officer and the main official channel between the island and Whitehall and Westminster. He was subject to the mandarins in the colonial office but he was appointed by the British monarch on the recommendations of the British prime minister. He had an advisory council made up of British civil

[30] Codrington, *A Short History of Ceylon*.

servants. He had executive and legislative powers, which he could use to control the colony and deliver revenues to meet the costs of running the country. The Library of Congress Studies says of the end of this period:

> By the early 1830s the British had almost finished consolidating their position in Sri Lanka and began to take more interest in securing the island's political stability and economic profitability ... a new wave of thought, influenced by reformist ideology (utilitarianism) articulated by Jeremy Bentham and James Mill ... promoted the idea of democracy and individual liberty. It sponsored the idea of trusteeship – new territories would be considered trusts and would receive all the benefits of British liberalism.[31]

The first step towards converting this philosophy into practical reality in Ceylon was taken in 1829. The British Colonial Office sent a Royal Commission of Eastern Inquiry led by W M G Colebrooke and C H Cameron.

The Colebrooke–Cameron Report, the result of the inquiry into how the country should be administered, was published in 1833. Among its recommendations was that the division of the country by 'racial' stereotypes – such as Low-Country Sinhalese, Kandyan Sinhalese and Tamils – be abolished and that all those living on the island be treated as a single people sharing a common land mass. This was the first attempt at creating a single nation of Ceylonese. Colebrooke also produced a charter of justice in 1833, which attempted to create a single system of justice out of the many different forms prevailing at the time. Many of the recommendations of the report were implemented. The country was divided into provinces and each province had its government agent. A new Supreme Court was established and district courts were also brought into being. In addition to putting in place these constitutional, legal and educational systems the British also began to develop the country in an attempt to improve health provision, communications and trade.

The powers of the governor were vested in an executive council, which appointed members to the Legislative Council. The Legislative Council included three representatives to represent the needs of the Low-Country Sinhalese, the Tamils and the Dutch Burghers. It recommended that the civil service employ local citizens and in 1840 the first Sri Lankan earned his place in the civil service by passing a competitive exam. It standardised the education curriculum and made English the 'new' common language of the country. For the first time the native-born had a common language of communication within the island that crossed linguistic barriers and linked them closer to their colonial masters. By the simple step of making English the common language of the country the Governor had, unwittingly, planted the seeds of future contention. An English-educated, privileged class came into being. This group

[31] Library of Congress website – *Sri Lanka, Modernisation and Reform*, 20 January 2005.

of people had also converted to Christianity, which gradually replaced Buddhism as the religion of the ruling clique who at that time were British and the English-educated Ceylonese. These English-speaking elite worked in the civil service and the professions and acquired the knowledge to negotiate their independence from British rule. The non-Christian and non-English-speaking Sinhalese and Tamils felt that their languages and their religion had been relegated to secondary roles in the affairs of the nation.

The political development of the island was set in motion by the Colebrooke–Cameron report and continued to evolve until the adoption of parliamentary democracy by the Ceylonese people on 4 February 1948. Over a period of about 120 years the British adapted and transferred their political and administrative systems to the needs of this, its first Crown Colony. In the more liberal political environment that followed the Colebrooke–Cameron recommendations (c. 1870 to c. 1910), various minority and aggrieved sectors of society formed into groups and agitated for equal status. The rise in the ranks of the educated Ceylonese released new elite groups who could act to secure adoption of their views using pressure groups. They earned various small concessions for their Buddhist brethren and they earned a small segment of the people the right to be represented in the legislative council, along with the representatives of minority communities. Democracy was taking root but it was a gift of the colonial ruler rather than something earned by the people. Perhaps this is the weakness of imposed democracies – the people do not value it in the same way as those who have fought for it. It is also questionable whether they truly understood its value to them.

The British managed to control the country without too much rebellion or protest from the islanders. However, from time to time, in response to harsh taxation for example, some of the island people would riot. Generally, these rebellions were quickly quelled. But sometimes, for example, in the Kandyan 'rebellion' in 1848, the British used brutal methods to suppress the rioters. This usually resulted in the recall of the governor, as happened to Governor Torrington after the Kandyan rebellion in 1848.

The unnecessarily harsh suppression of the riots of 1915 had more far-reaching consequences. Unlike in 1848, by this time, British policy in the island had created a new breed of Ceylonese who were articulate and knowledgeable enough to use argument and the political process to gain changes. Among those jailed during the 1915 riots was D S Senanayake who was to become the first prime minister of independent Ceylon. He was, in fact, trying to restore peace by mediating with the rioters at the time of his arrest. This ill-considered act gave impetus to the nationalist movements in Sri Lanka as the Amritsar Massacre in 1919 did in India.

The first sign of political activism was in 1919 when the Sinhalese and Tamils united to form the Ceylon National Congress. It was a political organisation that represented all the people of the island. It demanded a new constitution that would increase local control over the Executive Council and the budget. Although refused, the original constitution was revised in 1920 and again in 1924. The latter revision increased Sri Lankan participation in political affairs. A very small hole had been made in the dyke.

It was around this time (1921) that the early signs of how the balance of power between the Tamils and the Sinhalese would be managed became an issue. The English-educated Ceylonese of this period were:

> ...no longer a united group of all communities. Fear, not about how power might be wielded but for their very existence, felt by sections of the group, caused a split between the Tamils who had been intellectual leaders of the movement and the Sinhalese. Two leaders of the Tamil community – Arunachalam and Ponnambalam – left the Ceylon National Congress and founded the Tamil Mahajana Sabha in Jaffna ... the split came not on a question of a share of the spoils, but over special representation for the Tamils.[32]

In 1924, Ceylon was granted representative government. Thirty-four members were elected to the Legislative Council but they represented only four per cent of the population. However, the Governor had veto powers and could therefore ignore the views of the non-official members of the council. In effect control was still firmly in the hands of the Governor and the franchise was a sop to the educated Ceylonese who had argued for it. What is important, though, is that the fundamental principle of representative government was being gradually and grudgingly granted. Strangely, the reluctance to expand the spheres of influence of the Ceylonese in their own affairs came more from the British ruling group in Ceylon, who saw power slipping away from them, than from the UK. This constitution was rejected not long after by the Donoughmore Commission because 'it divorced power from responsibility.'

The Donoughmore Commission, led by the Earl of Donoughmore, studied the political situation in the island, and the commission, with a little help from Lord Passfield (Sidney Webb), recommended universal adult franchise and an experimental system of government. But the new constitution failed to embody the Colonial Office principles on how a multiracial colony should be governed – it was unable to ensure that 'the balance of powers [should be] so finely contrived that no single community can impose its will upon the other communities'.[33] Alas, Lord Donoughmore and Lord Passfield, being unaccustomed to the strong tribal instincts of the different communities in Ceylon, did not anticipate that, unlike their British counterparts who tended to vote on political programmes, the Ceylonese would vote on communal lines. So it was left to the voters – those over twenty-one years of age – to exercise their franchise for the good of the country and not for the good of their community. What was even worse was that these august gentlemen did not consider

[32] Ludowyk, *The Story of Ceylon.*

[33] Ludowyk, *The Story of Ceylon.*

whether the voters were able to determine what organisation or person would best represent their needs or whether there were political parties to contest the elections. In fact there were no political parties to contest these elections except the Labour Party.

> The politically uneducated voter presented it [the ballot paper] reverently to the great one of his area or the candidate of his caste. Practically all those returned to the two State Councils of 1931 and 1936 owed their success to their personal or family connections with the constituency rather than to any political considerations.[34]

This behaviour of the electorate was probably not very different to that of their British counterparts of a century earlier. The Donoughmore Constitution, despite ignoring the communally motivated voting tendencies of the electorate, helped the Sri Lankans take their first steps on the road to self-government. Over 1,400,000 people voted at the first elections to the State Council held in 1931. Although the British governor had to approve all legislation the legislative arm of government – the State Council – was both an executive and legislative body. The Library of Congress Country Studies says of this constitutional arrangement that:

> The system of executive committees did not lead to the development of national political parties. Instead, a number of splinter political groups evolved around influential personalities who usually followed a vision too limited or an agenda too communally partisan to have an impact on national politics.

Whether this is a result of the Donoughmore constitutional arrangements or an inherent tendency in the Sri Lankan psyche and society is not clear. My view is that it is a trait of the people. The constitution helped them exploit their tribal tendencies and personal loyalties to the fullest as it gave them the opportunity to settle disagreements between members of a party by leaving it and forming a new group rather than attempting to reform the existing group. Those in Sri Lankan politics found it almost impossible to handle the concept that a group of politicians with shared values and ideologies should formulate a strategy and collectively present it to the people and, if elected to office, implement it and be subsequently judged on how well they kept their promises. What they found easier to do was to leave a group as soon as it veered from a course they advocated and form a new group. Mr Bandaranaike's departure from the UNP (United National Party) to found the SLFP (Sri Lanka Freedom Party) is the most high profile defection of this sort, caused by his annoyance that the selection of the leader of the UNP was not by fair ballot but was dynastic. This raises also the issue of whether there is an

---

[34] Ludowyk, *The Story of Ceylon.*

ideological foundation for these political parties or whether they are really formed as acts of revenge or to pander to the vanity of its leader.

Between 1937 and 1944, four political parties designed to represent communal interests were formed: the Great Council of the Sinhalese by Mr Bandaranaike in 1937; the Burgher Political Association in 1938; the Ceylon Indian Tamil Congress in 1939; and the All Ceylon Tamil Congress in 1944, founded by Mr G G Ponnambalam. With the creation of these political groupings phase two in differentiation between the different communal groups had begun. The native-born Tamil community differentiated themselves from their Tamil and Hindu Indian-born brethren on the plantations and treated them as inferiors. During this period, parties sympathetic to socialism were established. Mr A E Goonesimha founded the Labour Party in 1931. The Lanka Sama Samaja Party was founded in 1935, and the Communist Party of Sri Lanka (founded in 1943) was a splinter group of the LSSP. These socialist parties, despite their limited appeal, were to play a significant role in the politics of the island. Many years later, although they were unable to gain power directly, they propped up the governments of Mr and Mrs Bandaranaike and used their bargaining power within those governments to put in place socialist measures that eventually destroyed the private sector in the country. Their state-sponsored alternatives sank into incompetence and were propped up by large injections of public money.

After the fall of Singapore in 1940, Sri Lanka was used by Britain as a base for its war efforts. The investment in the infrastructure made by the British at this time has sustained the country ever since. As much as a reward for unconditional support of the British war effort in the East, Lord Soulbury arrived in Ceylon in July 1944 tasked with the duty of examining a new constitution that the Sri Lankan ministers of the State Council had proposed. The new constitution that emerged out of his study gave Sri Lanka dominion status and eventually independence in 1948.

Independence was achieved through peaceful negotiations by a seemingly united people. Their leaders chose the democratic process of governance. This elite cabal of Sinhalese, Tamil and Muslim leaders negotiated with the British to win independence for the island. They were well thought of by the British, but Ponting is less generous about them. He says:

> The only area where the British faced few problems was Sri Lanka. Like the Americans in the Philippines they handed power to the local landowners in return for continued use of military bases.[35]

In other words, Ponting's view was that the country was not handed over to the people but to a small group who were sympathetic to British interests. D S Senanayake, the first prime minister of Sri Lanka, was a central figure in the

[35] Clive Ponting, *World History*, Chatto & Windus, 2000.

negotiations that eventually resulted in independence. He formed the United National Party, which incorporated the Ceylon National Congress, The Sinhala Maha Sabha and the Muslim League. Ludowyk says of the UNP at the time:

> ...the trouble with the UNP was that it was not a party at all. It was a group of personages brought together by the dominant personality of D. S. Senanayake, for the ad hoc purpose of providing a mode by which the Soulbury Constitution could be operated.[36]

The parliamentary democracy that emerged followed the British constitutional principles. There were two houses. The House of Representatives was made up of elected members. The upper house, the Senate, was made up of members appointed by the governor general or elected to it by members of the House of Representatives. The governor general was now a figurehead. There is no denying that the people who took over from the British, the new ruling clique, were the small group of English-educated landowning and professional classes. But they were also the best able to carry the burdens of forging a new nation out of a subject people. That they failed to do this is not the fault of the British.

For nearly eight years after independence, they basked in their new-found power but did little to pursue a new course that would keep the country united. They could have acted to heal long-felt and legitimate hurts of the people and position the country to take advantage of the world economy that was gradually getting into its stride after the Second World War. But they did not. At this juncture in its life, the country knew only 'Ceylonese people'. By failing to take control of the mood of the country they allowed various pressure groups to capture the minds and hearts of the people and to take them down a route that has left them with the chaos of today.

In modern Sri Lanka, the CIA's *World Factbook* lists twenty political organisations, but there are probably more, each representing single issues. *The World Factbook* also lists pressure groups of which the Buddhist establishment and the Tamil freedom movements are two. This tendency to form cliques is also prevalent among the Tamils. The Tamil freedom movement also has many faces – some opposed to the other. As Muttukumaru says, when in 1985,

> ...talks between the government, the TULF [Tamil United Liberation Front] and the militant groups took place ... apart from differences in attitude between the Government and the TULF, differences between militant groups also emerged which are traceable to ideology, political perceptions and to military strategies. Predictably therefore they did not form an united organisation.[37]

[36] Ludowyk, *The Story of Ceylon.*

[37] Anton Muttukumaru, *The Military History of Ceylon: An Outline*, New Delhi, Navrang, 1993.

What is yet to be proven is that the Sri Lankan people understand the spirit of democracy and work within it, rather than see it as a means of legitimately subjugating minority communities within the unitary state that is Sri Lanka. This issue is covered in Discussion Paper 1 in part seven.

Chapter 10

Building the Economy

The natural deep-water harbour of Trincomalee was a godsend to a British nation that had built its empire on the strength of its sea power. Tucked away in the north-eastern corner of Sri Lanka, and sitting on the sea ways between East and West, the harbour was a perfectly good haven for British warships. On those grounds alone, it made sense for Britain to hold on to the island. But the island offered more. So, having established a strong administrative system to manage the island, the British focused their attention on building its economy.

Historically, the indigenous people had depended primarily on an agricultural economy. Using very advanced water collection, storage and distribution techniques they had irrigated their fields and reaped rich harvests. But they had experienced famines too. The king, his courtiers and the Buddhist monasteries that owned the most fertile fields had devised a form of tenant cultivation to provide labour for their fields. Peasant communities were dependent on the land-owning group for their livelihood. But, they carved out areas from the forests to grow vegetables and keep cattle. The cattle were a source of milk and milk-based products, but they were not farmed for meat. A whole range of indigenous fruits that grew naturally provided islanders with nutritious food and the vitamins that sustained life. The coconut tree provided milk for cooking, and wood for homes and leaves for roofs and walls. The agricultural income of the country was supplemented by income from the export trade, which was managed by Arab traders. They bought and shipped many valuable goods from the island – pearl from the pearl fisheries, gems from the mines, cinnamon and other spices. Codrington, writing in 1929, says that during the first 1,000 years or so people lived 'in the north, south and south-east of the island' and that Anuradhapura, the capital of the Sinhalese kingdom:

> ...was of vast extent ... contained many parks, open spaces and monastic establishments ... a quarter assigned to foreign merchants in whose hands was most of the trade. About AD 500 we read of a Persian Christian colony; a Nestorian cross undoubtedly belonging to this community is to be seen in the Anuradhapura museum ... Traders from Egypt, subjects of the Roman Empire, visited the country, and small Roman copper coins of the fourth century at one time formed the bulk of the currency.

From 1505 to 1830 the Portuguese, the Dutch and the British made money from the very high quality cinnamon that literally grew wild in the southern provinces of the island. Money, it would seem, grew on trees. But in the early years of British occupation, cinnamon's appeal was waning and the British, realising that this feudal economy would not sustain the growing population and meet the financial criteria set in London – that all territories must pay their way – set about developing new revenue streams.

To make the island self-financing they set about developing a plantation economy. Between 1830 and 1869 the British invested in the development of a commercially run and managed plantation sector. The money to finance the plantations came from British civilians and military personnel stationed in Kandy. Land, for the plantations, was expropriated from the Kandyan peasantry, causing resentment and uprisings that were put down with ferocious energy. Coffee was the first new crop, and the first plantation was established in Gampola in the hill country in 1824 by George Bird, an army officer. Migrant workers from South India were brought in to harvest the crop. The success of the crop and the huge revenues it generated required and enabled the infrastructure of road and rail services to be built to link the plantations to the harbours of Trincomalee, Colombo and Galle. Codrington records that the road from Kurunegala to Kandy was opened in 1821, the road from Colombo to Kandy was opened in 1825, the road from Kandy to Matale was opened in 1831, the road from Kandy to Dambulla in 1832 and from Kandy to the boundary of Trincomalee by 1833. Ludowyk, writing in 1962, argues that:

> Coffee was the key-signature marking the transition from old to new Ceylon, and not constitutional and legislative enactments …coffee sent money downwards from the hills into the Western and Southern provinces. It brought into being practically everything associated with modern Ceylon – its characteristic economy, its changed social structure, its altered landscape and even its political development.

The coffee industry was hurt, however, by the coffee blight that started in 1869. It destroyed the industry in fifteen years. Contemporary figures suggest that 50,000 hundred weights of coffee were exported in 1836 and 856,570 hundred weights were exported in 1875. In 1886, as a result of the blight, only 179,254 hundred weights were exported. Coconut and rubber plantations had also been established during this time but coffee was the mainstay of the economy until tea replaced it in about 1870.

The people who paid the real price for the success of the coffee industry were the villagers who had established little hamlets right across the Kandyan kingdom and were moved out by the planters when they came to clear the land to plant coffee. Strangely, the issue that caused extreme anger among the villagers was not their distress at being moved out of their hamlets but the appropriation of lands belonging to the Buddhist establishment by the coffee planters. Such was the mindset of the peasants that they were willing to fight for the right of the Buddhist establishment to keep its landholdings. When the worldwide depression of 1846 adversely affected coffee prices, the government sought to recoup its lost revenues by imposing taxes on a range of things such as firearms, dogs, boats, carriages and bullock carts, a poll tax and a shop tax which hurt the indigenous population far more than it did the British. The peasant revolt – the Kandyan Rebellion of 1848 – which lasted four days and was nothing more than a spontaneous outpouring of anger at these iniquitous taxes, was brutally suppressed. But the incident caused the British Parliament to appoint a commission of enquiry. Peel, Gladstone and Disraeli were members of the commission. They concluded that Governor Torrington had overreacted, and he was recalled to Britain to his former job as Lord of Her Majesty's Bedchamber – a job, it is said, her majesty felt he was better suited to do.

The British planted tea as a replacement crop. The first tea plantation was established in the Ramboda district in 1867. It was not until 1873 or 1874 that the first packets of Ceylon tea were exported to Britain. Tea required a large resident workforce and this was predominantly brought into the island from South India. Ponting points out that:

> In the second half of the nineteenth century over 450,000 indentured labourers went from India to the British West Indies, others went to Natal, Mauritius and Fiji (where they became a majority of the population). Others went to Malaya to work in the tin industry or to Sri Lanka to work on the tea plantations.

Whole families came and established themselves in the tea plantation districts in the hill country. The British habit of moving people from different parts of its empire to provide labour for their plantation sectors, and its habit of creating unitary states out of previously independent tribes or ethnic groups, has resulted in ethnic problems in many parts of the world. And it did in Ceylon. This particular time-bomb is still ticking. The Library of Congress Country Studies website claims that:

> The census of 1911 recorded the number of Indian laborers in Sri Lanka at about 500,000 – about 12 per cent of the island's total population. In the 1980s they were a still substantial 6 per cent.[38]

The plight of the Indian indentured labourers was much greater than the problems the indigenous population faced when they were evicted from their hamlets. The Indian labourers lived ten to a hut that was 10' by 10' in conditions of near-servitude. In the 1840s, the death rate of these workers was estimated at 250 per 1,000 workers. The Christian missionaries who worked among them seemed more interested in their souls than their bodies because, although they

---

[38] Sri Lanka: Economic Innovations, October 1988. Library of Congress website, http://lcweb2.loc.gov.

sought to convert them, they were less successful in their attempts to pressure he plantation owners to improve their working conditions. It is my guess that they felt that any attempt by them to improve the conditions of the workers would have resulted in their being banned from the plantations and then they would not have been able to save either their souls or their bodies. However we must not forget that, at this time, the working and living conditions in UK factories and coal mines were not very different (see box for some examples). This is not to defend the situation on the plantations but to point out that the workers on the tea estates were not singled out for harsher treatment than their British counterparts in the UK.

English social history of that period, as evidenced by Trevelyan and Dickens among others, shows that the lives of English workers in the coal mines, the cotton mills and the heavy metal industries in Britain and those in the plantations in Sri Lanka were probably not too different. In other words, the insensitivity of the planters to their labour force and their neighbours was not a callousness born of racial supremacy so much as it was considered a necessary part of building profitable businesses. One may even venture to conclude that the harsh climate and the over-crowding of the English city made for an even greater hellhole than the hillsides of Ceylon.

The matchgirls working for Bryant and May

Davies, in his book on the British labour movement from 1880s to 1990s, says:

> On 23 June 1888 an article appeared in a small circulation weekly … called *The Link*. Written by Annie Besant, it was titled 'White Slavery in London'. She had written about their low wages, the regular fines and deductions to which they were subject and the horrors of 'phossy jaw', caused by the phosphorus used in the matchmaking process, which slowly ate away the girls' faces.

It must be pointed out that there were philanthropists too but the exploitation of women and children was also an unfortunate aspect of industry in the Victorian era.

Notwithstanding the human aspects of the commercial and entrepreneurial actions of the British planter, it is only fair that they be complimented on the management systems they developed to get the best from their investments. They established sales and distribution channels to get the produce to their end markets in the UK. They established 'Ceylon', probably one of the earliest global brand names, as a brand of excellence that tea drinkers worldwide came to trust. They designed and built machinery to change the dry tea leaf into a refreshing and aromatic cup of tea. Ramamurthy says:

> The battle for markets in the tea industry was always aggressive. Both the Ceylonese and Indian planters established organisations to represent their interests … the Planters' Association of Ceylon was established as early as 1854 … In terms of propaganda the Ceylon Planters' Association was on the whole much more forward-looking … At the 1888 Glasgow Exhibition, for example, the Ceylon planters not only organised their own tea house but also scored a trump card in Queen Victoria's public acceptance of a cup of Ceylon tea … in

> 1893 the Ceylon Association negotiated an agreement with J. Lyons, caterers to the newly opened Imperial Institute.[39]

British planters, by converting the sap of the rubber trees into valued crepe rubber, established a second source of revenue for the country. To support this agricultural economy, European and local businessmen set up support services in the form of banks, agency houses, engineering service businesses, law and accountancy firms, and suppliers of manufactured goods of all kinds. The liquid gold of coffee and then tea had been successfully harvested, and tea still provides considerable revenues to the Sri Lankan exchequer. Bernard Waites, in *Europe and the Third World*, points out that Ceylon was a successful trading nation whose economy was performing above the average for the region:

> As a proportion of national income, exports from colonial India were probably never more than the 11 per cent attained just before the First World War, when their per capita annual value was around £0.56. In the Dutch East Indies their estimated value in 1913 was twice as high (£1.15), but for a truly export-oriented economy in South Asia we have to turn to Ceylon, a small specialist tea producer with per capita exports estimated at £3.89.

In addition to tea, the British and many Sri Lankan families established commercial plantation crops, such as coconut and rubber. A very high proportion of the coconut estates and a much smaller proportion of the tea and rubber estates were owned by Sri Lankan families. This preference for coconut plantations was probably because, unlike rubber and tea, they were far less capital- and labour-intensive and were quite profitable.

There was no manufacturing industry on the island except that to do with the plantation sector. This contrasted strongly with India and China. Both these countries had established textile manufacturing industries, although the Indian textile industry was systematically dismantled by the British. Waites points out that a senior ex-official boasted to a parliamentary select committee in 1840 that they had:

> ...succeeded in converting India from a manufacturing country into a country exporting raw produce ... Sir Charles Trevelyan informed the same enquiry that 'we swept away their manufactures; they have nothing to depend on but the produce of their land'.

This policy may have been because of the textile lobby in Britain or because of the adoption of an economic policy that favoured a distribution of effort. The British Empire encouraged the use of different countries to be developed as specialised sources of raw materials. The high-value-added manufacturing was

[39] Anandi Ramamurthy, *Imperial Persuaders, Images of Africa and Asia by British Advertising*, Manchester University Press, 2003.

done in the UK. The image of Gandhi sitting at a spinning wheel encouraging the Indian people to again begin weaving their own cloth, besides harming the British textile industry, demonstrated the wider consequence of that policy on the psyche of the Indians.

In 1789, according to Dutch records, there were 817,000 inhabitants in the Dutch territories on the island. If the people living in the Kandyan kingdom were added there was probably a population in 1789 of perhaps 1.2 million. Between then and the time the British left, the population had expanded at least six-fold – to about 7 million in 1948. The plantation economy sustained this population expansion with money to spare. The government, in addition to bearing the costs of infrastructure building, had also been able to spend profusely on the eradication of malaria, the cases of which had fallen from 3,225,477 in 1942 to 1,350,521 in 1947. Ludowyk says that, 'Ceylon had come out of World War II with the very large sum of Rs. 1,260 million in blocked sterling balances.' But this state of economic prosperity could not be sustained unless the growth in the economy outstripped that of the population. To do this, value had to be added to the commodities grown on the island. This required the development of a manufacturing sector or a high-value-added services sector to convert the raw produce into high margin goods or services. But the British did not leave behind an industrial sector, because all manufactured goods were imported from Britain. This suited the economics of an empire where specialisation by country optimised the management and financial resources available to it. At independence, however, it was far from adequate for a fledgling democracy that depended on the vagaries of the commodities markets in London. The Sri Lankan people had to diversify their economy and capitalise on the economic base they inherited. This they have yet to do.

The successful nations of the Far East and Near East such as Singapore, Malaysia and India took the economic infrastructure that the Dutch and the British left behind and grew their current prosperity on it. Ceylon and countries like it are proof of the assertion that the countries that have failed have squandered their heritage and have no one to blame but themselves for their parlous state. The sad fact for the Sri Lankan people is that a country that in 1960 matched Singapore's GDP per head finds itself in 2001 with a disparity of US$ 20,650 (US$21,500 for Singapore and US$850 for Sri Lanka). It has not kept pace with Malaysia, either. Malaysia has 23 million people but enjoys a per capita income of US$3,330. The figure for Sri Lanka in 2004 was reported by the Central Bank as just about $1000. Only the most naïve would accept that the lower figure in Sri Lanka is due to the Tamil Tigers. The real reason is that the country still depends on agriculture and labour-based revenues, whilst Malaysia is now a highly industrialised country. It, too, has an ethnic mix of Malays and other indigenous groups (59 per cent), Chinese (29 per cent), Indians (7 per cent), Tamils and others. Yet it has managed to contain the differences and build a nation in which common aspirations for prosperity have overridden and contained ethnic tensions.

Chapter 11

Developing the Social Infrastructure

The British did much more than create wealth and establish a modern democracy in the island. They invested in the island in other ways too.

British scholars began to delve into the rich and ancient heritage of the island. The old chronicles were studied and the history of the island reconstructed and published. The jungles that had overgrown the old cities of Anuradhapura, Polonnaruwa, and Sigiriya were cleared, and the ruined buildings, irrigation channels and inland seas restored to their former glory. Today they are World Heritage sites. This work was supported and supplemented by learned societies such as The Royal Asiatic Society (Ceylon Branch) that sponsored and encouraged research into the history of the island. A museum and botanical gardens were established to hold and display the literary, archaeological and botanical wealth of the country. The skill and ability of the botanists at Kew Gardens in London were harnessed to help with the commercial crops such as rubber and to advise on securing the botanical wealth of the country. Ludowyk retraces the route by which the rubber plant became a significant revenue generator for the British. He says that in 1876, Henry Wickham, seized the opportunity to transport rubber seeds from Brazil to Kew Gardens. At Kew, the seeds were nurtured into rubber saplings ready for replanting. Sir Joseph Hooker sent 1,919 plants to the Botanical Gardens in Peradeniya, near Kandy in Sri Lanka. Some plants were sent from there to Malaya. The rest is history.

The huge knowledge explosion in Europe in the arts, sciences, commerce and industry was automatically transferred to the indigenous people. It was both a process of osmosis and design. Many of the famous Anglican, Wesleyan and Roman Catholic mission schools, and some government-sponsored secular schools, produced alumni with the knowledge and ability to compete with their European counterparts in the best universities of Europe and America. A small privileged group of Sri Lankans absorbed these skills and wove them into their own Sinhalese and Tamil cultures and values. They were, in effect, Anglo-Tamils or Anglo-Sinhalese. The University of Ceylon, established in Colombo towards the very end of British rule at the insistence of the Ceylonese members of the Legislative Council, trained Sri Lankans in medicine, science, law and many other areas of knowledge to graduate level. In the early nineteenth century the children of rich families were sent to Britain to finish their education. The first to be sent were the children of Mudaliyar de Saram, who attended Cambridge in 1811. Many returned with degrees from

Oxford, Cambridge and the London School of Economics. Thus fortified, they sought to take their place as equals with their erstwhile rulers among the nations of the world and play their part in the future of their country. They, and many others like them, became the professional and political elite of the country. Others joined the civil service and the many commercial organisations that supported the thriving economy. A few went on to play a significant part in the politics of the island before and after independence. But, as the management and leadership of their country had up to then been done by the Europeans, they were unable to exploit the gold of a new era in world prosperity. These British-educated Sri Lankans knew how to *rule* but not to *manage* or to *lead*. Maybe, in the final analysis, they failed their country as comprehensively as their less fortunate brothers and sisters.

The British formalised, updated and administered public services in a systematic and organised way. Hospitals were built in Colombo and the major towns and cities. Local government was set up, formalised and systematised and given the responsibility for managing the infrastructure services of major towns and cities. Telecommunications, electricity, gas, water and sewage services were made available to many people in the principal towns and cities. The earliest electricity generation plants were coal-fired but hydroelectric plants were also developed. The harbours in Trincomalee, Colombo and Galle became major ports and Colombo was a regular stopover for people travelling to the Far East and Australia in cruise liners and passenger ships. Government departments supervised the forestry, farming and the plantation sectors, and a public works department maintained the national infrastructure.

The systems of law enforcement and justice established by the Dutch were revised and added to by the British. The charter of 1 April 1801 created a Supreme Court for the Colombo district, a High Court of Appeal (consisting of the governor, the chief justice, the puisne justice, and the secretary to government) and civil courts were established in Galle and Jaffna. In 1802 more civil courts and provincial courts were created. The fiscal's court was renamed the Court of Justices of the Peace, one of whom sat daily and was styled the sitting magistrate. In 1810 the jurisdiction of the Supreme Court was extended to cover all the British settlements.

The system of justice was made more equitable, and all the people of the island were seen as having equal status under the law. Although the Sinhalese and Tamil communities had laws, they were subject to operation within a feudal system and subject to royal influence, which meant that they were not independent of the executive. So, although in its application, the law may have claimed to be 'blind', in reality the age-old tradition of special treatment and privilege for the ruling clique among the Sinhalese and Tamils came to an end only when the system of justice was administered by the European powers, particularly the Dutch and the British. During colonial times the administration of the law was probably influenced more by the prejudices of magistrates and judges than the institutionalised 'blindness' of the feudal system. This form of preference – a law for the ruling clique and another for the rest – only returned once the island regained its independence.

During the period of British rule, the law was enforced by a police force that was guided by statute. Their mode of working was modelled on that of the UK force. Their aim was to enforce the law and keep order. The army, air force and navy served the needs of the wider empire during British rule. After independence the role of the Sri Lankan Army, Navy and Air Force was mainly ceremonial. However, during periods of serious civil disobedience they supplemented the police and helped them restore order. The senior officers of all four services had the opportunity to learn their management skills at the respective officer schools in the UK.

The Ceylon civil service was a genuine gift to the people of Lanka. For the first time in their history they had a structured and systematic method of running the whole country. Management techniques that had helped the British hold together a vast empire were embedded in the process of governance of the island. The civil service was managed largely by expatriate British officers, who maintained the system and ensured its smooth running.

It is worth digressing to point out that many of the men and women who joined the colonial service were extremely talented and able people, and Ceylon got its fair share of them. According to Kirk-Greene, in the early years, appointments were often based on patronage but in later years the colonial service was the first to use formal and structured recruitment procedures that chose on merit. In the years 1927 to 1929, of the total graduate intake to the colonial service of 927 graduates 409 were from Oxford and Cambridge, 108 were from the University of London, 91 from Edinburgh, 48 from Glasgow and 41 from Trinity College, Dublin. They worked in the administrative service, education, finance, customs, legal, police, medical, agricultural, veterinary, forestry, various scientific, railways and survey and geological services – with one significant omission. During the colonial period the managerial layers were staffed by people from the ruling country. With independence, many members of the expatriate staff left. Many returned to Britain, but others were sent to other parts of the British Empire. In 1994, there were 9,437 overseas service pensioners, of whom seventy had worked in Ceylon.

When the British administrators left after independence they left behind a vacuum in managerial talent and capability that could not be filled by promoting the capable administrators who reported to them. The British officers were supported by Tamil and Sinhalese clerical staff who were employed to operate the administrative systems. They were supervised by their compatriots at unit and section levels. When the British officers left, they left a smoothly running and precise administrative system in place, but not the senior management capability to keep it running and to enhance it to meet the new needs of an independent nation. So it ran down and disintegrated, and suffered even more when political changes by the Sri Lankan government and the resultant communal riots forced the Tamil staff to leave the service, further reducing the number of trained officers.

During the 150 years of British rule, the major policy and administrative decisions to do with the island and its people were made by the British. To successfully drive the service in the future, the Sri Lankan people had to learn the skills of policy making and implementation; but the rational analysis of the needs of the country were diverted by pressure groups into unproductive sidings. The ruling clique that took control of the country at independence, lacking a strategy for managing a multi-cultural nation, took whatever action they thought would help them secure their powerbase. This meant that strategy formulation was transformed from a rational and logical process to an emotional competence and came to be dominated by the Sinhala Buddhist issue and its political appeal. The result was a set of policies that rational analysis would have shown would lead to the bankruptcy of the country and the destruction of any communal harmony that existed at the time of independence. This policy bias may have been dampened if the managerial talent in government departments matched up to the demands of a new country, but it did not. With no one to advise them of the folly of their ways, the ruling clique led the country into the snake pit of communal politics.

Chapter 12
Buddhism in Colonial Times

During the first 200 or more years of European occupation, the Buddhist establishment had watched whilst Portuguese and Dutch missionaries converted large numbers of Buddhists and Hindus – kings, lords and commoners – to Christianity. The most significant early convert was Dharmapala, the king of Kotte, and members of his court. He had donated temple lands to the Franciscans (although the people took them back) and had literally handed over his kingdom to the Portuguese. This meant that Christianity posed a serious threat to Sinhalese sovereignty over those parts of the island the kings controlled. Similarly the Buddhist establishment stood to lose adherents and income from temple lands.

The methods used by the Portuguese and the Dutch to convert the Buddhists and Hindus to Christianity were not always Christian. It is said that the Portuguese converted the people of the fishing community on the west coast, from about Chilaw right down to Moratuwa, often at the point of the sword. The Dutch, too, were not gentle in the way they converted both Buddhists and Roman Catholics to their form of Christianity. Despite the methods used by the Portuguese and the Dutch, there was a steady drift of people to Christianity. The Buddhist and Hindu priests and the kings found themselves fighting a losing battle against the Christian priests. Their only response seemed to be that of inciting their followers to riot and to withhold their labour so that it reduced the trading revenues of the Portuguese and the Dutch. In extreme cases, they destroyed churches and other Christian buildings to show their displeasure. The Catholics, who escaped persecution by the Dutch, found refuge in the Kandyan kingdom but they were not always safe there.

The king of Jaffna also persecuted the Catholics, but the Portuguese had made him pay dearly for his indiscretion. But those who converted saw real benefits come of their new faith. The Christian priests worked closely with the people. They often took their side when their European or Sri Lankan masters abused them and they got the help of the Europeans to prevent the Sinhalese kings abusing their erstwhile subjects. By these acts of solidarity with their flock, they won their confidence and their hearts to Christ. It looked as if the drift of people to the new faith was irreversible, and the Buddhist clergy feared for their faith and their own well-being.

Their fear was accentuated by their knowledge that the kings, their patrons and protectors, were themselves powerless to protect the sangha and Buddhism.

The practical impact of their impotence was fourfold. Firstly the sponsorship of the kings lacked real value because they were rapidly losing their power over the people. Secondly, the diminishing revenues of the Sinhalese kings resulted in a decline in their financial support and this depleted the temple treasuries. Thirdly, the tendency of the kings to build large Buddhist buildings and to donate lands as outward symbols of the intensity and sincerity of their faith also reduced. Unlike the Anuradhapura and Polonnaruwa kings, the kings who reigned during the period of European occupation built only a few monuments to Buddhism. The most notable new building was the Temple of the Tooth in Kandy. King Vimala Dharma Suriya II built the temple in 1697/98 so that the Dalada, an object of veneration to Buddhist worldwide, would have a permanent and secure home. Fourthly, the Buddhist establishment had to be renewed because it had suffered and the kings had to renew it by sending missions to other Buddhist countries. To do this, the kings had to get the permission of the Portuguese and Dutch authorities because they controlled the Maritime Provinces and restricted the king's access to the sea. The Kandyan kings sought and got permission in 1740 from the Dutch to send a mission to Siam, Pegu and Tennasserum and other centres of Buddhism so that they could find monks to renew the Buddhist priesthood on the island. Another embassy was sent to Siam in 1741, and in 1742 the Dutch East India Company was asked to forward letters by its own servants and at its own expense to Aracan and Siam for Buddhist priests and to bring back replies. The mission to Siam in 1746 did succeed, but was not acted on because Sri Vijaya Rajasinha died on 11 August 1747. Kirti Sri, who ruled Kandy from 1747–1782, was a devout Buddhist and he sent a new mission to Siam in 1750. This time it returned with a contingent of Buddhist priests who re-established the succession of the Theravada tradition. This new 'Siamese Sect', led by Weliwita Saranankara, took control of and managed the greater part of the old temples and their temporalities. Saranankara died in 1778. But there were fresh challenges ahead.

The pace of Christianisation accelerated once British rule was established on the island. A wave of missionaries from both America and Britain descended on the island, and began converting the 'pagans' to Anglicanism. The missionaries who preached and converted the Tamils and the Sinhalese were sincere people and believed that their souls were worth saving. So, with great determination they generously gave the Ceylonese the most valuable gift they believed they could bestow on them – rescue from paganism and the care and protection of a loving God.

The missionaries gave Anglo-Saxon and Portuguese names to the Ceylonese they converted to Christianity. One explanation given by a missionary to my forbears, although said tongue in cheek, may have had a ring of truth to it. According to him, the name change was considered necessary by his fellow missionaries so that God would be able to recognise the converts by name. It is more likely that the name change came about because the missionaries found it difficult to pronounce the long Tamil and Sinhalese names of those they converted. Whatever the reason, the missionaries who worked among the Tamils in the Jaffna peninsula gave them Anglo-Saxon surnames or first names. This resulted in a Tamil Christian community with surnames such as Abrahams, Benjamin, Brainerd, Cooke, Daniel, Hensman, Nelson, Niles, Paul, Phillips, Samuel, Thomas, Washington, Watson, Williams and Wilson among others. Those who did not wish to adopt these new Anglo-Saxon names, had their surnames anglicised or were given new 'double-barrelled' names where one name was Anglo-Saxon. Similarly, the Portuguese priests who baptised Buddhists and Hindus gave their converts Portuguese names. This of course meant that employers and others, some with malevolent intent, could identify Christians by name. Naturally, as most employers during the colonial period were Christian these new Anglo-Saxon names were a great advantage in the selection interviews.

Christian converts benefited in other ways too. The converted Hindu or Buddhist was certain of benefiting from an up-to-date education in one of the schools the missionaries had set up in the Jaffna peninsula in around the 1830s and in Colombo, Kandy, and other key cities. For example, St Thomas' College, Mount Lavinia near Colombo was founded in 1851. In fairness, it must be said that Christian schools did not exclude children of other faiths, neither was Christianity forced down the throats of unwilling Buddhist, Hindu and Muslim children. The other benefit was that Anglo-Saxon or anglicised names of Hindu converts, their Christian beliefs and their knowledge of English and mathematics gave them a head start in the new English-speaking Christian world being created around them. This advantage they exploited in the professions of law and medicine and in getting jobs in the civil service. Even though the cynic may claim that the exodus of Buddhists and Hindus to Christianity was done through fear or commercial prudence their sincerity and that of their descendents is shown by the fact that the Christian community on the island is still large and strong.

Gradually, those who professed and practised Buddhism and Hinduism felt displaced by their fellow countrymen and women who had embraced the faith of the Europeans. They felt that they no longer had a place in the new Europeanised secular society. Although the European religious establishment of the Church and the state operated independently of each other, there was a fraternity among those who professed the same faith. The result was that, intentionally or unintentionally, Christian Ceylonese got preference when European employers sought staff. This was naturally displeasing to non-Christians but the Buddhist clergy felt it most, because, under the Sinhalese kings, they had received the special treatment that they now saw their Christian fellow-countrymen and women getting. Then they had shared power; they had been part of the ruling clique, even though their influence was discreetly employed. Now they felt sidelined. A tradition going back nearly 1,800 years was broken, and it caused trauma.

Although the Christian missionaries did convert large numbers, they did not get even close to undermining Buddhism or Hinduism. Buddhism had deep roots. For over 1,800 years the Sinhalese had practised Buddhism and the Sinhalese kings had made it the religion of the state. Hinduism, the religion of the Tamils, had survived many thousands of years too. The inherent fluidity and tolerance of both faiths gave them an immense ability to absorb other beliefs and customs and transpose their own ritual and teaching into the religious practises of other faiths. For example, you do not have to be a Hindu to practise yoga and Hindus and Buddhists share places of religious significance, such as Adam's Peak, with people of other faiths. There were short periods when this amicable coexistence of Buddhism and Hinduism were challenged. Some of the Indian kings who ruled the island or parts of it attempted to impose Hinduism on the population. But those who converted returned to their Buddhist roots, because their conversion was not rooted in conviction and true belief, but in fear. The exodus to Christianity, however, was large enough to cause worry, and its impact was far-reaching and profound. In some cases the Buddhist priests were themselves subject to persecution. In other places they were completely displaced, as whole swathes of people changed to the new faith. But their worries increased when they found that the converted indigenous Christians became missionaries too.

The Buddhists saw that across the water in India, Hinduism had reabsorbed Buddhism and feared that Christianity, if preached by native converts, may attract an even greater following and displace Buddhism in Sri Lanka. The problem for the Buddhist clergy was that they had forgotten the strength and reach of the Buddha's message (see box at end of chapter) and had increasingly depended on the patronage of the Sinhalese kings. So, when, during the European period, the power of the Sinhalese kings declined and then disappeared altogether, they feared the worst.

But some among the clergy, such as the scholar priest Sri Sumangala Thera and Anagarika Dharmapala, set out to reassert and propagandise the benefits of Buddhism and Oriental values. In this effort they were supported by Colonel Olcott and Annie Besant. The cavalry, as usual, had arrived in the nick of time. Colonel Henry Steele Olcott was an American, an ardent abolitionist and president of the Theosophical Society. He came to Sri Lanka in about 1870, and set out to help the Buddhist establishment. With his help three Buddhist schools (Ananda College, Mahinda College and Dharmaraja College) were set up to educate Buddhist children to similar levels of academic excellence as those studying in the Christian missionary schools. The point about these schools was that they offered the opportunity for Buddhist children to acquire the knowledge necessary to actively participate in the affairs of the nation and benefit from the new opportunities it offered. Today the alumni of these colleges play a significant role in the administrative, political and commercial activities of the country. The founder also persuaded the British administrators to recognise Buddhist holy days and mark them with a holiday.

When the British left, there was an expectation that the new independent state of Sri Lanka would act to reinstate Buddhism and Sinhalese to their former status as the religion and language of the state. When this did not happen spontaneously, a segment of the Buddhist sangha decided to form a pressure group and push for its reinstatement as the prime creed of the country. Their demand is now embedded in the constitution. Despite this, this carry over from the colonial past – Buddhist Sinhalese chauvinism – is continuing to poison the well of religious and social harmony on the island.

So far, the ruling clique and the Buddhist clergy have used the people as pawns in their power game. The original objectives of those who spawned the Buddhist nationalist movement in the mid-1800s have been reduced to racism. Thus has human lust and greed for power and wealth reduced a noble objective to dross, as there is nothing noble or Buddhist about the current behaviour of their so-called descendents in the movement.

Regional Brotherhood of Buddhism

In India, the land of its birth, Buddhism has all but disappeared. The population census of 2001 showed that 82 per cent of the Indian people were Hindus, 12.1 per cent were Muslims, 2.3 per cent were Christian, 1.9 per cent were Sikhs and the balance 1.7 per cent (18 million people) were Buddhists, Jains and Parsees. The wonderful frescoes from Ajanta are virtually all that remain of Indian Buddhism today. In Tibet, the religion of which the Dalai Lama is head is suffering under the communist regime in Beijing. The status of the religion in China is not too clear, although before the Cultural Revolution it had a large population of Buddhists. Maybe in time the Chinese Buddhists will re-emerge as a powerful force. However, the Chinese Buddhists belong to the Mahayana Sect, unlike the Sri Lankan Buddhists, who belong to the Theravada Sect.

Other centres of Theravada Buddhism are Thailand, Myanmar, Cambodia and Laos. All five countries have very large populations of Buddhists. In Sri Lanka, 69 per cent of the population is Buddhist. 16 per cent are Hindus, 8 per cent are Muslims and 7 per cent Christians. Almost all the 65 million people of Thailand are Theravada Buddhists. The importance of the religion is underwritten by the fact that the head of Buddhism in Thailand, the Supreme Patriarch, is a member of the royal family. Almost 85 per cent of the 43 million people living in Myanmar are Theravada Buddhists. In Cambodia, 90 per cent of its 13 million and in Laos almost all its 6 million people are Theravada Buddhists.

But these countries are relatively far removed from the island and their political influence in the world is meagre. Myanmar's military regime is a pariah of the international community and the country a poor representative of the religion its military government belongs to. In the 1940s and 1950s the pattern of the worldwide Buddhist population was not very different from that in 2001. So the desire of the Sri Lankan Buddhists to involve themselves in the politics of the island to protect and nurture Buddhism is understandable.

Chapter 13
The Jaffna Tamils

The legends and traditions about Jaffna go back at least two millennia. According to legend the Lord Buddha is said to have visited Nagadipa (the Jaffna peninsula) on his second visit to the island to settle a dispute between the Naga princes, Mahodara and Chulodara, concerning a gem-set seat. This story, like many others relating to his visits to the island, is significant in that it suggests the presence of settlements on the peninsula dating back to the earliest times. Mendis makes the point that:

> The name Nagadipa (cobra island), given to the north-west of Ceylon, probably led to the growth of the legends of the *nagas,* who, like the *yakkhas,* according to Buddhist thought, were non-human beings.[40]

Nonetheless he does state that, 'The Jaffna kings were independent rulers, and had as their capital first Sinkai Nakarai (Sinhanagara) [city of the lion] and later Yapapatuna (Jaffna)'. The Tamils shared the whole island with the Sinhalese and the Vanniyars, a people who occupied the no-man's land between Anuradhapura and the Jaffna Peninsula.

The name 'Jaffna Tamil' applies to those Tamils who have made the northern strip of land called the Jaffna peninsula their home. The peninsula covers an area of about 1,262 square miles and is linked to the rest of Sri Lanka by causeways at Elephant Pass that allow train and road traffic. The Jaffna Tamils played a much greater part in the recorded affairs of the island during British occupation than they had done in previous centuries. They took advantage of the opportunities offered by the spread of education in this northern extremity of the island to acquire the knowledge and skill to work in the service of the government, in Sri Lanka and abroad, and to practice in the professions such as law, medicine, engineering and so on. They also played a leading part in the politics of colonial Ceylon. The Sri Lankan Tamil community now includes Tamils living in Colombo, generally called Colombo Tamils, and those living on the eastern coast, of whom the Batticaloa Tamils are the most numerous.

The Tamils and Sinhalese have been separated by their culture, religion, ethnicity and geography for most of their long histories. The Jaffna Tamils, although they share their religion and language with their South Indian cousins have evolved into a group that is distinguishable from the South Indian Tamils

[40] Mendis, *The Early History of Ceylon*.

by their insularity. For example, the Tamil they speak is in many respects different in vocabulary and pronunciation from that of the mainland Dravidians. In other words, the Jaffna Tamils are a distinct ethnic group with a unique identity and Sri Lanka is as much their homeland as it is that of the Sinhalese.

The story of the Tamils of Sri Lanka is almost always seen through the myopic lenses of the Sinhala traditionalists, as the earliest recorded sources are attributed to Scholastic Buddhist monks. These early Sinhalese historians focused on the Sinhalese Buddhist kings and people. The Tamils they referred to were mainly the Tamil-speaking Chola, Pandyan and Keralan raiders and invaders from South India rather than the Tamils in the north of the island. The world-view of the Tamils in Sri Lanka today is through the filter of a Sinhalese Buddhist government that paints them as a difficult people. In the espoused Sinhalese view, the Tamils should take their place as a subject people as behoves a minority community. This, the Tamils are unwilling to accept. What they are seeking in Sri Lanka is equality of status and opportunity; a phenomenon that is becoming an objective of minorities in many multi-ethnic democratic states. The reality is that the Tamils in the north boast a culture that predates that of the Sinhalese and they are, today, a people fighting to keep their national identity, culture and way of life alive. It would have been good if they could have achieved this without bloodshed, but it does take two to tango.

Their presence in the north grew out of trading settlements into settled communities before they grouped to become a sovereign state. The Jaffna Tamils have a folklore all of their own that explains their beginnings and their development into a self-financing kingdom. According to Katiresu the peninsula got its Tamil name of *Yalpanam* (Katiresu says *Yalpanam* became *Jaffanam* and was then anglicised to *Jaffna*) when:

> A certain Kaviveerarakavan from South India, an expert in vocal music and one skilled in the use of the instrument called the *Yal* so delighted the king NarasinghaRaja of Ceylon that he was pleased to present him with the Jaffna peninsula then a *manatidal* (literally sandy plain). The singer was called *Yalpady* and his land *Yalpanam.*[41]

Yalpady imported labour from South India in an attempt to harvest whatever he could from the land, which was arid and difficult to make fruitful. The immigrants established settlements and stayed on. Sadly, on his death, the settlers were ill-treated by the Sinhalese and were protected by King Koolanghai Singhaiaryan of South India. Katiresu says that in circa AD 104, Koolanghai:

> ...built a palace and flower garden at Nallore and became the first king resident at Jaffna ... during his peaceful reign some *Vellales* came from South India and

[41] S. Katiresu, *A Handbook to the Jaffna Peninsula, and a Souvenir of the Opening of the Railway to the North*, Asian Educational Services, 2004.

> settled in the villages. He built four temples: VeyiluvanthaPillaiarKovil to the East of the palace, ChaddanathanKovil to the North, VeeramakaliammanKovil to the West and KailayaPillaiarKovil to the South. The ruins of the palace are still [1905] seen. The temples were destroyed by the Portuguese. New temples with the original names have now risen on the old sites.

This story indicates that the Jaffna peninsula was probably a protectorate of one of the South Indian kingdoms and remained so up to about the twelfth or thirteenth century. Katiresu provides a sketchy lineage of kings from the time of Koolanghai to Sangili who was king when the Portuguese took control of the Jaffna peninsula in AD 1617. The most that can be drawn from this is that the Jaffna peninsula was not a permanent and integral part of the Sinhalese kingdoms. Some Sinhalese kings such as Dhatusena, Parakrama Bahu the Great and Parakrama Bahu VI did conquer it and claim sovereignty over the whole island but their hold on it was weak and short.

The kingdom of Jaffna first caught the attention of the Portuguese when the king of Jaffna massacred Christian converts on the island of Mannar in 1544. The Portuguese took their revenge in 1560 and occupied Mannar. However, according to Codrington, 'in 1591 the king of Jaffna was unwise enough to attack Mannar and as a consequence lost his life and throne at the hands of the Portuguese under Andre Furtado'. However, the kingdom did limp on until 1617 when the Portuguese invaded the Jaffna peninsula and, according to Codrington 'the kingdom was reduced to subjection, the native dynasty deposed, and Sangili himself captured and sent to Goa, where he was tried and executed'.

In fact, Sangili was the regent of the infant king of Jaffna. When the Portuguese captured Jaffna in 1591 and killed the king of the Tamil kingdom there, they installed a new king who was king in name only. This king died in 1615 and his infant son was put on the throne. It was during this time that the kingdom of Jaffna ceased to exist. In the fourteenth century, the Jaffna kingdom was again subject to rule from South India. Mendis suggests that the Jaffna kingdom was captured and held by Vijayanagara kings during the first half of the fifteenth century until it was conquered by Sapumal Kumara on behalf of Parakrama Bahu VI. But the kingdom reverted to the Tamils and remained in their hands until the Portuguese captured it. Portuguese occupation seems not to have benefited the Tamils in Jaffna. Katiresu makes the point that:

> The policy of the Portuguese was governed by territorial ambition, commercial greed and religious proselytism. This policy was prosecuted with bigotry and cruelty, which would be incredible if there were not the testimony of their own historians. The Roman Catholic form of Christianity was forced on the people. All the temples were destroyed...

The Portuguese period lasted forty years. The Dutch took it from the Portuguese on 22 June 1658 after a siege that lasted three and a half months. They introduced Reformed Dutch Christianity and persecuted the Roman Catholics. Anyone found harbouring or concealing Roman Catholic priests risked being subject to the death penalty. Despite this, during Dutch rule things seemed to be better. Katiresu says that the Dutch:

> ...developed cultivation and improved means of communication especially by canals. The education of the people occupied a good deal of official attention, as also their Christianisation through a staff of Dutch chaplains; the system of employing only Protestant Christians created many a hypocrite.

The British inherited it from the Dutch in September 1795. Katiresu says that since then, those in the Jaffna peninsula benefited from freedom of religion and speech, the system of trial by jury, the abolition of slavery of fishermen in 1840 and farmers in 1892, the setting up in 1845 of courts of requests for the settlement of small civil disputes, a police force introduced in 1866, a telegraph service introduced in 1869, twelve post offices and three sub-post offices, five hospitals and fifteen outdoor dispensaries and the provision of a comprehensive road network. Most important of all was the establishment of schools by Christian missionaries from America and Britain.

The official handbook that Mr S Katiresu published in 1905 to celebrate the opening of the railway from Colombo to Jaffna speaks of an area that was thriving. His book is, in many senses, a tourist guide akin to the better quality ones produced today. (Those wishing a more scholarly work should refer to Mudaliyar C Rasanayagam's *Ancient Jaffna* published in 1926. He challenges the folklore and offers researched alternative history that covers the period from early times to the coming of the Portuguese). Nonetheless the substance of established settlements going back to a period before the arrival of Vijaya is confirmed by him.

Katiresu writes as a man who is proud of his people and his land. The author says in his preface that he hopes the handbook will be 'useful to strangers desiring information of the hitherto isolated country to be opened by the Railway'.

Katiresu was writing about 300,851 people living in the peninsula. His figure is taken from the census of 1901. The official *Ceylon Manual* records that at the census of 1901 the indigenous population of Ceylon was 3,576,990 of which the Sinhalese were 2,330,897 and the Tamils (probably including those working on the estates as it does not distinguish between Jaffna Tamils and the rest) were 951,740. This means that roughly a third of the Tamil-speaking population on the island lived in the Jaffna peninsula.

This ratio of five Sinhalese to one Jaffna Tamil seems to have existed for a long time. However, the exodus of Tamils and the death of the young Tamil Tigers due to the current conflict may have changed this ratio in favour of the

Sinhalese, as there is the danger that in the future the diminution of the Tamil population could be a greater threat to the Tamils than the legislative actions of the Sinhalese. The Tamil population could fall to levels that would make them incapable of being economically or militarily self-sufficient and there would be inadequate young Tamils to refresh the population.

In 1901, the census states that there were 110 Europeans, 476 Burghers, 226 Sinhalese, 3,078 Moors, 60 Malays, 296,805 Tamils and 396 'others' living in the Jaffna peninsula. Of these 265,875 Hindus, 3,085 Mohammedans, 26,804 Roman Catholics, 1,059 Church of England Christians, 54 Presbyterians, 750 Wesleyans, 2,230 Congregationalists and 26 Christians of other denominations. Of the 78,793 wage earners 49,606 were owners of agricultural lands and cultivators, 6,267 were fishermen, 3,036 were goldsmiths, 3545 were toddy drawers, 1,909 were blacksmiths, 1,893 were cigar makers, 1,747 were clothes washers, 760 were government workers, 708 were merchants, 598 were teachers, 516 were Hindu priests, and 42 were missionaries and clergymen. The rest were made up of actors and singers, flower garland makers, cow herders and shepherds, boatmen, notaries and so on. In many ways the data showed a self-sufficient community.

The peninsula was not a land rich in resources. It was made up of low-lying sandy soil, which is predominantly a mix of iron and lime. The lime is primarily the result of eroding coral. As Katiresu points out, 'it is susceptible of successful cultivation and produces fairly good crops more due to the industry of the people than to the soil'. Despite this handicap, the inhabitants of the north succeeded in growing rice, dry grains, vegetables, breadfruit, jakfruit, groundnuts, chillies, pine apple, pomegranates, mangoes, tobacco, coconuts, palmyrah, tamarind, margosa among others. They also developed craft industries: the jewellers of Jaffna were and still are renowned for their skill as goldsmiths; the Jaffna cigar has commercial value – even though it is no match for the Cuban varieties, it did win a gold medal at the St Louis Exhibition in 1904. And this, in many ways, is critical to the type of people the Tamils have become.

Living off the land was not a soft option for those in the Jaffna peninsula but it was for the Sinhalese who lived in the most fertile parts of the island. The Sinhalese were blessed with two seasons of monsoonal rains and a higher annual precipitation, several rivers that rise in the highlands, fertile soil and terrain suitable for a range of crops. This made living in the north-western, central and south-western parts of the island far easier and probably accounts for the more relaxed lifestyle of the Sinhalese. The gem pits and graphite mines were situated in the south as was cinnamon. The plantation sector was limited to the hill country and the south. Coconut plantations in the north yielded half the crop of those in the south. The Jaffna Tamils brewed liquor in their backyards by fermenting the liquid drawn from the flower of the palmyrah palms whilst the much larger population in the south made retail businesses such as the sale of *arrack* very profitable. According to Kumari

Jayawardena the northern Tamils did not have the opportunity to accumulate capital from 'the liquor industry, plantations, graphite mining and the import and export trades'.

The primary assets of the Jaffna Tamil are hard work, thrift and the acquisition and use of knowledge. These are probably traits developed by people whose land lacked natural fertility and fecundity. As Katiresu points out, 'the land is responsive to systematic cultivation and is but imperfectly adapted for maintaining a constant succession of seeds and cereal production'. Even water has to be drawn from wells that are forty to fifty feet deep. Therefore, the arrival of American and British missionaries made a great difference to the well-being of the people. It helped them mine their only assets, their brains and their industry. Their knowledge of English was their passport to a better future. The British and American missionaries helped them develop these natural talents and transformed the lives of those living in the Jaffna peninsula. Katiresu says:

> Among the foreigners who with the assistance of Tamil scholars in Jaffna have enriched our literature must be mentioned Dr. M. Winslow whose Tamil-English dictionary is an admitted authority, and Dr. S. F. Green who published various medical works in Tamil, mainly translations from English.

The first educational establishment, Batticotta Seminary was opened in 1823 by American missionaries. Schools of that quality were not opened in Colombo until much later. The first such school to be open in Colombo was Royal College, which was opened in 1835, and St Thomas' College in 1851. According to Jayawardena, the Batticotta Seminary provided education at the very highest level. She says:

> The first principal was the Rev. Daniel Poor, a scholar and doctor of divinity; he was succeeded by a linguist and doctor of divinity, Rev. Henry Richard Hoisington. Apart from Christianity, the school taught English, Tamil, Latin, Greek, History, Geography, Mathematics, and philosophy; the language of instruction [except for Tamil language] was English. In 1833, the school acquired a professor of medicine, preparing students for medical studies abroad. By 1935, of the 147 students who had finished their schooling, 67 were teachers and 22 government servants in Sri Lanka and India, and 7 were tutors to local British families ... as a result, the levels of English education were higher in Jaffna than in the rest of the country.[42]

The missionaries encouraged information flows by sponsoring the publications of newspapers. Soon this small community had seven newspapers and six magazines and five public libraries.

---

[42] Kumari Jayawardena, *Nobodies to Somebodies, The Rise of the Colonial Bourgeoisie in Sri Lanka*, Zed Books, 2000.

The American missionaries in Jaffna started the first medical school in Sri Lanka. The pioneer was Dr S F Green (1822–1884) of Massachussetts, a graduate from New York. According to Jayawardena:

> He opened the Mission Medical School in 1848 in Manipay, hand picking students from the Batticotta Seminary, and giving them a three-year training. When the Ceylon Medical College was begun in 1870, many students from Jaffna transferred to Colombo ... by the late nineteenth century, many Jaffna Tamil doctors had made their mark in government service and in private practice.

Although the Batticotta Seminary was closed about 1857 new schools were opened that took forward its tradition of very high quality education. Jaffna College was opened in 1872 followed soon after by five other schools for boys. The Girls' Boarding School at Uduvil was founded by the American missionaries in 1826. Three other girls' school were opened in the peninsula as were two technical colleges. These schools prepared students for examinations carried out by English examination bodies such as the Cambridge local and similar Indian examinations, especially at university level.

Gradually, the peninsula, which had for centuries been a closed community, began to produce English-educated people in large numbers. Naturally, they found work in the Ceylon and Indian civil services and their children began to acquire the skills needed to compete in a Westernised Ceylon. Many families moved to Colombo and became indispensable players in the political arena of the country, the professional services and the trading communities. At the time of independence the Tamils were punching well above their weight. Many of the leading lawyers, advocates, doctors, engineers, civil servants and businessmen of Colombo were Tamils. This was why the policies advocated and introduced by Mr and Mrs Bandaranaike in the period from 1956 to 1965 were so deeply resented by the Tamils, and why they believe that their future lies in a separate state.

At independence, despite misgivings about how the Sinhalese and the Tamils would exercise the power they inherited, the British handed the country to the ruling clique which in 1948 comprised members of the Sinhalese, Tamil, Muslim and Burgher communities. But the Sinhalese have used the democratic process after independence to treat the Tamils as a subject people rather than as co-owners of the island and as neighbours and friends. In other words, the forced marriage of the two groups under British rule was not consummated and, until the railway was opened in 1905, the people who inhabited the peninsula continued to remain physically and mentally 'distant' from those in the south. Today, despite the rail, road, sea and air links, the mental separateness of the two communities continues because politicians on both sides feed the separatists' mood. The current troubles, accompanied as they have been with bombs and suicide bombers, the violence of riots by racially or criminally minded civilians and members of the security forces, have separated both communities. An attitude of hate and distrust, that both communities have nurtured about each other over the last forty or so years, makes reconciliation and forgiveness so much harder. But the history of the north and of the island people as a whole shows that the level of hate and animosity prevalent today was *not* a feature of their relationships during British rule or before.

In fact, during British rule the Tamil and Sinhalese elite became close allies. This 'alliance' was not one that was biological or cultural but one of expediency. They collaborated to grasp what they could of the reins of power by demanding participation in government rather than responsibility for the divisions and actions of government for which the British, as rulers, were responsible and accountable to the world community. The culmination of this collaboration was the Pan Sinhalese ministry of the 1930s. The executive committee system of government enabled the Sinhalese (who had manoeuvred themselves with the help of the Tamils to the position of ministers in charge of the committees) to frustrate the workings of the executive, which was almost exclusively composed of the British. The chairmen of the various governmental committees, as non-executive members, were able to stall and prevaricate at the policy levels of the administration. This cosy arrangement cased on 4 February 1948 – Independence Day. Since then, the Tamils and Sinhalese have drawn further apart and are now on divergent courses.

The war between the Sinhalese and the Tamils has severely affected the people living in the Jaffna peninsula and elsewhere on the island. The land is a desolate waste. Most of the infrastructure of the peninsula has been destroyed. Many people have left it for good, finding homes in other lands. Rebuilding the territory will require levels of investment that are beyond the financial resources of the country. Inward investment from foreign sources will only bear fruit in a climate of peace and generosity. However, there is no doubt that, given the acorns, the Jaffna Tamils will grow oak trees.

It is so sad to think that this innate ability of the Tamil people should now be used to wage war against their Sinhalese neighbours. Both communities, in an attempt to gain narrow advantages, have sacrificed their common heritage and impoverished their common futures.

Chapter 14

The Sources of Discontent

The period of foreign occupation and rule of 443 years had eventually ended. The country had changed but not matured. The older feudal ways had been replaced by newer, more egalitarian approaches to justice and the equality of people under the law. But old customs, caste structures, religious beliefs and ethnic divisions had not.

At first, it seemed that the spirit of the new constitution would be observed and, in view of Lord Soulbury and many others who knew him well, it may have been if D S Senanayake had not died so early in the life of the new nation. His death created a power vacuum. The scramble to fill it resulted in otherwise reasonable and honourable people compromising their integrity.

The social veneer of nationality – one nation, one people – that had matured during British rule crumbled under a Buddhist Sinhala chauvinist/nationalist movement that claimed the island for itself. It became apparent after independence that the term 'Ceylonese' only applied to a very small group of Western-educated and Western-minded Sinhalese, Tamils, Muslims and Dutch Burghers. The rest of the island people, probably 95 per cent of them, retained their separate ethnicity. The nationalist movements appealed to them. The fears and frustrations of this very large group that had simmered under the surface during the European period were brought to the surface and used by politicians such as Mr Bandaranaike to achieve their personal ambitions. Mr Bandaranaike is claimed to have said in an interview in 1956 'You know my dear fellow (smiling broadly), I have never found anything to excite the people in quite the way this language issue does.'[43] How right he was.

Under the searing heat of language and religion, the glue of the independence struggle that had held the Ceylonese ruling clique together melted. The politicians encouraged the people to separate into their ethnic identities. Consequently, the people lost their sense of nationhood. They began squabbling amongst themselves and the disagreements accelerated into open warfare between the Sinhalese and between the Sinhalese and the Tamils.

During British occupation a collaborator sub-group appeared. Its members grew rich by becoming intermediaries between the British administration and the people. This group of people – the most successful of whom were the

---

[43] Manor, cited in Bush, *The Intra-Group Dimensions of Ethnic Conflict in Sri Lanka.*

Sinhalese, because of the large populations in the south – earned their income from a range of activities essential to the development of the island economy, and for earning tax revenues for the British exchequer. Among these were those Sinhalese and Tamils who facilitated trade within the island by providing land- and sea-based transport; those with craft skills, such as carpenters, building constructors, blacksmiths, and those who provided financial services such as Ceylonese and Indian moneylenders and financial risk underwriters who underwrote risks for the foreign bankers, lent money in their own right and facilitated the import/export trade. The opportunity for exploiting their fellow countrymen and women was not missed by them. A small group of Sinhalese built up a portfolio of revenues based on farming rents, paddy rents, fish rents, toll rents and, most profitable of all, *arrack* rents. These rentiers who bought monopoly rights to retail their products to the people from the government became the richest and most powerful families during British rule. They had married into the feudal families and were the people who formed the ruling elite after independence. And they continued to exploit the people, but this time they used race – with horrendous consequences for the people, but not for them.

During foreign occupation, another rift had opened up. A new class of English-educated Sri Lankan had emerged. This sub-group made up of Sinhalese, Tamils, Muslims and Dutch Burghers had benefited disproportionately during the European presence. This small group took easily to European attitudes and values, just as their modern counterparts absorb the American culture as exported by the American movie industry and as embodied by branded products such as Nike and McDonalds. The European-oriented English-speaking Sri Lankans saw their compatriots who still retained their Sinhalese and Tamil traditions as a lesser breed. The non-English-speaking majority (Sinhalese and Tamil) who had been left out of the gains of European occupation had nursed their resentment for nearly a century. Their resentment turned into anger and spilled over into envy and hatred and this cocktail of negative emotions warped their judgment. The actions they took to redress the balance rebounded on them rather than on those they intended to harm. Instead of using the English-educated people as links between the past and the future and between the island and the international community, the politicians chose to vilify them and ignore the contribution they could have made to the country's prosperity. The result was that a large number of the English-educated left to build new lives in 'foster-countries' and to work for more appreciative and rewarding employers in English-speaking countries. This loss of talent was an unnecessary drain at so crucial a stage in the country's development, and could have and should have been avoided.

The British attempt to create, for administrative reasons, a single nation out of the different races on the island failed because they failed to create a new people who saw each other as equals. Although the British considered that everyone on the island was a subject of the British monarch, the islanders did not. So the artificial nation of Ceylonese they created on paper and attempted to reinforce by creating a unitary state disintegrated. All that the new unitary state of Ceylon did was to make all its citizens subject to the *democratic process* but not to each other. But because the democratic process is subject to the wishes of the majority, the Sinhalese were able to seize control of the island and rule everyone on it. And that is what they set out to do. In other words, when the British installed the democratic process on the island, they also handed the Sinhalese something that their kings had not aspired to in the past and which they were not entitled to in the present or the future. They tied the hands and feet of the Tamils and delivered them up to the altar of Sinhalese Buddhist chauvinism.

The Sinhalese and Tamils realised this and the Sinhalese acted at once to consolidate the gift they had been given. At independence, the separateness of the people was accentuated by the flag chosen to represent independent Ceylon. The flag of the new nation was too ethnocentric. It was a Buddhist Sinhala flag and stated in no uncertain terms that they were the 'masters' now. A people who wished to build consensus would have chosen a 'neutral' flag, like the Stars and Stripes, to name an example. True, they were the majority people, but this blatant statement of their position stirred the chauvinism that had lain dormant in the Tamil breast. Unlike the constitution of the United States of America, the mechanism in the Sri Lankan constitution that protected minority interests had no teeth, in that the minorities did not have an arbitrator to whom they could express their grievances and get them debated and, if need be, corrected. As Roberts in his book on the history of the world points out, the success of the civil rights campaigns in the United States:

> ...stemmed from decisions of the Supreme Court in 1954 and 1955. The process thus began not with legislation but with judicial interpretation. These important first decisions provided that the segregation of different races within the public school system was unconstitutional and that where it existed it should be brought to an end within a reasonable time.[44]

Such a mechanism was an absolute necessity if peace was to prevail. Its omission meant that it was left to the magnanimity of the majority to ensure fair play. Alas, that was asking too much. The rest is history.

The British ran the country as a secular state, and religions of all communities and faiths were practised as a personal and private activity. There was no apparent tension between the adherents during British rule. However, during British rule, the indigenous religions of Buddhism and Hinduism had lost their primary status. Christianity had taken root in the island among the ruling clique, although it rarely challenged the supremacy of Buddhism as the religion of the majority Sinhalese community. There could, therefore, have been no doubt in

---

[44] Roberts, *The Penguin History of the World.*

the minds of those directing the country's future that the democratic process would favour the Sinhalese Buddhist majority, and that Buddhism would reassert itself as the religion of the state. An astute political leadership would have created the conditions for this transformation to take place peacefully and with the agreement and collaboration of the other communities. In the atmosphere of post-independence euphoria a negotiated settlement acceptable to all communities could easily have been struck. Instead, it was ignored at first, and then resurrected to serve the political needs of aspirants to the prime minister's job. Used in this way, the democratic system became a vehicle of advancement and Sinhalese and Buddhism were used as differentiators in the power struggle that followed independence. The result was disastrous. It highlighted religious and racial differences. It provided a platform for the bigot, the racist and the opportunist in all communities and, marked the Sinhalese Buddhists and the Buddhist establishments as racial supremacists.

The British also left behind a group of stateless people – the Indian Tamils, as they were called – who were imported by the British from India to provide labour for the coffee and tea plantations. Although they were unwelcome guests at the table of the Sinhalese and the Tamils these 'coolies', as they were called, were the backbone of the island's economy. The labour of these unfortunates produced the 'two leaves and a bud' that became the liquid gold of the country's economy for over a hundred years. Their lives on the plantations were really awful. But they came because it was better than the life they had in India. Waites makes the telling point when discussing the expansion of the agricultural market economy in Asia. He says:

> About 4.9 million Indian labourers migrated to Ceylon between 1843 and 1903 (some 1.5 million permanently) and a large proportion going from Madras were from the servile castes. Though conditions on the tea estates were harsh, they were an improvement on the outcaste's misery: one month's pay equalled two years' income at home.

Life for them was, indeed, harsh. Indian women left their line huts early in the morning to collect the baskets, which, suspended from their heads, would hold the two leaves and a bud that eventually ended up in our tea cups and mugs. The idealised picture of these women in tourist pictures and on the tea packets of most tea producers belies their true existence. They were no more than slaves caught in a vicious trap. These large families lived in line huts. Their sanitation was of the most primitive kind. They drew water from standpipes and used communal latrines. The older women, their lives and bodies wasted on the precarious slopes of the tea estates, cared for the children of their daughters when they left each morning to pluck the tea. These women and their male colleagues, who did the heavy work on the plantation, were answerable to their gang masters, who often robbed them blind and from whom they and the planters in their big bungalows demanded sexual favours. Women continued to pluck tea late into their pregnancy, and some suspended their work only for long enough to deliver a baby before returning to continue their shift in the harsh heat of the tea slopes.

The whole country depended on these people and survived on their sweat and blood. And then, having wrung the lifeblood from them, the Sri Lankan government made them stateless people in 1949 and forcibly repatriated a proportion of them a few decades later. Nobody blinked. The Indian government took them back, but it is not clear what happened to them then. The Sri Lankans should have given these people citizenship and welcomed them as fellow countrymen and women. After all, they had contributed so much to the island and deserved to be treated better. Such blatant discrimination, condoned by the Tamils, opened the way to policies that currently impact the country in its civil war.

The British left behind a thriving private sector made up of the local branches of major British, European and American companies. These local offices not only offered all the skills and technologies of their parent companies, they also ensured that the management methods and practices adopted by them were of the best available in the UK, Europe or America. They also provided high-quality jobs for able Sri Lankans with the opportunity to develop careers that were global rather than national. These companies bred capable managers and administrative staff and were sources of new knowledge and competence. So, at independence, almost all the most lucrative and prestigious businesses were in foreign hands. There were many successful family businesses that belonged to the Sinhalese, Tamils and Muslims too, but these businesses were 'closed shops' as regards career opportunities for those who did not belong to the extended families of their owners. Sinhalese- and Tamil-speaking individuals were effectively locked out of both sources of employment because fluency in English was a critical requirement. This form of discrimination had to be eradicated, but to do it by nationalising or limiting the scope of operations of these businesses, and using import controls to throttle the family businesses, was not the way to go about righting the balance. When these businesses were nationalised or constrained for reasons of revenge or ideology, large quantities of talented managers of major global corporations were lost to the economy, together with another large quantity of Sri Lankans who had to go abroad to find careers and futures. The decimation of the private sector effectively removed whole layers of jobs, some of which moved to the nationalised industries and fell into the hands of politicians who then gave them to their friends, cronies and constituents. The result was instantaneous and devastating to the economy. A more practical approach would have been to encourage these organisations to grow and build their businesses on the condition that they reinvested a reasonable percentage of their profits in the island and its people.

During the 150 years of British rule, the major policy and administrative decisions to do with the island and its people were made by the British. To successfully drive the civil service and the country the Sri Lankan politicians had to learn the skills of policy making and implementation. But policy, to be effective, needs an ideological framework and rational analysis. Except for the socialist (LSSP) and communist parties (CP) the other collections of individuals who came together under the banner of a 'political party' lacked any ideological basis for so doing. They gathered under a leader who they believed would enable them to take power, and would as easily have joined any other leader who offered them a better opportunity to take office.

This desire to gain power purely for personal benefit rather than to achieve benefits for the people as a whole accounts for the preponderance of pressure groups and their tendency to fill policy or ideological vacuums with their own needs. Consequently, strategy formulation was transformed from a rational and logical process to an emotional competence. Lacking a vision and desirable goals the political group drifted from idea to idea and eventually came to rest in a convenient harbour where it propped up a lame-duck government. So, in this policy wilderness, the only issue with any electoral promise was the Sinhalese Buddhist one. So it became both the means and the ends. The result was a set of policies that rational analysis would have shown would lead to the bankrupting of the country and social unrest.

Chapter 15

The End of Colonialism

When Dom Lourenco de Almeida arrived with his fellow countrymen in November 1505, he came to a country whose glory and achievements were in decline. When the British left in February 1948, the country had been transformed. The economy was sound. The country was competitive and matched many of its neighbours. Palden Jenkins criticises the British because he felt that:

> Insufficient attention was given [by them] to nation-building in the colonies, assisting new political and social cultures and initiating appropriate modernisation.[45]

As we have seen in Part Three, his criticism is not entirely fair. The British had moved the country towards democracy in many different ways. There was a large group of Oxford, Cambridge and LSE-educated Sri Lankans from all ethnic groups who were working hard to take the reins of power from the British. The literacy rate of the Sri Lankan was very high. The constitution was drafted by this Sri Lankan elite, and the people had voted in State Council elections. All of this had been done to prepare the Sri Lankan people for self-governance. It must also be remembered that:

> Neither the Dutch nor the English company sought territorial dominion in Asia, but by the 1760s both were ruling extensive lands beyond their factory enclaves and exploiting indigenous populations in new ways. Both were instances of 'expansion without design'.[46]

In other words, the British, the Dutch and the Portuguese went to the East to make money, not build nations. As it turned out, they not only made an impact on society, they also created successful money-making machines. Their legacy was such that the Sri Lankans had the skills and the foundations on which to build a strong and independent nation.

There were excesses and there was exploitation by the Europeans, but it is difficult to know if these exceeded those the population, as a whole, had suffered under their own leaders, who subjected them to summary justice, or the caste system that allotted people at birth a life of privilege or abuse.

[45] Palden Jenkins, *Healing the Hurts of Nations,* Gothic Image Publications, 2003.

[46] Waites, *Europe and the Third World.*

Besides, it is hard for an impartial observer to take a good hard look at Sri Lanka today and conclude that the lot of the island people is better now than it was under their European rulers. It is also unclear how the transition of the island from the Lanka of 1505 to the Ceylon of 1948 would have happened without the significant input of political, legal, managerial, financial and technological expertise that the Europeans introduced to the island during the intervening 450 years. To suggest that the feudal Sinhalese and Tamil people could have evolved at their own pace stretches credibility.

The challenge for the people of Sri Lanka was not European occupation but how the Sri Lankan people would use the European legacy to their advantage. They took the economic and infrastructure benefits for granted and projected a prosperous future, in the same way that the children of wealthy parents expect their inheritance to last for ever, and devote their time to squandering it. But there is much more to keeping a country prosperous, and the people have yet to learn how to go about it. Its future prosperity was not improved by the competing power groups who made its governance almost impossible. The Buddhist fundamentalists who had seen Buddhism superseded by Christianity set out to reclaim lost ground. The Western-educated Sri Lankans wanted very much to keep things the way they were. The huge rural poor who associated themselves with the Buddhist clergy wanted change – particularly a transfer of the wealth that a small group in Colombo had accumulated. The Tamils and Muslims wanted equality under the law. What was needed was a strategy that blended all these elements. Instead, what emerged was a series of single-issue pressure groups that, whilst they were controlling the politicians, forced them to take a lopsided view of the future direction of the country. The unintended consequences that followed are still dogging the country.

Independence did not bring freedom. In the globally interconnected world of today, no country is entirely free to chart its own course. The foreign policy needs of the major powers impinged on each and every country and increased the pressure on them to think and act globally. Unilateralism, even for the most powerful, is an impossible dream. Learning to live in this new American- and Soviet-dominated world was a challenge for which it was unprepared. Continuing to belong to the Commonwealth did ease some of the burden. But the reality was that Sri Lanka's politicians and its senior civil servants had to learn how to keep the country afloat. They had to swim in the shark-infested waters of international politics and deal with the so-called impartial international bodies such as the World Bank, the UN and its many agencies who usually only responded to the tune of 'Yankee Doodle Dandy'.

Besides this, Hollywood was doing a great job dictating the cultural agenda for the rest of the world. It portrayed the USA as a land of plenty, the Russians as wicked, and the rest of the world as burdens on Uncle Sam. This US cavalry view of the role of 'Uncle Sam' was the hallmark of many American movies. It is true that the USA helped Europe recover after the Second World War and helped many developing nations. But there was another side too.

Hollywood failed to point out that Uncle Sam was a reluctant participant in many world events. And it failed to point out that Uncle Sam could be a mischief-maker too, and looked unkindly on those who did not sing his tune. Neither did it point out that Uncle Sam, to satisfy his own foreign policy objectives, was capable of financing and encouraging insurrections and other forms of dissidence, whilst playing the 'innocent' at home in order to keep the American public believing in his benignity.

Governments do, however, sometimes have to act in ways that their people may not fully approve of in order to protect the people from their own naivety. Governments do sometimes preach freedom whilst acting undemocratically. Unfortunately, many countries with dubious human rights records have sought refuge in democracy and Sri Lanka is no exception.

Whether they liked it or not, whether they wished to or not, in 1948 the Sri Lankan people were part of a worldwide community and they either had to keep up or fall far behind. There was no middle ground. Whether they wished to be or not they were part of the foreign policy of the major powers and would have been dragged in anyway. In this situation the country needed to face outwards in unity.

Part Four

The New Imperialism

Summary

This part focuses on the new imperialists who took over from the British. This group of Western-educated, well-connected Sri Lankans, mainly Sinhalese, were the new patricians of independent, democratic Sri Lanka. They represented a new ruling clique drawn from families that had prospered during British rule. Time would show that they seized control and then ran the country for their benefit. They held on to power by being ruthless, power-hungry, self-serving and single-minded. They created a political culture that institutionalised their right to rule. Kumari Jayawardena, in her book about the rise of a Sri Lankan ruling class during British rule, shows the interconnectedness of the post-colonial leaders of Sri Lanka from before independence to the present time and explains how they succeeded in establishing a 'dynastic democratic leadership'. After independence, to consolidate their position, they formed political parties that represented family interests. This resulted in the creation of what Hague and Harrop call an 'elite political culture' which they define as one that:

> ...consists of the beliefs, attitudes and ideas about politics held by those who are closest to the centres of political power. The values of elites are more coherent and consequential than are those of the population at large.[47]

It was vital that this patrician group took control because they had to safeguard huge investments in land and revenue rights they had accumulated during the colonial period. Their wealth and social standing were gained by exploiting the new opportunities for enrichment and social mobility created by the British. The British needed intermediaries to help them run the country and harvest their revenues and a group of 'Westernised' Sinhalese, Tamil, Muslim and Burgher families took on the role and benefited in both status and wealth. Others exploited the financial opportunities offered by British rule, but remained neutral or challenged their rulers at the margins. Those who cooperated were honoured by the British in the usual way. They received titles. Many were given local titles such as mudaliyar, maha mudaliyar, muhandiram, gate mudilayer and the exceptionally cooperative were honoured by the king or queen. Kumari Jayawardena says of one cooperative family – the Bandaranaike's – that when Mrs Kumaratunga's (president of Sri Lanka 1994–2005) grandfather received a CMG from the King, a former governor of the island, Sir Joseph West Ridgeway, wrote, saying:

---

[47] Hague and Harrop, *Comparative Government and Politics: An Introduction*, fifth edition, Palgrave, 2001.

> You have indeed given very valuable assistance and loyal cooperation, and your services have been justly recognised by the King. I hope that further honours are in store for you and if I can be of any use to you in this or any other matter, please command me.[48]

Indeed, he was knighted in 1907 and received a KCMG in 1925. His son, S W R D Bandaranaike, switched allegiances after independence, took up the Sinhala Buddhist cause and propelled himself, his wife and daughter to the highest office in the land. All, as they say, is fair in love, war and politics.

The ruling clique created what Hague and Harrop call 'a parochial or subject political culture'. In such a culture it is 'the views of the elite which exert the most direct effect on political decisions'. And, sadly, the view of the ruling clique was and is of a two-tier country – themselves and 'others'. The political culture created by the ruling clique consolidated their powerbase but it alienated the 'others' (the rest of the population) and increased instability. According to Hague and Harrop there are three tests that can be applied to assess the potential for stability in a society. These are whether the elite have faith in their own right to rule; whether they accept the notion of a national interest, separate from individual and group ambitions; whether all members of the elite accept the rules of the game, especially those governing the transfer of power. Sadly for the country as a whole, the ruling clique fails on all counts. The ruling clique believes that it has a sovereign right to rule. Secondly, the ruling clique has governed the island to ensure that its individual and group ambitions remain paramount. And thirdly, the different factions of the ruling clique have worked hard at preventing a transfer of power except between the favoured 'families'. They have used presidential vetoes and the manipulation of the democratic processes to override the wishes of the electorate, to extend their stay in office and to remove potential challengers to that office from the political arena. This has been done within the democratic process to appease the international community whose money is vital to the country's current quality of life.

The instability may have been contained if another powerful group, the Buddhist nationalists, had not sought to exert its influence on the newly independent island. They, with the help of the Buddhist clergy, sought to create a different country; one that better fitted their image of an independent Sinhalese Buddhist state. The champions of the Buddhist nationalist movement were drawn from an entrepreneurial group of Sinhalese Buddhists and were supported by Western movements like the Theosophical Society. They wanted a country that reverted to Buddhist/Sinhalese values and took steps to make their wishes reality.

In their original message, the Buddhist nationalists had called for self-suffi-

---

[48] Kumari Jayawardena, *Nobodies to Somebodies, The Rise of the Colonial Bourgeoisie in Sri Lanka*, Zed Books, 2000.

ciency, the creation of an industrial sector and a return to Buddhist values. The movement was personified in Anagarika Dharmapala and his family. The power the movement had was its ability to exercise considerable influence on the voting intentions and behaviours of the electorate. Although, at first, the ruling clique ignored the Buddhist nationalists, it did not take them long to realise that it paid to take he Buddhist nationalists seriously. It became clear that the political group that the nationalists supported stood a very good chance of taking control. The politician who realised this first was Mr Bandaranaike. So he decided to make them an electoral asset and also prevent the UNP from using them. He promised to further their cause and drew on the Buddhist nationalist movement's strength to influence the majority electorate and win power.

By doing this, he gave a political voice to the Buddhist establishment. Its most vocal propagandists abandoned Buddhism and Buddhist values and donned robes of political debate and Western democratic aspirations. So, by clever political manoeuvring, Mr Bandaranaike, the leader of one political family within the ruling group, created a secular state that did their bidding and clothed it in the saffron robes of Buddhism and Sinhalese to gain mass support. By championing the forces of nationalism, Bandaranaike had tainted the nationalists, diverted their influence to help him become prime minister, and set in motion his dynastic ambitions. The 'people', whom democracy was supposed to empower, found themselves powerless under the combined onslaught of the ruling clique, the Buddhist nationalists and the Buddhist establishment.

Those outside the ruling clique were unable to exercise their democratic rights by using the political institutions, because the political institutions belonged to the ruling clique. By co-opting the Buddhist nationalists to fight his cause, Bandaranaike deprived the 'others' of a voice in the affairs of the nation, and their frustration at being politically neutered eventually erupted as civil strife and drove a wedge between the Tamils and the Sinhalese. This suited the ruling clique very well.

Having set the 'others' to fight among themselves in a racial war, the ruling clique continued to reap the benefits of power. They used the state, in Hague and Harrop's words, as '...a seam of scarce resources to be mined for the benefit of the rulers, their family, their constituents and their ethnic group'. Hague and Harrop say that such behaviour is endemic to 'much of the developing world, where economic resources are scarce and state institutions are weak'. How right they are. Many on the island, as well as impartial observers, would agree that the Sri Lankan ruling clique act like politicians and officials in some post-communist countries who, in Hague and Harrop's view have 'rediscovered a role: defrauding the public purse while flying the flag of transition to a market economy' and of failing to 'generate criticism rather than a mere shrug of the shoulders' when corruption is discovered. Both are part of the elite political culture of the island. Only the dispossessed and disadvantaged Sinhalese and Tamil youths revolted at this gross abuse of democracy.

Now, after almost fifty years of indoctrination the 'people' have lost the plot. Tempted by the ruling group, who saw them as a political threat, one faction of the youth revolutionaries has exchanged its arms for the ballot box. But they are finding that coexistence with the ruling elite does not necessarily mean that they have 'real' power. Another faction has called a truce. Both revolutionary groups, however high-minded their original intentions were, seem now to be self-serving and are losing their status as the champions of the 'others' in Sri Lanka. So, the 'others', the vast mass of the people, are still lost. They have no one to lead them or help them define what suits their own best interests so they continue to act according to the wishes of the ruling clique and the Buddhist nationalists who have now transformed themselves into racists. The result is that, after nearly sixty years, the divide between the Sinhalese and the Tamils has been institutionalised and each community is unwelcome in the territory of the other. The poor remain poor and the young have little future.

In Part Five we will explore the country that the ambitions of the ruling clique created. In this part we explore how the ruling clique took and held on to power.

Chapter 16

The New Imperialists

On 4 February 1948, a band of Tamil, Sinhalese and Muslim, English-educated, Western-orientated politicians, businessmen and landowners took control of the island and the people. There was no freedom struggle, just a peaceful handover. As Ludowyk says:

> What was obscured in 1947–8 in the paean of self-gratulation by His Majesty's Government, the Colonial Governor and the Ministers of Ceylon, was that the island had been identified with the Ministers. The corollary of this was the suspicion of a large number of people outside the charmed circles of power that independence was a private negotiation between the British and the 'nobodies', [Sri Lankan term for the *arriviste*] in which the high contracting parties arranged things to their own satisfaction.

Ludowyk's view is supported by Kumari Jayawardhena who points out that the political clique of the 1920s did not:

> ...attempt to develop, as in India, a mass movement for independence ... the very narrow franchise of the 1920s enabled members of bourgeoisie [the ruling clique] to take a firm grip on local politics. They entrenched themselves to such an extent that they were able to perpetuate their political authority as the 'natural' representatives and leaders of the people.

So, at independence, they slid smoothly into the chairs of office vacated by the British and became the new colonial masters of the country. It was a coup against the people, executed with elegance and dexterity. Since then, their descendents have ruled the country although they have had to align with a range of others to take and keep power. So, although the composition of the ruling clique has changed as it absorbed or annexed essential bedfellows to keep power, their objectives of self-preservation and exploitation have not.

There is no evidence that the original group had any clear aims or overarching goals for the new country. They knew that there were various disaffected factions within the majority community – the Buddhist nationalists for example – whose expectations had to be managed. And they knew that the Tamils were uncertain of where they stood vis-à-vis the majority community. These were all real issues that needed to be addressed and controlled. This task fell on the UNP who were the only realistic political grouping the people could vote for immediately after independence. It had gathered under its wing the leaders of other special interest parties and it had therefore the ability to build a united nation. But it failed to live up to its name.

At first, the politicians who had gathered under the banner of the UNP and the socialist parties took the view that parity of status for all the citizens of the state of Ceylon was a desirable objective. But nepotism within the UNP and the impact of the Citizenship Acts drove some politicians to leave the UNP and form their own political parties. These new parties had to find a competitive edge that would win them votes. Mr Bandaranaike chose to politicise the Sinhalese Buddhist cause to win votes. The leaders of the Tamil political parties, seeing that the winds of change were blowing them further away from their objective of gaining equality of status and treatment from the Sinhalese majority, campaigned on a Tamil nationalist slogan and sought a federal state. The UNP continued to appeal to its traditional electorate but realised, too late, that Mr Bandaranaike had stolen their clothes.

From then on – the early 1950s – the political map of the country polarised. The Sinhalese Buddhist majority had the choice of the UNP and the SLFP and the Tamils the Federal Party and the Tamil Congress. The socialists and the communists who were primarily the urban workers were represented by trade unions affiliated to the Communist Party (CP) and Lanka Sama Samaja Party (LSSP). Although the representation of the CP and LSSP in Parliament was small they were willing to align themselves with the SLFP – Mr Bandaranaike's party – to help him achieve a majority in Parliament provided he implemented some of their policies. The representatives of the plantation workers and the Muslims, understandably, allied themselves with the party that protected their people's interests. Consequently, ever since independence, because only the UNP and SLFP could muster a ruling majority in Parliament, the families who led the UNP and the SLFP took turns to govern the country.

Control of the UNP has passed to other hands but the SLFP has remained the property of the Bandaranaike family since its formation but may not remain so for much longer now that Mrs Kumaratunga is no longer the president. In the main, the supporters of the UNP were foreign and local businessmen, professionals, the landed gentry and others closely associated with them. They were quite happy for the new state to continue along the lines set for it by its British rulers, and the UNP leadership was happy to oblige. The SLFP claimed to be the party of the 'people' and appealed to that segment of the electorate who wanted the country returned to its indigenous roots, which to them meant a country that was primarily Sinhalese Buddhist and free from Western influence. Mr Bandaranaike and, after him, Mrs Bandaranaike presented themselves as, and were accepted as, the champions of the Sinhalese Buddhists. And once in power they acted to prove their sincerity.

They asked the British to vacate their bases in the country, nationalised or severely constrained the scope of foreign-owned businesses and the businesses of those rich local entrepreneurs who supported and financed the UNP. By doing this, they simultaneously appeased their socialist allies and their supporters and harmed the financial interests of the UNP. Revenge was sweet, but it had the bitter aftertaste of racial disharmony and economic decline. The UNP exploited every opportunity Mr Bandaranaike gave them to drive him down a blind alley by forcing him to make good his promises to the Sinhalese Buddhist majority who had voted him into office. After his death, his wife continued to follow his policies with renewed vigour and determination. And their daughter carried the flame until she stepped down as president in November 2005 at the end of her second term.

So the battle between the UNP and the SLFP to gain and retain power continued, but the promises these two parties made to the voters – that they would enjoy improvements in security, peace, the opportunity to earn a living wage, the ability to feed and clothe themselves and their families, educate their children and maintain their health – did not materialise. During the leaderships, of Mr Bandaranaike and then Mrs Bandaranaike the economy suffered. As a consequence, the generation of Sri Lankans born during and after the Second World War suffered most. They faced a future devoid of opportunity. Only the children of the ruling clique escaped this fate. So, the frustrations of the disadvantaged of all races erupted into violence. As The Library of Congress Country Studies commentary on Sri Lanka says:

> Sri Lanka's decent into violence was especially disturbing because for many years the nation was considered a model of democracy in the Third World. A nation with one of the world's lowest per capita incomes, Sri Lanka nevertheless had a nascent but thriving free-market economy that supported one of the most extensive and respected education systems among developing countries. Sadly, in 1990 the recollection of a peaceful and prosperous Sri Lanka seemed a distant memory.

Despite their appalling performance as legislators and politicians, and their failure to deliver peace and prosperity, the ruling clique held on to power by blaming their failures on others. Favourite among these scapegoats were the colonial powers, Western and local industrialists and the Tamils. Their one dubious achievement in the years since independence was to do what their forebears had failed to do for over two millennia – create a single united nation by uniting the people. In a period that was a mere hair's breadth in the context of its long history; they converted this once peaceful island into a cauldron of hate and despair.

It would be charitable to suggest that the ruling clique had not planned it this way and that they had not wanted their hunger for power to be cannibalistic. The charitable may claim that they were caught in a catch-22 situation. To stay in power, they had to appease the Buddhist lobby, but in appeasing the Buddhist nationalists they had to cede the moral high ground. This Faustian bargain has no victors, just victims. So, although they could appreciate the benefits that collaboration, cooperation and peaceful co-habitation would bring them, they persisted in creating winners and losers because that seemed the only way to keep power.

The less charitable would claim that they knew exactly what they were doing. To keep power, they kept racism high on the political agenda and were grateful to the Buddhist nationalists for keeping the issue alive in the rural communities. This meant that they could appease the racists and Buddhist fundamentalists and benefit from the voting power they received in return for their betrayal of the other groups in society. Machiavellian it may be, but the practical outcome suited the ruling clique very well. It helped them keep power. And this they were very good at doing. Today, the rural Sinhalese youths who staged two insurgencies have been neutralised and absorbed – but not changed. The Tamils, having resisted the efforts of Sri Lankan and Indian governments to destroy them, have called a truce even though their deeply felt sense of injustice remains.

The current conflict keeps the Buddhist Sinhalese majority on side and gives the ruling clique the best chance of holding on to power. They know that the racists who hide their racism under the Buddhist nationalist umbrella are still there and carrying on their gruesome work by holding the Damocles' sword of 'appeaser of the Tamils' over the heads of those willing to give peace a chance. A new pressure front is being opened by the Muslims, who fear that any accommodation with the Tamils will be at their expense. So the President, as the representative of the ruling clique, has another excuse to delay meaningful talks with the LTTE (Liberation Tigers of Tamil Eelam) and achieve peace. It seems that, ever since the new Parliament was elected in April 2004, the peace talks have stalled. Since December 2005 the LTTE and the Sri Lanka armed forces seem to have resumed where they left off three years earlier.

President Kumaratunga, like her father and mother before her, seemed content to let the status quo rest. Her father took office by beating the racial drum, her mother nurtured it and she keeps the racial flame alight because it helps her keep the presidency. Of course she would deny this. For example, TamilNet.com of 20 May 2005 quotes her as saying, 'The government may fall ... I might lose the presidency but those things are not of national interest unlike bringing lasting peace to the country.' The implication is that she would risk her presidency to win peace but it is more likely that by then she knew her attempts to hold on to power by constitutional or judicial manoeuvring had failed. But as the same article points out:

> ...given her determined efforts to retain political power over the past several years, her threat is not being taken seriously. It is widely acknowledged that President Kumaratunga's central political project is to abolish Sri Lanka's Executive Presidency and replace it with a powerful Prime Minister's office, for which she would be entitled to compete, unlike a third term as President.[49]

[49] 'Joint mechanism mired in Sinhala politics', Tamilnet.com,

Key events listed in the BBC Timeline on Sri Lanka provide proof of her desire to hang on to office, even at the expense of the peace process. It states that:

> [In] 2001 July – President Kumaratunga suspends parliament for two months to save her minority government from defeat in a no-confidence vote. 2001 October – Kumaratunga dissolves parliament hours before a no-confidence vote which her Marxist-backed minority government seemed likely to lose. Elections set for 5 December. 2003 November – President Kumaratunga dismisses three ministers, suspends parliament. She had been at odds with government over peace process. Parliament reopens after two weeks but negotiations with Tamil Tigers are put on hold. 2004 April – Early general elections held amid political power struggle.[50]

Mrs Kumaratunga and the ruling clique continue in power by persuading the Sinhalese Buddhist majority that the price the Tamils are asking for peace is too high a price to pay. The reality, which the ruling clique have so cleverly hidden from the majority of the Sinhalese Buddhists, who are suffering the deprivations and depredations of the war and its economic consequences, is that the struggles of the Tamils and the Low-Country Sinhalese youth for what Sim calls, 'the preconditions for normal existence'[51] is their struggle too. What average Sinhalese Buddhists need to realise is that their real enemy is the ruling clique and that by continuing to elect them to office they are postponing the day when they and their children can benefit from the wealth and resources the ruling clique have been robbing from them these last fifty-seven years. The ruling clique is indeed the real villain of the current unrest because they have prevented the growth of true representative government in the country. The two insurgencies staged by the Sinhalese youth and the current conflict with the Tamils, with their consequent heavy cost of lives were and are awful and unacceptable, but they were and are attempts to wrest power from the ruling clique.

In many ways the country is still bound to its feudal ways and the members of the ruling clique behave like 'lords of the manor'. Kumari Jayawardena points out that the image of Sri Lanka as an island paradise is an outdated view based on its colonial period. According to her and many other commentators on the island, the reality is 'of war, underdevelopment, authoritarian rule, caste consciousness and women's subordination'. In her view, the reality for the mass of the population in both the colonial and post-colonial periods '...has been one of persistent poverty and continuous rule by these changing layers of "Somebodies", [the ruling clique] in a situation of continuing ethnic strife'.[52]

Those who took control of the island sixty years ago still control it now

---

<http://www.tamilnet.com/art.html?catd=79&artid=14858, 9 May 2005.

[50] *Country profile: Sri Lanka*, BBC News, www.bbc.co.uk, 18 November 2005.

[51] Stuart Sim, *Fundamentalist World*, Icon Books, 2004.

[52] Jayawardena, *Nobodies to Somebodies*.

through their descendents. They could be forgiven for ruling it for their benefit, but they cannot be forgiven for having created a dysfunctional country to keep power. Those who trusted them have been horribly let down. The chaos they have created has occasionally rebounded on them, but, in the main, they have risen above the chaos. The people they rule continue to live in it.

The ruling clique knows that to gain peace they may have to undo the emotional damage and the inequalities of past policies. They will also have to denounce and punish the racial supremacists who organised and used civilian thugs and vigilantes and a subgroup of members of the security forces to indulge in communal violence. But it is unlikely that this will happen. Mrs Kumaratunga, like her predecessor presidents and prime ministers, claims that she has tried to rein back the excesses and rebuild national unity but is finding it difficult to do so due to the intransigence of those involved. These 'troublemakers', she claims, are preventing her from unravelling the knotted thread of social unrest. She and the ruling clique she represents claim that, despite the obstacles, they have done the best they can to keep some semblance of fairness in Sri Lankan society. And there is some truth in this.

What is clear is that there were interest groups hampering her attempts at peace. But it is not clear that she and the ruling clique really wanted peace or that they were willing to challenge these groups, take control of the political agenda and create a climate for peace. The reason for her reluctance was that she needed their support to stay in power.

The island needs, but has not as yet produced, an Alexander the Great to cut the Gordian knot. Ranil Wickramasinghe who, by all accounts, was on his way to resolving the issue and returning peace and democracy to the island, is now in opposition because the government he headed as prime minister incurred the displeasure of the President. So, on 3 November 2003 she removed key ministries from it, dissolved Parliament on 7 February 2004 and held fresh elections on 2 April 2004 and appointed a compliant prime minister, Mr Mahinda Rajapaksa. Her current hate seems to be the JVP (People's Liberation Front), the very party that helped her government take power in April 2004 and has now left the coalition. At a July meeting of the SLFP, Mrs Kumaratunga has made it clear that she:

> ...is not ready to consider any agreement with the JVP as they were responsible for 'all the mess' the country faces today. 'It was the JVP and some of our own people [SLFP supporters] who forced me to take over the three Ministries and dissolve the UNF [United National Front] government.[53]

It seems that, unable to tame the JVP, she is back in her familiar role as 'protector of dynastic ambitions'. However, time has run out for her.

---

[53] Colombopage.com, 10 July 2005.

Chapter 17
The Dynasts

A small group of educated and financially self-sufficient Sri Lankans took over when the British left. Although the leadership of this group reflected the electoral mix power actually passed from the British to the sons of the Sinhalese ruling elite.

D S Senanayake belonged to one such Sinhalese family. He was elected the first prime minister of independent Ceylon. He had distinguished himself in Sri Lankan politics since about the 1930s and was the leader of the state council in the years leading up to independence. He had the family connections, the money, political stature as the leader of the United National Party (UNP), which he founded in 1946, the ability and the ambition to pursue a political career that would culminate in being the leader of the country.

> He studied in Colombo, worked on his father's rubber estate. Entering the Legislative Council in 1922, he founded the co-operative society movement in 1923, and was elected to the State Council in 1931, where he was minister of agriculture for 15 years.[54]

Senanayake was older than Bandaranaike and, as the leader of the group that negotiated the liberation of the island from the British, established his right to take the office of prime minister. He also had earned the admiration of the people he would later lead and who would affectionately dub him 'the father of the nation'. The nation commemorated his contribution to it by naming the largest artificial lake built after it won independence in his honour. The Senanayake Samudra, as it was called, lay within the 62,936 hectares of Gal Oya Park west of Amparai in the eastern province. His stature among the people was high, perhaps as high as that enjoyed by Nehru in India. If not for his untimely death, he would certainly have kept the office of prime minister for many years, and, like Nehru and Lee Kuan Yew, he would have provided the steady hand an emergent democracy needed.

D S Senanayake expected to be prime minister for a long time and wanted it to be his son's office too. When he took office in 1947 as head of an interim government he had expected to keep his pre-eminent position of prime minister until his death or when his son was ready to take over. But fate took a decisive hand. One morning, he fell off his horse, and the fall was fatal for him and his country.

---

[54] The Penguin Encyclopaedia, 2004.

Even whilst he was alive and the leader of the UNP, the quality of leadership shown by the party was inadequate to forge forward and optimise on the country's heritage. In Ludowyk's words, the UNP was 'not a party at all. It was a group of personages brought together by the dominant personality of D S Senanayake'. The UNP was the only political party with the size and constituency to field enough candidates to win a majority in Parliament. So they took power. The first UNP government included ministers from all races and creeds as befitted a multi-ethnic ruling class and a multi-ethnic nation.

The party had no vision of a future Ceylon and showed a marked reluctance to change what they had inherited. The UNP was led by men and women who often wished to be more British than the British. So, under their governance the country seemed to continue to be British, except that now it was run by Ceylonese grandees to whom independence purely meant a transfer of power from the British to them. They were the new masters in an independent Sri Lanka and intended to run the country to suit their needs.

In the meantime the 98 per cent of the population watched in dismay as their lives became increasingly worse rather than better under their own leaders. This was a state of affairs that had to change, but they saw no sign of it happening and probably, in those early days, did not know how to wrest the reins of power from the elite unless someone gave them the means. They would have been content to see slow change, but one with a forward thrust and a clear vision that would deliver a better and fairer society for all the islanders, not just its elite.

But politicians with the ideas and ability to deliver for all the people were thin on the ground. Some, such as the leaders of the Lanka Sama Samaja Party (LSSP), subscribed to socialist ideologies and championed the creation of a socialist state. But they did not have the following to put their ideas into practice. So, at this time, the country had a group of political leaders who, except perhaps for Mr Bandaranaike, did not know how to exploit the sound economy and administrative system the British had left them. They could go everywhere and do everything necessary to create a thriving country but they went nowhere and thought there was nowhere to go except to be where they were. There was no vision, no imagination, and no drive. The elite already had what they needed so they squabbled among themselves and called it politics.

When D S Senanayake died, the dynastic machinery of the United National Party shuffled chairs and put Dudley Senanayake in the premier's seat (1952–1953) long before he was really ready for the job. It was in this dynastic spirit of bequeathing the highest office in the land to his son that D S Senanayake had groomed Dudley Senanayake. But Dudley Senanayake did not demonstrate the same drive and ambition as his father. Dudley Senanayake gave the impression of a man who felt it his duty to take on the burden of high office, more to humour his father's and his extended family's ambition to establish a dynastic right to the job, rather than because he had a deep ambition to rule the country. Ludowyk says that Dudley Senanayake was:

> Naturally modest and open, he was respected and liked. In his youth he had been a sportsman, good at cricket and boxing; he had a scholarly mind and had taken a good degree at Cambridge. His entry into politics in the early thirties seemed so far from the predilections of the young man he was that it was probably the result of that mixture of impressionability and conscientiousness so characteristic of him.

But there were others, like Mr Bandaranaike, who could also claim the right to lead the country. Bandaranaike was by far the more politically astute and ambitious of the two and believed that governance of the country was his by right. The untimely death of D S Senanayake gave Bandaranaike the opportunity he needed to seize control.

When Dudley Senanayake resigned in October 1953, following widespread protest at his measures to increase the price of rice by reducing the Government subsidy on it, the party shuffled again, and this time his cousin, John Kotelawala (1953–1956), became premier. Sir John Kotelawala was primarily a playboy. A man of independent means, he made sure that he enjoyed life to the full. In his vanity, arrogance and total self-assurance he failed to read the signs of the times and took his re-election for granted. There was scope for a new beginning and Bandaranaike was ready to deliver it.

Mr Bandaranaike had set up his own party, but joined the UNP under D S Senanayake's leadership in 1946. He believed that this move would add impetus to his political career. He was appointed Minister of Local Administration, a post that brought him into contact with people right across the political and social spectrum and helped him to understand the mood of the country better than his colleagues.

Solomon West Ridgeway Dias Bandaranaike was born into opulence in 1899. He was a true blue-blooded aristocratic Sinhalese, son of a KCMG, an English-educated Oxford graduate, a one-time Anglican and a strong anglophile who bore the name of the British Imperial Governor – J West Ridgeway, his godfather. As a member of a very small band of super-elite, super-rich, and super-privileged Ceylonese, brought up to believe that he was a prince among men, he felt certain he could control any monster that his actions created. His was not the fantasy of a doting mother but the realistic expectation of a family that had position, money, education, caste and past achievement on its side. From childhood he had demanded and got obedience. He was schooled for greatness. Like so many children of the Sinhalese and Tamil elite, his mother tongue was English. He was educated at St Thomas' College, Mount Lavinia, the premier English-medium Church of England school in the country, and graduated from Oxford University. On his return from Oxford in 1925 he converted to Buddhism and exchanged his Western clothes for the sarong and long white cotton shirt that became his sartorial trademark ever since. He was now ready to keep his date with greatness, if he did so desire. And he and his powerful extended family did. They had the wealth and social position to finance and support a political career dedicated to achieving high office in the 'service of the country'.

Bandaranaike and his family had excelled at being at the right place at the right time, sporting the right garb and the right beliefs. Swapping faith to exploit the prevailing wind seems to have been a family tradition. By allying and collaborating with the ruling power during the Portuguese, Dutch and British periods, his Sinhalese aristocratic forbears ensured that the family fortunes and position was enhanced. It seems that every generation of the family had a man for all seasons – a Richard Rich – to safeguard its interests. This ingrained sense of timing or opportunism had helped the family in the past and was going to do so in the future.

Bandaranaike decided that he would leave the cousins – Dudley Senanayake and Sir John Kotelawala – to play musical chairs, and form his own political party. So in 1951 he created the Sri Lanka Freedom Party (SLFP) and used it as the platform to make his bid to be Prime Minister by promising to release the country from its colonial past for ever. And the policy is still working as first his wife and then his daughter ruled this broken fragment of a country, manipulating the democratic process and allying themselves with whomsoever fitted their purpose at the time.

As a Christian who converted to Buddhism, Bandaranaike was able to legitimise his claim to be the Buddhist champion and to call on the Sinhalese Buddhist majority – who had been agitating for some time for changes in the way the country was run – to support him. This groundswell of emotional energy was there to be tapped and used, especially in a democratic system where the power really came from the people, however misguided and ill-informed they were. So, he took up their cry. As Bandaranaike's biographer says:

> These things indicated to many that for Bandaranaike, Sinhalese chauvinism was more a tactical ploy than a matter of conviction. They were essentially correct, but his chauvinism was no less dangerous for that.[55]

He argued that it was time to drop the colonial baggage and resuscitate the Sinhalese Buddhist heritage of the island. In this single simple message he had found the 'open sesame' to his dreams.

His second hurdle was to overcome the fact that the UNP was seen as the natural party of power, and Bandaranaike had to create a mood swing that would favour him. He formed a coalition with other, smaller political parties and entered the election as the leader of the Mahajana Eksath Peramuna (MEP). Supported by the Buddhist clergy and the racists among the electorate, he won hands down in 1956, despite the UNP unleashing its well-funded and well-organised party machinery with its network of offices across the country to thwart him. The UNP's attempt to entice people to vote for it by providing transport for the willing, and bribing and intimidating the unwilling, failed. And their grandees, for the first time, found that they had lost their power to

---

[55] Manor, *The Expedient Utopian: Bandaranaike and Ceylon.*

influence the voters. Instead, the people had listened to the Buddhist monks, who had preyed on their fears by telling them that their heritage was in danger and only a change of government would help save and revitalise it. The people heard this call and voted for Bandaranaike, whom they saw as the saviour of the Sinhala/Buddhist cause. Bandaranaike came from nowhere to win forty-nine of the ninety-five seats, and the UNP won just eight seats. Sir John had realised too late the power of the Buddhist clergy to influence the voting intentions of the people. Kotelawala collected his knighthood and drove off into the sunset in his white Cadillac, and into political oblivion – which, as it happens, was his farm in the Kent countryside. It was a decisive rejection of what the UNP stood for – the status quo.

The voters had replaced one set of feudal overlords with another. This new breed of politicians depended on politically inclined Buddhist monks for their power. The monks, having tasted power, moved in for the kill and, as the new powerbrokers, claimed their place at the high table of the island's politics from then on. Managing them would test the most able politician. And Bandaranaike was not that politician. He had not learnt how to win consensus, only how to order it into being. He could sway with the breeze and bend with the wind, but the storm about to engulf him and his country was of hurricane proportions and neither he nor the people had any place to shelter from it.

His political ambitions lived on in his wife, son and daughter. The son failed to live up to his father's image or his mother's expectations. He rolled from one political party to another and gathered no moss. Mr Bandaranaike's wife and daughter, however, grasped the opportunity that fate presented them, but failed to meet the challenge Mr Bandaranaike left them – of restoring the peace he had destroyed for personal gain. They have deepened the wounds and piled new agonies onto the lives of the misguided voters. Despite the abysmal performance of mother and daughter, the Sinhala Buddhist majority has voted them into office and kept them there. Perhaps the death wish of the Sri Lankan voter is insatiable... or maybe the ruling group know their people better than the people know themselves? They have kept control of the levers of power for nearly sixty years. The methods they used were varied, but all were effective.

Chapter 18

The Governor Generals, Presidents and Prime Ministers of Sri Lanka

The Ceylon Independence Act of 1947 formally transferred power from the British Crown to the ruling clique of self-selected Sri Lankans on 4 February 1948. The 'people' of Ceylon had no say in how the new independent state of Sri Lanka should be governed. The new constitution was drafted, negotiated, modified and agreed by a group of leading politicians drawn from the different ethnic communities. It took them four years to arrive at an acceptable compromise. The new constitution created a unitary state. The British monarch was the head of state and was represented in Sri Lanka by a governor general until the constitution was changed in 1972.

The post of governor general was held by the Right Honourable Viscount Soulbury between 1948 and 1954. Lord Soulbury was head of the commission that scrutinised and approved the constitution under which the people of Sri Lanka would be governed. He left after the visit of Queen Elizabeth II in 1954 and his place was filled by Sir Oliver Goonetilleke who was governor general from 1954 to 1962. Mr William Gopallawa took over from Mr Goonetilleke and held the office from 1962 to 1972 and then became the president from 1972 to 1977.

The system of governance between 1948 and 1972 was made up of an appointed House called the Senate and a House of Representatives made up of parliamentarians elected by the people to represent them and their interests. The prime minister was usually the leader of the party with the highest number of seats in Parliament. During this time executive power resided with the prime minister and the cabinet.

Ceylon became the Republic of Sri Lanka in 1972 when the constitution was changed. It replaced the post of Governor General with that of a president whose role was mainly ceremonial. It abolished the Senate and the House of Representatives and established a unicameral National State Assembly in their stead. The decisions of the National State Assembly were final as it precluded the judiciary from scrutinising and if necessary rectifying any injustice its acts and actions may have caused to an aggrieved party. Executive power resided in the prime minister.

There were significant risks associated with this constitution as it gave the prime minister the ability to behave like a dictator, particularly if circumstances allowed the prime minister to use emergency and special powers. In 1978, the government of Mr Jayawardene revised the 1972 constitution. The new constitution gave the president executive powers and immunity from prosecution from any official or private action carried out when in office. Tamil was given status as a national language. This new arrangement made the prime minister subordinate to and dependent on the president. This is the constitution under which the country is currently governed. Mr Colvin R De Silva, an able and much respected politician, is reported to have said at the time, 'Both Parliament and prime minister have been so heavily devalued that the only thing that I can think of comparing them to is our rupee'.[56]

This chapter lists, in chronological order, the prime ministers and executive presidents who have led the country since independence. It also lists some key policies and statutes passed during their time in office that had far-reaching implications for democracy and racial harmony in the island. The primary data for this chapter was drawn from the Sri Lanka government website and supplemented with information from the website of the Library of Congress Country Story for Sri Lanka and Ludowyk.

The final comment on their stewardship are the words of a tour guide who told a journalist, 'We haven't found any good politicians since 1948'.[57] It is a sentiment expressed by the majority of the people living in Sri Lanka.

[56] Matthews, quoted in Bush, *The Intra-Group Dimensions of Ethnic Conflict in Sri Lanka.*

[57] Michelle Jana Chan, 'Embers of Empire', *Telegraph*, 9 July 2005.

Prime Ministers of Sri Lanka from 1948 to now

P M/PRESIDENT	KEY SOCIAL AND ECONOMIC POLICIES INFLUENCING THE COURSE OF THE COUNTRY SINCE 1948.
Mr D S Senanayake (PM) 1948–1952	Mr Senanayake was the first prime minister of Ceylon and known as 'father' of the nation. During his period in office, the Citizenship Acts of 1948, the Indian and Pakistani Residents (Citizenship) Act of 1949, the Ceylon (Parliamentary Elections Amendment) Act of 1949 were passed. He introduced various welfare measures that helped the country to maintain its investment in human capital at a higher level when compared with other developing countries and was responsible for lifting the human development status of the country.
Mr D Senanayake (PM) 1952–1953	Dudley Senanayake was the son of D S Senanayake. His term of office was short. The Central Bank of Ceylon, responding to the findings of the International Bank for Reconstruction and Development (1952), advised him to reduce the subsidy on imported rice. He took their advice. The country revolted and he resigned.
Sir John Kotelawala (PM) 1953–1956	Sir John was the nephew of D S Senanayake. Hosted Queen Elizabeth II's visit to Ceylon in 1954. Ceylon joined the United Nations.
Mr S W R D Bandaranaike (PM) 1956–1959	S W R D Bandaranaike successfully wrested control of the country from the UNP, of which the three preceding prime ministers were leaders. As leader of the SLFP he formed an alliance with other political parties and fought and won the election of 1956. He campaigned on a promise to make Sinhalese the official language and kept his promise by proclaiming it the official language in June 1956. In 1958 racial tension burst its banks with disastrous consequences. Other initiatives were the Paddy Lands Act of 1958 protecting the rights of tenant farmers. His administration established an Employees Provident Fund Scheme for public sector workers so that they would have pension rights. The government lost control over wages to the trade union movement, which flexed its considerable muscle to correct, what it believed to be, huge disparities in income and living standards between workers and management. The ports were nationalised as a first step in his policy of state managed enterprises as outlined in the State Industrial Corporations Act in 1957. British naval and air force bases were closed. He was assassinated by a monk.

Mr W Dahanayake (PM) 1959–1960	Presided over a caretaker government. The SLFP began to fragment during his period as its leader and it prompted the party grandees to ask Mrs Bandaranaike to take on the leadership late in 1960.
D Senanayake (PM) March–June 1960	Short-lived term of office.
Mrs S Bandaranaike (widow of SWRDB) (PM) 1960–1965	The world's first unelected woman prime minister. The government website says that 'Mrs Sirimavo Bandaranaike was appointed prime minister as a member of the Senate'. She was strong-minded and came from the Kandyan elite. Anxious to implement her husband's policies she attacked the task with vigour. She enforced the Sinhala Only Act. She passed the Language of the Courts Act of 1961 that made Sinhalese the official language of the courts and refused to allow court records in Tamil-speaking areas to be kept in Tamil. She contained protest by declaring a state of emergency and curtailing the activities of Tamil politicians. She took over state-assisted denominational schools, most of which were set up by Christian missionaries, thus losing the support of the Christian community. Nationalised foreign-owned oil businesses and limited the activities of others. This lost her government the goodwill of foreign governments and destroyed large number of careers. It antagonised the United States when she merged the assets of Shell, Esso and Caltex into a newly formed State Oil Corporation. She further alienated Western governments by importing oil from Russia and other countries. Foreign Exchange controls were introduced in 1963. This placed a moratorium on the repatriation of profits and dividends and restrictions in foreign travel including going overseas for education. The curb on education hurt the Tamils more as the policy of 'Sinhala Only' limited their learning opportunities at home. Imports were also severely restricted. This heightened increase in government control, opened up the opportunity for patronage, bribery and corruption and discrimination at all levels. She attempted to nationalise the Daily News Group of Newspapers and appoint a press council, but this failed. She extended the concepts introduced by the Paddy Lands Act to encompass other agricultural property by redistributing estates. She broke up well-run plantations and parcelled them out in one-acre smallholdings and limited individual ownership of plantations to maximum of fifty acres. Theoretically, the rural poor were supposed to benefit but in practise no one did. Her economic policies included high taxation, import controls and foreign exchange controls. The economic decline hurt the youth even more due to a lack of 'good' jobs and other opportunities for betterment. The government website says also that

	she 'contested her first seat in Parliament in March 1965 from the electorate of Attanagalla (her husband's old seat) and was returned by majority votes', but she did not get a majority in Parliament.
D Senanayake (PM) 1965–1970	The intensity with which Mrs Bandaranaike had pursued her socialist policies had literally bankrupted the country. Mr Senanayake had a major challenge on his hands to rebuild the economy. He focused on reversing previous economic measures and made the economy and country attractive to foreign investment. Rice and food subsidies seemed to be his Achilles heel. The increasing cost of rice in world markets and a decline in commodity prices made him take action that made him unpopular. Although investment in tourism increased during this time the economic damage was too deep-seated to be corrected in one term. With an increase in tourism other evils surfaced. The price of food escalated as the hotel industry swallowed up what the local food industries could produce. Some youths learnt that they could live off certain types of foreign visitors and it bred a new type of criminality. He received huge support from Western governments and the World Bank and Asian Development Bank. Some enterprising businessmen with links to the ruling UNP group tried to initiate new industries but other economic factors hampered the recovery. To appease Buddhist sentiment he made full moon days holidays. The Federal Party supported him, but this hurt his re-election chances. He died in 1973.
Mrs S Bandaranaike (1970–1977)	Formed a coalition with the LSSP (a socialist political group) and CPSL (a communist political group), who then saw their chance to implement their socialist agendas. The Business Acquisition Act was passed in 1971. It gave the government the right to take-over any private sector business by notification. Restrictions were imposed on agency houses, through which foreign companies managed the plantation sector. Land Reforms, introduced in 1972, restructured land ownership by imposing a ceiling of fifty acres on nationals. The excess was vested in the state. The government also took over foreign-owned plantations by negotiation. While most of this land was kept under state companies, some effort was made to set up collective and co-operative farms. One stated aim was to support national liberation movements but not necessarily those operating within the country. She renamed the country Sri Lanka and made it a republic in 1972. She used the change of status to extend her leadership of the country by two extra years and set a precedent for further constitutional abuse by political leaders who followed her. The new constitution had little or no provision for the protection of minority interests. It vested the legislative, executive and judicial branches in the National State

	Assembly, which meant that the judiciary could not rule on government actions. This meant that the citizen had no recourse to the law against government harassment. Buddhism was made the state religion in the new constitution. She promulgated laws that openly sanctioned universities to give special preference to Sinhalese students by effectively demanding higher standards of academic performance from Tamil students. Most of her policies seemed to make the economy worse and disadvantage the youth. This resulted in the emergence of the JVP in 1971, a strong Sinhalese chauvinist movement, hell-bent on removing her lawfully elected government. Sinhalese youth, under the banner of the JVP, revolted. The resultant insurrection cost many lives and inflicted irreparable harm to the psyche of the nation. But it gave her a legitimate reason to use emergency powers and stifle the freedom of the individual. The people as a whole found that their democratic rights were being whittled away by those in power with the connivance of Parliament and the judiciary. For the first time, it seems, the people saw through her. She lost the next election decisively. The website[58] suggests that her 'greatest achievement was perhaps the staging of the 1975 Non-Aligned Movement's Conference in Colombo.' A poor reward indeed.
Mr W Gopallawa (President) 1972–1978	Titular head, executive power was with the prime ministers Mrs Bandaranaike and then Mr Jayawardene
Mr J R Jayawardene (PM) 1977–1978 and (President) 1978–1989	He changed the constitution to make the president the executive head of the country with extensive powers that included immunity from prosecution for any act committed by the president in private or public capacity. Under the new constitution, the president was all-powerful and returned the country to pre-colonial days when the king was a despot. Introduced the proportional representation system. In the words of the website, 'led to a situation where no party was likely to gain a two-thirds majority in the future, which would prevent a change in the constitution.' In 1983 he got Parliament to require all MPs to take an oath to the unitary constitution of Sri Lanka, knowing that the Tamil United Liberation Front politicians could not do so and would therefore be expelled from Parliament. The TULF was, at that time, the principal opposition to the government and the sole representative of the Tamils in Parliament. His actions meant that

[58] Sri Lankan Government's website, www.priu.gov.lk/. See sections on Presidents and Prime Ministers.

	the Tamils were not represented in Parliament. It is no coincidence that that was also the year when the militant groups began to use extra-political means. On the one hand, he made Tamil a national language and removed the discriminatory university entrance criteria. On the other, he passed the Prevention of Terrorism Act in 1979 that gave the security service carte blanche to search and arrest at will, and it did so when there were serious riots in 1977 and 1981. The real problems, however, began when in 1983 the Tamil Tigers ambushed and killed thirteen Sinhalese soldiers. This resulted in reprisals of bestial brutality on innocent Tamil civilians living among the Sinhalese in the south. Jayawardene did not act to stop or express remorse for their actions. He brought in Indian troops under the terms of the Indo-Sri Lankan Accord to contain the Tamil Tigers. It was a shrewd move, as it neutralised any support the LTTE got from Tamil Nadu. But Mrs Bandaranaike, among others, fomented resistance to it and eventually the Indians, having achieved little, decided that discretion was the better part of valour and left. Her actions were reminiscent of Mr Jayawardene's with regard to the Bandaranaike–Chelvanayagam Pact, which was an early attempt at negotiating a peace with the Tamils but was stillborn primarily due to Jayawardene's actions. Tit for tat behaviour is commonplace in Sri Lanka politics. Statesmanship was needed at this and previous periods to right the economy and the racial inequality but it never came about. Mrs Bandaranaike was accused by Parliament – at the instigation of Mr Jayawardene – of a range of illegal acts and lost her civic rights. Resurgence of the JVP in 1987 resulted in further unrest. The country and economy was in complete disarray although valiant attempts had been made to encourage private enterprise and to remove barriers to foreign investment. Some of this paid off. But the industrial base of the country was still very weak and insufficient to sustain a fast growing population.
Mr R Premadasa (PM) 1978–1989 and (President) 1989–1993	Prime minister during Mr Jayawardene's period of office as president. He demanded the withdrawal of Indian Troops from the Island, which at the time amounted to about 45,000 officers and men. He attempted to broker a peace accord with the Tamil Tigers but met with strong resistance from the Sinhalese and by resurgent Tamil Tigers who took advantage of the withdrawal of the Indian troops to reassert their authority over the north and east. Held nation's first parliamentary elections in eleven years. Unfortunately, assassinated whilst electioneering.

Mr D B Wijetunge (PM) 1989–1993 and (President) 1993–1994	
Mr Ranil Wickramasinghe (PM) 1993–1994	
Mrs C Bandaranaike Kumaratunga (PM) Aug–Nov 1994 and (President) 1994–2005	Appointed her mother as prime minister, thus giving her mother, Mrs Bandaranaike, a third term from 1994 to 2000. Failed to make any inroads in bringing about peace, although she got little cooperation from the Tamil Tigers. Adept at keeping her job as president. Her husband was assassinated in 1988 and she survived an assassination attempt.
Mrs S Bandaranaike (PM) 1994–2000	Mother of President
Mr R Wickremanayake (PM) 2000–2001	
Mr R Wickramasinghe (PM) 2001–2004	Although the job of prime minister seems almost redundant in the context of the executive presidency, as the office is subject to presidential discretion, Mr Wickramasinghe declared a unilateral ceasefire, opened the main road between the south and the north and allowed the free flow of goods and people. He visited Jaffna and also signed a joint ceasefire agreement in February 2002. He actions for peace won him support in the West and made him enemies at home, especially President Kumaratunga who saw him as a potential challenger. Mr Wickramasinghe lost his job, when the President dissolved Parliament and sought fresh elections on the grounds that he was giving away too much to the Tamils.

	Alas, Mr Wickramasinghe seems to have taken a back seat at present. He lost the presidential election held in November 2005 by a whisker. The difference was the result of the LTTE instructing the Jaffna Tamils (who would certainly have voted for Mr Wickramasinghe) not to participate in the elections.
Mahinda Rajapaksa (PM) 2004–2005 and (President) 2005–present	
Mr R Wickremanayake (PM) 2005–present	

Chapter 19

Holding on to Power

There is no denying that the leaders of the country faced major challenges when they took over from the British. They had to build a unified country. They had to build an economy that would support a growing population. They had to learn to live in a post-war world in which the superpowers were the USA and the USSR. They had to learn to deal with a whole host of international organisations whose help depended on putting forward a strong case and winning the arguments. The new world was a fiercely competitive one and they were alone in it.

The people had never had an opportunity to determine how they would be governed until Sri Lanka became a democracy. The leaders knew the theory of democracy but did not know how to run one. What they did know was that they were now in control of a multi-ethnic country. And they knew that a whole host of repressed wishes and wants would surface as every sector of the community came to believe that their real or imagined wrongs could be righted.

To deal with these external and internal challenges, the new leaders had to have a clear view of where they were taking the country and how they would achieve their aims. Since they could not achieve their dreams alone, they had to persuade the people to share it with them and work with them to achieve it. This, in turn, meant that they had to manage the ethnic diversity inherent in the population and harness it for good. They had to build a political system that was responsive to the needs of all the people and to offer the people real choices – choices they could understand and vote responsibly for. But very little of this happened.

What did happen was that, for their own selfish ends, they used any potential flashpoint to gain advantage for themselves, their families and supporters. This meant that they surrendered where they could without repercussions to their self-interest, and diverted and denigrated when surrender was politically unacceptable. And when all else failed, they manipulated the political system to take and keep power.

Surrendering to Troublemakers

Holding on to power is never easy. It requires many skills, but among these, probably the most important is the ability to keep control of your powerbase. The ruling clique, especially when they were led by Mr and Mrs Bandaranaike, lost control of their powerbase to the Buddhist nationalists and the socialists who helped them to win power. Unable to control the powerbase, they pandered to it. They should have anticipated the coming troubles and bared their teeth. Instead, when under threat, they opened their doors and let the 'troublemakers' in, hoping to neutralise them. The Buddhist lobby forced them to pass and enforce laws that divided the country. So a united, peaceful, multi-ethnic, country that was governed by a unitary state became a battleground.

The Buddhist nationalists won their wish and Sri Lanka became a Sinhalese Buddhist state. The socialists won their wish and got the government to implement socialist economic policies. But then, it would not allow any government to give the Tamil nationalists a state of their own or to remove the burdens that prevented members of the Tamil minority from living fruitful lives. The ruling clique found they were trapped in the middle, unable to balance the demands of both groups so that they could end the fighting and get on with enjoying the fruits of power.

Neutralising the 'Reasonable Man'

It is puzzling that the 'reasonable man' seems unwilling or unable to take control of his destiny. It may be that he is too naïve to see that the many interest groups who have played a major role in creating unrest and instability in his name are manipulating him for their personal benefit, but that is very unlikely. The majority of voters may not be intellectual geniuses, but they do know what is best for them and their children. As Louis Menand points out in his book, *The Metaphysical Club*:

> Effective working of democracy does not depend on an educated or intelligent populous just one that is rich in life's experience, discernment and wisdom i.e. natural common sense ... critical faculties, does not mean high intelligence, or education. It means the experiences of life that enables people to intuitively judge the 'rightness' of a cause or assertion.[59]

Sri Lanka has more than enough people who can make such judgements. The problem is that the reasonable man, especially of the older generation, has been confused by hereditary loyalties to the 'lords of the manor', the priesthood, the tribe, caste and social hierarchies to decide and act on those things that best meet his and his family's needs. This was truer in the first fifteen or so years of independence. The insurrection of his children in 1971 put paid to that tradition, but shocked him nonetheless, and made him ready to give power to those he considered his 'betters' so that they would return peace to his life. But they have failed and he still lives under the shadow of terror – this has kept

[59] Louis Menand, *The Metaphysical Club.*

security and stability uppermost in his mind. Consequently, he is, for the present at least, less concerned with a thriving economy, education, health, the provision of essential utilities such as water, sewage, and power, and the creation of jobs for his children. If he felt that he could gain all these things by sharing power with others, he would probably do so willingly. But what is a priority for him is less so for the ruling clique because they already enjoy these desirable benefits and can continue to do so only as long as they keep power. And to do that, they have proved, over and over again, that they will sacrifice anything and anyone that is not part of their clique.

Denigrating Tamil Leaders

Because the democratic process made it almost impossible for the Tamil politicians to gather enough votes to make a difference to government policy, they were not a threat to the ruling clique. So the Sinhalese politicians ignored the Tamil politicians and moved Tamil concerns far down the list of priorities, sacrificed them or ignored them completely. This distanced the Tamil leaders from their own people, as they could not deliver benefits to them. But, because the Sinhalese politicians gained their knowledge and understanding of the Tamil communities through the Tamil politicians and the Colombo Tamils, they were not fully able to understand the strength of the resentment of the majority of the Tamils who lived in Jaffna and its surrounds. Besides, the northern Tamils had disowned their Colombo cousins. The ignorance of the Sinhalese politicians (the UNP and SLFP, who represented the ruling clique) of the effect of their actions on the Tamil community resulted in their using their parliamentary muscle incautiously. By 1980, the ruling clique had stripped the Tamils of even the little political influence they had had and made the Tamil politicians irrelevant.

The result was that Tamil political parties that championed the Tamil cause could not influence legislation or stop the flow of legislation and executive action that disadvantaged the Tamils. Their sidelining by the Sinhalese politicians made it easy for the militants, such as the LTTE to offer themselves up as credible alternatives to the Tamil political elite and to claim that it was time to stop talking and to start fighting.

The claim of the Tamil militants that the Tamil politicians were impotent was confirmed when, in 1983, the Jayawardene government excluded the Tamil United Liberation Front (TULF) from Parliament, even though it was the largest opposition party and represented all the Tamil constituencies. By that one act, Mr Jayawardene condemned the Tamils to rule by LTTE and the country to twenty years of chaos. Since then, most Tamils in the north have had no choice. They were victims of the arbitrary and autocratic use of the power of democracy by the governments of Sri Lanka and then ended up under a 'military dictatorship'. The ordinary Tamil citizen, one who is not of the LTTE or the ruling group, has suffered the most.

Laying False Trails

The ruling clique have diverted the attention of the 'reasonable man' by creating distractions and scapegoats and blaming these conjured-up bogeymen for the failure of the country to realise the great hopes that independence had promised the people. Sadly, the ruling clique, to keep power, used any means at their disposal to keep these 'bogeymen' current. These means include: sustaining the myths of ethnic vulnerability; dismissing prime ministers who may have solved the current problems of ethnic conflict by accusing them of 'giving away too much' (however that is measured); changing constitutions, extending periods in office and collaborating with other political groups to create coalitions that harm the country but keep them in power. The problem for those left out of this charmed circle is that the only way they have of winning control or gaining things that matter to them is to use force.

Winning Votes with Foreign Aid, Loans and Grants

Unable to use locally raised funds because there aren't enough of them, and unable to spend the tax revenues from the rich, because their money is not in the country to be taxed, successive governments have drawn on the generosity of the aid agencies and international bodies like the World Bank and foreign governments. This ability to 'shame' Western governments to donate money, so that the ruling clique can live lives they have got accustomed to but cannot afford, is one of the great skills of the Sri Lankan government and many others around the world. The bureaucratic nightmares that result in long delays and the centralisation of decision making play into the hands of those who use these mechanisms of government for personal gain. All of this is well known and understood by international institutions and aid agencies that accept the inefficiency and corruption as the 'natural cost of doing business on the island'. Western governments, who know that their money often flows into the private pockets of politicians and senior officials, also turn a blind eye, probably feeling that it is much harder for their industries to earn a living in the developing world without compromising their standards or acting illegally. There are signs that Western governments and aid agencies are beginning to flex their muscles, but it is essential that they do this with caution.

If foreign aid comes with conditions that distance the people from their institutions, it increases the powerlessness of the people and strengthens the hold of the ruling clique. Besides, in an import/export-led economy, foreign aid enriches a small group of intermediaries and feeds the lifestyles of the ruling clique. A conversation with people from Sri Lanka often confirms the view that there is a great dependence on aid to finance infrastructure projects and an expectation of more aid to pay for the maintenance, consumables and fuel for these projects where that is necessary. The problem here is that the government escapes being held to account for its incompetence, but gets praised for its ability to get more aid and loan funds from the international community. The people who benefit most from this are a small import cabal, who make commissions on purchases made with loan and aid funds, and who wish to keep the situation unchanged for their own personal gain. This group will, no doubt, benefit enormously from the tragedy of Boxing Day 2004.

Managing International Opinion

A country like Sri Lanka, which depends on foreign financial assistance, needs to be perceived as operating within the accepted norms of behaviour expected of a democracy: maintain a good human rights record; manage its money well; be free of corruption, and so on. It was more successful at this in its first eight years of independence than at any other time.

During the eight years of Bandaranaike rule between 1956 and 1965, the country fell out of favour with the West. The British were asked to vacate their bases on the island, British and American companies operating there were nationalised or constrained, and the country adopted a neutral or Soviet-friendly stance.

Conciliatory moves by successive UNP governments restored some of the goodwill, and aid funds and loans began to flow back into the country. However, by then, the laws that created social division and disadvantaged minorities were firmly in the statute books. The most that countries sympathetic to the plight of the minorities could do was turn a blind eye to groups gathering funds and support for their rebellious cause. That is a simple view of things and makes it appear as if the international community was absent in the crucial years. The critics of the West may claim that it took a neutral line because, by the late 1960s, the country had lost its strategic value. However, defenders of the policies of the international community argue that a more even-handed approach to injustices perpetrated by governments against segments of the people may have resulted in the West being frozen out completely, as the country was, at that time, flirting with socialist ideologies.

It seems that the country's leaders are now fighting shy of international visibility. Daya Gamage, reporting in Asiantribune.com on 18 April 2005, points out that Sri Lankan diplomacy in the United States has hit an all time low and that the President of Sri Lanka was unaware that the United States Senate had presented a bill to give tariff concessions to Sri Lanka's apparel exports, or that the Norwegian deputy foreign minister, Vidar Helderson, visited Washington to discuss the troubles in Sri Lanka. Perhaps the government of Sri Lanka takes foreign aid for granted and does not believe that it needs to do anything to win help and support. Or, perhaps it is embarrassed by the troubles on the island and finds the whole process of explaining their racist behaviour to foreign governments unpalatable. The same article claims that the LTTE played host to Democratic Congressman Danny K Davis and that Mr Davis was of the opinion that the 'Sinhalese government is a blatant violator of Tamil human rights'. (This remark is reported in an article in Asiantribute.com of 15 April 2005 under the caption 'Tamils Want Peace With Dignity and Justice – says US Congressman Who Toured Sri Lanka')

Manipulating the Opposition

The policy of appeasement that the different governments representing the ruling clique have adopted has resulted in their creating a rod for their own backs. When the ruling clique unconditionally accede to the demands of a pressure group, the same group will then make new and more unreasonable or onerous demands on it. This escalating cycle of acquiescence and demand had to be reversed, but this needed all political parties to act in harmony. But this rarely happened. Every concession a 'reasonable' government of Sri Lanka proposed to make to the minorities to solve the problems was used by the opposition. It would pick on a special interest group like the Buddhist nationalists and, with their help, embarrass the government. Since no Sinhalese Buddhist politicians wanted to be identified as working against the interests of the Buddhist majority, it was a charge that politicians could level at each other in order to weaken their opponent's electoral appeal – and this often happened. But it did play into the hands of the ruling clique who found, in this behaviour, a means of showing their good intentions but were able to avoid taking steps that jeopardised their hold on power.

Coalition Politics

The UNP and the SLFP hijacked the country from the 'reasonable man' and, for nearly sixty years, made it their fiefdom. The SLFP has proved extremely adept at gaining and keeping power by forming alliances with socialists, Marxists, the JVP and any other political grouping or pressure group that came along that were able to give the SLFP a majority in Parliament and help it win the presidency. Very often this has been done by the ruling group aligning with some highly questionable allies. Today, the JVP are willing participants in this game of musical chairs. The JVP is guilty of horrendous crimes against the innocent and, by all accounts, their leaders should be branded as murderers and be in jail. Instead the ruling clique has allied with them to keep power.

It is unclear what the JVP is really about, and because of this they have received help from Tamil pressure groups. In its early political life, the JVP championed the cause of oppressed peoples, among whom they counted the Tamils in the north and the plantation Tamils. But in the late 1980s, the party began to voice anti-Tamil slogans to gain the ear of the Sinhalese Buddhist voters. And this tactic worked. In 1987 they sided with Mr Premadasa, who wanted the Indian peacekeeping forces to leave the island.

By 2001 they had emerged as a powerful political force, capable of delivering the racists' vote. In other words, they were beginning to steal the SLFP vote. This frightened Mrs Kumaratunga into an alliance with the JVP when the country next went to the polls in 2004. Now they have linked up with the SLFP and are propping up the President. They are undoubtedly playing one group against another. They seem better at gaining power through alliances than the SLFP and will probably take power whilst the UNP and SLFP continue to see each other as the 'enemy'.

This form of double-dealing designed to satisfy personal ambition harms the country. Obviously, the government of Sri Lanka has failed to grasp that these former insurgents (terrorists) could turn on their benefactors. President Kumaratunga's invitation to the JVP to join her at the high table has sent a signal to the LTTE and other disadvantaged minorities – Tamil, Sinhalese or Muslim – that the way to achieve their aims is through force.

Constitutionally Approved Dictatorship

Being out of control but in power is a very uncomfortable position to be in. The prime ministers and presidents of Sri Lanka have sought to remedy this by acquiring more power. The current constitution makes the president a dictator in all but name. The first constitution with its counter-balancing power bases was done away with and replaced with one that transformed the titular role of the governor general as head of state, to, in 1977, an executive presidency with such wide ranging powers and legal and statutory protection that it is now all powerful and above the law. It made the president omnipotent, infallible and irreproachable.

By this means, the ruling clique have consolidated their position. The president cannot be removed from office without the consent of the president unless force is used. Although the president must present him or herself for re-election every six years, the president can stop such elections by using a whole series of constitutional means. Mr Jayawardene used the instability caused by the war with the LTTE to postpone elections. He held a referendum instead to confirm an extended stay in office. Mrs Bandaranaike changed the constitution under the guise of changing the name of the country to buy more time as prime minister. If, for example, Mrs Kumaratunga decides to postpone elections due at the end of her second term of office on the grounds that continuity of government would be the most effective way to help the country recover from the ravages of the tsunami, it is difficult to see how she could be removed. The fact that she did resign suggests that she has lost her political powerbase and the voters' affections.

By giving the president such unlimited power, the ruling clique have protected their interests and protected the incumbent of the office but they have not, as yet, calculated the price. And the price is very high. It threatens the democratic process at its core. Without the troubles of 1971 and after, the president may not have asked and got such far-reaching powers. Therefore, there is no incentive for the president to resolve the conflict. And the ruling clique will not force a change of president because if the presidency fell into the 'wrong hands', all the members of the ruling clique would be at risk. So it's a question of the devil you know being the choice by default.

Use of Emergency Regulations and Anti-terrorist Laws

It is right that governments should have powers to suppress revolt, insurrection and violent social and communal unrest. In most cases they can exercise this power within the rule of law and the democratic process without invoking these dictatorial or martial processes. However, there are times when, as in Sri Lanka, riots and civil disturbances last for days and it becomes essential to impose curfews and emergency powers as temporary defensive measures to suppress unrest and reinstate law and order in society.

What seems wrong to most observers is that these laws should be used as oppressive weapons against segments of the community or that they should be operated as they were in Sri Lanka for extended periods of time. When the Sinhalese insurgents and the Tamil Tigers began showing their claws, the government of J R Jayawardena passed the Prevention of Terrorism Act of 1979 and enhanced its power to arrest and indefinitely imprison, without trial, people it thought were arousing racial hatred. Almost all those held were Tamils. Rarely, if ever, were those in government who espoused the racial cause and facilitated racial unrest detained under these laws. This rather one-sided use of the laws by successive governments served the purpose of entrenching the rights of the ruling elite and their powerbase, showed the governments to be strong and decisive to its supporters and enabled them to duck the key issue of resolving the causes of conflict and returning peace to the island by the use of political means. Eventually, these laws became the political means of gaining and holding on to power.

Whatever, their private views, the modern crop of politicians in both main parties have acted to safeguard their own interests, and the nation's interests have taken second place. Given this mindset, it is easy to see that it was difficult for the politicians to stand above the issues and argue for tolerance and magnanimity from the people in order to remove the causes of dissention. So, whilst a small segment – primarily the ruling clique and their henchmen and women – grew in power, wealth and status, the rest languished. Even when the dam broke and a tidal wave of resentment – of much greater ferocity than the tsunamis that hit the island on Boxing Day 2004 – drowned the whole country in the floodwaters of bitterness, envy and hate, it did not touch the ruling clique. Everyone, except they, lost and are still losing; proving, perhaps, that holding on to power is more important than knowing what to do with it. The ruling clique has proved without any doubt that it is possible to have power and avoid responsibility and accountability.

Chapter 20

The Post-colonial People

Once the islanders gained independence and the country was handed over to the ruling clique, the people thought that their new leaders would lead them to a socioeconomic nirvana. They assumed that their lives would improve. But that did not happen. What did happen was that those who had benefited under British rule continued to benefit in the 'new' Sri Lanka. The small, privileged group of English-educated, Western-orientated Sinhalese, Tamils, Muslims and Burghers slipped smoothly into politics, the professions, government service, the armed forces, agency houses and the branches of foreign-owned organisations and other highly prized occupations. A new class of Sinhalese entrepreneur called *the mudalali*[60] – the most famous of whom were the *bus mudalalis* – joined the long-established entrepreneurial sub-group of Tamil and Muslim merchants. Together, they held the power and the purse strings. The government that represented their interests – the UNP – pursued policies that widened the power and economic divide in the country.

For this privileged group life was idyllic. They lived in the principal towns and cities. Their children went to the best schools and automatically got the best jobs because they were the best trained and had the connections to secure them. As time went on, and the Buddhist nationalists began to exert greater influence in the affairs of the country, the leaders of the movement and the Buddhist priests who supported them joined the small band of rich folks and revelled in their new-found status as members of the ruling clique.

At the same time, a small but influential middle class, supportive of the ruling clique and drawn from the electorates of ministers, was created as the Sinhala-only language policy began to take effect and the government's preferential employment policies locked out the Tamils, Muslims and Burghers. This policy favoured the Sinhalese-speaking majority and gave the Sinhalese Buddhists new opportunities in government service and the state-controlled sector. But the economy was unable to sustain the steep increase in the population. Neither was it able to sustain the 'make work' jobs that ministers created to absorb the unemployed in their electorates. Consequently, those living in the rural areas found that, despite improving their levels of literacy, they remained disadvantaged and isolated. Nothing had changed for them. In fact, in emotional terms things had got worse because the people they trusted to improve their lot had let them down. The ruling clique had, in Mr

[60] The word *mudalali* refers to a Sinhalese businessman/entrepreneur.

Abeyasekera's words made Sri Lanka, 'The Country of Deep Sorrow!' As he goes on to say:

> Over half the population live below the poverty line. About 5% are Croesuses having milked the State and continue to fatten on it. The sad thing about the ugliness of the situation is that it is shrouded by a veneer of apparent prosperity and a public desensitised into a helplessness beyond the ability to care.[61]

Even the things that had worked well during the colonial period were beginning to fall apart by the late 1960s, and import controls made matters worse. There was more work as the wheels of government needed people to keep it turning. The masters and their wives and children in the towns and villages needed domestic help, and the children and youth of the village found work in the homes of these better off people. Some were treated well; others were treated like slaves.

Today, these same people earn foreign exchange approximating $1 billion for the country as domestic workers in the Middle East. Their new-found income has transformed their lives but not their burdens. The lack of new wealth creating enterprises meant that economic growth in poorer areas was almost none existent and this exacerbated inequality within the country.

Alas, sixty years on, the rural poor have the vote but not much else. A recent World Bank report on the island says that, 'ninety per cent of Sri Lanka's poor live in rural areas'.[62] The World Bank country brief claims that the rural population who form the largest segment of the island's people are among the poorest households. It says that, 'only 38 per cent have electricity, 55 per cent sanitation, and 61 per cent access to safe drinking water'. The report also points out that 'the availability of modern learning materials in remote areas is low'. Perhaps it is making the point that, although the village schools provide a higher standard of education than the old temple schools, the schools in the towns prepare their students for brighter and more lucrative careers. The magic of the web and the computer have yet to penetrate the village communities who are most likely to benefit from computer-based learning systems. Despite this, the literacy rate is high. Today it is around 92 per cent (94.8 per cent male and 90.0 per cent female), suggesting a population that is eager to learn and to develop.

All Sri Lankans value education. They see it as the way out of the poverty trap. 'The British Council Library in Colombo is the busiest British Council Library in the world, with half a million book loans a year.'[63] This immensely valuable service is not available to the rural youth who live too far away and whose command of English is too poor for them to benefit even if it was available in their village. And yet it is among the youth of the rural poor that

---

[61] Henry Abeyasekera, *Sri Lanka under a Brahamana Curse*, Vijitha Yapa Publications, 2002.

[62] *Country Brief, The World Bank in Sri Lanka*, http://www.worldbank.org/lk, updated July 2005.

[63] Foreign and Commonwealth Office, http://www.fco.gov.uk/, 19 May 2004.

most effort needs to be expended to increase their ability to learn and develop marketable skills so that they can compete in the fast changing world of today. Fluency in English is a vital element in this education.

All this points up the key fact that, given the opportunity, the youth of Sri Lanka have the intellect, the dedication and the drive to build their own futures. The problem they have faced for nearly sixty years is that there is *no home for their skill and expertise*. The country lacks the job opportunities and the careers necessary to fulfil the dreams of its young. As Andy Mukherjee says in his excellent article in Bloomberg.com:

> Leaving too many people out of work for too long means sooner or later some of them will discover guns. And that isn't a risk Sri Lanka should run ever again.[64]

How true! But the risk is still there. As Mukherjee points out in his article, '636,000 jobs are needed to clear the backlog of unemployment.' In addition there are risks of nearly 600,000 potential job losses in the garment industry if the policy decision of the US government to abolish the concessionary multi fibre agreement is implemented on schedule. Fortunately, this did not happen. In the light of the tsunami disaster, the US government decided to extend the concessions. But this must be seen as a response to the tsunami and not a permanent state. So the risk to these jobs is still there. The youth of Sri Lanka are doomed to a life of servitude and low wages unless the government focuses on building a viable economy that can use the skills and intellect of these 'acorns'. But what has happened is very different.

In an import/export-based economy only the ruling clique, a small group, benefit. The glad-handing and self-feeding greed of the import cabal made up of politicians, Buddhist monks, public servants and intermediaries who call themselves businessmen siphon off the inheritance of the rural poor into their greedy hands and foreign safe-haven bank accounts. It is robbery on the highest scale, and it is condoned by self-interested groups at all levels in and outside the country. The World Bank report points out that 'over 50 per cent of active lending to Sri Lanka totalling $545.1 million as of June 2003 is in rural development and the areas of health and education.' If, to this, is added the huge sum of '$2.87 billion in support of development efforts as of July 2002', the rather unfortunate state of the rural population is hard to explain. No doubt some of the money was recycled to the West to buy expensive capital equipment and expertise, and some of it was spent on local contractors. The location of the balance could be guessed at, but not proved. So, one way or another, the money that does flow into the country from its many well-wishers seems never to get past the hands of the rich and powerful in Colombo.

Though good people, who saw what was happening, were incensed, it was the young of all races who were hurt most by the rape of their inheritance. But

[64] Andy Mukherjee, 'Sri Lanka Is Repeating Past Socialist Follies', Bloomberg.com, 14 October 2004.

they had no champions and no voices to legitimately express their grievances. As the economy declined, power became the social currency by which individuals achieved their objectives, but in a strongly power-based hierarchical and socially immobile society, power was the prerogative of the few. Of these few, the majority were increasingly the Sinhalese-educated elite among the ruling clique who now had the best jobs and the best futures. However, those favoured with these jobs were only a small minority of the Sinhalese youth. This was an unsustainable situation, and the JVP-led insurrections in 1971 and again in 1988 were the direct results of a society that was deaf and blind to the needs of the disadvantaged majority. Only this time, the disadvantaged were created by those post-colonial governments, especially that of Mr Bandaranaike and his family, that claimed they were helping by making Sinhalese – their language – and Buddhism – their religion – the paramount social forces so that they, the dispossessed in earlier times, would reap the greatest benefits. Unfortunately for them, the fruit they plucked from this new tree was rotten at the core.

Whilst the country was being misled, mismanaged and ravaged by the ruling clique, other forces were at work too. The people believed that when Britain left, the new superpowers that befriended the new nation – namely, Russia and the United States – would help them in many ways. They thought that they would act as brakes on the super-powerful in their own country, i.e. the ruling clique. And they thought that the superpowers would help them mature at their own pace and that the developed world out there would help them along. But what they and their leaders did not realise was that they had entered a new, interconnected world and were subject to the foreign policy objectives of the superpowers – the USA and the Soviet Union and the international institutions such as the UN and the World Bank. Whereas, before independence, they had a single conduit to the wider world as members of the British Empire, suddenly they had to manage multiple influencers with multiple and often contradictory objectives. British politicians had been answerable to their own public and to the international community for their actions in the colonies, but these new influencers could dabble in the affairs of the newly independent countries of the 'Old Europe' without having to take any responsibility for the chaos they might create. Ellen Ray and William H. Schaap, writing in *Covert Action – the Roots of Terrorism* point out that American interference in developing countries they judged of strategic importance to their foreign policy objectives created some monsters and distortions. They point out for example that:

> During the cold war, Pakistan's military regime, under General Zia ul-Haq, was embraced by the United States for its anti-Soviet zeal (as was Anastasio Somoza's Nicaragua, Augusto Pinochet's Chile, Suharto's Indonesia, Mobutu's Zaire and many other allies of convenience), which, if nothing else, proves that the United States has no permanent friends, only permanent interests.[65]

[65] Ellen Ray and William H. Schaap, *Covert Action – the Roots of Terrorism*, Ocean Press 2003.

They also point out that America and the majority of its people are unable, or more likely, *unwilling* to link cause and effect. They say:

> The United States is the only country in the world where the terrorist attacks on September 11, 2001, are not viewed as a consequence of US policy.

This may be a sweeping generalisation and unfair to many deep-thinking Americans who can join the dots. But, they say, the cause may be due to the American nation and its people suffering selective amnesia.

> In official and media circles in the United States, almost no memory evidently exists of the policies of just a few years ago, in the Reagan and first Bush administrations that promoted radical, fundamentalist Islamic "holy warriors" as "freedom fighters" against the Soviet Union. Yet these, or their younger brothers, are the very people who are the core of the al-Qaeda network and its supporters.'

This new form of superpower foreign policy, in which surrogate colonialism is the norm, where responsibility is not accepted for the consequences of meddling – and one power in particular goes even further and denies or conveniently forgets its complicity – was the world into which the fledgling democracy of Sri Lanka was launched. Certainly, neither its politicians nor its people could either comprehend or develop the diplomatic skills to play 'these Greeks bearing gifts' at their own game. Their background of governance did not prepare them for this. The new leaders could read their own people, and manipulate them, but not the foreigners in their midst. Here, then, was a new world in which foreign aid bought subservience, and independent-minded rulers became fair game for removal by superpower-sponsored resistance movements.

But the presence of the Russian bear and the American eagle had a different effect on the literate but unemployed youth. The films of Hollywood and Bollywood introduced them to lifestyles that contrasted with those they were leading. When they compared the glamour and material wealth of the societies they saw on film with their own, the disparity shocked them into the realisation that they were missing out in many ways. But they, like their parents before them, may have accepted this situation if they had not seen that the children of the ruling clique did not suffer the same deprivations that they did. It was the gap between their lives and the lives of the ruling clique that stirred their drive for betterment. Surely, they thought, if the ruling clique can lead lives like those we see in the films and read about, then so can we. That was the turning point. They believed the propaganda of the superpowers.

Each power extolled the virtues of their particular system of governance and set out to convert the most vulnerable sectors of society. Socialism and Marxism had already entered the country through a previous generation of Sri

Lankans who had studied at the London School of Economics. The new generation of inquiring and impressionable minds were not only exposed to Marxist ideologies at home; some were indoctrinated more deeply when they got scholarships to Russian and other foreign universities.

Those who went to Russian universities, such as the Patrice Lumumba University, in Moscow, learnt that revolutionary movements had displaced the established feudal systems with political systems that were supposedly people-friendly. They were taught that the socialist system was superior, as it was run for the people rather than for vested interests, such as the capitalist classes. This message struck home. These students had experienced the disparity between the rich and the poor in Sri Lanka and wanted to close the gap. Communism appealed because it redistributed wealth and power, or so they thought. They also saw that, at that time (in the 1960s and 1970s) Russia was a world power. The educated youth from the rural communities succumbed to the rhetoric and set out to create their own revolutions. Both the Tamil Tigers and the JVP have Marxist/Leninist roots.

The capitalist message peddled by the United States, despite its more friendly face and much deeper pockets, did not capture the minds of the rural youth because they did not think they could benefit from the capitalist system. They believed that it favoured those already in power. They also felt that capitalism was unlikely to deliver a fair and equitable society as it was founded on an ideology that rewarded avarice and selfishness. What discouraged them most about embracing it was that it represented what they had come to despise in the ruling clique. Besides, having bought the rhetoric of the Russian bear, they believed that the United States of America was expert at manipulating the international institutions – which, to a large extent, they bankrolled – to help its foreign policy.

So, from the viewpoint of the rural poor, the world was a bleak place. It offered no hope and no future except the drudgery of the past. Before the arrival of the Portuguese, the people of the island were ruled by kings. Now there were no kings, but there was a ruling clique. Much of the chicanery – princes killing each other, chieftains breaking treaties and so on – had in pre-European times been limited to the court, but now it spilled over into their lives and they had no control over its effects on them. Although the rule of law had replaced the arbitrary rule of kings, they realised that the law operated differently depending on where you sat in the hierarchy of power in the new independent state. And they were the bottom rung of the ladder and the ruling clique stepped on them as they ascended to their privileged place. Democracy was supposed to replace succession and usurpation as means to power but that was not what happened. The ruling clique was busy building a dynastic system to replace the one the British had destroyed in 1815. So the people in the rural areas, and increasingly in the urban areas too, lost faith in the new state.

In this new world that was so rich with promises and so short on results, who could the electorate believe, and what could they believe? The priests, who were their spiritual mentors, perhaps? The country squire whose forbears had dominated the village for generations, perhaps? Or the politicians, who came touting for their vote? People in the cities and towns thought they knew, but were no wiser than the village communities. The rural population knew that they constituted the majority and it was their vote that would determine the fate of the country. The sad truth was that they were not equipped to unwrap the package of promises presented to them and see the skeletons within. Palden Jenkins blames this on the British:

> As the empire declined, Britain failed to help subject people build their post-colonial foundations. When independence came, many countries lacked political experience and social readiness, depending heavily on charismatic leaders who started as visionaries and later became corrupt dictators. A culture of inter-tribal impartiality, consensus and trust had not been formed, and the British had favoured some groups over others.[66]

Much of this is true. But it must be pointed out that Ceylon, as it was then called, did have people who could carry the burden of self-government. The problem was that the electorate did not know how to use its new-found power and the ruling clique made no attempt to teach them. The people were unaccustomed to defining their futures. In feudal times, they had played no part in how they were governed. In modern times, they did not really understand how to decide what was best for them and how to bring it about. So they looked to their elders and betters and trusted them to lead them. Because the transition was peaceful, the ruling group did not have to invoke the help of the people to help them remove the imperial power in their midst and therefore felt no obligation to the people. It seems unfair to blame the British if those they handed the country over to chose to hold on to it and treat it as their fiefdom. Besides, the British Empire was, in reality, a huge trading block. The British stumbled into the role of empire builder because, in order to exploit, they had to manage, and to manage they had to control, and to control they had to conquer. It certainly was not an education charity that went around the world teaching people how to govern themselves.

What the rural youth realised was that the new leaders of the country saw power as a means to achieve their personal ends rather than those of a nation. The rural youth saw, too, that the power was with them but that they had been deceived by the false promise that adopting Sinhalese and Buddhism was, in itself, adequate to improve their well-being and the well-being of their children. This was the crunch. The Buddhist nationalist movement hijacked the political agenda and persuaded the rural poor to vote those who preached this message into power. The leaders realised that by appeasing the Buddhist nationalists, they could win power. So that is what they did. Sadly, these

[66] Jenkins, *Healing the Hurts of Nations.*

leaders found that in satisfying one group they would incite the others to revolt, or at the least, withhold cooperation.

Dictatorial rule may have contained the situation but none of its leaders chose that route, although they have manipulated the electoral system and the constitution to serve their own personal ends. Here, to some extent, was the problem. The personal ends of winning power through the democratic system made them lean towards the group that could deliver the vote, even though they knew that it would be a pyrrhic victory. Having won the vote and the power, they could not persuade their followers to be satisfied by a gradual change of social structures. The majority community wanted everything – and they wanted it now and at any cost. So they chose to divide and rule.

The post-colonial peoples of Sri Lanka needed to be united to win in a world of greater complexity; instead they, like the Sinhalese kings before them, bickered and quarrelled among themselves and squandered a rich heritage, and the world was too busy to notice until it was too late…

Part Five

Modern Sri Lanka

Summary

When the British left in 1948, it appeared that the Ceylonese were, despite their multi-ethnicity, a united people. To continue as a united people in a unitary state, it was essential that race and religion were subsumed by the wider goals of prosperity and peace. Sadly, there were vested interests, and power overrode all other considerations.

The ruling clique, torn between holding on to power or taking the tough decisions needed to maintain the integrity of the unitary state, chose self-preservation. To keep the power they usurped at independence they allied themselves with the Buddhist nationalists who were able to deliver the votes they needed to be in power and created a world in which they and the Buddhist establishment held supreme sway.

In this new world, the Tamils, Muslims and Burghers became merely bit players and interlopers and people who were not entitled to claim equality of status. These ethnic groups, however, claimed, and justly, that they had made significant contributions to the common struggle to return Sri Lanka to its people and expected now to join the Sinhalese in enjoying the benefits the island had to offer. The ruling clique ignored their pleas and introduced legislation to ensure Sinhalese supremacy. This meant that the ruling clique and the Buddhist establishment had the cake and the rest had to live on the crumbs.

The resulting social inequalities erupted into the insurgencies of the Sinhalese youth and the freedom struggles of the Tamils. Ever since then these two groups, seeking to achieve a more equitable society in which they, too, could benefit, have taken the blame for the island's troubles. The ruling clique has avoided any blame for their part in creating an unequal society in which they have prospered.

Dare I say it, those who used Buddhism to gain power have not followed the Lord Buddha's eightfold path in the way they conducted the affairs of state. All the trappings were there but the substance was missing. What characterised leadership behaviour was a set of policies, attitudes, misjudgements, deliberate manipulation of the people, the abuse of the processes of justice, law and democracy, the exploitation of privilege, the shortfall in leadership and the general mismanagement of the island in the fifty-six years following independence on 4 February 1948. But it all began so well and so auspiciously.

The problem was that the people of Sri Lanka had democracy thrust upon them and they did not know how to use the power it conferred on the electorate. Succeeding prime ministers adopted policies that appeased special interest groups and ideologies and indiscriminately destroyed both good and bad inherited capabilities.

The result was that:

- the sense of nationhood was shattered and nationalism was born;
- socialist policies, a fad of the times, destroyed the economy and heightened class tensions of the 'haves' versus 'have-nots' variety;
- the introduction of democracy and workers' rights exacerbated the downward spiral. The trade union movement fuelled worker unrest and undermined the efficiency and profitability of commercial enterprises. Whilst everyone clamoured for their rights, no one worried about their responsibilities. Few worried about how these rights would be funded or introduced without harming the rights of others as long as their needs were met;
- the selfishness of the ruling clique ensured the widening of the gulf between the races, employers and employee, the haves and have-nots, the Westernised minority and the rest;
- each group wanted greater recognition of their culture, language and religion;
- the politicians gave in to the majority demands and introduced policies and practices that did irreparable damage to the country and the people;
- politics became subservient to the Buddhist nationalists and the rulers forgot their real duty to the people;
- the mentality of patronage and dynastic ambition meant that merit and ability was replaced with nepotism;
- moral and humane values eroded as both sides to the conflict lost their sense of propriety, justice and fairness, and began to resort to means odious to most people;
- the corrosive impact of corruption in every artery of the life of the nation (justice, law, the civil service, nationalised industries, public and private service providers, politics and religion) fed instability and poverty;
- rulers fomented racism to hold on to power, ignoring racial abuse of minorities and using 'democracy' to legalise racial discrimination and institutionalise racism;
- the language policy disadvantaged the children of the poorer, less Westernised families who lived mostly in rural communities, by isolating them from the global employment marketplace and creating a time bomb of disaffected youth of all racial groups;
- the nationalisation or containment of foreign and private Sri Lankan

businesses discouraged enterprise and entrepreneurial behaviour and created high unemployment among the young, diminished the stock of Western trained managers and access to Western managerial systems, practices and techniques;

- the seeding of Tamil areas with Sinhalese families as part of population redistribution, although laudable in its intention, had the potential to create tensions. Natural migration can work. Forced migration rarely does, as both groups resent the coercive nature of the action;
- the destruction of the economic inheritance of European occupation, led to an extended period of economic decline and hardship, with the imposition of import controls, foreign currency controls, increased bureaucracy and corruption;
- the growth of an underclass made up primarily of unemployed youth of all communities whose idle hands turned to militancy;
- succeeding governments perpetuated the racial divide and created the conditions in which a Tamil separatist movement could take root and thrive;
- the continuing conflict traumatised the vast majority of people of the island to the point that it sapped their will and put them in a catatonic state;
- the internal and external displacement of both Tamils and Sinhalese resulted in a brain drain and destroyed communities and families;
- the scarce economic resources of the country were diverted to buy arms, maintain a larger than necessary security function, and not invested in cities, towns, villages and the infrastructure that supports them;
- leaders failed to rule on behalf of all the people;
- centralised control increased, and weakened the democratic process to the point where democracy is now purely an exercise in window dressing and spin, but not of real substance.

Alas, history records that this once resplendent isle lies impoverished in the sorrow of the strife and enmity of its own making. Was this where two thousand or more years of history was to lead it?

Chapter 21

Using Race for Political Advantage

Racial or caste-based segregation was well established on the island. When the Portuguese arrived on the island in 1505, there were three kingdoms on the island: Sinhalese kingdoms based in Kotte and Kandy and a Tamil kingdom in Jaffna. By 1550, the Sinhalese kingdom of Kotte had split into three, resulting in there being five kingdoms on the island. The Portuguese and the Dutch dealt with these separate kingdoms as separate entities. The unitary state left by the British had merit. Among these, the most important was that it enabled the creation of a single nation on the island.

In general, all three ethnic groups had not only willingly shared places of worship; they also coexisted in the major cities and towns. In these mixed communities, people of different faiths celebrated religious festivals that were unique to them without let or hindrance. They and their children fraternised with their Sinhalese and Tamil neighbours. It was, therefore, vital for the future peace, security and prosperity of the island that this tradition of peaceful coexistence was maintained and built upon.

But the concept and acceptance of being part of a single nation required that all the people were treated equally and fairly, irrespective of their ethnicity. This meant equal opportunity and that the rule of law was applied impartially throughout the island. After independence, a range of laws and executive actions ensured that the majority Sinhalese community benefited disproportionately. Eventually, the Tamils found that what was on offer was nothing more than a subordinated life with little future.

Many people see parallels between the problems in Northern Ireland and Sri Lanka. It is possible to trace similar routes to the wars of discontent in both countries. I have resisted the urge to go down that route but I do think that Gerry Adams' view applies to the current conflict in Sri Lanka.

> A settlement where the poor remain poor and the dispossessed remain dispossessed would not be a real change of lives. A cobbled together political settlement and an end to killing are not enough.[67]

I believe that the Tamils of Sri Lanka and their immediate Sinhalese neighbours will agree wholeheartedly with that view. But in the politics of the island, the picture is very different. The racist elements among the Buddhist

[67] Adams, quoted in Whittaker, *The Terrorism Reader*.

Sinhalese of Sri Lanka do not wish to give the Tamils the opportunity to live rich and fulfilled lives. Buddhism, which at one time was *the* civilising influence, is now being used to achieve racist ends. And the political elite has supported the racists because racism keeps them in power. The demands of the Tamils for a separate state became strident only after the laws passed in 1956 disadvantaged them and the communal riots over the last fifty years dispossessed them.

These events made it more difficult for people to intermix and heightened the sense of vulnerability among the Tamils. Under threat, the people regrouped according to their ethnicity. This naturally led to the Tamils asking for territorial separation. Many Sri Lankans see partition as a means to an end but it is more likely to create new causes of strife. If separate states were to come about, it is likely that the Tamils and Sinhalese would war over territorial boundaries, fishing rights, mineral rights, alliances with foreign governments – such as the strong ties of the Sri Lankan Tamils to Tamil Nadu – because there is now no goodwill between the races. In fact, the Sinhalese would probably condone actions by the government to expel the Tamils from the island.

This sorry state arose when the seeds of discontent were sown by the Buddhist nationalist movement. The Government could have anticipated that the racist elements in the Buddhist nationalist movement would set out to use race for political or personal objectives. There was adequate evidence of this risk. The attitudes and actions of the Nazi Party in Germany were fresh in everyone's memory. The riots in which millions of people were killed when, after independence, imperial India was partitioned into India and Pakistan was another reminder. Even if the government of Sri Lanka thought that Sri Lankans would not resort to such means, it had an obligation to keep an eye open for any overt moves that would take the country down a racist route.

But the ruling clique learnt, very early in the life of the new independent country, that racial disharmony was a very powerful political weapon. Mr Bandaranaike used it during the election campaign in 1956. Mr Bandaranaike and the Buddhist clergy beat the Sinhala Buddhist drum loudly and succeeded in persuading the Sinhala Buddhist majority that only he could make their wishes a reality.

His message was conveyed by rural influencers, such as village headmen, teachers in rural schools, purveyors of native medicine and the unemployed youth. Significantly, by using the unemployed youth, he aroused another group who would return to haunt Sri Lankan politics. Since the UNP had ignored the Sinhala/Buddhist issue completely up to then he was the only plausible champion they had. But there was an expectation of worldly benefits too. The Sinhalese Buddhists, mostly the unsophisticated poor in the hinterlands, believed that from that one act of renewal (reinstating Sinhalese and Buddhism to their paramount status) abundant material blessings would flow. Their children would have jobs and they would have more money in their pockets. So they voted Mr Bandaranaike into office.

He had achieved his purpose. He had won power from the UNP and broken their stranglehold on the political system. Once in office, he passed The Sinhala Only Act of 1956 and confirmed Sinhalese as the official language. Buddhism and the Buddhist establishment became part of the ceremonial of the state and major public occasions such as the opening of all state functions and state-sponsored public gatherings. The Buddhist clergy also wielded great influence in the corridors of power. The adherents and proselytisers of the prince who abandoned his throne had gained a kingdom and had become the super-rulers. This of course meant that the Buddhist clergy were in great demand as power brokers and as preferred guests at private functions. A new and lucrative revenue stream was created to feed the already overflowing tax-free coffers of the Buddhist establishment. Finally, in 1972, when the Republic of Sri Lanka was created, its constitution made Buddhism the official religion and Sinhalese the official language. The Buddhist clergy had won the battle, but the war was far from over.

The Buddhist clergy had regained their lost status and prestige. But, collectively, they condemned the country to poverty and created the climate for the uprisings among the Sinhalese Buddhist youth in the 1970s and 1980s and the Tamil freedom struggles. By focusing on this single – and, to most independent observers, a secondary issue – Mr Bandaranaike subordinated and completely removed other objectives, such as international competitiveness; economic growth; national security; mobilisation of all the people into a powerful resource; holding the people together as a single nation; keeping and building on the goodwill of other nations; and the sustaining and building of its inherited infrastructure from the collective consciousness.

Having won these concessions, he expected the clergy to move on and allow the country to realise its rightful place in the world community. He expected to be allowed time to build a vibrant economy that would bring prosperity to the people and to find ways to create jobs for the burgeoning ranks of the young so that they could make a positive contribution to their own and the country's future. He expected to help the youth to draw on the knowledge of the world and to grow the intellectual stature of the people. Instead, the racist elements in the Buddhist nationalist movement stayed in the political arena and became pawns in the politicians' power game. The king-makers became the bait. They were trapped in their own conceit and greed. The politicians continued to champion the Sinhalese Buddhist cause to retain their hold on power and the Buddhist clergy became their greatest publicists. This was a house of cards that would collapse the instant they stopped supporting it – and collapse it did. The promised material benefits did not flow. The monks were called to account and they looked to the man they had promoted.

Bandaranaike had not planned to meet the challenges of the unintended consequences of his election-winning manifesto. Those who put him in power now wanted him to deliver. He was the servant now and not the master. His strings would be manipulated by others to satisfy their own specific personal aims. His rise to the top was based on expediency, not on an overarching vision born of conviction. He had no foundations on which to build. He scrambled to find a foothold but his feet fell on loose soil and he slid further back, battered and bruised by his encounters with a range of insatiable demands. His fragile new party of coalition politics began to unravel and he found himself isolated and alone. All he seemed able to do was watch as his ambition crumbled to dust. He was reluctantly taken down a path that would divide a once united country in which racist and religious feelings had been damped down, to one where they became the main measure of political effectiveness. The genie was out of the bottle and running wild.

To contain it, Mr Bandaranaike proposed a compromise solution, which he called the Bandaranaike-Chelvanayagam Pact. In conjunction with leading Buddhist monks, Bandaranaike proposed that those parts of the country where there was a majority of Tamils should be given the autonomy to manage their own affairs, and to conduct their lives and government business in Tamil if they so wished. He also proposed amendments to the constitution that would safeguard minority rights and interests. If his proposals, made soon after he came into office and at the height of his power, had been taken on board and espoused by the whole political movement, Sri Lanka would be a thriving and prosperous country today. Instead, politicians of all persuasions joined the 'race game'. After much haggling, he did achieve a compromise that was formalised and published as the Bandaranaike-Chelvanayagam Pact. But it failed to win through.

When the initiative failed, the Tamil politicians, led by Chelvanayagam, the leader of the Federal Party and his cronies, decided to mobilise the Tamils to resist Bandaranaike's message – forgetting completely that they did not have the voting power to make any difference to the governance of the country. So they fretted and fussed and alienated the sympathy and support of the majority of the Sinhalese and made it even harder for those Sinhalese politicians who would have willingly given a little to regain a united country.

The UNP took political advantage of the situation. Having been routed at the polls, the party was now leaderless and rudderless, but opposition to the measures proposed by Bandaranaike was just what they needed to rally the party and regain its following. Taking a leaf from Bandaranaike's book, it beat the racial/religious drums loud and long, and destroyed any chance that Bandaranaike had of getting his proposed measures through both houses of Parliament. J R Jayawardene was the prominent agitator of the UNP's anti-government stance. To raise his and his party's profile, he led a symbolic march from Colombo to Kandy, the last capital of Lanka and the home of the Dalada. The symbolism of the march was that Jayawardene was recalling a period of Sinhalese Buddhists greatness, a period when the priesthood and the state had worked closely to sustain and grow the island as a haven of Buddhism. That drove the final nail into the coffin of the multi-ethnic elitist society over which the UNP had presided and opened a hairline crack in the nation's unity, which, by the time Jayawardene became president, had become a yawning chasm.

Jayawardene had whipped up a political storm of huge violence and Bandaranaike's attempts to still it failed completely. He had tried to lead the country back from the brink of racial disharmony, to create a fairer society for all the citizens of the country and suggested that with a little give and take on all sides the people could have their cake and eat it but his pleas fell on deaf ears. Compromise was not in the air. The victory was too complete and the winners wanted their pound of flesh.

Was it wrong for Mr Bandaranaike to read the mood of the electorate and use it to gain power? Perhaps not, if he had known how to control the forces he had unleashed. His fault was that he failed to lead them once he had won power. He was a great and gifted follower, but he did not know how to lead. So, whilst he prevaricated and vacillated, the rabble-rousers and fundamentalists stole his clothes – they wrested power and leadership from him. The rest is history. The rush to oblivion had begun.

Myopic Sinhala/Buddhist fundamentalists pursued their single-issue politics, oblivious to the fact that the flimsy raft they were travelling in was being ripped apart by the sharp rocks and fast rapids of hatred and bigotry. They seemed willing to pay any price to gain their objective of claiming the island for the Sinhala/Buddhist majority. The minority selectively joined with them in the hope of winning temporary gains. The Jaffna Tamils abandoned the hill country Tamils and the Muslims in their rush to plead their cause, and were run over by the Sinhala Buddhist juggernaut. The good people of the island were mortified by the harm that was being inflicted on others and on them and their loved ones but felt unable to act lest they be labelled betrayers of their race and their religion. A form of mass sadomasochism had gripped the country and was taking it over the precipice of reason. The great Hindu and Buddhist traditions of tolerance and peaceful coexistence were now replaced by the drumbeat of hate. And it was a Buddhist monk who assassinated Bandaranaike at his residence one fateful morning in 1959. The monk shot him even as the Prime Minister bowed a reverential greeting.

Chapter 22

Divisive and Repressive Laws

The laws that were passed by the government of Sri Lanka during a period of twenty years, beginning with the Ceylon Citizenship Act of 1948/49, the Sinhala Only Act of 1956, and others, undermined the foundations on which a peaceful, secure, economical and humane society could have been built. They separated the people. They shifted their values of tolerance and peaceful coexistence. These laws and those that followed were bad laws because they were forged in the white-hot heat of political expediency and lacked the checks and balances necessary to ensure fairness and equality in a multi-ethnic country.

These divisive and repressive laws were to do with citizenship: giving legal and constitutional preference to the Sinhalese language and the Buddhist religion; making these two things a major criteria for admission and promotion within the government services and government-owned businesses; biasing the university entrance criteria in favour of Sinhalese students; nationalising or constraining foreign-owned businesses that were, in most cases, biased towards the UNP and inclined to employ people on merit rather than ethnicity as their concern was primarily profit; reforming landownership in an attempt to distribute private estates by splitting them into small units and giving them to local people; and taking state control of schools receiving government assistance, which essentially meant the taking over of Christian schools except the few fee-levying ones. The impact of these measures was greatest on the Tamil community, who found a whole stream of employment opportunities denied to them. In that sense, whether intended or not, the laws had the same effect on the Tamils as the policies of the Nazi Party in Germany had on the Jews and other minorities in the years leading up to the Second World War. But the unintended consequences of these laws were felt most acutely by the Sinhalese Buddhist youth, who expected so much and received so little.

Citizenship and Belonging

The first steps on the road to division and civil war were taken when, very soon after independence in 1948/49, D S Senanayake, the prime minister at the time, passed three separate bills in Parliament. The first, called the Ceylon Citizenship Act, was passed in 1948, and in 1949 the Indian and Pakistani Residents (Citizenship) Act and the Ceylon (Parliamentary Elections Amendment) Act were passed. These bills effectively disenfranchised 800,000

Tamil plantation workers who were born in Ceylon. They were the descendents of the Indian Tamils brought to Ceylon by the British as labourers for the tea estates. They became stateless persons and lost the right to vote – a right that they had had during British rule.

Making them stateless achieved other important political purposes. It strengthened the position of the Kandyan Sinhalese politically and commercially. They were able to gain seven extra seats in Parliament. It weakened the bargaining power of the poorly paid plantation workers employed by UK-based limited liability companies and Sri Lankan landowning families. A redrawing of the electoral districts based on population included these plantation workers even though they could not vote, thus giving the Kandyan elite a monopoly right to those seats. This gerrymandering went unchallenged by the other political parties. The Sri Lankan and Indian governments argued over the status of the Indian Tamil workers for many years but the overall effect has been to reduce the population of plantation workers from 12 per cent of the population in 1953 to 5.5 per cent in 1981. From then on the plantation workers had to secure their needs through the trade union that represented them rather than the political processes of the country.

The slow process of eroding away the rights of minority groups had begun, and the precedent that it set would be used against the natural-born Tamils a few years later. The Tamils showed a level of unquestionable short-sightedness and stupidity in not fighting this policy on humanitarian grounds, as the act legitimised forced deportation and disenfranchisement and was immoral by all human standards. By fighting it in the international arena they could have claimed and held the moral high ground and would have gained international support for their stand. By doing the 'right' thing they would have made other similar measures less likely.

The Official Language Bill (Sinhala Only Act)

The next step in separating the people was taken by Mr Bandaranaike when he passed the Sinhala Only Act on 5 June 1956. The act was a statement of intent. Its implementation was open to interpretation. It was implemented to give preference to the Sinhalese. It made Sinhalese the official language of the country and required that all dealings with the government and matters to do with the law had to be in Sinhalese after a small settling-in period. This meant that it disadvantaged those who did not speak the language. The Tamil politicians expressed their displeasure by staging a peaceful protest, *Satyagraha*, on Galle Face Green. This act of silent, non-violent protest sought to emulate the tactics used by Gandhi against the British. But whereas Gandhi understood the psyche of the British, the Tamil politicians of Sri Lanka did not understand their Sinhalese counterparts. A band of thugs beat up the Tamil politicians whilst the police guarding the House of Representative across the road watched. The government of Mr Bandaranaike trivialised the episode and succeeded in diverting attention from the real issue – *imposition* of majority wishes on the rest of those living in the island. The behaviour of the Tamil parliamentarians was held up to ridicule, the true significance of their unhappiness was clouded, and this act of wilful disregard for the feelings of the Tamils by the government was lost on those who considered it to be a storm in a teacup.

The Sinhala Only Act had other repercussions. Children in English-medium schools were placed at an instant disadvantage, as they had to sit most subjects in Sinhalese or Tamil, even though for most of their school years they had learnt all subjects in English, which had become the de facto mother tongue of many of the English-educated in Sri Lanka. This policy also had significant detrimental effects on those in public service. During the period of British rule, a disproportionate number of Tamils (measured on the basis of those eligible to do the jobs rather than total population) had come to dominate the administrative services of government, and also private businesses. They demonstrated fluency in both Tamil and English and were able to converse in Sinhalese to get their views heard to Sinhala-only speakers. The Sinhalese officers were fluent in Sinhalese and English. The lingua franca of the office was English, which they all spoke. The Sinhala Only Act, in one fell swoop, destroyed the careers of those who could not, even if they wished and wanted to, learn Sinhalese to a level of competence necessary to conduct government business. So the older Tamils in the government and commercial sector were presented a hurdle that most could not leap.

As the Tamil and Sinhalese languages have different roots, use different alphabets and the letters of the alphabet are written differently, the challenge facing a Tamil wishing to learn Sinhalese to the level of sophistication needed to conduct government of commercial business was extremely high, and something that was genuinely beyond those already in middle-age. And, those who passed the laws that made Sinhalese the official language knew that they were setting an insurmountable hurdle for those Tamils in government service. The result was that many Tamils lost their jobs, which was what those who passed the laws had expected and hoped would happen. It might have helped if the government had offered compensation that made it easy for the older Tamil government servants to retire with dignity, but it did not. Today, Tamils living and working in Sinhalese areas and in the professions speak and write Sinhalese fluently. Phased implementation of the policy may have been accepted without incident.

Like all things done to gain short-term advantages, the policy began to misfire when, five to ten years later, children who had learnt all their subjects in Sinhalese or Tamil found that, outside their immediate circle, a lack of competence in English was a handicap. They found it hard to benefit from training in European and American universities and institutions as they found it difficult to keep up with modern developments that came mostly from America and other Western countries. This was not a handicap shared by children of the ruling clique, as their parents could afford to teach them English to the level needed to further their careers. Those who graduated with Sinhalese or Tamil degrees found that there were inadequate home-grown jobs. So they swelled the ranks of the unemployed disaffected Sinhalese and Tamil youths. These frustrated young people became easy targets for the recruiters of the various freedom movements that were springing up in rural areas of the country. Soon the government of Sri Lanka would be fighting not only the Tamil liberation movements, but the Sinhalese insurgents too.

Language of the Courts Act

The Language of the Courts Act, passed in 1961, made Sinhalese the language of administration in the courts of law. This act further alienated non-Sinhalese-speaking minorities. The government was adamant that court records had to be kept in Sinhalese even in Tamil-speaking areas. During British occupation, English was the language of the courts and non-English-speakers were unable to understand the rationale behind the judgements handed down by the courts, as they could not follow the proceedings. Now, in the changed circumstances of an independent Sri Lanka in which there are no subject people, it seemed that justice was being denied to the non-Sinhalese-speaking population and they interpreted it as an act of vindictiveness rather than of administrative convenience.

The University Entrance Examination Standardisation Scheme

The University Entrance Examination Standardisation Scheme introduced during the premiership of Mrs Bandaranaike was a blatant attempt to ration the number of places given to Tamil students in the country's principal universities. This was a double whammy for the poor Tamil student. The first was to disadvantage them from gaining a high proficiency in English so that they could circumvent this handicap by studying for examination conducted by English institutions. The second was to use the powers of this act to limit the entry of Tamil students to Sri Lankan universities so that the number of Tamil graduates declined even though their entrance examination results justified their acceptance over Sinhalese students. The knock-on effect of this was a reduction of job opportunities for Tamil students, even if they were proficient in Sinhalese, because fewer of them had the opportunity to gain higher education.

Schools Takeover

In 1961 the government of Mrs Bandaranaike took over all state-assisted schools. This left only a few private fee-levying, mostly Christian schools outside the government schooling system, even though they were subject to the education policies of the government. Those most affected by this were the

Roman Catholic schools and the Church of England (later Church of Ceylon) and Methodist schools. Was this necessary? Perhaps a Buddhist Sinhalese establishment felt that it had to be done for policy reasons. But the prevailing view was that the move was vindictive and aimed at the Christian community.

Nationalisation and Operational Constraints on Businesses

The nationalisation and constraining of foreign-owned businesses gathered pace in the mid 1960s during the premiership of Mrs Bandaranaike. This was done more to appease the socialist members of her coalition government than as a considered policy of indigenising the industrial and commercial base. State or semi-state bodies were handed responsibility for petroleum distribution, fertilisers, life insurance, personal banking, shipping and bus transport among others.

These changes resulted in thriving and profitable businesses becoming bogged down in bureaucracy and the inefficiencies spilled over into poor service. New monopoly ventures such as the Ceylon Steel Corporation, the Ceylon Milk Board, the Ceylon Textile Corporation, the Ceylon Cement Corporation, the Ceylon Hardware Corporation, and the Ceylon Ceramic Corporation, among others, were created, often with foreign government grants or loans, but they were invariably located in Sinhalese areas. The only exceptions were the Ceylon Cement Corporation in Kankesanthurai, the Eastern Papermills Corporation at Valachenai and the Paranthan Chemicals Corporation in the Jaffna district. These acts of state control led to the political patronage of these organisations. This meant that a whole new set of opportunities for bribery and corruption from the top to the bottom of the organisations and laterally to various politicians had been created. The real cost of these takeovers was that their inefficiency and incompetence eroded the economic performance of the country, increased unemployment and forced economic migration of the better qualified young men and women.

In 1971 Mrs Bandaranaike's government passed the Business Acquisition Act 1971. This act enabled the government to take over any private sector business by notification. It imposed restrictions on Agency Houses who managed foreign-owned plantations. This Act had the effect of reining in private sector firms, especially those that may have been tempted to use their influence with the public or foreign governments and institutions from briefing against the government.

Land Reform

A series of land reform acts came into effect in 1972. The Land Reform Act effectively broke up the large estates of the rich families except, it was claimed and generally accepted at the time, those of the members of the government who pre-empted the Act and retained their land holdings. Members of the government were reputed to have used their 'insider knowledge' to share out their better and more profitable lands with members of their families and close friends who held them as trustees. The rest lost large tracts of property and land that their ancestors had bequeathed them or they had bought with profits from other ventures. The impact of this was to fragment these estates into fifty-acre blocks and to release the rest in one-acre blocks to the local community, chosen more for their political affiliation and their value to the party organisation than for their ability to make commercial sense of such small tracts of land. The effect of this policy was to further impoverish the plantation sector and the economy of the country. Those who received these small plots of land did not have the knowledge, money or the competence to manage them. Besides, the plots were too small to be economically viable except in the hands of those with adequate income from other sources to subsidise these holdings.

In this new implacable and vengeful mood everyone lost their sense of justice, fairness, humanity and understanding. The public mood was such that a mixed group of starving Sri Lankans, offered a bowl of rice, would fight over the bowl and not the rice. The form became more important than the substance, and the laws set out not to create the climate for change, but to install racial, linguistic and religious supremacy. The laws declared that the Sinhalese Buddhists were the chosen people and would be legally entitled to the enjoyment of the country's riches. The others, if they wished to stay, could eat the crumbs. In effect, this was the same attitude as that of the white supremacists in South Africa, but it did not attract any global attention because, alas, the Tamil community did not have a Nelson Mandela or a Rev. Trevor Huddleston to argue their cause.

But the discriminatory laws, policies and actions that successive governments had set in motion led inexorably to apartheid. Another result of these laws was that the Muslims and the Tamils shamelessly exploited each other's situation to gain short-term benefits for themselves rather than coming together to present a common front of opposition to policies that they considered odious. They stood by and sometimes supported the government when minority groups, such as the Dutch Burghers, the plantation Tamils and others were discriminated against. All communities behaved shamefully during this period, but the lack of an opposition from the Buddhist clergy or other groups whose views would have mattered most and were based on the sound moral principles drawn, perhaps, from the four religions (Buddhism, Hinduism, Christianity and Islam) of the country made the situation worse.

There is no question in my mind that the silence of the international community towards the deliberate acts of discrimination by the majority Sinhalese people against the Tamils and other minority groups has contributed to the crises of the last twenty or so years. Pressure – such as the total withdrawal of aid – from the United Nations or the United States and the then Soviet Union would have stopped the process in its tracks and provided an excuse to the moderate leaders of all communities to make bolder moves towards a more equitable conclusion to the ethnic conflict that, in those early days, was no more than seeds of discontent.

This same phenomenon now prevails in multicultural and multi-ethnic communities in the West. For some inexplicable reason, injustices by the white races against the coloured races gain an inordinate amount of publicity. The reverse, like the injustices suffered by the white planters and farming community in Zimbabwe, or the arbitrary nationalisation of foreign-owned businesses in Sri Lanka, have caused no more than a ripple of awareness in the world's consciences, and are less loudly publicised or condemned. Eventually, the 'white' communities will rebel at always being the scapegoats for the 'disadvantaged minorities' in their midst. If people of all races are required to act in ways that are humane and fair towards their 'brothers and sisters', then any injustice by any group should be loudly condemned and, if necessary, punished in accordance with the laws and statutes of the country in which they take place. Civil rights groups must act even-handedly if all races and colours are to live together amicably. The injustices of ethnic groups to each other seem to attract even less attention until they create disasters so horrendous that they cannot be ignored any more.

Chapter 23

A Failure of Governance

A prime function of any government is that of creating the climate in which people can live true to their beliefs and moral values. If, instead, the government creates a climate in which people are forced to take sides and required to compromise their values and standards, it erodes the social fabric and creates social conflict. This is doubly true in multi-ethnic democratic societies where a disproportionate number of one ethnic group places the others at a disadvantage. In such states, every citizen should be able to champion the rights of their fellow countrymen and women to gain equality under the law irrespective of colour, race, language, religion, sexuality, gender, education, disability, finances or other discriminating features without recrimination by the government or their fellow citizens. This may be a naïve expectation, but the people of some nations expect and get governments that strive to meet this higher standard. As is well known, the founding fathers of the USA considered it so important that they made it the overriding condition of their constitution. And it is a standard that is now embodied in the Charter of Human Rights, and many nations voluntarily agree to be judged by its code.

This higher standard of conduct that many governments aspire to attain provides the essential conditions for peace and prosperity, because a troubled people are an unproductive people and unproductive people cannot create a prosperous society. Moreover, a failing economy almost always hurts the young and the poor most and, having nothing to lose, they take revenge on those who seem able to buck the trend and enrich themselves. In such a climate, any action by a government to deliberately single out a group for special treatment – praise or censure – will initiate a backlash that physical force alone may control but not cure. However tight the lid, resentment will simmer and boil and eventually spill over.

The visible outlets for these suppressed emotions do not always manifest themselves in riots and insurrections. Very often, they appear in the form of individual acts of violence towards people and property. In this form they are reduced to issues of law and order. Yet harsher punishment and imprisonment seems not to correct the trend – just to stall it until it reappears in another guise. The disharmony that follows affects all the citizens. The real solution lies in restoring value to people's lives. Oliver Twist is not only still with us, he has grown into a man with resentment in his heart and the strength born of desperation in his arms and legs. Such powerful forces must be diverted to productive use, not bottled up so that the container blows up as fragments of glass and metal that lacerate and kill.

The patterns of behaviour that the Sinhalese kings displayed have been repeated by their descendents. The prime ministers and presidents of post-independent Sri Lanka have acted more like kings than democratically elected leaders, whose power comes from the people. Dynastic ambitions have been sustained despite decades of misrule. The law and the constitution have been used as personal tools for personal ends. Ideology has been used to sustain power rather than to defuse tensions that were in place long before disunity became such an implacable issue. Similarly, the opposition politicians in the late 1950s were happier to quarrel among themselves for petty gain rather than combine to create a political climate that would have prevented the current bloodshed. Their self-serving actions created hate and distrust among the people, and it is this and not an invader that threatens the island. Richard Armitage picks this out as an issue to be addressed:

> It is clear that if Sri Lanka is to continue moving forward, the Government must move together as one. No individual, no single political party can carry this burden alone. This must be a concerted effort by the President, the Prime Minister, and the parties.[68]

This is a form of collaborative effort that is beyond the politicians of Sri Lanka. The UNP and the SLFP, the only two parties with the power to act, have always worked against each other. If President Kumaratunga, the person who has suffered more than most and who has the power and the moral authority to ask her people to sacrifice self-interest in the cause of peace, was, despite fourteen years as president, unable to join with all the other parties that represent the majority community of Sinhala Buddhists to devise a solution, what chance does anyone else have? Her courage and her desire to achieve peace for her people – despite losing her father and her husband to violence associated with these issues, and losing an eye in a failed assassination attempt – are not in question, but her judgment must be. She, above all, should understand that the only defence available to the Sinhalese and also the Tamils is not the force of arms – because that would inevitably lead to genocide and ethnic cleansing and brutalise the people – but the force of reason implemented through the rational and collective use of the democratic process. Was it not her father who started the troubles when he appeased the Buddhist clergy to seize the throne? It is time she reversed the trend and created one nation out of the people her father divided. Now that she is not shackled by political objectives she can become an ambassador for peace in her own country.

[68] Richard Armitage, *Sri Lanka: Prospects for Peace*, Presentation to the Center for Strategic and International Studies, Washington DC, 14 February 2003.

After independence, the democratic process – very specifically, the ballot box – was the principal defence mechanism the people had against irresponsible leaders and against their own irresponsibility and excesses. When properly used, democracy helps individuals defend themselves from exploitation by the state because it gives them the legal right to expel their leaders when they fail. And it helps mature, reasonable and humane majority communities to ameliorate injustices so that they and their fellow countrymen and women can live in peace and prosper collectively. But in Sri Lanka the politicians, with the connivance of the racist element among the Buddhist clergy and laity, have compromised the decent, tolerant, law-abiding and generous majority, along with the democratic process, to such an extent that they have succeeded in denying the people the power that democracy ought to give them. A few unscrupulous politicians and priests have persuaded these decent people that the protection of Sinhalese and Buddhism is synonymous with their own well-being. Won over by this rhetoric, the people have sacrificed their own safety and security and accepted reversals in their economic, educational, medical and infrastructure standards, in the belief that they are doing this for the sake of Sinhalese, Buddhism and their children's future. The reality is that continuing to beat the drums of ethnic supremacy only satisfies the needs of the politicians and priests who wish to keep power and money in their hands rather than in the hands of the voters.

In his book, *Emergency '58,* Tarzie Vittachi highlighted the sheer ineptitude of the government of the day, run by Mr Bandaranaike, to stop the bloodlust of rioters who picked on Tamil homes in Colombo. He was not thanked for documenting both the causes and the results. But it has not been above the government or those associated with a government in Sri Lanka to foment trouble and feed rioters. Mrs Kumaratunga admitted as much to Tim Sebastian in the interview she gave him, although she used the usual caveat of, 'Not I, sir – him, sir'. The relevant extract from Mrs Kumaratunga's interview with Tim Sebastian of the BBC is provided in the box in this chapter.

The country is now gripped in a vicious cycle – a downward spiral in which the troubles play into the hands of the politicians of all communities. They are using the troubles that they have fomented to hide their abysmal performance. They use the troubles to deny freedoms that a democratic society has the right to enjoy. They proscribe politicians and groups that challenge their sincerity. They amend the constitution and the law to please their purpose, and they even go to the extreme of dissolving Parliament purely to protect their self-interest.

The most extreme excess is when the constitution places the president above the law. The only group who could have prevented this is the Buddhist priesthood, but they have not because they are also now – by virtue of the fact that they can control the outcome of an election and therefore have the president compliant to their wishes – above the law. When to this is added the indiscipline of those appointed guardians of the island's peace, the army and police forces, who when under pressure become a rabble instead, and act indiscriminately to abuse the people, we have a cocktail of apocalyptic proportions.

The desire for power on the part of the politician and the bloodlust of the rabble-rousers combine to create an ungovernable conflagration in which the poor and the innocent pay the ultimate price and genocide and ethnic cleansing blot our humanity. Who will care for the people if the people will not care for themselves? That is the question that gave rise to the Tamil Tigers and the JVP, and that will arise again unless the island gets leaders who can think for the people and not for themselves.

So, how do a naturally peaceful and tolerant people, who are committed to harmony in body and spirit, allow themselves to condone the extreme behaviour of a rabid minority among them? It is certainly *not* because they are a horrible bloodthirsty lot – by no means. Most of them are honest, honourable, compassionate people who abhor what is done in their name, and succour those who suffer the injustices of racial and religious disharmony. If they stay publicly silent, yet help individually, it is because the climate of recrimination and intolerance forces them into silence. It is an awful hell that they suffer, knowing and wanting to do what is right yet being disabled by a rabid minority who brand all those who expose their inhumanity as disloyalty. To help them bring peace to the island, the government and the Buddhist sangha must preach and practise the virtues of tolerance and inclusivity so that 'one people' can once again listen to each other and act to create the conditions in which they can live in harmony. If it was possible in the past under foreign rule, it must be possible now and in the future.

Evil of the kind practiced by the racist elements in all communities must be condemned as morally reprehensible by the clergy and severely punished by the legal processes. The government of Sri Lanka and the Buddhist establishment must not be above the law, but should instead be its exemplars.

Tim Sebastian of the BBC, interviewing Mrs Kumaratunga, the President of Sri Lanka, in October 2001.[69]

Q: It's okay when you say that not once have you allowed any physical excesses against the Tamil people, you said this in a BBC interview the other day. You would stick by them? Not once have you allowed any physical excesses...

A: Not once have we promoted...

Q: You say that you have allowed...

A: I said this in a very specific context, in a context of what happened during the last government which was in power fraudulently for seventeen years, where the government organised its own mafia, and policemen and military men in

[69] *Hardtalk*, BBC, 31 October 2001.

civil to attack innocent Tamil civilians five times over and the fifth time was a huge pogrom carried out against the Tamil people in July 1983.

Q: But Tamil civilians have been attacked under your rule...

A: No, never

Q: Never?

A: Never.

Q: Simply doesn't accord with the facts...

A: —

Q: Let me quote the State Department report on your human rights practices: 'Since April '95 at least several hundred persons have been killed extrajudicially by the security forces, or have disappeared after being taken in to security forces custody, they're presumed dead.' That doesn't accord with your, 'not once have you allowed any physical excesses against the Tamil people'.

A: Well, that's exactly what I was coming to. This is as opposed to what the last government did where hordes of their, of government mafia, ran on the streets burning down houses, burning down business places belonging to Tamil people—

Q: So you are saying that it was intentional under the last government? And you are saying this is just carelessness under yours.

A: No, that's not what I'm saying. They burnt people alive, I was witness to some of these, as I tried to stop it, whereas what the type of thing they are talking about is something that happened in 1995, there has been absolutely no violence against the Tamil people, or any people at all encouraged or promoted or given a hand to by my government.

Q: But it's happened nonetheless. Or is the State Department completely wrong on this? Is Washington lying?

Chapter 24

A Compromised Democracy

The issue of achieving a balance of power in a multiracial society is still unresolved in Sri Lanka. Natural justice would not begrudge the majority community the right to use their mother tongue and to practice their religion. But should they deny other groups that right too? It certainly does not make them more Sinhalese Buddhist by suppressing Tamil and Hinduism. The solution to this problem is more in the mind of the majority community than in its constitution. It is vital that the constitution is above party politics. Its prime role is to protect the citizen from the executive. For this to happen, judicial independence and integrity is essential, as that is the only way that every individual becomes equal under the law. If this prerequisite is lacking, as it seems to be in Sri Lanka (see Chapter 25), the people of the island have no means of protecting their human rights from acts of Parliament that discriminate against named groups and arbitrary acts of vengeance against a people for imagined past wrongs.

Democracy has not matured in Sri Lanka. It is still a sectarian implement that enables the majority community to 'legitimately' harass and intimidate the other groups living on the island. This raises the horrendous issue of whether democracy can ever be an effective means of electing leaders in a multiracial state.[70]

After independence, Sri Lanka chose to adopt the British parliamentary system of democracy. The flowering democracy of Ceylon functioned in a lopsided way. The vast majority of the voters cast their votes as they were told by those on whose largesse their lives depended. Most villages had one or more grandees and the villagers tended to vote to please them out of a sense of duty, respect and dependence. Therefore the votes gathered were not necessarily representative of the views and opinions of the people but those of their masters. As the UNP represented their masters' interests, the 'democratic' process smoothly completed the lock-in needed for the party to be re-elected. As Ludowyk pointed out in 1962, these early elections were going to be 'decided as they had been in the past – by voters expected to choose the right man according to considerations more important than those of party programmes: those of caste, religion and community.'

The early signs that the power conferred on a majority by the democratic process would be abused came in 1949. The legislation that made the Indian

[70] See Discussion Paper 1.

Tamils stateless highlighted that just below the surface, this 'single' people were a crazy paving of poorly cemented fragments representing race, religion, caste and ideology. It also showed that the government would use its power to tilt the electoral balance in its favour so that it can hold on to power. The Delimitation Commission of 1946 had taken special care to ensure that in sparsely populated areas the minority vote would matter. But the UNP knew that the plantation workers were unlikely to vote for them, so the Citizenship Acts were a 'democratic' way of making them stateless and 'voteless'. The reason given was that India had, after independence, by definition, disenfranchised plantation Tamils who were born in Ceylon, but whose parents were born in India, but who were living in Ceylon. This type of abuse of the democratic process would become a feature of succeeding governments.

The trade unions also began to abuse the democratic rights they were given. They became pressure groups and attacked employers ruthlessly. An impartial observer could not be blamed for concluding that the trade unions were acting as political parties rather than as associations aimed at improving the lot of their members within a viable commercial sector. And it is fair to suppose that the left-leaning political parties were fuelling the discontent of the urban worker through the trade unions.

Personality politics was blossoming in the country. Parties were a convenience for individuals to pursue personal ends. In this game of political snakes and ladders, every time an able politician with leadership skills moved up the board on the ladder of personal ambition, the nation slid down the snakes and ever closer to chaos. The Ceylon Tamil Congress that had formed in 1944 split. Mr S J V Chelvanayagam and some of his friends left it to form the Federal Party. His message was clear. He wanted a federal state for the Tamils in the north of the country. Mr Bandaranaike left the UNP in 1951, ostensibly on the grounds of irreconcilable policy differences but more likely because he felt that he would not lead the UNP and needed his own platform. He made race the deciding issue in 1956 and it has been ever since.

Sentiment also plays a part in the way the electorate vote. It is generally accepted that Dudley Senanayake was voted into office in 1952 partly on his own merits, but also because of the sympathy people felt for him at his father's untimely death. Similarly, Mrs Bandaranaike's victory over Dudley Senanayake in 1960 was due, in large part, to the sympathy people felt for her following the assassination of her husband the previous year. The newspapers dubbed her the 'weeping widow', but she certainly won the people's hearts and votes and proved no pushover once in office. It is suggested that Mrs Kumaratunga's re-election as predisent in 2000 was also due to a sympathy vote following an attempt on her life on the last day of campaigning.

Such a decision process makes a mockery of the principles of democracy, which require freedom from inbuilt bias if the system is to be fair. The ruling group wins the power to rule on the quality of their objectives and their ability to deliver them. When followers believe that they are being misled, they vote their leaders out of office and appoint a new set of leaders. Each set of leaders gain their position on the basis of the number of people voting for them. Those who gain the most votes get the right to govern all the people, irrespective of whether or not they voted for this set of leaders. But politicians who do not get the highest votes can still govern the country. They do this by forming alliances with other political groups so that their combined votes make them the largest political grouping and thereby earn the right to govern. For much of the post-independence period, the SLFP has depended on alliances to gain a majority. In other words, the SLFP has rarely gained power on its own. Therefore those political groups who helped the SLFP gain power must also share the blame for the current ills of the country. The UNP, on the other hand, has won the right to rule on its own merits and is responsible for the problems too.

But democracy is not just a numbers game in which the winner takes all. Hague and Harrop state that 'the development of democracy requires more than just competitive elections'. Democracy also requires:

> ...the enforcement of legal restraint on state power, protection of civil rights, the establishment of relatively uncorrupt and effective bureaucracies, and the imposition of democratic control over potentially authoritarian forces such as the military and the other security services.[71]

By these mixed criteria, the various governments that have ruled Sri Lanka over the last fifty or so years have failed to consolidate democracy in the island.

This is not to suggest that democracy is perfect in other parts of the world. It certainly is not. Like most systems that depend on people, it suffers from human frailty and failings. There is concern in the West that it is losing its lustre; fewer people are taking the trouble to participate in the political process and, consequently, governments are losing their legitimacy as instruments of public purpose because they are not representative of a majority view. The presidential elections in the United States of America in 2000 had its fair share of drama, and there are those who claim that Mr Bush did not receive a true majority vote. But there is no doubt that he was the clear winner in 2004. There are also those who claim that the huge sums of money (about $120 millions for each of the main candidates) needed to fight a presidential election makes a mockery of democracy. Perhaps it limits the choice available to voters but it does not deprive them of their power as electors.

The general election in Britain in 2001 was won by Labour with a majority of 165 seats in Parliament on the votes of only 24.1 per cent of the electorate. Only 59.4 per cent of the electorate tuned out to vote, and Labour received only 40.7 per cent of the votes cast. Despite this, the Parliamentary system of democracy practised in the UK enabled Mr Blair to take the country to war,

[71] Luckham and White, quoted in Hague and Harrop, *Comparative Government and Politics: An Introduction.*

even though a large proportion of the public did not wish him to and showed their displeasure of his intentions very clearly by organising anti-war marches, the largest of which is supposed to have had over a million participants. Based on these numbers, the UK government can enter into treaties and ratify and adopt European Commission directives without further reference to the public. So, in the end, the preferences of a small elite determine the way the British people live their lives. The only – and this is a very big 'only' – means they have is to vote a party and a government out of power if they do not like the way they govern. However, this raises another issue of great importance, one of choice. Unless the people are offered credible leaders, they end up having no choice but to vote in the 'best of a bad lot'. This, too, undermines democracy. So it would be unfair to condemn democracy in Sri Lanka as flawed because democracies all the world over are flawed, and the alternatives to democracy are even worse as mechanisms of power sharing in a community. The point about Sri Lankan democracy is that it has been hijacked by the racists to dispossess and disenfranchise the minority communities.

Although some people in a democracy will be ruled by people they did not vote into office and with whose political objectives they disagree, they have a right to expect, bar unintended consequences, to be treated as part of a homogeneous group rather than as a heterogeneous group. That is to say that all the citizens should have an equal chance of benefiting from policies adopted by the leaders because the policies do not differentiate by category of person. If, on the other hand, leaders deliberately choose policies that disadvantage some of the citizens, the political system in force is much closer to being a semi-democracy or even an oligarchy by proxy. The political system operating in Sri Lanka fits either definition. A semi-democracy is defined by Hague and Harrop as a political system that has:

> ...democratic and authoritarian elements in stable combination. Although rulers are elected, often helped by control of the media, they govern with little respect for individual rights and often harass opposition or even non-official groups.

Although the strict definition of an oligarchy is 'rule by a few', in Sri Lanka 'the few' are in fact a class of persons, a ruling clique, who took power at independence and have held on to it ever since. They used race, language and religion to win votes and made the Buddhist monks fellow conspirators. The Buddhist sangha became the publicists for a small, fundamentalist clique of the Sinhalese Buddhist majority who hijacked the political system and began to use it to discriminate and differentiate one group of people from another. The British might have wanted to prevent this from happening, and the Soulbury Commission anticipated it, but could not find suitable safeguards.[72] As Lord

[72] See Discussion Paper 1.

Salisbury points out in his preface to BH Farmer's book on Ceylon,

> the reconciliation of Tamils and Sinhalese will depend not on constitutional guarantees but on the goodwill, common sense and humanity of the government in power and the people who elect it![73]

As we have seen, democracy is an imperfect tool because the views that matter happen to be those of the people with the power to implement them; the rest have to suffer the frustration of their ideas and views being stillborn. This creates a mindset of winners and losers and breeds discontent, dissent and discord. In mature democracies, politicians and the systems of policy implementation attempt to even out the greater discrepancies by providing constitutional and legal safeguards. For example, in the UK there are legal safeguards against the discrimination of individuals on the grounds of their race, colour, gender, sexual orientation and religious affiliation, among others. Despite this, discrimination does occur, but when it does the institutions of the state recognise the right of an individual to obtain redress.

So the right to equal treatment has been institutionalised. This prevents the majority from using the democratic process unreasonably or unfairly. And when redress for wrongs done cannot be corrected by the legal systems of the country, individuals can take their case to the European Court of Justice. In some cases, the majority population are finding that these safeguards are being abused by the minorities and used as sticks with which to beat the majority community. The minority communities have learnt to suborn the law to their advantage by shouting 'foul' at the least provocation. If this were to happen too often, the credibility of their cause and of the legislation would suffer adversely and harm the minority groups more, as the well-intentioned among the majority will find that they are unable to protect those who are genuinely disadvantaged. So again, as is often the case in human affairs, nothing is perfect and every good intention falls at the hurdle of the manipulative micro-population of exploiters and abusers.

In Sri Lanka, the Sinhala Buddhist community, drawing on ethnic loyalties, have used their majority vote to institutionalise the dominance of their religion and language. Having done this, politicians continue to use it as the touchstone of loyalty and continue to be elected to office for espousing it. But it disenfranchises the voters who believe that it is time to govern the country using a wider perspective, one that involves a mix of issues that provide a balanced and successful economy and social climate. This sophisticated use of the voting system, however, is denied them because the voting system is susceptible to corruption and fear, and not because the electorate of Sri Lanka are fools or illiterate. The opposite is the case.

The voters are able to take a wider perspective and would, if allowed to do

[73] BH Farmer, *Ceylon A Divided Nation* Institute of Race Relations, OUP 1963.

so; but they are prevented by social pressures created by a variety of sources. The media, sensing the mood of nationalism in society, feed it for profit. Specific individuals convert personal obsessions into public hysteria, like McCarthyism in the United States. At such times, reason is suspended because to think in ways other than that of conventional wisdom is to stand out as not being 'one of us' and therefore being seen as 'one of them' and being branded as a 'bad guy'. This, of course, is now becoming a routine means of winning support, and even leaders of the more powerful countries in the world have used it to augment their case for war. Simple-minded or Machiavellian politicians put into power by a set of puppet masters tend to reduce complex issues into political correctness to get their way.

In Sri Lanka, the puppet master is the Sinhalese Buddhist lobby, which is dominated by the Buddhist priesthood. It is claimed that they are choosing to step out of the political arena. However, their past behaviour dumbed down an electorate of whom 92.3 per cent (90 per cent of the women and 94.8 per cent of the men are rated literate). This means that besides being able to read, write and speak their native tongue they are also able to comprehend the effects of policy on their lives and to vote for things that matter to them. So although they are not all scientists, nor do they all hold PhDs, they know what matters to them, their children and their grandchildren and will support the political group that they believe will deliver their needs. The vast numbers of Sri Lankan men and women when they meet socially carry on heated debates about the political issues of the day. And some, emboldened by toddy or *arrack*, will attack others who have a different view and even kill them. So whilst the discussions do not take the sophisticated approach favoured by the Western media they still take place and still inform. But their discussions can only be based on the information that they get from 'trusted' sources, and there is no more 'trusted source' than the local clergy, whether Roman Catholic, Muslim, Hindu, Buddhist or Anglican. It is they who control the floating vote.

It is within the power of the Buddhist clergy to incite or placate the intemperate wishes of the Buddhist laity. This is because the Buddhist clergy have a stranglehold on the thoughts and actions of the village communities where most of the voting power resides. In these village communities, the Buddhist monks can fulfil the role of rabble-rousers, troubleshooters or pacifiers. The Buddhist sangha has used the Sinhala Buddhist majority's concern for their religion and language to take control of the levers of power. By adding the votes they can deliver through their influence to the stronger and more dependable voting base of loyal supporters, they enable politicians in Sri Lanka to win power. And the politicians have perfected the art of using bigotry, bribery or fear – or all three – to win the floating vote.

Unfortunately, this is also the vote that is against any accommodation with the Tamil movement for autonomy or equality of opportunity, so the country is doomed to be at war. This is why the democratic system in Sri Lanka fails to deliver a peaceful and stable country. So the wheels of peace may turn, but the peace-loving Sri Lankans, who probably amount to 70 per cent of the population, have their wishes usurped by the bigoted, corrupt or timid floating voter. Because of this, the democratic system denies the law-abiding citizen a voice to redress legitimate grievances or to steer the agenda into other fields that matter to them more.

In most countries what matter to most voters are things like personal security, safety, jobs, medical help, education, food and clothing. These things matter more in poor countries. It is only after these necessities of survival have been secured that the debate moves on to the higher plains of human rights, or equal rights for minority groups, or the macro issues of economic performance, incorruptibility of officialdom, justice that is fair and equitable, the quality of public services, freedom of expression provided it is within the law and *habeas corpus* among others. Fortunately for the Sri Lankan people, they inherited these survival and higher elements from the British. All they had to do was build on it. By raising the Sinhalese Buddhist issue so early in the new nation's life and by implementing it in such a strident manner, the government of Mr Bandaranaike created an impediment to harmonious living. And all Sri Lankan governments since 1956 have, by failing to ameliorate the adverse effects of his policy, failed the people.

But the voters still vote for a party that beats the Sinhalese Buddhist drum loudest and longest as if it is an unfinished task. This must be because they believe the rhetoric and the slogans that say that any ills they suffer are because of the discontented actions of the minority Tamils. Since those who preach this are often the racists among the Buddhist clergy and their subordinated politicians, it tends to be believed. Mrs Kumaratunga, too, was not above playing this particular tune. When it suited her she blamed all the ills of the country on the Tamil Tigers. To her they were the scapegoat. And when she could not blame them, she blamed the international community for supporting them. The lacklustre performance of her parents and her own incompetence in tackling the issues she promised to resolve when she took office in 1994 are never mentioned. When challenged in 2001 on these points by Tim Sebastian of the BBC, she chose to blame the previous government instead. At least in this one respect she acted like most politicians.

So, the people do, indeed, have the government they deserve – and the government the clergy it wants and cultivates to help it stay in office. The clergy and laity of all nations have fallen into this abyss from time to time. The trick is to get out of it fast, before the digging takes those affected further and further into the void and away from the sunlight of reason and tolerance.

So deeply embedded is the Sinhala Buddhist issue in the minds of the rural voters that it stifles the beneficial debate that democracy ought to enable and encourage. To return the island to true democracy, it is essential to implant a new set of beliefs about the 'ideal' state, rather than allow the complexities of modern living and global communications to warp and distort it into one the country cannot provide now. It is important that politicians and other opinion-formers place the lives of celebrities, images from films and other visual inputs as well as peer group opinions in a context that makes sense for a country still reeling from internal strife and economic decline. It is vital that they give the young a reason for living. It is important to reinstate the values of a caring society so that future leaders will be chosen against a new template that focuses on economic and social achievement rather than on Sinhalese and Buddhist chauvinism to win votes.

Unless the politicians project a vibrant new image of the future, they will not be able to harness behaviour that will help people to regain balance in their lives and remove the sense of despair that they feel today. The democratic process must again offer people a legitimate and peaceful means of expressing their discontent and of righting wrongs in a peaceful and legitimate way, whilst recognising that, in an imperfect world, all our endeavours can only deliver imperfect solutions. If this is not done the serpent that always resides in the garden will offer the apple of wish-fulfilment and disaffected people, mostly the young, will bite the apple of discontent and don the mantle of revolution. If this continues to happen in Sri Lanka, the blame must fall on a compromised democratic process that is manipulated by a ruling clique who use the racists to win votes.

As long as the racists hold on to the levers of power, people will not step forward to sell this vision of a new nation. Indeed, parties that decide to focus more on improving the economy, rebuilding infrastructure, working for peace, individual and collective prosperity, health care, education, social welfare, law and order, justice, freedom of speech, and so on will continue to lose at the ballot box. Those who wish for these things will feel excluded from the political process because their legitimate grievances about the economy, safety, equal opportunity and so on will never get heard and corrected. Eventually, frustrated and disillusioned by the democratic process they will seek redress in violence – the usual outcome of ill-conceived, misapplied and debased democracies.

Freedom of independent thought, long seen as the prize of a truly democratic system, still eludes the Sri Lankan people. The electorate does not, as yet, choose a government on the strength of the case made by potential leaders. Neither do the electorate or the politicians understand the concept of a political party – a group of people with a common ideology who work together to deliver a programme of work. Both these fundamental drivers of democratic politics are still many decades away. What the current democratic process does is ensure that an individual occupying the highest seat in the land and those sharing power with that individual can be removed from office if the people so wish. In other respects, all the old feudal constraints of race, religion, servitude to a proprietary class such as the clergy, the stratification of caste, a judiciary that cowed by the state and is partial to its wishes, a political elite that changes the rules or allies itself with any group to help it stay in power, and a self-seeking mercantile class ready and able to exploit the money-making opportunities that the social unrest brings, are hallmarks not of a democratic country under the rule of law, but a 'bully state' legitimised by the democratic process. Using the majority vote and determined to appease the extreme elements that control the voters' minds it imposes its will, not by overt physical force but by the subtlety of the ballot box. Such a sophisticated and distorted use of a liberating system reflects a mindset that is, as yet, unable to comprehend the true measure of the huge responsibility for fairness and equality that democracy demands of it. Nonetheless, the process is in place, and one hopes that over the succeeding decades its rough edges will be smoothed and the people will see it not as a means to an end, but as a desirable end in itself and one that it is worth sacrificing individual self-interest to secure.

Chapter 25

Corruption of Morality and Justice

In the power politics of the governance of a country, corruption manifests itself in many different forms. However, the primary issue with the corruption of individuals in the service of the public is not that some people gain an unfair advantage, but the fact that they abuse their position of public trust for personal advantage. To avoid punishment and to meet their obligations, they involve others and create a sense of collective guilt, which, over time, institutionalises corruption in society. By this means, too, the wrongdoers avoid punishment or censure, and, by default, legitimise corrupt and corrupting behaviour, which gradually erodes the integrity of the state and the nation.

Although such claims cannot easily be proven, no one will deny that it takes place in Sri Lanka. But it is worth asking what other purpose middlemen play in an economy in which government departments and public corporations are the sole purchasers of most capital goods and services used in the construction of infrastructures, the provision of arms and of utility services. The *Daily News* of 24 September 2004 reported that:

> A member of parliament and three others have been remanded in connection with the alleged possession and sale of galvanised sheets valued over Rupees 2 millions imported from India to be distributed free to 128,000 poor families.[74]

ColomboPage.com reported on 22 September 2004 that a high ranking police officer:

> was arrested yesterday by Bribery and Corruption officers on charges of graft. It would seem that the officer was 'unable to account for more than Rs. 3 million in assets.[75]

Gulf-news.com reported in October 2004 that 'A senior Sri Lankan military officer has been arrested after he failed to declare as to how he amassed a large amount of wealth during the past seven years.'[76]

It may be that they are innocent of these charges, or it may be that the arrests are politically motivated. Or perhaps, there is a wind of anti-corruption

---

[74] *The Daily News*, 24 September 2004

[75] ColomboPage.com, 22 September 2004.

[76] Sinha Ratnatunga, 'Top Sri Lankan Military Officer Arrested for Corruption', Gulf-news.com, 13 October 2004.

blowing over the island; perhaps it is a cynical ploy to appease the international community. Whatever the reason, if such senior figures are involved, it is likely that the rot is widespread and that the barrel will be completely empty when the rotten apples are taken out. The question is: will these arrests result in a clean-up or will they, like many such exercises in the past, stop as soon as 'sensitive' senior political, government and commercial figures are fingered by those arrested now? What the country needs is a clean sweep, but who will run it when the clean up is completed?

If the large sums in grants, foreign aid and loans received over the last fifty-six years for infrastructure and utilities projects are aggregated, the shortfall between the actual money spent and that received will show a large gap. Part of this gap could be attributed to incompetence, as there is much of that too, and another part to the destructive effect of the internecine wars. But in the main it represents money siphoned off into the hands of policy makers and those implementing and administering policy via untraceable routes.

This is not a phenomenon unique to Sri Lankan politicians. It does happen the world over, even in countries that are considered to be above institutionalised corruption, politicians and policy makers may sometimes tilt the balance in the favour of their sponsors and financiers. In the United Kingdom, for example, the issue of pension rights and entitlements is being hotly debated. Ian Cowie, the personal finance editor for the *Telegraph* writes that Members of Parliament, using their privileged position, have voted themselves a better pensions package than most other employees in the country. According to him, an MP working for the same period of time as a public sector or a private sector worker would be significantly better off than both. In his example, an MP working for twenty-six years would be entitled to a final pension of £93,000 per annum whilst a private sector employee working for the same period of time is only likely to earn a pension of £22,300 per annum. In his view, 'Such a stratospheric pension is almost equal to the maximum available to politicians and is likely to remain beyond the wildest dreams of most MPs' constituents.' His point is that:

> MPs voted to improve the benefits of their pension two years ago, so that it accrues at a rate of one fortieth of final salary for each year. They also increased their contributions into the scheme to nine per cent of salary.[77]

In this instance it would appear that the MPs have used their position of trust to unfair advantage. In another article, Cowie's final point is most telling. He says when he suggested to a Conservative MP that his pension should be calculated in the same way as that of his constituents, 'he just laughed'. As Cowie says, 'And these jokers expect us to take them seriously.'[78]

---

[77] Ian Cowie, 'For £1 million, you too could retire in the style of an MP', *Telegraph*, 13 October 2004.

[78] Ian Cowie, 'Comment: Put not your faith in politicians - they do not share our problems', *Telegraph*, 16

Politics has become a gravy train for many people who, by conforming to the wishes of the party bosses, benefit from incomes well above their ability. In December 2004, the Labour government decided to act to reduce the pension rights of government servants but failed to do so for MPs. This is interesting. When there was public protest at MPs voting themselves pay increases that exceeded those of workers generally, the issue was resolved by linking MPs' pay scales to those of civil servants, thus ensuring that any benefits and salary increases the civil servants won for themselves were automatically also paid to ministers and MPs. It also did mean that any downgrading would be equally applicable. But it seems that it is not so.

A strange form of corruption occurs in Sri Lanka because of the respect accorded to those of mature years. The most obvious and visible expression of respect for the 'older, wiser head' was the appointment of Mrs Bandaranaike to the office of prime minister between 1994 and 2000. On the two previous occasions when she was prime minister, she presided over the social unrest that has plagued the country since 1958 and the economic decline of the nation. She was voted out of office in 1977. When she returned in 1994 to carry that heavy burden again, the country was experiencing a period of considerable unrest. Despite being much older and frailer, she soldiered on until 2000. In the view of many, she was unequal to the challenge.

The suspicion was that this time her appointment to the office was less to do with the respect for wiser heads and more to do with the political survival of her daughter, who was uncertain of her position and did not dare to risk having a more energetic and aspiring individual in the job of prime minister. If Mrs Kumaralinga had taken her responsibilities for the welfare of the country more seriously and had the self-confidence to do the job she had sought and won she would have persuaded her mother to enjoy her retirement and let a younger person run, rather than hold, the heavy office of prime minister. The country must surely have suffered. But this was not an isolated incident. Mr J R Jayawardene (born 1906 and died 1996), a veteran politician, took his seat as prime minister in 1977 at the age of seventy-one and then the executive office of president from 1978 until 1989 when he was eighty-three. It could well be that age is respected in Sri Lanka, as it is in India, but it leads to the wrong choices. The issues facing the country (the war and economic decline) had been created by these, now aged, politicians whilst in office and in opposition, and they were certainly not the people to resolve them. To elect people long past their prime to the office of prime minister of so troubled a country was a strange irony indeed.

Most external commentators will admit that the electoral system in Sri Lanka is a process that bends to the lure of money, and the pressure of physical force. Administrative gerrymandering and clerical mishandling and counting by officials makes a mockery of the secrecy of the ballot box. The US State Department website note on Sri Lanka, issued on 17 May 2004 says:

October 2004.

> Sri Lanka has a long history of democratic institutions and processes, but its elections have historically been fraught with violence, and government capacity [presumably to contain it] at the district and local levels is weak.

Again, it is important to remember that a democratic system of governance is open to the abuse of bribery. Politicians who appeal to the self-interest of segments of the voting population, particularly those that espouse and support a welfare state, tread a fine line between concern for the disadvantaged and buying votes. There is always a narrow line between helping those in need and giving handouts that create a dependency culture. Similarly, any attempt at rationalisation or abuse control is used to scare beneficiaries into voting in the government that sustains the status quo. In time, state help has the same effect as drug abuse – it creates dependency and increases the craving. The problem in some countries, including Sri Lanka, is that such forms of handouts are part of a deliberate policy of bribery.

Press Freedom

Colombopage.com of September 23rd 2004 reports that the Free Media Movement (FMM) has urged the government not to shackle investigative journalism after five contempt notices were issued against *Sunday Leader* journalists after the paper published a series of critical articles against the Chief Justice. These notices refer to articles in 2001 and 2002. The FMM claims that 'we also find the fact that all five notices have been issued after the *Sunday Leader* published a series of critical articles on the Chief Justice of the Supreme Court of significant note, and believe that this does not augur well for the independence of judiciary.'

The judicial system in Sri Lanka is corrupt in that its opinions and decision are biased towards political expediency. Again, there is the potential for this to happen in any democratic state. In Sri Lanka, the judges are used by the politicians to curb protest and at other times to curb other politicians whose utterances are unwelcome. The Asian Human Rights Commission, in a news bulletin issued when Justice Mark Fernando resigned, said that his resignation 'is of grave concern'. Why? Because in its view:

> Justice Fernando has consistently upheld the rights of Sri Lankan citizens, especially those of the victims of human rights violations. Since joining the Supreme Court in 1988 he has observed the highest levels of independence and integrity, maintaining principles of impartiality, fairness and justice at all times.[79]

It goes on to state that: 'His premature retirement can only have an adverse effect on the rule of law in Sri Lanka and may further diminish the citizens' trust in public institutions.'

[79] 'Senior judge's resignation a warning of deteriorating judicial independence and rule of law in Sri Lanka', AHRC, http://www.ahrchk.net/statements/mainfile.php/2003statement/119/, 29 August 2003.

It would seem, according to the bulletin, that such an exemplar was being excluded by the Chief Justice 'from hearings relating to the constitutionality of bills before the Parliament'. The tone of the bulletin leaves the reader with the impression that the Chief Justice bows to his political masters to keep his office. This is why Amnesty International expressed concern when Sri Lanka decided to reinstate the death penalty. Gina Wilkinson's report from Colombo published in the Australian Broadcasting Corporation's website abc.net of 25 November 2004 says:

> Amnesty International warns it's highly likely that innocent people will be executed, given serious failing within the Sri Lankan justice system, including frequent reports of police using torture.

It would seem the State Department of the United States is also concerned about brutality by the forces of the government and the lack of action to bring the perpetrators to justice. The extract in the box at the end of this chapter from Tim Sebastian's interview with Mrs Kumaratunga justifies Amnesty's fears.

But justice is corrupted in a different way too. The law of the land is not applied evenly across the country or across social groups. From infringement of the traffic laws to more serious crime, influence determines who is held accountable under the law and who is not.

There is a history of the abuse of power in Sri Lanka. The same State Department website note quoted earlier comments that:

> ...political infighting within the Government between the President and Prime Minister, resulting in the President's decision to call early elections in April, was also an obstacle to attaining stability and democracy.

The President's reason for calling early elections was probably to prevent the Prime Minister from upstaging her by consolidating the peace. Instead, to subvert him, she claimed that he was giving too much away to the Tamil Tigers. Richard L Armitage, in his talk to members of the Center for Strategic and International Studies in Washington, says of the Prime Minister she effectively dismissed:

> We owe much of that [peace process] progress to the Government of Prime Minister Ranil Wickremesinghe, who continues to take bold steps in the direction of peace.

But the abuse of power is not limited to Mrs Kumaratunge alone. In 1983 Mr Jayawardene and the UNP, his party, were reaching the end of their first terms. Jayawardene decided that he and his party should remain in office longer than the voters wished so that he could enjoy the majority that he had won in 1977 and enjoy the unconstrained power it gave him. So he postponed the general elections and held a referendum instead which he won by an affirmative vote of 37.8 per cent of the electorate. But even before this, Mrs Bandaranaike had used a cynical ploy to extend her term in office. They had both extended their terms of office by sleight of hand. Technically their extended terms were obtained by bending the rules.

Leaders in the political arena in Sri Lanka believe that they are above the law. The members of their immediate and extended family, and their close friends and relatives also claim immunity. The corrupting influence of this attitude, which at times becomes a demand, destroys probity throughout society. Everyone, from the lowliest to the highest, invokes whatever influence they have to advantage themselves and their kith and kin. The result is a state of near anarchy. In consolidated democracies, no member of the political elite is exempt from the law. The president of the United States can be impeached for certain actions, but he cannot be dismissed by Congress because he disagrees on matters of policy. Also, the judicial branch of the federal government can and will act to mediate between the president and Congress. The sovereign heads of European governments are expected to live within the law, and if they fail, to pay the price of failure. Theirs is not a perfect system – no system is – but accountability is demanded and exposed when it is found to be wanting.

Patronage

Transparency International Sri Lanka has claimed that 'the government that assumed office after the 2 April General Election has made several incorrect and inappropriate appointments to key posts, based mainly on favouritism and not in the interests of the state.' It goes on to state that 'qualified persons who should be appointed to such key high posts are deprived of this opportunity due to politicians appointing their political stooges to these positions.' The other issue it flags up is that when these appointees fail, 'ministers are reluctant to "pull up" any such appointees mainly due to party affiliations.'

ColomboPage, September 22, 2004

Few prime ministers or heads of state of major democracies will be able to force legislation through their governmental processes that will place them above the law. But Mr Jayawardene did just that. When the UNP was voted into power by 85 per cent of the vote, the government and certainly Prime Minister J R Jayawardene did what they pleased. The prime minister made Sri Lanka a Republic, appointed himself president and then ensured that his office was above the law. Section 35 of the Sri Lankan constitution, as published in the government website on 10 September 2004, says:

> Whilst any person holds office as president, no proceedings shall be instituted or continued against him in any court or tribunal in respect of anything done or omitted to be done by him either in his official or *private* [my italics] capacity.[80]

[80] www.priu.gov.lk.

When to this is added the fact that the president appoints the cabinet, has direct control of the armed forces and appoints the judges, among other executive rights ceded to the president by the constitution, we have a very powerful office and one that is equivalent to a dictatorship. Naturally, one would not expect the president of a country to act outside the law or immorally. However, even presidents and heads of state are fallible and are held accountable for their criminal actions when in or out of office, but the president of Sri Lanka is not.

Similarly, heads of state of consolidated democracies would not proscribe a political opponent, especially the only one able to challenge them at the polls, without proving misconduct that warrants such proscription. In Sri Lanka, Mr Jayawardene did just that by passing legislation that set up a tribunal to try Mrs Bandaranaike for alleged abuse of power while in office and when it found her guilty deprived her of civic rights and prevented her from participating in the political process until Mr Jayawardene lifted the suspension in 1986. Ostensibly, his actions were legal but his motives were questionable as indeed was the judgement of the tribunal. It would seem that it took him a long time to realise that the 'pot was calling the kettle black'. Such acts create resentment and personal animosity. No doubt Mrs Bandaranaike bore a grudge that wove itself into the political arena with detrimental effects, because power passes between a narrow group of often related families and personal animosities enter the political domain and sour it. So when in 2003, the President (Mrs Bandaranaike's daughter) constrained the government led by Mr Ranil Wickramasinghe (Mr Jayawardene's cousin's son) and then dissolved Parliament a few months later it is hard to imagine that her motives were governed purely by the political considerations prevailing at the time.

When Mr Jayawardene was president he used his large majority in Parliament – one that he held at the time by political subterfuge – to amend the constitution (the sixth amendment), so that any person or organisation could be banned from participating in the Parliamentary process if they encouraged or advocated the establishment of a separate state for the Tamils. By this pseudo-legal means, Mr Jayawardene was able to expel the lawfully elected opposition party, the TULF, and proscribe the JVP in 1983. Bush points out that 'it reflects a pattern of political decay in which members of the legal opposition political parties are harassed and intimidated while legal recourse is simultaneously closed to them due to political manipulation.'

Against these huge abuses of power, the abuse of privilege indulged in by senior government officials and their families, and politicians and their families, is merely chicken feed. The abuse of privilege occurs because these 'exalted' individuals are unable to distinguish between private and public property. They will unashamedly use their position in office to gain personal favours from private individuals and from foreign organisations. Nepotism, too, is rife in many government and private sector organisations where appointments are made on the basis of kinship, electoral expediency and money rather than merit.

Thus does a corrupt state create a corrupt nation.

Tim Sebastian of the BBC, interviewing Mrs Kumaratunga, the President of Sri Lanka, in October 2001.

Q: You say one incident – the State Department cites a variety of methods of torture that are used: electric shock, beating, suspension by the wrists or feet, burnings, slamming testicles in desk drawers, near drownings. They don't say one incident. June last year – I'll give you an instance as cited by the state department – June last year, police at Kantale near Trincomalee arrested and tortured five Tamils, one died as a result. December last year, the bodies of seven Tamils have been, who have been tortured and killed by the army in Mirusavil were exhumed after one person escaped and notified authorities. A commissioned officer and eight soldiers were arrested.

A: Exactly. We have arrested them and they are before a trial at bar in the same way that we have put the people who raped this one lady for trial at bar which is a very special legal procedure – judicial procedure much more expeditious than the usual one. Because we want to punish these people.

Q: You want to punish but they say little progress has been made in resolving many cases of extrajudicial killings or disappearances. Don't you see little progress?

A: I don't accept it.

Chapter 26

Abandonment of Politics for the Gun

The Sri Lankan people experienced intense militancy from both the rural Tamils and the rural Sinhalese, proving that not all the militancy was racially motivated. In fact the insurgencies in the south by the JVP could be attributed to a group of disaffected Sinhalese youth. In both communities the frustration of a poor lifestyle and an indeterminate future erupted into violent protest. A responsive, sensitive ruling clique could have prevented the heartache and bloodshed.

In those democracies where elections are fought and won on a range of issues, voters can choose the party that most closely espouses the causes they are interested in. If their party wins, they accept that they gain some and lose some. If their party loses, they have the consolation of knowing that the winning party is unlikely to follow policies that are so different as to cause discontent. If it does, voters have a range of options, including that of forming a pressure group, knowing that their peaceful and legitimate protest will be picked up by the media and forced into the public consciousness. Or they can create or join single-issue political parties that are sympathetic to their cause and vote for them. This has happened in the UK with the Referendum Party, the Green Party, the British National Party and the UK Independence Party. These organised voices of dissent force issues that are of concern to a segment of the population on to the agendas of the mainstream political parties, where they stand a better chance of being resolved. If citizens are denied such safety valves, their discontent becomes dissent and eventually leads to discord. A particularly good and early example of the power of peaceful but persistent protest was the success of the anti-slavery movement in the UK during the early decades of the nineteenth century. As Niall Ferguson says:

> This was the birth of a new kind of politics, the politics of the pressure group. Thanks to the work of zealous activists armed only with pens, paper and moral indignation, Britain had turned against slavery. Even more remarkably, the slave trade had been abolished in the face of determined opposition from some powerful vested interests.[81]

However, the success of peaceful protest rests very much on the cry of the protest group being taken up and satisfyingly dealt with by those with the

[81] Niall Ferguson, *Empire: How Britain Made the Modern World*, Penguin Books, 2003.

power to change injustices in society – governments, the judges and the electorate that empowers them. But what happens when these three forces are compromised and the protest falls on deaf ears. In the context of a democracy that is weighted against minority racial groups, peaceful protest will only work if the Government acknowledges its obligation to the minority groups and tries to accommodate those interests as best they can within the wider framework of a multi-ethnic, multicultural population. Governments need to show that they have genuinely attempted to resolve the issues. Governments also need to show that the solutions they eventually arrive at are the best possible given all the circumstances, and they need to win the approval and support of the whole population if they hope to successfully implement their solutions. This is a hard job. If, instead, governments ignore or refuse to consider and respond 'reasonably' to the needs of legitimate dissent, they run the risk of fomenting revolt. Democracy breaks down. Those who feel most disadvantaged or ignored feel excluded, take exception, and react most strongly even to the point of exploding into revolt. No one benefits then. In *The Story of Parliament,* John Field illustrates this point very well when he discusses the 'Irish issue' of the 1820s. He says:

> Daniel O'Connell's inspired tactic of mass gatherings for non-violent disruptive protest has been imitated by repressed peoples worldwide, most notably in India and South Africa ... the absence of any sign of political concessions provoked the outbreak of Fenian terrorism in the 1860s; a second modern political tactic was born.[82]

Field goes on to point out that when Gladstone introduced the Second Home Rule Bill in 1892 it was passed by the Commons but was lost in the Lords by a majority of 419 to 41, and that:

> The second rejection of Home Rule had two consequences: the birth of the Sinn Fein movement and a delay of 20 years before Asquith's Liberal Government had the courage to pick up the time bomb again.

In other words, he suggests that a more reasoned and reasonable response may have prevented almost a century of discord and violence. It would seem that by ignoring peaceful protest and driving people to act militantly, those who are against an equitable solution in the first instance claim that the intractability of the protestor has justified their stance all along. And they now have a new pretext to deny the discontented redress for their grievances by claiming that they will not talk to terrorists. In this way, intolerance breeds intolerance and escalates the violence until both groups are shedding innocent blood. The resulting militancy of the wronged prevents reasonable people from acting to

---

[82] John Field, *The Story of Parliament.*

correct any felt injustice because their pleas for fairness get drowned out by the cries for vengeance.

In Sri Lanka, the Buddhist response to the request by the Tamils to be treated fairly and with respect should have been that of the *dharma*. The Sinhalese should have sought a 'middle way'. A democracy operating along Buddhist principles should have listened to the voices of disgruntled minority groups and worked towards a mediated, amicable settlement designed to ensure long-term peace and stability. The government of Sri Lanka should not have created the discord in the name of Buddhism. It should not have created new wrongs in order to redress past wrongs. By doing so in 1956, it set the foundations for the militancy and bloodshed that followed. With every riot and every period of tension, the gap between the communities widened until it reached the point of 'irreconcilable differences' in the minds of those most affected. As a result, the flame of discontent and disaffection will smoulder on as long as the underlying issues of discrimination and institutionalised racism that lead to economic deprivation is legitimised by the ballot box.

In his excellent book, *In Defence of Politics*, Bernard Crick justifies using an example from Sri Lanka to illustrate the point that democracy can be misused by a majority community, but that they can hide behind 'just' causes to justify their actions. He says of Mrs Bandaranaike:

> Democratic nationalism, the myth of the sovereignty of the people, can be the most intolerant to minorities. It thrives upon the confusion of national government with popular government and uses both sticks – is possessed by both extremes – to beat a divided people into a unity. Only three years ago [the first edition of the book came out in 1962] the Government of Ceylon stirred up a civil disobedience campaign among the Tamil minority by attempting to suppress its language. Ceylon should be one nation. On 26 April 1961, in justifying the declaration of a state of emergency, the Prime Minister [Mrs Bandaranaike] said: 'At times like these we must lay aside political and religious differences. This is the hour for everybody to unite against the enemies of the nation and of the people.' Here is the worst plausible rhetoric of nationalism. Mrs Bandaranaike is saying that politics is to be thrown away in order to achieve a national unity and that those who wish for political compromise are enemies of the people.[83]

In the meantime, the LTTE has been branded the enemy of the people by Sri Lankan politicians so that they can avoid dealing with the root causes of Tamil disaffection. As Crick points out:

> This category of man [enemy of the people] was the terrible invention of the Jacobins, and still thrives happily: an 'enemy of the people' loses all civic rights, he is literally an outlaw – cast beyond justice; it is a small step then before he

[83] Bernard Crick, *In Defence of Politics*, fifth edition, Continuum, 2000.

> loses all human rights. What sort of man [or woman] can willingly, wilfully, be an enemy both of the nation and of the people? The answer may, of course, be simply – a politician. *The Times*, on 3 May 1961, reported Senator S Nadesan, a prominent Tamil leader, as saying: 'that the true solution to the problem facing Ceylon could not be found by a resort to armed force. There had to be a political solution to the language problem if Ceylon was to go forward.'

Mrs Kumaratunga, Mrs Bandaranaike's daughter and president of Sri Lanka for twelve years, agreed that only a political solution would work. When she came to office in 1994 she promised to bring peace to the island. Ten years on, she can claim a partial success in that a ceasefire has lasted two and a half years. But many commentators credit Mr Wickramasinghe, the prime minister at that time, for his achievements in setting the peace process in motion. He was not honoured by his country for his achievement; instead, Mrs Kumaratunga took away some of the portfolios from his ministerial colleagues and then dissolved Parliament, claiming that he was giving too much away to rebel forces. So her speech to the fifty-ninth United Nations General Assembly Sessions at the UN Headquarters in New York on 21 September 2004 (ColomboPage.com of Wednesday, 22 September 2004), where she argued a case for negotiated settlements to internal and international conflicts, did not ring true to many people. She was experiencing selective recall, as she did when she appeared on the BBC programme *Breakfast with Frost* some years ago and failed to mention then that the current conflict originated during her father's and her mother's periods in office as prime minister.

The Tamil National Alliance (TNA) responded to her speech by saying that the 'speech at the United Nations General Assembly does not reflect [the] true factual position'.[84] They pointed out that 'hundreds of thousands of displaced Tamil people in the north-east yet continue to languish away from their homes'. They are indicating that the peace is not 'a done deal' until normalcy returns to the affected areas and the Tamils can again exercise the same levels of autonomy as their Sinhalese neighbours. It seems that since the elections in April 2004 she has not restarted the peace talks. As the TNA points out:

> We urge the President to refrain from rhetorical statements and focus on resolute action that would enable the recommencement of talks and meaningful consensus building that would ensure the success of the negotiation.

Even now, there is a suspicion that the talks have been delayed because the Sri Lankan government is colluding with the breakaway group of Tamils based in Batticaloa, in the hope that with their help the government will be able to crush the Tamil Tigers. The question is, would any government negotiate with the LTTE if it could crush the Tamil Tigers and subjugate the Tamil

[84] ColomboPage.com, 24 September 2004.

people? Probably not. Faced with the reality that the Tigers were able to survive despite the efforts of the Indian peacekeeping force, which towards the end of their period in the island numbered between 60,000 and 80,000 troops, the Sri Lankan government really does have no choice but to talk and to eventually arrive at a compromise solution. But the Sinhalese chauvinists on whose vote presidents and prime ministers depend will obstruct the government at every turn.

There is another aspect to resolving the mood of militancy. The government of Sri Lanka, whatever its complexion, must attack the system that creates the undesired social situation. If it only focuses on the perpetrators rather than controlling them and simultaneously uprooting the underlying causes, the weeds of militancy will resurface with greater virulence. So antisocial acts must be treated as systemic failures, and the solutions aimed at modifying the system, because the system usually shapes the belligerents. In Sri Lanka, the majority of the electorate, including the opinion formers, do not understand this distinction. So when Sinhalese Buddhist youth protested at the lack of opportunity in a declining economy and revolted, the first response of those in power was to attempt to subjugate them, not to attack the causes of their belligerence by righting the economy.

When that approach failed, the governments led by Mr Jayawardene and Mrs Kumaratunga bought peace by offering the leaders of the disgruntled youth new lives as political leaders. However, when Tamil Hindu youth protest at the lack of opportunity in a declining economy made worse by discriminatory legislation, the government does not act to ease their burden. It vilifies them and their leaders.

When Tamil militant groups carried out bank robberies and killed police officers in the formative year of the LTTE in the 1970s, the problem could have been controlled using normal security measures and the intervention of Tamil politicians who had the ear of the LTTE hierarchy. But the government's hard-line response convinced the LTTE that they lacked champions in the legitimate peaceful mainstream. So the Tamil youth joined a freedom movement that offered to get them out of the hole of despair, even when the price of joining was to voluntarily give their life. This immensely valuable, once only resource is, as the rebels see it, sacrificed at the altar of governmental intransigence. And the fight will go on unless the underlying causes of a lack of jobs and careers are corrected by revitalising the economy. Then people with something to lose will not engage in destructive behaviour. Support for this solution comes from Hague and Harrop, who say:

> A long research tradition claims that economic well-being is the key to democratic consolidation. In *Political Man* (1983, first pub. 1960), Lipset famously concluded that 'the more well-to-do a nation, the greater the chances that it will sustain democracy'. He showed that stable democracies scored highest on such measures as income per person, literacy and the proportion of the population

> living in cities. Following Aristotle, Lipset believed that a large middle class opposed to extremism was conducive to democracy.

Correcting the political and social systems that keep the rural population in poverty will cure many ills. Helping them to acquire the knowledge and savvy to educate and work their way out of their 'rural traps' would complete the process. But should peace come before prosperity or will prosperity banish belligerence?

In the meantime, the reality is that the country Mrs Kumaratunga has ruled as executive president for twelve years, a country she promised to bring peace to, continues to suffer the ravages and uncertainties of war. And although there is a ceasefire, there is no immediate prospect of a permanent peace. But the opportunity for peace is still alive and must be nurtured into being.

So there is a challenge for the government of Sri Lanka, but it is also a challenge for every democracy. It must adopt a proactive and constructive policy of listening and responding constructively to the voices of dissent if a hard won future peace is to result in sustained stability. All democracies must create safety valves through which the minority communities in their midst can release their frustrations and invoke the magnanimity and tolerance of the moderate majority. It is only then that the moderate majority can act to ameliorate the dissonance in their societies without incurring the wrath of the more militant majority. In Sri Lanka, the moderating voices of the majority Sinhalese and the Buddhist sangha must be encouraged to preach tolerance and inclusivity so that peace and harmony will bring prosperity. It is only the Buddhist sangha that can highlight the bankruptcy of the politics of past years and reroute the politicians along a peaceful and prosperous path. Until they do, the slow diffusion of discontent by the many will continue to be gathered, harnessed and activated by the few. The overflowing resentment will explode over and over again and the venom will remain to recycle and poison the body politic. It will progress from anger through a sense of injustice to hate, intolerance, disharmony, riots and eventually civil war. Along the way it will encrust and soundproof each new generation with an impenetrable barrier of bigotry.

The result of the last thirty or more years of fighting is that the people have, at best, only lived a half-life in a country that promised an abundance of riches. Thus were the people of Sri Lanka banished from Eden, for eating of the forbidden fruit of religious and racial bigotry.

Chapter 27

The Buddhist Monk as Racist Politician

By attempting to make their religion the foundation of the secular state, the Buddhist clergy converted a sacred objective into a political one and handed control to a small group of self-serving monks and lay activists (see box below) who, to satisfy their greed for worldly power, wealth and status, distorted its message. That this has happened is evident to impartial observers. The sad fact is that their continued influence and growing wealth are witness to the fact that they have fallen from the high standards expected of them. By their continued insistence on the primacy of Buddhism and Sinhalese and their unwillingness to share the island with those of other faiths, they deny the teachings of the Buddha. By using their power to influence votes, a small minority of the Buddhist clergy have involved themselves in politics and claimed and exercised the role of kingmakers under the pretext that in so doing they are acting to preserve Buddhism. Were the Buddha to come among them now he would be ashamed and disgusted by their behaviour and their lust for power and wealth. And he would point out to them that the blood of the innocent and the belligerent on all sides is on their hands and still staining them. It is time for the Buddhist establishment to cleanse itself, and, failing that, for the political establishment to cleanse it – as the Sinhalese kings did in past times.

> *Monks Influence Lankan Politics*
>
> 'Sri Lanka … is emerging as a hotbed of Marxist monks. Hundreds of monks walk behind huge cut-outs of Marx and Lenin during JVP May Day rallies. A state campaign for a mass ordination of 1,000 monks four years ago was cancelled after a poor response. Saffron-robed monks lead political demonstrations … even though the Buddhist majority nation faces a severe shortage of clergymen for theological work. All mainstream Sinhalese-majority political groups have a band of monks loyal to them. The world's first all-clergy party of Buddhist monks, the JHU or the National Heritage Party, won nine seats in the Sri Lankan Parliament at elections last year. The entry of monks into politics has sparked a public debate but the legislator monks use theology and history to justify shift from the pulpit to politics. However, there is no religious conflict in the country where Hindus consider Buddha to be one of their gods. National leaders pay obeisance to the Buddhist hierarchy before launching any new venture and even diplomats posted to Sri Lanka call on Buddhist monks after presenting their credentials to the president.
>
> (Amal Jayasinghe, DAWN International, June 10 2004)

But are the politicians or the Chief Priests big enough to take on this role? The acid test must be how the Buddhist community on the island would answer the Buddha, were he to come among them now. How would they answer if he asked them why they made his teaching a racist tool? How would they answer the charge that they have denied those of other faiths their right to coexist on the island? What would he say to those among his monks who lust for power and wealth? How would they answer if he asked them why their hands were red with the blood of the innocent? What would they say if he asked them why they did not stop the bloodshed and return peace to his island? How would they answer if he asked them why they had spent the last fifty years working hard to win him a kingdom when he had abandoned the one he had? What answer would they give if he accused them of converting a sacred objective into a political one? How would they answer if he asked them why they were dabbling in politics and why they used his teachings to take control of a secular state? What answer would they give if he asked them why they had handed control to a small group of self-serving monks and lay activists whose prime purpose was to satisfy their greed for worldly power, wealth and status and were willing to distort his message to achieve their worldly ends?

They could not deny any of these charges, as it is evident to impartial observers that this has happened. The sad fact is that their continued influence and growing wealth are witness to the fact that they have fallen from the high standards expected of them. All those who have knowledge of Buddha's teachings will be able to take a very good guess at the answers he would give and the opinion he would have of the people who took and continue to take his name in vain.

It would seem that a philosophy of peace and goodwill, of self-abnegation, modesty, poverty, chastity, charity and good intentions has been turned into a political weapon and as such has instigated genocide, hatred, greed, envy, malice, and destruction on the island these last fifty years. Change can only come about if the Buddhist establishment redefines it objectives in the light of recent constitutional changes that have made Sinhalese and Buddhism the language and religion of the state. They must now play the role of peacemakers. They must take on the role of being the custodians of democracy not its abusers. They must be the scourge of those who preach and practice racial and religious bigotry. And through the balm of their influence, sacrifice, and benignity they must heal the nation's wounds. That is the new role that the Buddhist establishment must arrogate unto itself. The responsibility and obligation to cleanse its stables; wash its hands of the blood of the innocent, and to return the country to a place of Buddhist tranquillity must lie with the Buddhist clergy. They must not fail the people but their behaviour to date does not hold out too much hope.

As we have seen in previous chapters the Sinhalese kings sponsored Buddhism and the Buddhist establishment by providing *Viharas* (Buddhist monastery complex) with lands to ensure that they had an independent source of income to support the work of the priests who resided within them. We also saw that, from time to time, they had to intervene to renew Buddhism on the island and to ensure that the Buddhist hierarchy kept to the teachings of the Buddha and did not abuse their privileges such as the use of revenues from temple lands for personal purposes. The British governors too had to intervene in this way. In 1853 the government attempted to disentangle itself from Buddhism by setting up independent organisations whereby village dignitaries could appoint chief priests to administer property. But this arrangement did not work too satisfactorily. As owners of temple property these chiefs could use its revenues and assets as they wished with little or no interference from the laity or other clergy. The result was that some chief priests abused their trust. The problem resurfaced in 1876 and a commission was appointed to look into the way the chief priests administered the *Viharas*. The commission reported that it found widespread misappropriation of temple revenues, corruption and fraud. The proposal to vest management of the *Viharas* in a government appointed supervisory commission was rejected by the Secretary of State. Another attempt was made to prevent chief priests from abusing temple property in 1886 but this attempt also failed. It is not clear that the situation is any better today.

The Buddhist clergy enjoy special privileges and considerable freedom in the way they run their affairs. By all accounts they have long since abandoned the mendicants bowl. As indeed a new breed of fundamentalist Buddhist priests and laity have abandoned peace and tolerance too. It seems that these politicised priests and their followers are bent on cleansing the country of non-Buddhist Sinhalese. Their political arm, the JHU, is creating a mood of intolerance towards Christians and the Christian community on the island is being persecuted. There is a move to amend the constitution to ban conversion of Buddhists to other religions – particularly Christianity. The National Christian Evangelical Alliance of Sri Lanka reports that, in the last two years, there have been one hundred and forty-six acts of violence against Christians – churches have been burnt to the ground and pastors and followers persecuted.[85] This is all very reminiscent of the way the persecution of the Tamils began in 1958 and we know where that led.

[85] www.cswuna.com, 14 May 2006.

Chapter 28

Communal Violence and Intimidation

Communal violence and intimidation of the Tamils in Sri Lanka began in 1956. The first incident related to racial issues was the Satyagraha staged by the Tamil Members of Parliament following the introduction in Parliament of the Official Language Bill on 5 June 1956. The Federal Party had written to the Prime Minister, Mr Bandaranaike, warning him that they had planned a peaceful protest against the Bill on the steps of the House of Representatives. The Prime Minster replied that such a demonstration (albeit peaceful) in the premises of the House would cause 'a breach of the peace'. To stay within the law, the federal party changed the venue to the open area known as Galle Face Green immediately outside and opposite the House of Representatives.

On the orders of the Prime Minister and the Speaker, police surrounded Parliament, but none were deployed to protect the Tamil Members of Parliament and the group of protesters involved in the Satyagraha. The peaceful protest was turned into a violent event when a mob comprising mainly of workers from the docks nearby and hooligans beat up the Tamil MPs. It was alleged that the mob was encouraged and even led by Leftist elements who were part of the coalition that made up Mr Bandaranaike's government. After beating up the Tamil MPs, the mob looted the shops of Tamils in the nearby commercial district known as the Pettah the constituency of Mr Keuneman. When a Tamil Member of Parliament, Mr Vanniasingham of the Federal Party, walked into the Chamber of the House of Parliament with his head bandaged following the beating he received at the hands of the mob the Prime Minister, Mr Bandaranaike greeted him with the words, 'Honourable wounds of war', a parody on 'Honourable Member of Parliament'. His remark reflected his cynical disregard for the safety of the Tamil MPs. The debate in Parliament that followed the incident further underlined the point that Mr Bandaranaike had not taken any steps to protect the Tamil MPs and seemed unwilling to acknowledge a failure of law and order. He seemed also to have treated the incident more like a 'schoolboy prank' than a serious breach of the peace and a precedent for future similar actions. (See box for extract from the Hansard of that time.) Time would show that it was the beginning of the rule by racists.

Extract from Hansard[86]

MR KEUNEMAN: Now, Mr Speaker, the real crux of the matter is to find out from the Hon. Prime Minister what exactly he is doing or intends doing apart from the general assurance that he has given that he will handle the situation. May I say that this is necessary because today what is uppermost in the minds of a large number of Tamil-speaking people in the City of Colombo and particularly those who have been subjected to this reign of terror in the Pettah is that they can expect no protection from the government? Many of them think that the government is not prepared to lift a finger when this sort of thing is happening to them. That is indeed a sorry state of affairs. I am not accusing the government of adopting such an attitude. But it is a very sorry state of affairs that this feeling is widespread... Is it correct that the general orders given to the police were that if anybody is assaulted they should try to stop it but not apprehend the aggressors in case it might instigate the crowds to further riots?

THE HON. S W R D BANDARANAIKE: Certainly not.

DR COLVIN R DE SILVA: I do not think it is proper to read the newspapers during such an important discussion as this. [Dr De Silva had raised a point of order that the PM was reading a paper]

THE HON. S W R D BANDARANAIKE: Oh! Shut up.

MR KEUNEMAN: Today when I met a number of these people [those beaten by the rioters] from the affected areas they all had one complaint. I shall quote the words of one person. "These people attack us; the police come and tell them not to do so, to stop doing so; but when they continue to do so, the police stand back and look on." I want to ask whether the police are merely expected to do some general propaganda about the undesirability of looting and beating up people who happen to speak a different language or belong to a different race. Surely, one has a right to ask the Prime Minister this specific question?

[The general tone of the whole debate suggests that Prime Minister Bandaranaike was irritated by the situation and by the fact that he was being asked to explain why nothing was being done to stop the rioting and looting and to arrest those involved particularly as the criminals were easily identifiable. Those familiar with the behaviour of the police in later years know that in the 1980s onwards the police were willing participants in the rioting and looting of Tamil shop and homes.]

---

[86] Hansard, p.863–864.

This was followed in December 1956 by an act of provocation designed to bait the Tamils into acting rashly. The government introduced a new number plate system for cars and other motorised vehicles. The old system had used various combinations of the name Ceylon, by which the island was known during British times, as alphabetic prefixes to the number. CE was followed by CY, CL, CN, EY, EL, and EN. Following that pattern the government decided to use Sri (from Sri Lanka) as the prefix. The Tamil politicians protested by claiming that *Sri* was a sacred word to the Hindus and should not be carried on the number plate of motor vehicles. A little give and take on both sides could have established a precedent of future goodwill. Instead, the Sinhalese welcomed this move and the former prime minister, Sir John Kotelawala, used his influence to ensure that he was the first person to use the new numbering system when he registered his new Cadillac under this scheme. It was a test of good faith among the two ethnic groups and a statement of future intent and they all failed at the first hurdle. The issue was considered too trivial to warrant any real support and the Tamil leaders lost credibility. As time would show, the Tamil leaders' tactics of picking a quarrel over every issue rather than those with true moral content weakened their ability to gain effective support.

In 1958 Sinhalese mobs burnt and looted the shops and homes of Tamils living in Colombo.[87] Mr Vittachi's vivid and honest account records the extent of the carnage and damage done to property and the relationships between races during those few horrendous days. The riots were organised and executed by thugs in the pay of vested interests. It is they who lit the fuse and let the fires of hatred and intolerance rage. Again, the government of Mr Bandaranaike stood by and watched this happen and did little or nothing to stop it. His inaction was either due to incompetence, callousness or because he was happy to allow the rioters to do their worst. His actions seemed almost as if he, again, did not have any part to play in maintaining law and order in the country. It demonstrated a strange detachment, as if he felt he was too much of a gentleman to dirty his hands by intervening in a bloody brawl. Ludowyk say of the riots of 1958:

> Communal violence began on Thursday, May 22nd … when the racialists were convinced that the police were powerless to take action against supporters of the government. All over the Southern, Western, and North Central provinces there were lootings, burnings and savagery on such a scale as had not been known before … the Governor General took over. He administered the country, while the military maintained order. That he had taken over … was clear only to those who at a time of press censorship knew what was happening in the country.

Both UNP and SLFP governments are guilty, not only of condoning such

[87] Tarzie Vittachi, *Emergency '58: The Story Of The Ceylon Race Riots*, Andre Deutsch 1958.

'spontaneous' occurrences but also of creating groups to supplement the work done by the security services and then allowing them to go on rampages. Various governments consistently ignored or justified blatant acts of revenge by the security services when they acted more like vigilantes than disciplined soldiers. The Government also failed to act when the organisers of riots distributed electoral registers so that Tamil homes could be identified and burned or looted.

There are many more such events. One mentioned by Bush was of 'a group of 100–200 policemen who went on a rampage in Jaffna town.' But the real issue here was that:

> Present in Jaffna throughout the police rampage were the Minister of Lands and Land Development, Gamani Dissanayake, and the Minister of Industries, Cyril Matthew, perhaps the most virulent anti-Tamil Sinhalese chauvinist in the UNP government. The presence of these two Ministers, in addition to a Brigadier General and the Inspector General of Police, and the flooding of Jaffna with an externally recruited police force only days before the rampage, led many observers to conclude that the attack was organized and planned in advance. The fact that not a single suspect was charged ... suggests either state complicity or the abrogation of state responsibility for security and the rule of law in the North.

He does make the point that even when the perpetrators were known to the security forces no action was taken by the government to arrest and punish them.

There are instances where political prisoners awaiting trial have been summarily executed by a mob of fellow prisoners. There were two such occurrences that received publicity. The first was on 25 July when thirty-five Tamil detainees were killed. The second was on the 27th after the President had given instructions to prevent any recurrence. Undoubtedly, the prison officials and the security service chose not to obey the President's instructions or believed that he did not mean what he had said i.e. that it was window dressing for the world's consumption but not directed specifically at them. A Commission of Inquiry was appointed but according to very well informed sources in the prison service 'it fizzled out due to non-prosecution'. It would seem that the prison officials and the soldiers were not held to account for complicity in the killing or for disobeying the direct orders of the President. Neither is there any reference to the punishment the prisoners were given for this horrendous act. The tendency of the government has been to punish those who put their heads above the parapet to denounce and identify the perpetrators.

But of all the issues that this behaviour of the government raises, the most horrendous is the one that justified imitative behaviour by the LTTE and the Sinhalese insurgents. Each side created more abominable atrocities in an attempt to outdo each other. In the end, the young followed the terrible example that the government and their mentors perpetrated on each other. The massive destruction of lives, livelihoods and property, the human misery and the destruction of communities and peaceful neighbourhoods was utterly meaningless and achieved nothing of any value. But it did give the bloodthirsty and the criminal an excuse to go on the rampage. And the forces of law and order joined in the orgy of bloodletting. If any of the armed forces of any Western government had acted in the way the Government and the security services in Sri Lanka have over the last half-century they would have been condemned and had to account to the world's press and governments. The Sri Lankan government seems to have continued to get aid and foreign loans and a sympathetic ear whilst these acts of common criminality were done and condoned by it.

The US Department of State website points out that despite the peace process that is stumbling along, there are human rights issues that need to be addressed. It points out that the 'National Human Rights Commission [which the US government funds] has more than 2,500 cases of alleged abuses pending.' It also points other shortcomings in the government's approach to ensuring human rights in the country. For example it says that:

> [The] Government's arbitrary arrest of citizens under the Prevention of Terrorism Act (PTA) has been a serious human rights problem. Although the PTA is no longer used to detain new suspects, 65 Tamils remain in jail on PTA charges.

Bush gives us a measure of the scale and arbitrariness in his book:

> The wide-ranging emergency regulations facilitate systematic human rights abuses by state actors. State authorities were permitted the following: arrest without warrant; incommunicado detention; the taking of persons 'to any place' for interrogation; the restriction of an individual's movements and activities; detention without trial for up to 18 months in any place, under any conditions ... security force disposal of corpses without inquest or post-mortem; and seizure of property and vehicles. Thousands of Tamils were rounded up and brutally interrogated.

Tim Sebastian taxed Mrs Kumaratunga about human rights abuses in Sri Lanka perpetrated by the police and army personnel when he interviewed her in October 2001. An extract from the interview appeared at the end of the last chapter. It needs no explanation except to say that her predecessors in government were probably twice as culpable.

By allowing racial hatred to take root, the ruling clique was able to keep power. It diverted attention from the real issues. It gave them an excuse to use emergency powers to silence dissent and criticism and to subvert the rule of law. The problem was that a small group of influential racist extremists created vigilante groups who planned and executed the most horrendous crimes, claiming that they were doing it for Buddhism and the Sinhalese cause. Those Buddhist nationalists who felt strongly about the resurgence of Buddhism and Sinhalese and argued most vehemently for action to be taken to resurrect what was left of their culture and civilisation; were compromised by the racists even though they were not racially motivated and did not condone the racists' actions.

By cleverly entwining racism with the Buddhist nationalist cause they bought immunity and put those who objected rather than themselves on the defensive and in the wrong. They should have been stopped immediately and the plotters and their operatives brought to justice. But they were not. Instead, the ruling clique turned a blind eye to their activities and often benefited from the actions of this pernicious and violent group. Besides some of the ringleaders were their friends. So they were allowed free rein.

Tim Sebastian, in a BBC *Hardtalk* interview with Mrs Kumaratunga, refers to this and Bush, drawing on the documented research of many Sri Lankan and foreign authors, provides ample evidence that at various times during the last fifty years the governments of Sri Lanka were responsible for or condoned organised violence by vigilante groups. So successfully has the racist element camouflaged its activities that it is the Buddhist nationalist movement that has carried the racist tag for so long. This does not exonerate the Buddhist nationalists because they, like the majority community and the ruling clique, have condoned the activities of the racists. However, the failure to maintain a united country rests not with the pressure groups, but with the politicians who allied themselves with the racists to keep power.

Chapter 29

The Government at War with Sinhalese Youth

Well-meaning Sri Lankan politicians of the 1950s and 1960s believed in the socialist theory of the redistribution of wealth and adopted policies that would make redistribution a reality, only to find that it failed those they most wanted to help: the poor. Sadly, the poor did not know how to use their windfall to increase their meagre wealth. If they knew how to use money they would not be poor. Whatever they got they spent rather than nurtured.

Wealth redistribution by politicians makes people believe that money grows on trees and all they have to do is get the politicians to pluck and distribute it to them. So the more handouts they get, the more they expect and extort through the clever use of their voting rights. Eventually, such policies end up creating a dependency culture, in which more and more people find it more expedient to queue for benefits than to work for a living. It also makes those who work for a living and pay taxes wonder why they bother at all, if their hard earned but meagre income is used to maintain the feckless. Those who end up paying the most are the wage earners, whose income is taxed at source and have little opportunity to plan their income so that they can avoid punitive taxes. They also have the least influence over what politicians do once they take office. The net result of this policy of 'tax and spend' usually is that it impoverishes everyone, although if those things on which it is supposed to be spent – such as education, medical care, infrastructure or security – do materialise, it would help the wage-earner most. Unfortunately, incompetence and dishonesty combine to ensure that the promised benefits do not materialise and the wage earner loses out most. The worst affected are their children whose futures are impoverished. It was this cycle that was unleashed in Sri Lanka in the 1950s and 1960s.

Sri Lankan society recognises a power hierarchy. It still expects respect for elders and authority. In traditional Buddhist homes, it is not unusual for children to kneel and touch their parents' feet before they leave the house for the day. Ordinary villagers will be deferential to the leaders of their community and to people of rank, to an extent that people in more egalitarian societies would find hard to understand. Some of this deference may have eroded because of the social influence of foreign films showing more egalitarian lifestyles, but at heart the power hierarchy still functions. Where these power distance differences are high, it takes considerable courage or anger to express disagreement. So the young who want their grievances heard and resolved will tolerate any injustice they feel until their frustrations rise to a climax of dismay and erupt into violence. It is only in such a state of dismay that the young may find the courage to make their feelings known. By then it is too late. The cauldron of hate boils over, and the powerless find power through anger and the expression of anger. And, having discovered its potency, they adopt it as a means to an end, and then are adopted by it to the extent that acting in anger becomes the norm.

The Sinhalese youth have every reason to be angry. However benevolent and well meaning the economic policies of the governments led by Mr and Mrs Bandaranaike during an initial ten-year period from 1956 to 1965 and again from 1970 to about 1977 they hurt those they intended to help most – the rural poor. The rural poor also had to contend with the partially corrupt and managerially incompetent political elite who systematically robbed those whose cause they were championing. By nationalising and constraining foreign businesses, Mrs Bandaranaike struck, she thought, a deep blow to the colonial powers; but she hurt the island's economy instead. Their Sri Lankan holdings, although material in the context of the island's economy, were irrelevant in the context of their global businesses. By redistributing the large land-holdings of rich families, she thought she was helping the rural poor to become self-sufficient. But the outcome was the creation of huge swathes of unproductive land. By introducing crippling taxation, she fed the bloodlust of the envious but gathered money that was poorly used, because it ended up subsidising once profitable and self-sufficient businesses now in state hands, and not infrastructure, where it would have done the most good. Exchange control policies throttled businesses that depended on imports and ensured that foreign earnings were kept abroad. At the same time a black market in foreign currency was created which damaged the economy even more. It pleased the ideologues that everyone's life was being made miserable and ordinarily, honest people were being forced to act dishonestly. Most of these rules and constraints did not apply to government ministers, their relatives and friends; but the rest paid heavily for these bankrupting policies, as they got poorer by the minute.

Unfortunately, the ministers were completely ignorant of the resentment they were creating among the rural poor, or if they knew, they chose to ignore it. What interested them most was that, once nationalised, these well-paid and highly desired jobs in the private sector came under their control and could be handed out to their relatives and friends and the clerical jobs to their constituents.

Thus the democratic political process was used by governments to provide 'jobs for the boys' and secure their votes. Overmanned organisations ground to a halt as employees tripped over themselves in an effort to make work. They buried themselves in the tar of bureaucracy. Everyone became a queen bee and there were no worker bees to bring honey to the hive.

The worst effect of these policies was that they damaged the competitiveness of the island. No attempt was made to find ways of increasing the revenues of the country so that the ever-increasing population could be fed and offered careers and futures. The *Hindustan Times* website of 13 December 2004 makes the point that Sri Lanka, unlike India, has taken no steps towards industrialisation. It says:

> So far, successive governments in Colombo have not only chosen to take the easy option of importing the country's needs, but have been under the influence of an entrenched import lobby – a comprador class as it were.

What is rather interesting is that it goes on to say:

> Industrialization got no encouragement in the island throughout the Colonial period. But immediately after independence in the early 1950s a cement factory was started in Kankesanthurai on the northern Jaffna coast and a chemical factory in Paranthan in the southern part of the Tamil-speaking northern peninsula. These ventures were the brainchild of the famous Tamil politician, G G Ponnambalam of the All Ceylon Tamil Congress.

The ethnic disagreements stifled Tamil enterprise and diverted it into creating, funding and maintaining a military capability that has tested the will of both Sri Lankan and Indian armies.

Similarly, the ability of the rural Sinhalese youth had also been diverted into insurrection. By a strange quirk of fate, the island now had youths of all ethnic groups who saw only the same bleak future ahead of them. Trapped in this common predicament, the Sinhalese Buddhist youth and the Tamil Hindu youth came together to help each other against a common enemy – a government of the few, for the few. The JVP, whilst it was still an insurrection movement, made up as it was of disaffected Sinhalese youth, argued in favour of the plantation Tamils and their Jaffna compatriots. However, now that the JVP has been absorbed into the mainstream they have taken on the rhetoric of all the mainstream Sinhalese Buddhist parties.

Those who suffered most were not the English- or Sinhalese-educated politicians living in their comfortable homes in Colombo, or their children, who continued to be English-educated, but the children of the rural poor. They, the Sinhalese-educated majority, were unable to learn or develop any skills that labour markets in Sri Lanka or overseas valued. Their years of learning took them to a literal and actual dead end. The result was that poverty stared them in the face and they had nowhere to go. The promised future dripping with nectar failed to materialise and they felt cheated. Bored, frustrated, and fed up with the empty promises they had been fed by their self-seeking elders, they built a movement to challenge the state and usurp its power. Huntington, in *The Clash of Civilizations,* says:

> In Sri Lanka, Gary Fuller has shown, the peaking of the Sinhalese nationalist insurgency in 1970 and of the Tamil insurgency in the late 1980s coincided

> exactly with the years when the fifteen-to-twenty-four-year-old 'youth bulge' in those groups exceeded 20 per cent of the total population of the group.[88]

This was the context in which the JVP insurrection needed to be viewed.

The first insurrection of the JVP found its voice in the late 1960s when it attracted predominantly young unemployed and disaffected Low-Country Sinhalese Buddhist youth. In 1971 they acted to unseat the government of the day by force. They had the backing of the younger elements of the Buddhist establishment and therefore had political clout. When the fighting, the carnage and the atrocities stopped, and the leaders had served a respectable period in jail for their insolence, the majority political parties treated them as 'one of us' and absorbed them into the mainstream of Sri Lankan politics. The website of the People's Liberation Front (JVP) says of the 1971 insurgency:

> Janatha Vimukthi Peramuna (JVP) of Sri Lanka was founded on the 14th of May 1965. The 1971 April up-rising took place as an exercise of self-defense [sic] during the continuous capitalist state suppression in which nearly 10,000 members of the movement were slaughtered and about 20,000 members were held in detention in prisons.[89]

The JVP insurrections of 1971 should have alerted the complacent politicians to the reality of how bankrupt their language and economic policies were, but it did not. They ignored what was obvious: the Sinhala Only Act was producing young people whose literacy was limited to a language that had no market value. The best jobs – most jobs – still went to those who were able to speak, read and write English with some fluency, because that was what the commercial, professional and scientific world spoke. The JVP uprising was ruthlessly suppressed and large numbers of its members were indefinitely incarcerated under powers granted the government by the emergency regulations. But the underlying causes of a lack of careers and financial deprivation brought about by a failing economy were not corrected.

The JVP had caused severe problems for the Sinhalese Buddhist community but succeeding governments forgave them, thus condoning their brutality and lawlessness. The UNP government led by Mr Jayawardene released their members, apparently because the emergency powers had lapsed. In reality it was probably a wish to defuse the JVP and bring it into the mainstream political process to prevent it from undertaking future acts of terror. Its leader, Wijeweera, contested the presidential elections of 1982 and came third, albeit with 4.19 per cent of the votes. (The UNP got 52.91 per cent, the SLFP 39.07 per cent and the balance was spread among a few other

---

[88] S. Huntington, *The Clash of Civilizations and the Remaking of World Order*, Simon & Schuster, 1996. Gary Fuller's findings are entitled 'The Demographic Backdrop to Ethnic Conflict: A Geographic Overview' in CIA RTT 95-10039, October 1995. As quoted earlier in 1969 the figure was 45 per cent in Sri Lanka.

[89] 'About us', The People's Liberation Front, http://www.jvpsrilanka.com.

parties.) The honeymoon did not last. The UNP government proscribed the JVP after the 1983 riots on the dubious pretext that the party was behind it, driving the movement underground where it simmered and fermented to resurface with heightened virulence in 1987. This second insurrection, although under new leadership, followed the same cycle of disaffection, indiscriminate violence and terrorism, stalemate, rapprochement and absorption.

The catalyst, this time, was the Indo-Sri Lanka peacekeeping pact signed by Mr Jayawardene in such haste and secrecy that it pre-empted any debate or dissent. This time, government forces and JVP followers exceeded every imaginable level of atrocity until the movement was crushed, and its leaders summarily executed by agents of the state.

The Sri Lankan Army had always been ambivalent about controlling the JVP. In a sense, they were 'brothers' because the Sri Lankan Army, except for the officers, was manned exclusively by rural Sinhalese youth. But the JVP made the mistake of threatening the families of members of the armed forces and increased the intensity of the determination of the army to rid the country of them. The cost in innocent lives was horrendous but the objective was gained. To quote Bush:

> From 1987 to early 1990, the Sinhalese south of the island was paralysed politically, socially and economically by the seemingly limitless levels of brutality and violence committed by security forces and the JVP. No one was immune; children, the elderly, women and monks were all victims ... legitimate targets later expanded to include 'social deviants' such as illicit alcohol sellers, alcoholics, and husbands who beat their wives.

Today a revived and revitalised JVP is thriving. It shares power with the ruling party, and became a fully integrated force of the political system. For the second time, the JVP was admitted into the fold. The same JVP website says:

> After having discussions for more than 10 months the PA [Peoples Alliance] and the JVP formed the United Peoples Freedom Alliance (UPFA) in January 2004. Having won the election held on 2nd April 2004 the UPFA formed the government. The JVP won 39 seats in the Parliament. The JVP won 80 seats at the Provincial Councils Elections held in 2004. The JVP for the first time in its history is now a partner of the Sri Lankan Government.

But the economy is still failing and the lack of opportunity is building a new group of disaffected youth who will rise up in its stead and repeat the cycle of violence. Already the drums of chauvinism are beating. Nanda Wickramasinghe in the World Socialist Web Site of 15 October 2004 points out the fact that a group called the North East Sinhala Organisation (NESO) is beginning to flex its muscles. The NESO, according to Wickramasinghe:

> ...was established in 1996 amid the country's bitter war and draws its support from layers of Sinhalese businessmen, government officials, the military and Buddhist clergy. [90]

The party has filled the space vacated by the JVP when it succumbed to the bribery of office. The JVP, fearing that it will lose its constituency and its potency is therefore showing signs of belligerence. Wickramasinghe says:

> The JVP has been caught in a bind. It is in office for the first time but faces the prospect of being outflanked by other Sinhala extremist organisations. The JVP's leaders have threatened to leave the UPFA [United People's Freedom Alliance] and bring down the government if Kumaratunga agrees to the LTTE's demand to negotiate on the ISGA [Interim Self-Governing Administration].

The most worrying comments in her report are:

> The communal politics of the ruling elites – Tamil, Sinhala and Muslim – has already turned the eastern province into a political powder keg. The NESO campaign comes on top of protests by Muslim organisations opposed to the LTTE...

It appears that the issues still remain. A new chauvinist force has arisen to take the place of the JVP and the cycle of despair will, it seems, be re-enacted by every generation that follows this one.

The issues that caused disaffection among the Tamil minority, however, remain and now absorb the attention and sparse economic resources of the country. Until this is resolved the country will be unable to bury its past and find its future.

The Tamils have claimed the north and east of the island as their own. They see it as their plot of land over which they have sovereignty and on which they wish to build their lives, bring up families, combine in communities and grow into a nation that offers them and their descendants the opportunity that others have and enjoy. It is not an unreasonable request and is a mirror image of similar requests elsewhere in the world. Surely a compromise can be found?

[90] Nanda Wickramasinghe 'Communal protests inflame tensions in eastern Sri Lanka', World Socialist Web Site, 15 October 2004.

Chapter 30

A Government at War with the Tamils

The Official Language Bill of 5 June 1956 set in motion a train of events that would irreparably divide the nation. A consequence of the Act was that children were taught all subjects in their mother tongue, except those that could only be taught in English. This meant that children in mixed community areas, who up until then had studied in classes made up of a mix of children of different ethnicities, were segregated into Tamil and Sinhalese medium classes. Muslim children could choose to study in either the Sinhalese or Tamil stream; Burgher children had a difficult choice to make as their mother tongue was English but there were not enough of them to warrant providing an English stream for them – consequently, many chose Sinhalese. Suddenly the Ceylonese had divided into Tamils and Sinhalese and Muslims and Burghers, and this difference was being inculcated into them from their kindergarten years. Children who had spent their lunch interval playing in mixed groups now only played with their Sinhalese or Tamil classmates.

Sensing that they had no future in a Sinhalese Buddhist country, the vast majority of the Dutch Burgher population who could prove European antecedents left for Australia and Europe. All the others settled into the new routine until the communal riots of 1958 forced the Tamils to reappraise their position in the country.

Tamils living in Colombo and its environs were attacked by Sinhalese mobs. Some Sinhalese living in Tamil areas were also attacked. The cycle of retaliatory killing and looting became the normal response from then on.

The people had turned against each other and the tinder of racial disharmony had been lit. It was not until the governor general of the time, Sir Oliver Goonetilleke, declared a state of emergency and imposed martial law and gave the army orders to shoot looters on sight that the riots died down. But its scars were broad and deep. Tarzie Vittachi's book, *Emergency 58* records the horror of these times in chilling detail.

The immediate effect of the riots was that many Tamil families relocated to Jaffna. Overnight, the classrooms of the Tamil students in Colombo schools were bare, and remained that way. The fathers eventually drifted back to Colombo and their government jobs. But they lived in ghettoes for economic and security reasons. Besides, their days in government service were limited by the need for them to be fluent in Sinhalese. The very small number of racially minded Sinhalese realised that terror was working – the point that Dershowitz so eloquently makes in his book on terrorism.[91] But the point Ray and Schaap make in theirs is that the conditions for terrorist activity is often created by a flawed and partisan government and the government of Sri Lanka is a prime example. The decision of Prime Minister Bandaranaike to put divisive policies in place and, by his inaction and unwillingness to punish the leaders of the mobs, signal to the belligerent minority that it was 'OK' to bash the Tamils was unquestionably the key factor in all that followed. It was not as if a carelessly doused campfire had burnt down a whole forest. These riots were the result of malicious fundamentalists pouring kerosene on a flickering flame and fanning it into a forest fire. The vast majority of well-meaning and decent Sinhalese helped their Tamil neighbours and protected them when they could. But they kept public silence lest they be branded sympathisers and were beaten and robbed too. The situation had moved from racial enmity to state-sanctioned communal terrorism. These same scenes were repeated in the 1960s, in the 1970s and again in 1983, and added to the volume of youth with idle hands and resentful hearts.

Consequently, Tamil children were now marooned in Jaffna with only a future of poverty, ignorance and disenfranchisement. What followed was inevitable. They began to feel like refugees in the land of their birth and looked for a champion to lead them out of this impasse. Because successive governments had made sure that the legitimate Tamil political parties were marginalised or, worse still, ignored and humiliated, it enabled the belligerent Tamil minority to claim that political means were not working and that progress towards equality and fair treatment could only be won through the sword. The belligerent Sinhala majority did not anticipate that the Tamils would be able to finance and organise such a lethal weapon as the Tamil Tigers. It is also likely that the Tamils did not expect the fight to last as long as it did. The Tigers' military prowess was supplemented by the propaganda skills of the political arm of the liberation movement. And its ranks were swelled by young Tamils who had been denied a future and therefore had very little to lose by joining the militants.

The War for Liberation

A well-trained and armed Tamil army declared war on the Sri Lankan government in 1983 by killing thirteen soldiers. This act was of a different magnitude to the previous unrest. This action by the Tigers unleashed an orchestrated ethnic cleansing of the Tamils in Colombo and its periphery and sealed the conflict to come in the blood of both races. The Tigers rationalised their actions as an act of war on a trained and armed military force. The Sinhalese could not justify their actions except to claim that it was retribution for the lives of the thirteen soldiers. Thus legitimised, the Sinhalese thugs

[91] Alan M. Dershowitz, *Why Terrorism Works*, Yale University Press, 2002.

walked the streets of Colombo, using the electoral registers to identify Tamil homes and businesses and destroy them and the people in them.

On the face of it, it did not make sense for the Tamil Tigers to arouse Sinhalese anger, because the impact on the Tamils in the south was predictable. But, the Tamils in the north and east did not see the Tamils in the south as worthy of their protection. They considered the Tamils in the south as a separate group, like the Tamils living on the plantations. The Tamils in the south had integrated themselves into the Sinhalese societies in the south and were seen as traitors by the Tamils in the north and east. To the Tamil Tigers, they were as Sinhalese as the Sinhalese. Their view was that if the southern Tamils suffered pain at the hands of those they were cohabiting with, they had only themselves to blame.

The challenge posed by the Tamil youth in the north was of very different dimensions to that posed by the JVP. The Tamils wanted greater autonomy to minimise or eliminate the disadvantages of living in a country that increasingly favoured the Sinhalese majority. The Sinhalese, on the other hand, saw it as more than an issue of land. They saw it as a loss of sovereignty, security and safety. They may have been willing to lease the north and east to the Tamils but not hand over real control to them. So they acted to deny Tamil aspirations for a homeland. Since an amicable solution seems unlikely, both sides believed that only a military solution would break the impasse.

The Sri Lankan Security Forces were authorised to do whatever they deemed necessary to destroy the Tamil Tigers and seize control of territory that the Tigers claimed as theirs. In 1987 the Sri Lankan Army took on the Tamil Tigers and were close to annihilating them; but the Indian government, sensitive to the feelings of the 50 million Tamils in India's south, signalled that it would not tolerate genocide or ethnic cleansing of the Tamils in the north of Sri Lanka. This it did by airlifting food to the Tamils, and later, at the request of Mr Jayawardene, sending troops to oversee a ceasefire. But that backfired on them as the initial force of 6,000 soldiers built up to nearly 60,000 as they, in turn, found themselves at the receiving end of Tamil bullets. But during the fighting the Sri Lankan Security Forces had, in the view of some, used excessive force (see box at end of chapter).

The US Department of State website points out that:

> ...serious problems remained in some areas. These included torture of detainees by the military and police as well as the deaths and rapes of prisoners. Despite government investigations in some cases of past abuses, impunity remained a problem. Discrimination and violence against religious minorities increased, and discrimination against persons with disabilities as well as ethnic discrimination against Tamils persisted. Violence and discrimination against women, child prostitution and trafficking in women and children were also serious concerns.

The Tamil Tigers similarly believed that they, too, could do anything they pleased to repel the Sri Lankan Security Forces, and their actions, too, are singled out for censure by the US Department of State, which says that:

> The LTTE continued to commit serious human rights abuses including extra-judicial killings, disappearances, torture, arbitrary arrests, detentions, extortions and recruitment of child soldiers ... [and are guilty of] the assassination of political opponents and harassment of the minority Muslim population.

In the middle, a whole host of innocent malnourished civilian non-combatants suffered the indignity of being abused by both sides on the spurious argument that they were supporters of the other side. And well they might be, when forced to under threat of annihilation. Are they all innocent of the charge? Of course not, but neither are they guilty of such a charge. They are forced to live in a moral limbo. They are involved because they are there and could not be anywhere else. But it has become common and accepted military strategy to destroy whole villages and towns to demoralise the enemy, deny them support and justify the action by claiming the villagers were harbouring enemy personnel and people sympathetic to the enemy. Richard Armitage points out that on a recent visit to the island:

> Sadly, I have had the chance to see the costs of war up close. Last summer, I travelled to the Jaffna Peninsula. We first flew over the area in a helicopter and saw below us a blasted landscape, pockmarked with thousands of bomb craters and shell craters. For me, that view reminded me strongly of my time in the service in Vietnam. I really don't think I've seen anything quite like it since. And I am talking about the physical devastation and the sense of futility that was unmistakable on the ground. We ventured into one of the cities that had been largely destroyed, where people were nonetheless starting to return, trying to reclaim lives many have hardly remembered. Today, some 300,000 internally displaced people have returned to the northern and eastern parts of the country, even though these areas lack sanitation, clean water, and other basic amenities.[92]

Mr Armitage will be heartened to learn that Nisthar Cassim reported in the website of peaceinsrilanka.com that 'the once battle besieged Jaffna town is now bustling with trade and demand, a development driven solely by the two year plus ceasefire.'[93] However, he does point out that there is a lack of white-collar jobs.

The longer the war lasted, the longer the atrocities and destruction continued until there was very little left to destroy. Over 64,000 lives have been sacrificed already and over one million people, representing perhaps a fifth of

---

[92] Armitage, *Sri Lanka: Prospects for Peace.*

[93] Nisthar Cassin, *Trade Bustling in Jaffna*, www.peaceinsrilanka.com/insidepages/stories/PaperDoc220704.asp.

the people living in the affected areas, have been displaced. The damage to property and the number of people driven to destitution are another set of horrendous statistics. The young will carry these emotional scars to their grave. Many will also carry their hatred of the other side to their graves. Some will live in a hell of distrust all their lives and others still will not be able to love or be loved for fear of betrayal. This is where the political ambitions and religious bigotry of a few have led the nation.

But new monstrosities came into play. Suicide bombers became part of the Tamil Tigers' armoury, and children were requisitioned by the LTTE, armed and sent out to fight because there were fewer and fewer adults to do the fighting. This, it was argued, became a necessity in the small community of the Tamils, who had proportionately lost more civilians and military personnel in the fighting. The CIA's *The World Factbook* entry on Sri Lanka states that there are just over four million Sinhalese fit for military service, which is the equivalent of the *total* Tamil population.

The cycle of hate has not ended; it has just moved on. And history will repeat itself unless the government of Sri Lanka takes Richard Armitage's warning to heart. He says:

> The Government of Sri Lanka must institute reforms that address the legitimate aspirations of the Tamil people. This means allowing Tamils the simple right to stay in their own homes and to pursue a living, such as fishing in coastal waters, without prejudice or harassment. But it also means protecting the full range of human rights for all the people of Sri Lanka. In particular, the burden will be on the Government, military and civilian officials alike, to prove that they can accord these rights to residents of the northern and eastern parts of the nation, including the refugees returning to the area. And that they will hold officials accountable for their conduct.[94]

His reference to fishing rights for the Tamils is about the establishment of a 'no-go' area along the coastline of the Jaffna peninsula. It was created by Mr Jayawardene's government in 1984, presumably to prevent the smuggling of arms and supplies, but it effectively prevented Tamil fishermen from pursuing their traditional way of life. This, of course, meant that the resentful and now idle fishermen and their children were willing recruits to the Tamil Tigers' cause.

It would seem that the period of peace the north has enjoyed in recent years has resulted in the resurgence of the northern economy, but Mr Armitage's challenge must be met if peace is to be permanent. In time, with the help of foreign aid, the bricks and mortar will be replaced, perhaps with better-looking houses and public buildings, provided the generous donations of well-wishers are not spirited away into the coffers of the carpetbaggers who will surely arrive and try to siphon off the lion's share. But the heart of the people will

---

[94] Armitage, *Sri Lanka: Prospects for Peace.*

remain damaged for much longer and the distance between the Tamil and Sinhalese people may never be bridged. Like their ancestors in pre-European times, all that the island races can expect is an uneasy peace that any little spark might turn into a conflagration. Some wounds may never heal; they will not even fade away.

Having paid the unacceptable price of lost loved ones, the tendency is to want revenge, not accommodation. The same politicians who created the divisiveness that exploded into belligerence will have to work as a single group and with a united voice to win the peace. That is their debt to society and they must pay it willingly.

But if future governments do not, every new generation will be doomed to be born and grow up in a culture of hate and distrust. Every new atrocity and every act of retaliation from either side, whatever the cause and whatever the justification, will widen the chasm between them, and hate and distrust will fill the void. Money for arms to fuel the conflict would be sourced through intimidation, robbery and organised theft in the island and amongst the diaspora of Tamils around the world – a population swelling by the minute as a result of government policies both old and new. The government would use scarce development resources or foreign loans and grants to arm its forces. The faltering economy will shed unemployed and disillusioned youth, almost exclusively sourced from village communities, onto the battlefields. But these poor, unemployed and unemployable boys and girls will be shedding their blood to feed the bank balances of those involved in satisfying the demand for arms and infrastructure. A whole new breed of ministers, government servants and intermediaries will continue to get wealthy on the blood of innocent bystanders and government peacekeepers and army personnel caught in the crossfire of their greed. The bloodbath has and will prove profitable for some, and this profit will buy them bolt holes in foreign lands and regal comforts at home.

But surely, some would say, the fruits of peace will obliterate the horrors of war. It might, for those things that can be repaired or rebuilt; but the tenuous emotional ties will stay broken, each disconnected end dangling in free space unable to connect in order to reform the spider's web of life. The people who once willingly shared the island amongst themselves and lived at peace with their neighbours of all racial groups will be wary of doing so again. In the meantime, new problems have emerged. The US Department of State websites points out that:

> Multiple attacks on Christian Churches in Sri Lanka during 2003 led the United States to express deep concern. The United States also expressed deep concerns about draft legislation targeting so-called 'unethical conversions', noting that the campaign for such legislation as a contributing factor in the deterioration of the religious freedom situation in the country.

Since the peace process between the Tamil and Sinhalese communities began, the Muslims, who make up 7 per cent of the population, now find themselves the 'new people to hate'. The Sinhalese do not need their help and the Tamils resent them for sitting on the fence when they were 'persecuted'. When will it all end?

The reality is that the army and the Tamil Tigers have lost the will to keep on fighting. After the terrorist attacks on the World Trade Centre in New York, Western governments began to reappraise their policy of tacit support of 'freedom fighters'. As a result, there has been less and less money and support available to the Tamil Tigers to keep the fight going. Similarly, politicians and army officers have been siphoning off large chunks of money that ostensibly was earmarked to provide for the army, with the result that the army do not have the competence or the materiel to bring the war to a successful conclusion. Aided by these hard facts, the President and Mr Ranil Wickramasinghe, the prime minister at that time (although there was no love lost between them), and a Norwegian intermediary, collaborated to bring a temporary truce into being. Despite the daring raid on the airport and the bomb in Colombo there has been peace on the island for two and a half years now. Hopefully the peace will be more permanent and the presence of the Indian peacekeepers in the late 1980s can be relegated to history, allowing the Sri Lankans to take a fresh look at their populous neighbour.

Now, after twenty years of relentless belligerence from both Sinhalese and Tamil youths, there are signs that exhaustion is setting in – necessity has intervened to quiet the clamour. The representatives of the Sinhalese youth are now part of the government. The government and the representatives of the Tamil youth are now involved in talks and more talks. Despite the occasional suicide bombing and military action, the northern peninsula is showing signs of material recovery. Realism has entered the negotiations, and pragmatism may win out at the end. The emotional wounds will take much longer to heal. The belligerence of the last forty years has meant that the hate is multi-directional. Sinhalese have hurt their fellow Sinhalese, and Tamils have hurt fellow Tamils. People have separated by region, and new battles for supremacy have been fought between racial groups and will be the next wave of antagonism and hate. Slowly and surely, the war economy will be replaced by the peace dividend, but the patchwork quilt of the policies and actions of the past fifty-seven years will not blend into a single colour for decades. The island is doomed to be a collection of independent clans from now on. Peace is still far away. It is achievable only if the Buddhist establishment cedes the high ground and accepts that it will be just one among many communities who are entitled to the care and protection of the state, or, more probably, states within a federated system of states.

Interview of Mrs Kumaratunga, the President of Sri Lanka, conducted by Tim Sebastian of the BBC in October 2001[95]

Q: But in most cases they say there was no investigation or prosecution, given the appearance of impunity for those responsible for human rights violence. In most cases…

A: That is not true. Wherever there has been any evidence there has been.

Q: You have to take this up with the US Government.

A: I haven't seen this report, which you're talking about.

Q: You haven't? Then I will give you a copy of it. Twenty-four pages here.

A: I would like to have that. But wherever it has been reported to the government, I mean to the authorities, the police or whoever, we have taken the strictest action.

Q: So they're involved? They are simply involved?

A: These are exceptions. I think you are taking it out of context; these are exceptions to the rule as opposed to what happened previously, and every one of those cases we have taken or we will take action, and very expeditiously. But what I want to underline and highlight is that when the police was made to take people up in the middle of the night, 50,000 young Sinhalese people were killed off; nothing to do with the ethnic problem, people from my party, democratic parties, simply because they opposed the government in power then, they used to be picked up in the night in unlicensed vehicles with the unlicensed number plates, or without number plates, it was the police or military that used to go in civil, in civil dress, kill them, they used to be, you know this was called … I don't know, necklacing or something, and rubber tyres put around their necks and…

Q: And you are saying the situation is better than what it was, there is one case which is causing huge alarm, which is the case of the journalist, Mr Nimalarajan. He worked for the BBC, a much respected contributor to the BBC programme. You ordered an inquiry but nothing has happened. Many people were deeply troubled by the lack of progress. Even the judiciary in your own country has commented on the apparently unenthusiastic approach by the police. How do you explain that? This is something we have taken a direct interest in.

A: We had ordered an inquiry; people had not come up with sufficient evidence which could be due to intimidation, from whoever has done it. There are people in the security forces. After I came in to government, about thirteen or eighteen young Tamil boys were picked up on the roads, and I heard that Tamil boys were disappearing and I was shocked, for normally it cannot happen, without the knowledge of the state, and then they were killed and their bodies were found floating along a river, which flows through Colombo, and we discovered

[95] *Hardtalk*, BBC, October 2001.

that it was a group of people of the special task force, which is a military body of the police, and the man concerned was in the personal security in what we call the close protection of the leader of the opposition who was before me the prime minister.

Q: —

A: We have got rid of them; we have taken serious action, but you know we are a democratic government, they were taken to court, and the case is taking years to be resolved.

Chapter 31

A Lost Opportunity for Peace

The way the country was governed by the ruling clique and the current mindset of the people is amply illustrated by the chaos surrounding the response of the politicians to the recovery programme following the devastation caused by the tsunami on Boxing Day 2004.

In the introduction, I stated that despite the awful consequences of the tsunami, the catastrophe gave the people of Sri Lanka a chance to unite and work together to speed up the recovery of their shattered lives. The principal actors to any accommodation are the president and the politicians and the leadership of the LTTE. Sadly, a year later, it would appear that the recovery effort has ground to a halt because the politicians have failed to arrive at workable solutions. Consequently, the huge show of goodwill and support shown by the world community and the large sums of money ($3 billions) made available by it to help the island people remains, according to reports, largely unspent. The *Telegraph* of 29 May 2005 reports that very little has happened due to bureaucratic inertia, incompetence and corruption. The headlines of The *Telegraph* of 28 May 2005 were quite emphatic: 'Tsunami victims still wait for aid to arrive'. Its opening paragraph said:

> The generosity of millions of Britons who gave money to help the victims of the Boxing Day tsunami is being betrayed by Sri Lanka's army of bureaucrats. ... Five months after the tsunami struck, killing 40,000 and leaving 500,000 homeless in Sri Lanka, more than 100,000 of the poorest victims are still living in tents or crude temporary shelters.[96]

Page four of the same paper carried more dispiriting news. It told of the despair and desperation of those still living in tents that are 'hot enough to turn the pages of a reporter's notebook to a useless pulp'. [97] According to Peter Foster's report, £1.75 billion of aid (almost 12.5 per cent of the annual GDP of the country) allocated to relieve the suffering in Sri Lanka remains unused. In its view, the central government has managed to achieve a state where:

> Shipping containers remain stuck at ports, vital building plans await approval and incompetent officials ignore the advice of specialists ... corruption is also holding things up as cartels of builders demand exorbitant 'UN prices' for work

---

[96] Peter Foster, 'Tsunami victims still wait for aid to arrive' *Telegraph*, 28 May 2005.

[97] ' "Why have we been left to rot in this hell?" ' *Telegraph*, 28 May 2005.

> that should cost half as much ... the Irish Sri Lanka Trust Fund is considering withdrawing its money after receiving a £300,000 VAT bill for engines to be fitted to 890 boats.[98]

Chandra Monerawela, the Irish Sri Lanka Trust's Sri Lankan-born director, echoes the views of the frustrated majority when he says that:

> This hard-earned money was raised by schoolchildren and old folk to help the people of Sri Lanka. It was not raised for the Sri Lankan government to swipe 15 per cent for itself.[99]

The BBC News website ran an article with the title 'Oxfam pays $1m tsunami aid duty'[100] pointing out that Oxfam had to import twenty-five Mahindra vehicles to help its workers reach the poorest villages who lived in remote locations. It would appear that Oxfam had missed the duty-free window that existed between January and April 2005. It is not clear whether this was the result of government servants prevaricating over the paperwork or whether Oxfam failed to apply in time. What seems clear is that Sri Lankan 'customs had charged $5,000 a day while the vehicles were being processed'. It would be interesting to know how many rich Sri Lankans took advantage of this moratorium to update their fleet of vehicles and how fast the customs processed their paperwork. The editorial in the *Telegraph* of 28 May 2005 says that the only way to unblock government incompetence and corruption is to:

> Hold up the Sri Lankan government to the ridicule and contempt of world opinion. As it happens, Bill Clinton arrives in Sri Lanka today: perhaps he is the man to do it.[101]

Mr Clinton did not ridicule the government but his presence seems to have galvanised the government and some international bodies to inject fresh resolve and speed to right this state of inertia. It has prompted the World Bank, after five months of silence, to condemn the government for placing bureaucratic obstacles in it way. And it forced the president of Sri Lanka to make a determined effort to create the joint mechanism that the international community demanded before they would release the money the island people need to rebuild their tsunami-shattered lives. One can only conjecture that if they had not, Mr Clinton would have taken them to task and the UN, already reeling under the 'oil for food' fiasco in Iraq will have more than one angry American president calling them to account. As it is, he seems to have left the international agencies and the NGOs the clear message that he expects the

---

[98] Foster, 'Tsunami victims still wait for aid to arrive'.
[99] Ibid.
[100] 'Oxfam pays $1m tsunami aid duty', BBC News, 17 June 2005, http://news.bbc.co.uk.
[101] 'Sri Lanka's shame', *Telegraph*, 28 May 2005.

UN to take responsibility for accounting for the money they will be spending on behalf of the world community in the tsunami affected areas and prompted the Sri Lankan government to work to relieve the suffering of all the people. He is quoted in the *Mirror* as saying:

> Might it have a positive impact on the peace talks? Sure. Because any time people do things together as human beings, instead of scream at each other as political actors, good things happen.[102]

Mr Clinton, ever the good diplomat, congratulated the government of Sri Lanka for achievements in other areas. As the *Mirror* reports, he pointed out that: 'You have lost no children to starvation or disease. You have had no mass outbreaks of an epidemic as a result of destruction of your water and sanitation facilities.' In private, one hopes that he did take the Sri Lankan government to task for allowing the situation to reach its current sad state where, in the words of the *Mirror* reporter, 'Almost all those rendered homeless are still living in temporary wooden shacks or tattered tent camps strung out along the island's coast.' The UN Office for the Coordination of Humanitarian Affairs report 'Humanitarian Situation Report – Sri Lanka: 20–26 May 2005' also points out that some progress has been made in the areas of health, water and sanitation, education, the provision of means of livelihood and protection.[103] However, judged against the larger canvas, the general opinion is that it is far too little and far too late. In many ways what has happened follows the usual pattern of post-independence Ceylon.

For almost fifty years the ruling clique have failed to optimise the gifts and donations of well-meaning people and international institutions. Some of that money has been wasted, misapplied or misappropriated. Despite this, international institutions have continued to bankroll the government by granting it more aid in the form of loans and grants. Rarely have the Sri Lankan government, the international institutions or the donor governments had to account to their taxpayers and benefactors for the billions of dollars that they have given successive Sri Lankan governments as loans or grants. The Sri Lankan governments, the ruling clique and the foreign organisations have accepted that the misuse of funds 'was the cost of doing business in the developing world'. As if it was wrong to expect higher standards of probity from politicians, government servants and businessmen and women in these countries.

The sad fact is that the longer it takes for the money to be spent, the better the chance that those responsible for seeing it well spent can avoid blame when it is discovered that the funds have been misapplied or misappropriated. This is because those responsible for initiating the projects (both officials in the international organisations and the politicians in the recipient country) are

[102] Bill Tarrant, 'Clinton backs tsunami aid deal with Sri Lanka rebels', *Mirror*, 28 May 2005.
[103] www.reliefweb.int/rw/rwb.nsf/db900sid , 27 May 2005.

rarely around to explain the overexpenditure and the under-achievements. This lack of 'real' accountability – identifying and punishing those responsible – has allowed the administration of the time and their henchmen to enrich themselves at the expense of the poor in their own country and tax payers (mostly middle-income and lower-income groups) in donor countries.

It was therefore heartening to learn that Mr Clinton wants more accountability and transparency in how tsunami money is spent by the government and the aid agencies. One can only hope that he will hold the government of Sri Lanka accountable for the money that it holds in trust for their people and that by rigorously advocating the auditing of expenditure and reviewing the projects the money finances he satisfies the donor community that tsunami money was honestly and meaningfully spent.

What many who criticise the government for its slowness in responding to the needs of its people often overlook is that when its own selfish interests are at stake the ruling clique can display a remarkable turn of speed in getting things done to suit their ends. Then bureaucracy takes a back seat. Resources flow in and action becomes the watchword. The ColomboPage website of 19 January 2005 gives us a staggering example of how this can happen. It says that:

> In Prime Minister Mahinda Rajapaksa's home district of Hambantota, an organisation has been formed to see Hambantota come alive after tsunamis devastated the coast on December 26 … According to sources at the Prime Minister's office, these organisations [13 foreign and local relief agencies and several government departments] have undertaken to construct nearly 4,000 of the 6,223 houses that are to be newly constructed.[104]

The speed at which the Prime Minister was able to harness the aid agencies, advisory bodies and other necessary groups and the large sums of money needed to help rehabilitate 'his home district' is commendable. The point is that this contrasts so sharply with the plight of the fisher families in Parssekudah reported in TamilNet.com on 1 February 2005 and the plight of those in the *Telegraph* report of 28 May 2005. Parssekudah, according to this report was once a thriving tourist resort reduced to rubble during the fighting and thought by the locals to be littered with mines. The tsunamis devastated the homes of the fishermen living there, destroyed their boats and made them destitute in a matter of minutes. The government response to their plight seems to be different to that in the Prime Minister's home district. The local MP, Mr Jayanandamoorthy, is pleading for well wishers to contribute a paltry US$ 25,000 to buy land on which he can re-house 183 families. Mr Erambamoorthy, the president of the Pasikudah Mariamman Temple, speaking for the people, says:

[104] ColomboPage, 19 January 2005.

> The government has offered us land in Vembu, which is a barren spot four kilometres from the sea. All of us have depended on the sea for our livelihood for generations. Where do we keep our boats if we are that far from the beach? Also, we set out to sea at night. If we live in Vembu, we have to walk through the military camp area, which is very risky after dark.[105]

Maybe following Mr Clinton's visit things will change. He is reported to have said: 'I've attempted to nudge along the process of resolving the buffer zone in my talks with government.'[106]

No doubt he saw the absurdity of the government's proposal, which many believe was prompted by security considerations rather than its concern for the comfort of the people whose lives were so tragically affected. The security forces believe, and probably rightly, that wide uninhabited swathes of the coastline will help them to more effectively prevent the smuggling of arms by the rebels. No doubt that is a laudable objective and one that is necessary to achieve, but reality and common sense dictates that this cannot be achieved at the expense of the livelihood of thousands of people who have earned their living from the sea for generations.

In the broader context of getting help to all regions it must be remembered that there are a large number of such contrasting situations across the island and the government cannot be everywhere at the same time. Choices have to be made and people will be disappointed that they are not at the top of the list. What was needed here was a carefully structured plan and a structured set of criteria against which relief effort would be expended. Then the vast army of aid workers, commercial organisations and government bodies could have acted in concert to meaningfully use that money. The issues should have been debated extensively in Parliament, the criteria established with its consent and published so that the people and the foreign donors could see how their money was being spent and judge the equitability of the actions taken. In addition the government should have, through some agreed price mechanism, ensured that those with scarce resources did not make extortionate profits from the misery and suffering of others. But it seems these precautions were not taken, probably because the Members of Parliament were unable to set aside their sectarian objectives in the pursuit of much higher goals.

The plan that the Sri Lankan government issued so rapidly after the events on Boxing Day were found by many to lack comprehensiveness and cohesion. It was, reportedly, drawn up by a small group of undoubtedly able people but it failed because they were unable to scope the scale and needs of so widespread a disaster without consultation with all those affected and without setting the ground rules so that the efforts of the various relief agencies are optimised. Sadly, wider consultation would have hit the roadblock of political

[105] 'No sunny times for east coast idyll', TamilNet, 1 February 2005.

[106] Bill Tarrant, 'Clinton backs tsunami aid deal with Sri Lanka rebels', *Mirror*, 28 May 2005.

intransigence that characterises much of Sri Lankan politics today.

An independent group, Rebuilding Sri Lanka Limited, points out what happens when these simple steps are not taken. It says that the demand created by the aid agencies, which are unknowingly competing with each other for the limited heavy machinery and labour on the island, is pricing both out of the market and enriching those who least need the money.[107] In addition, they suspect that it may prevent local farmers, who were willing to pay the higher price to harvest this year's bumper crop of paddy, from paying the same high price to plant next year's crop, which, if it fails may bankrupt them. This may lead to a shortfall in next year's paddy crop and the same aid agencies that are pricing labour out of the market now will be calling for food aid then. Even if these criticisms are only partially true the lack of coordination of the effort of a whole raft of volunteers will mean that the money of millions of well wishers is likely to be wasted or purloined by the unscrupulous who view this as a once-in-a-lifetime opportunity to make money and to feather their political nests.

But there is another side to this appalling situation. And that is the political infighting inside the ruling clique. A report in TamilNet.com of 9 May 2005 provides a more detailed insight into the situation surrounding the use of aid funds:

> International donors, who withdrew their backing in 2000, frustrated with her then People's Alliance (PA) government's failure to resolve the ethnic conflict and poor 'good governance' performances, are now [at long last] standing firm that there must improvements in these areas. Reconciliation with the LTTE and neo-liberal economic reform have thus become strong conditionalities for their backing.[108]

The President, backed by a opinion poll result that said that two-thirds of Sri Lankans backed a joint mechanism, wished to set up such a mechanism. She was not only anxious to get the money but to also show that she is a woman of her word. Establishing such a joint mechanism with the LTTE, 'despite her barely disguised repugnance for dealing with the LTTE',[109] would prove that she meant it when she promised in December 2004 in a BBC interview[110] that aid funds would be distributed according to need rather than race. Unfortunately for her, the JVP – her partners in government – realising that the two-thirds majority hid the fact that only 51 per cent of the Sinhalese community approved of such a joint mechanism, argued against its establishment. The JVP's intransigence was matched only by the belligerent mood of a group of hard-line monks called the Jathika Hela Urumaya. The UNP held its silence,

---

[107] Case Studies – Consequences of duplication and uncoordinated relief efforts, February 2005.

[108] 'Joint mechanism mired in Sinhala politics', TamilNet, 9 May 2005.

[109] Ibid.

[110] BBC News broadcast, 26 December 2006.

vindicating the claim of the TamilNet article that, 'The only certainty is further political turmoil as Sri Lanka's main parties put their political ambitions before ordinary people's welfare'.

However, by 19 May 2005, the President had won the support of the UNP and neutralised, perhaps temporarily, the JVP whose members, according to a TamilNet.com report on 19 May 2005, 'attended the event, uncharacteristically wearing suits and ties'.[111] This situation amply illustrates the rather shambolic and self-serving way the governments of Sri Lanka have served their people these last fifty-seven years.

However, to give credit where credit is due, the President, the Buddhist establishment and peace-loving Sri Lankans seem to be uniting in an effort to bring realism back into Sri Lankan politics. It is difficult to know whether this is a new and lasting mood or whether it is a pragmatic step designed to get the $3 billions on offer released. The Venerable Galagame Dharmmaransi Thero addressing a rally of the National Anti-War Front (NAWF) chastised those political parties (primarily the UNP and JVP) for their reluctance to support the President in her efforts to create the conditions for peace. He is reported to have said:

> The decision to get the cooperation of the LTTE to deliver aid to the tsunami-affected people of the North and East on equitable basis should not be viewed from a political angle. Instead of finding reasons and shortcomings to criticise the Joint Mechanism proposal, all political parties should support the implementation of it for a proper distribution of relief and rehabilitation in the affected areas.[112]

These words of the Thero were taken up by the Reverend Father Anslem Silva OMI, director of the Centre for Society and Religion. He is quoted as saying:

> Sri Lankan society did not have a sense of urgency. Political parties were engaged in squabbles while tsunami victims are languishing in makeshift shelters. Over 70,000 young men and women died during the JVP insurrection, 60,000 died in the ethnic war and more than 30,000 died in the tsunami national disaster. But our politicians are still engaged in squabbles, quite unwilling to take decisions on vital national issues.[113]

The chairperson of the NAWF damped down fears that the Tamil Tigers and the government would use aid funds to finance the war effort by assuring the meeting that the joint mechanism would have 'limited powers' and that 'there was no room for misuse of the relief assistance for military purposes'. He seemed to be of the view that 'Fears expressed on this are baseless.' However,

---

[111] 'Sri Lanka's President invites JVP, CWC for talks', TamilNet, 19 May 2005.

[112] ColomboPage.com, 30 May 2005.

[113] ColomboPage.com, 30 May 2005.

they cannot be discounted either. It behoves all those involved to identify and prevent such abuses by either side.

The most reassuring action of all is that of the President, who, at an exhibition held at the Polonnaruwa Royal Central College grounds, said:

> The Tamils have reasons to fight as the governments since independence have neglected them. In 1995, we [she] took the first step and Ranil Wickramasinghe took it forward. As Buddhists we entered into a dialogue with the enemy. The LTTE could be made amenable only by getting them to work within the framework we have drawn up, to which they have agreed. It will pave the way for a peaceful settlement.[114]

She also slapped down her coalition partners by pointing out that:

> The JVP should remember that they were given the opportunity by the SLFP [her party] to enter into mainstream politics, and they should be grateful for that. They should honour it and dedicate themselves in the nation building.[115]

One would imagine that such a mood change and such forthrightness in Polonnaruwa – a place that suffered much from LTTE incursions – suggests that the President has found a new confidence and that the 'good' people of the island are at last being heard by those who matter – their political, religious and lay leaders. Sadly, that is not the case. Within days of her statement, the country was pitched into political chaos by Buddhist monks who decided to protest about the joint mechanism.

> Nearly a hundred Buddhist monks led by Jathika Hela Urumaya (JHU) parliamentarian Ven. Omalpe Sobhitha Thera are to launch a fast-unto-death campaign tonight at the Sri Dalada Maligawa against the Signing of the proposed Joint Mechanism with the LTTE.[116]

The fast was called off on 11 June 2005 when the President assured the Buddhist establishment that she would 'consult the monks before deciding on the plans for distributing $2bn of aid'[117]. The same report says that 'analysts believe the bigger threat to Mrs Kumaratunga lies with her coalition partner, the Marxist JVP party, which says it will pull out if the shared aid plans go ahead'. This is the same JVP that donned Western dress and obediently followed 'their master's voice' a few weeks earlier at the formal talks. On 13 June 2005, however:

---

[114] 'Solid foundation for peace has been laid', ColomboPage.com , 30 May 2005.
[115] Ibid.
[116] ColomboPage.com, 6 June 2005.
[117] 'Sri Lanka monk ends hunger strike', BBC News, bbc.co.uk.

> More than hundred policemen ... fired tear gas and used water canons to disperse monks and university students who were protesting in front of Colombo Fort railway station in support of Ven. Dambara Amila Thera ... who started a new fast unto death campaign on Saturday against the Joint Mechanism.[118]

Despite the belligerence of the monks, Mrs Kumaratunga attempted to win support for the government's stance on the joint mechanism by lobbying politicians of all political persuasions. Unfortunately for her, the JVP, members of her ruling group, opposed her actions and decided to leave the government on 16 June 2005, significantly reducing her majority. They may have hoped that the opposition would strive to remove the present minority government from office, but they have not. So, it seems that although a group of intransigent monks and politicians are struggling to divert the President from following the course she has chosen she, despite the vulnerability of her government, is standing firm. She is reported as saying:

> There are 28,000 Bhikkus in this country. Only just a handful of Bhikkus and a few political parties have opposed the JM [Joint Mechanism]. It is not the view of the majority. Hence as early as possible, JM work has to begin.[119]

The report also says that she:

> Reminded the Bhikku audience that the JVP was responsible for their behaviour as a terrorist group in 1971. They were the first group to spread terror in this country ... the LTTE had their first lessons of armed struggle from the JVP.

Perhaps the island people have at long last come to their senses and their leaders, sensing their mood, are willing to bring in a new era in which the silent majority, who for years have wished for peace, stability, safety and security, will get their way. But there is much to do to institutionalise these new values among the people and encourage the electorate to vote for them in the future.

---

118 'Police use tear gas to break up monks' protest in Colombo', TamilNet, 13 June 2005.
119 ColomboPage.com, 18 June 2005.

Part Six

Beyond Spices and Suicide Bombers

Summary

In February 1948 the country was well placed to secure a bright future. But its political leaders coveted the seat of power that Britain had recently vacated. To sate their lust for power, they used the highly charged emotional levers of language, religion and envy. This destabilised the country in three important ways. Firstly, it passed power from the politician to the racists and, even now, the politicians are governed by the racists who purport to represent the Buddhist nationalist lobby. Secondly, socialist policies won votes but destroyed the economy and the natural enterprise of the people. Thirdly, the youth of all races found themselves with no future, and, as their needs were ignored by the ruling clique, resorted to violence.

In 2006, the task of picking up the pieces of fifty-eight years of mismanagement and of building a united and prosperous nation must be approached as a new challenge by a 'new' people who have shed the baggage of past years. This is easier to do now that the generation that took over from the British are all dead or long past their active political life. Their children have had their turn and now the future belongs to *their* children. It would be madness for them to continue the failed and discredited policies of their forefathers. They must chart a new course. One that is more inclusive and free of the prejudices and the racism that currently bedevils the island. To achieve this they will have to moderate and control the Buddhist nationalists, racists and opportunists who still wield power over the country.

By using religion and language as war cries the racists not only differentiated one group of people from another, but they also used the emotional content to attract supporters and convert them into activists. As Hague and Harrop say:

> In the developing world religion has become the culture of the dispossessed and is a major device through which those who feel distanced from society can articulate their frustration.

It is the emotional driver that facilitates the step change from ethnic identity to nationalist movement and from nationalist movement to the reality of political power and self-determination. After independence, the Buddhist nationalists worked hard to gain greater autonomy for the Buddhist majority and achieved both self-determination, and, by gaining constitutional changes, sole sovereignty over the island.

Sri Lanka is now a Sinhalese Buddhist unitary state in which Tamils and other non-Buddhist Sinhalese can live only on the terms laid down by the

Sinhalese Buddhist majority. This means that the Tamils and the other non-Buddhist Sinhalese who are citizens of Sri Lanka are, for all practical purposes, subjects of the Sinhalese Buddhist majority and subservient to their wishes. In addition, their status as second-class citizens has been institutionalised by legislation passed during the Bandaranaike years. As a result, the Tamils are living in a two-tier society in which they are denied equality under the law because they are Tamils and for no other reason. As Bernard Crick points out, 'The Tamils, like the Jews, are being punished for what they cannot be, or for what they are not even allowed to be.' Having tried to correct this by peaceful means for nearly a quarter of a century, the Tamils resorted to war in 1983.

The war has, naturally, increased the animosity between the Tamils and the Sinhalese but it has not corrected the injustices felt by the Tamils or subjugated them. The situation is now a stalemate. Some form of autonomy for the Tamils seems like the only way out, but it is unlikely that the racist lobby represented now mostly by the JVP and the JHU (a political group formed by the young Buddhist clergy) would agree to share power or to retreat from the current position of institutionalised preferment. This does suggest that in the long run the pressure by the Tamils and others for separate states will remain strong and the conflict will continue. Any move to give the Tamils a state of their own will give rise to a similar demand by the Muslims and a new cycle of discord will start all over again. Consequently, the impasse will reinforce old prejudices and every new generation will be haunted by them. The future stability of the country demands that some policies and attitudes adopted during these lost years are reversed or subordinated:

- the Buddhist clergy should abandon politics and return to their role as spiritual rather than political guides.

- The economy should be grown so that the young of all races are given a fair chance to carve out careers and futures consistent with their abilities and desires.

- the electorate should 'wise up' and vote politicians into office on the merits of their achievements rather than on their patronage of Buddhism and Sinhalese.

- politicians should be rewarded for bringing knowledge, food, clothing, homes, health, sanitation, mobility, honesty and integrity into public life; facilitating interracial communication and cooperation; achieving security, safety and economic growth and for enshrining equality of status in such things as opportunity and justice. And if the politicians fail to do this, then the electorate must teach them by voting into power those who will travel this harder road with them.

- the ethnic divide should be treated as the smokescreen it is and the bogeyman that is India and Hinduism – as manifest in the northern Tamils – should be put to rest for ever.

- the country should cast off its dynastic tradition and encourage instead a meritocracy where achievement and personal competence, rather than the accident of birth, are rewarded.

Unless these shifts occur the country will continue to languish in poverty and strife. Lasting peace will only follow if these issues are firmly addressed.

To change this, it would require that the country revert to being one where all citizens enjoy equality of status. Unless the Buddhist clergy take the lead and create the conditions needed for reconciliation and peaceful coexistence, and guarantee that they will fight to protect minority interests in order to secure a peaceful and prosperous island, nothing will change.

The action plan that will get the people on this new path to freedom, peace and prosperity has four main themes:

- establishment of strong ethical and moral values in the country so that the endemic corruption is rooted out by the individual's moral conscience. This must be provided by the different religions – and Buddhism, because it is the ruling philosophy for the vast majority, must take the lead. It is only then that the law can become effective;

- provision of unselfish leadership the country needs at this critical time;

- the political education of the people so that they can determine how they want to be led and who should lead them, rather than allow themselves to be led by the self-serving. It is time they reasserted their democratic rights to rule their lives;

- rationalization of relationships with India. The country will benefit from India's industrial know-how and enable Sri Lanka to piggyback on its global reach. It will also bring in the huge financial investments and technical skills and resources needed to transform the island's economy and fully use the skills of the Sri Lankan people. Other countries, such as China and Japan and power blocs such as the USA and Europe, will all wish to invest in a peaceful Sri Lanka. There is room for them all, but India's close association of thousands of years provides the closest cultural fit.

The chapters that follow are designed to trigger discussions on all these issues. It is only if the country progresses along this new moral and ethnically inclusive road that it will be able to secure its future. Corruption will wither and justice will reassert itself. The finances will fall into place when the people work together for their common good. And then their future will be brighter than their past has ever been.

Chapter 32

Old Scores and New Beginnings

Parts Four and Five have discussed the way the country has been run since independence. And, frankly, they show that Sri Lankan management of the country has been very poor, and that the Sri Lankan people have no one to blame but themselves for the appalling mess they are in. Much is wrong with the country and there is much to do, but the foundations on which a recovery can be mounted are still in place. For instance:

- The country has remained democratic even if it is a form of partial democracy. Its leaders have had to justify their stewardship and justify their suitability to be elected or re-elected to high office.
- Despite two attempted coup d'états, the country has not fallen into the hands of a dictator or tyrant.
- The justice system has its flaws, the police and the security services may not be totally even-handed in their treatment of those they arrest or fight, but at least they are answerable to a civilian administration.
- The economy is a mess but, despite the population growing from about 7 million to 20 million in fifty years and the heavy cost of the war, the people are not starving, nor have they suffered from famine.
- The two insurrections by the Sinhalese youth, and the 'civil war' with the Tamil liberation movement in the north and east have been contained, albeit at the great cost of lives, livelihoods.
- The civil administration may be overburdened by procedure and paperwork and susceptible to corruption, but it does still function and its operational efficiency can be improved and integrity restored.
- The expanding population may have eaten into the forests and reduced them, but the country still has its game reserves.
- The physical infrastructure may be on its last legs, but can be resuscitated.
- Buddhism has been used as a political tool by racist groups, but the Buddhist establishment has not descended into the fundamentalism shown by the Taliban or the clergy in Iran in the early 1980s, nor have the fundamentalists been allowed to take the reins of political power.

So a new, forward-thinking generation can rebuild the country their grandparents ruined. To repair these crumbling foundations and build a new peaceful and successful country, however, requires a new mindset. Sadly, every new generation learns the old songs and imbues them with new vigour. The result is that every new generation carries forward the prejudices of their parents. At the superficial level the new generation of skirts, jeans and T-shirt wearing Sri Lankans appear to be different from their parents and grandparents. Modern communications technology has opened their eyes to the wider world outside the island's shores and created in them a wish to emulate the lifestyles of those they see on TV and the films of Hollywood and Bollywood. But those who believe that they will absorb the egalitarian views that the films and soap operas portray need to consider the fact that the political socialisation of children begins in early childhood and that the views and opinions they form then, tend to stay with them all through their lives:

> Political loyalties are formed when young. Childhood learning is 'deep learning' because it provides a framework for interpreting information acquired in adulthood...
>
> Learning a political culture is very different from acquiring an academic skill ... It involves the development of political emotions and identities (what is my nation? my religion? my party?) ... For example, children's attitudes towards politics will be influenced as much by their experience of authority at home and at school as by what parents and teachers say their views should be.[120]

Observers of the political process will support these views. The reality is that the majority of people tend to be lifelong supporters of a political party – often the one their parents voted for – and will tend to vote the same way election after election, irrespective of what those leading the party do. Unquestionably there are exceptions to this rule. They are the people who vote tactically. Politicians work very hard to influence tactical voters, even though they are few in number when compared with the total voting population. They know that winning them over can win them seats and majorities. But they are also aware that it is very difficult to shift loyalties. Supporters who are angry with the party they have supported all their lives are more likely not to vote than vote for another party. The winner gains from the silent protest of a vote withheld.

Based on these views we must accept that the outward appearance of the new generation of Sri Lankans does not reflect their inner feelings and that it is fair to assume that the children of Sri Lanka will, despite seeing alternate lifestyles and even imitating them at the superficial level, fall back on their tried and tested sources of guidance when they have to make the big decisions such as 'protecting' their ethnicity. Then they will take a lead from their parents and their religious leaders as their parents and grandparents did before them. So, although they may recognise that the country has lost its way and

[120] Hague and Harrop, *Comparative Government and Politics: An Introduction.*

wish for a better future, it is more likely that they will continue along the same route their parents and grandparents took before them to correct the situation. They will increase the tempo and intensity of their actions in the hope that that will change things for the better. Their increased desire for change eventually escalates from frustration to protest, to anger, revolt and to war.

Lasting change will only come about when there is a shift in mindset. People have to think differently and find new emotional levers to motivate them in new directions. To achieve W S Senior's vision of a multi-ethnic unitary state of Sri Lanka (see box on right) it is vital that the emphasis on Buddhist Sinhala chauvinism gives way to the reality of the modern world and for the people of Sri Lanka to accept that multi-ethnicity is now a global phenomenon and that perfecting the art of peaceful coexistence and collaboration offers them the best hope of a peaceful and prosperous future. As John Gray points out in his book:

> But most shall we sing of Lanka
> In the brave new days that come,
> When the races all have blended
> And the voice of strife is dumb;
> When we leap to a single bugle,
> March to a single drum.
> March to a mighty purpose,
>
> One man from shore to shore,
> The stranger become a brother,
> The task of the tutor o'er;
> When the ruined city rises,
> And the Palace gleams once more.
>
> *From 'The Call of Lanka', by Walter Stanley Senior*

> Toleration was practised many centuries ago in Buddhist India, in the Ottoman Empire and the Moorish kingdoms of medieval Spain, and in China. There is nothing particularly liberal, western or modern about the peaceful coexistence of communities having different values and beliefs.[121]

And this is true for the Sinhalese and Tamils in Sri Lanka too. The Sinhalese people must learn again to harness the diversity in their midst and use it positively. They must realise that if they are to find their place in the world again, the past sixty or so years of retrospection must be set aside and a new maturity must light the future. It is time the 'reasonable man' took charge of the politicians and provided them with an agenda that will drive the country towards the achievement of its long forgotten dreams. This means changing their self-centred politicians into statesman because the quality of governance is so important to the recovery of the island's fortunes. The key steps to recovery are within the grasp of the people. They, especially the young, need to take charge of their futures and drive forward a new agenda of hope, reconciliation and peaceful coexistence. This requires them to:

[121] John Gray, *False Dawn*, London, Granta Books, 2002.

- Re-establish the traditional Buddhist, Hindu, Christian and Muslim values of good neighbourliness.
- Consolidate the truce to deliver a new era of peace and security.
- Establish a fair and equitable society in which Tamils and Muslims are again able to trust their Sinhalese neighbours to treat them as 'brothers and sisters' and not aliens. This will be a slow process and will hit obstacles from time to time but it must be achieved if there is to be any hope of achieving and sustaining peace on the island.
- Slowly recover the legitimacy of the sovereign state of Sri Lanka to rule over the whole island. Since this is unlikely to be achieved by force in a democracy, it is vital that the government persuade all its citizens to voluntarily accept its legitimacy to rule them as a single nation.
- Take immediate steps to manage population growth. The island has already reached the limits of its ability to sustain the people living on it. The different ethnic groups must abandon any attempts to out-populate the other.
- Recover the island's economy so that all its people can live dignified lives. This means gradually moving from being providers of cheap labour to becoming a nation that creates high valued-added jobs consistent with the literacy rate of the people.
- Avoid bidding in world markets for scarce resources such as oil. This suggests that industrialisation is not an option, as it will require the country to compete unsuccessfully with other huge consumers of energy – a rapidly depleting resource – such as the USA, China, India, European countries, and some South American states. Instead they should build a knowledge-based economy.
- Avoid the temptation to live beyond their means, as that makes Sri Lanka a debtor nation and puts it under arbitrary rules of its creditors.
- Act prudently. If they were to strike it lucky and find oil or some other resource, it would be wise to invest the revenues in infrastructure rather than on conspicuous consumption.

Achieving this requires the help of the Buddhist clergy, good political leadership and the willingness of the people to take control of their lives and manage their politicians.

Chapter 33

The Bhikkhu as a Moral Leader

The world is experiencing a severe clash of cultures. When the values and beliefs of a people are undermined by imported and 'alien' cultures there is and always will be a backlash. The country with the most prolific influence on the cultures and values of the young in all nations is the United States. It is also, coincidentally, the country with the largest gathering of political and religious fundamentalists in the world. Through the vast output of its film industry and television broadcasts, it exports its culture, values and lifestyles to the rest of the world. Through the industry's distorted lens a version of the truth is exported that sometimes unfairly presents the values and beliefs of other people and nations.

Unfortunately, few people are able to absorb the best of what they see and discard the rest. People, especially young people, living in countries where life is still hard and ambitions stunted by a lack of opportunity, are seduced by these imported lifestyles and succumb to them. But they lack the maturity to handle the psychological dissonance that such submission creates. As a result, their expectations from life far exceed their own (or their country's) ability to deliver. Their frustration bubbles over into dissatisfaction with themselves, their elders and those who set out to provide the balance in their lives. In Sri Lanka, those most able to provide this balance are the Buddhist clergy. If they fail to preach and gain acceptance for the 'middle way' fundamentalist thinking will take root and flower. What follows then is often unthinkable. It is against this backdrop that the *bhikkhu* has to follow his calling.

The *bhikkhu* is the heart of the Sinhalese Buddhist community. As he moves among the people in his yellow robes and his close-shaven head he remains a permanent and ever-present reminder of the teachings of the philosopher prince Gautama, who is now venerated as the Lord Buddha. He is an influential figure. He can shape the thoughts of the Buddhist laity to love or hate their neighbours. He can persuade them to vote according to his wishes. He can still the storm of their anger or arouse it. And he can fill their hearts with tolerance and magnanimity. Such is his influence that he carries a heavy burden and, to ease it, is guided by the *Dhammapada*[122] which tells him in unambiguous words what his duty is to himself, his flock and his fellow clergy.

[122] A collection of sayings and teachings of the Buddha accepted at the Council of Asoka in 240 BC.

First he needs to remember that:

> All that we are is the result of our thoughts; it is founded on our thoughts and made up of our thoughts. With our thoughts we make the world, if a man speaks or acts with a harmonious thought happiness follows him as his own shadow, never leaving him.[123]

And also that:

> Let no man think lightly of wrong doing: 'It will not touch me.' Drop by drop is the pitcher filled, and little by little the fool becomes filled with folly.[124]

Then that:

> Hating can never overcome hatred. Only love can bring the end of hating. This is the eternal law.[125]

And finally that:

> All the holy words you read and all the holy words you speak are as nothing if you do not act upon them. Even if you read little and say little but live the right was, forsaking craving, hatred and delusion, you will know truth and find calmness and will show others the path.[126]

And also that he should:

> 'Hurt none by word or deed. Be moderate in your eating. Live in inner solitude. And seek the deepest consciousness.' This is the teaching of the Buddha.[127]

The role of the *bhikkhu*, then, as decreed by his master the Lord Buddha, is as a mendicant and a servant whose role is to minister to his flock and help them follow the true path as decreed by the Lord Buddha. To remain true to his lord, the Buddha, the *bhikkhu* should stay within the spirit and the letter of the law through self-examination and by eschewing worldly desires. It is not for him to enter the realms of politics as a politician or to crave political or secular office. That way opens him up to temptation and to sin. He will then be twice judged, as a man and a *bhikkhu*. Failing these tests, he will debase his calling and become like any other man – judged not by the law of the Buddha but by the laws of men. Once subject to the laws of men, he will lose his power as a *bhikkhu*. Far better, then, for him to follow in the footprints of the Buddha and

[123] *The Dharmapada*, The Choice, verse 2.
[124] *The Dharmapada*, Trouble verse 12.
[125] *The Dharmapada*, The Choice, verse 5.
[126] *The Dharmapada*, The Choice, verse 20.
[127] *The Dharmapada*, The Awakened One, verse 185.

be the guiding light of politicians and lay persons alike as they struggle to travel the true path of peace, and to chide, admonish and correct them when they deviate. This is his higher calling. And most monks strive to meet its demands, although sometimes they falter and stumble.

In Britain, the Anglican Church, except for its ceremonial role, has long since moved to the periphery of political life. When it speaks on political issues it is as a provider of moral and ethical guidance. In Italy, the Lateran Treaty, signed by Mussolini for Victor Emmanuel III and Pietro Cardinal Gaspari for the Pope, laid to rest issues that arose in 1870 to do with the temporal power of the Pope over Rome and its surrounds. It recognised the Vatican City as a separate and independent state within a state, with its base in Rome. In Spain, the government of Mr Zapatero is seeking to reduce state financial sponsorship of the Roman Catholic Church. Maybe it is time something similar happened in Sri Lanka. It would certainly be inappropriate for Sri Lanka to become a state ruled by *bhikkhus* or to continue to finance an institution that is rich with taxpayers' money for political gain.

The *bhikkhu* should redeem himself and his flock by leaving the secular sphere to the politicians, but watch them from afar and admonish and chide them when they step outside the *Dhammapada*. The monks who work and live among the villagers must work to moderate the extreme views and actions of the intemperate and, acting as guides and mentors, show them the true way. The monks who head the major temple complexes and their fellow monks should avoid intimate involvement with the political establishment except when the political processes deviate from humanity and justice. They should use their financial independence, derived from the revenues of temple lands and donations, to act as impartial referees in matters that affect their flock. They have it in them to encourage the village elders and the people to pursue peace. They are therefore a force for good or ill and should not allow themselves to be used as political tools, nor should they use the politicians as their tools. Similarly, the *bhikkhu* has a role in eliminating corruption within the political and public and private sectors of society. It is their voice, more than laws and judges, who will return justice and the rule of law to the country.

Their influence is too valuable to be squandered along party or partisan lines. As an integral part of the social fabric of society the Buddhist monk fulfils an important role in the lives of all the people of the island, thus showing that Buddhism helps people in this life as well as the next. Although he has passed on his role as doctor and teacher to others, he still carries the heavy burden of teaching and propagating Buddhism among the people in order to provide spiritual balance to their lives. *Bhikkhus* have to live up to the veneration, respect and support they receive from the laity. But their duty goes beyond what they owe their followers. Their message must reach across all religions and all races if they are to be the harbingers of peace. The worldly monk can do none of these things and will stand condemned by the Lord Buddha. The unworldly monk will shed light on the frailty of human existence; the value of obeying the Buddha's teaching, and highlight the blessings of following the *Dhammapada*.

It is such a monk that Sri Lanka needs as it seeks to abolish for ever the problems of racial and religious bigotry. He should preach the abiding value of tolerance and benevolence. He should preach the *dharma* and he should show the way to the unbeliever. Then, and only then, will Buddhism flourish and its message enrich the world beyond the shores of Lanka. With the help of such a *bhikkhu*, the nation can be rebuilt.

The most promising sign so far that this is beginning to happen is that the heavyweights of the Buddhist establishment are beginning to work for peace. The Maha Nayake Thera of the Malwatta Chapter, the Most Ven.Thibbottuwawe Sri Siddhartha Sumangala Thera, has met the Tamil National Alliance and asked them to participate in the National Advisory Council for Peace and Reconciliation. He has met the Indian Ambassador and is also putting pressure on the UNP to find a workable solution to the north-east ethnic conflict. Here, at last, is hope of a real kind, a lifeline for any political leader who wants to grasp it. The other hopeful sign that the Buddhist clergy are awakening to their true role is the resignation of the Ven. Sumangala Thera from the JHU. In his resignation letter, he stated that he has decided to quit party politics, saying that he finds politics unsavoury and disgusting.

It seems that some Buddhist monks have recognised that involvement in the political process violates the values that the Buddha taught and which they have promised to uphold at all times.

Chapter 34

Political Leadership for a Resurgent Nation

Sri Lanka today is a vastly different country from the one that the British vacated in 1948. It's a traumatised place. Years of communal riots, insurgencies and wars have depleted its people's reserves of drive and enterprise, of neighbourliness and goodwill towards others. The rural poor are still poor. The huge global opportunities have drifted by and a people well able to exploit it lie shattered and bruised and sapped of the energy necessary to benefit from it.

Hopefully, the negotiations that the Norwegians are chairing will deliver peace to the island. During the period of change that will inevitably follow peace the country will experience significant social and structural change as it recovers from these decades of enmity and grief. At times like this, leadership matters most. Stability demands only that you maintain things as they are. Change demands adaptation, an openness of mind, and the ability to handle a never-ending cascade of disorientation and dislocation. Above all it demands hope and faith: hope that the future will indeed turn out better, and faith that they can bring that better future about. In this transient environment there are no maps, but there are traps for the unwary. There are no finishing posts, just journeys and adventures. And the timid must be supported. Those unable to adapt fast enough to be in tune with the present reality must be carried part of the way. It is a long trek to the Promised Land. Old habits will have to be shed and only the weary, the dispossessed and the dispirited will have the motivation, the endurance and the constitution to make it to the end. The meek will indeed inherit the earth; the proud will be consumed by their folly.

Because of their proximity to the community, religious leaders and politicians of all races, religions and groups are best placed to be the transformational forces that guide their followers through these transient times. It seems strange to suggest such a role for people who hold strong views and beliefs. But if those values and beliefs are to flower into a peaceful and prosperous nation it is vital that the highest standards are forged from the best these many faiths and ideologies offer. Collectively, they would be irrepressible forces for good. Parliament, local authorities, local councillors, the judicial system, the security services, civilian authorities NGOs and those who work in them have a higher calling as custodians of the future of their communities, not as self-seeking opportunists. A lack of leadership from these institutions will debase them to being purely places where careers are forged or livings earned. And then they would have lost their purpose – they would be measured against the baser metal of cost and not of value.

Leadership extends from the individual to the community at large. There are four stages in this leadership paradigm. The first is individual leadership, as embodied in the effective follower. Without effective followers, the whole societal and organisational edifice will collapse. The next challenge is to create individual and team leadership in the institutions that govern the people so that collectively they achieve more than the sum of their parts. Thirdly, leaders – politicians, managers in commercial and government NGOs and local government departments – and their motivated and committed employees must jointly build leading institutions: exemplars of the values that their society wishes to see fostered and sustained. Finally, effective leadership by the elected representatives of the people should build a leading nation that is admired by others to the extent that they wish to emulate their example. At the heart of such a community one would see a deep sense of ownership, noble common values, a spirit of sacrifice, a will to work for the common good and to build on individual strengths.

The government and Parliament have a role to play as forces for good. They should be the exemplars of social aspirations, values and means. They should be the incorruptible core of the new nation. They should provide the fundamental social and physical infrastructures that enrich and empower communities and the individuals in them. Their value to the community lies in the quality of life that people grow up, live and die in. Above all, they should run a country to which all citizens are proud to belong and to which they gladly offer their loyalty so that each and every one can walk tall in the community of nations that is the world.

Within a changing community, the state, through its agents, remains the focus and the foundation stone of life in it. It cannot afford to be marginalised, ostracised or made impotent because there are no other institutions to take its place. And if it dies, its people will have no hope and no champion to give it better homes and schools, crime-free streets, uncongested roads, safe playing fields, jobs and careers, health services, help for the aged, libraries as food for the mind, and the host of other facilities that enrich and succour those within its bounds. Above all, these services should not be driven by the motive of profit but by the greater motive of human kindness, opportunity and generosity of spirit.

Nevertheless, the resources entrusted to the state and its agencies by the community must be harnessed and spent wisely and well – but not on schemes that satisfy the technocrat, the bureaucrat, the faddist, the opportunist, the gentleman, or government-sponsored thief. The first duty of a good government is to use the money entrusted to it by the people to build the solid foundations fundamental to a modern society. The baubles, bangles and beads can follow. The government is the nation's banker, not only of its money but also of its aspirations, hopes and dreams, and has the banker's duty to account for every penny and to return it on demand, albeit transformed from base metal to human worth. The governments of Sri Lanka have not as yet matched up to these high values but future governments can if they want to.

It would be nice to again hear the people say that their representatives at all levels of government use their money wisely. It would be nice to know that a broad range of people are genuinely grateful to the government for enriching their lives, for rewarding those who cherish their environment most, by giving them more, and that the government does more for people than they expect. Most importantly of all, government must influence public opinion so that the hard decisions are implemented without acrimony, communal disharmony or shouts of bias. Similarly, it would be nice if government is the prime mover in fostering and supporting innovation, developing potential, providing safe and secure environments in which the able-bodied and the disabled could experience life to the full. And that the government is willing to challenge and disturb the status quo to achieve this. Finally, it would be nice if the public acknowledged that all those who worked in all areas of the state were highly dedicated men and women with such a strong sense of community and an even stronger public service ethos that it engenders honesty and integrity in them.

None of this is possible without good leaders at every level and in every walk of life. The state cannot do all this on its own. The people need to join in provided the government takes the lead and sets the standards. Good governance begins with the president and the ministers and filters through to the country through their elected leaders and others in authority and with influence. But they must have a cause to fight and vision to chase after.

My own research into leadership shows that good leaders consistently display eight characteristics irrespective of the role they play at the time. The research findings are based on the views of 998 people (husbands, wives, parish priests, local officials, friends, strangers in foreign lands, bosses, colleagues, scout masters, and exercise fanatics in the sports field or the gym). Their leaders were not paragons of virtue. They were flawed human beings who wore the mantle of leader because of their willingness to carry a burden on behalf of others. They were followed despite their frailties. The study also showed that leadership was most needed during times of trouble, dislocation, disorientation and when people, events, resources and expectations had to be combined in a holistic and systematic way to derive benefits that satisfied the needs of many people with differing views of what is best and right. Most people experience leadership every day in many different ways but fail to recognise it because their minds carry an image of leadership that is to do with power and great deeds.

The study showed that anyone could be and often is a leader. Effective leaders were those who *protected* their followers. They were people who could be *trusted* because they were honest and had integrity, and they were people with an *adventurous* spirit who could innovate and envision new approaches and things and win others to the newer approach. Effective leaders were people who were *purposeful* in that they were able to implement their ideas by focusing on distant objectives and planning the route to take them there. Importantly too they were tenacious and showed great endurance. These leaders were *self-assured,* not in a boastful way but in a way that gave others confidence and a sense of security so that they felt able to follow their leader even when the going got tough. Effective leaders got *involved* with those they led. They were in touch with their followers and because of their emotional proximity could empathise readily with their needs, moods and aspirations. Similarly, these leaders *respected* their followers and treated them with fairness and consideration. And finally, effective leaders were *inclusive* in that they saw their followers as part of their 'team' and as people who had knowledge and skills to offer. Most importantly, they involved them in those decisions that affected their lives. In other words, they were democratic in both attitude and action, and in the spirit of the words' original meaning in a way that is rarely seen in democratic societies today.

There is nothing earth shattering about these findings. Their reproduction here is to aid recall. As Darwin pointed out when on one of his collecting forays '...how easy it is to overlook phenomena, however conspicuous, before they have been observed by any one.'[128]

It is time that the politicians and the priests and all those others who have designated roles as leaders recognise the greatness within the people as they continue to live honest, gentle and considerate lives under the harshest of conditions – conditions that their 'leaders' have created and now have difficulty correcting because their egos block the way. Despite the handicaps their leaders have created for them, the fathers and mothers in poor rural settings will continue to give life and love to those around them. They are capable of showing mercy and kindness to those they now call 'enemy' if only the public ethos will allow them. All it takes is good leadership to switch on these engines of peace.

The message to them is simple. They may think that they are small cogs in the huge wheel that is the politics of their country and that they have nothing more than a vote to contribute to it. This is wrong and it is time they were given a greater purpose than survival. It is the small cog that makes the big wheel go round and it takes great leaders to admit that and persuade others that they have a contribution to make that is collectively greater than their own puny attempts. It is time that the little drops of hate that have washed away the island in a torrent of rushing water are changed into tiny drops of forgiveness that will wash away the encrusted hate of half a century. And the renewed spirit of hope and peace is captured and used by leaders who care more for their flock than themselves.

Poor politicians, those who are ego- and power-centred, believe that voters exist to keep them in office, to emerge from their huts every five or six years,

---

[128] *The Autobiography of Charles Darwin, From The Life and Letters of Charles Darwin*, Francis Darwin (ed.), Project Gutenberg etext, 1999.

vote them into office, and blend back into the scenery. To these politicians, the voter is purely an object that is wooed into life at elections and returned to their 'place' once their vote is cast. Others see them as objects to be moved around until they find their preferred seat. And others still use the voters as the scapegoats for their uncharitable behaviour or blame them when unintended consequences mar their grand designs. And then there is the politician who sees in every grain of sand a mountain of difficulties and conjures up gremlins as excuses for their lack of imagination and perseverance. These are not the type of leaders that the Sri Lankan people need – now or ever.

The leaders Sri Lanka needs now are those who can put the past behind them and genuinely reach out for a new future and, when they know its shape, size and texture, to persuade all the people that it is worth working towards. They need to be able to distinguish between the cultures of the people and encourage them to take pride in these and live according to the values and beliefs these cultures foster – yet they must create the climate in which different cultures can coexist in harmony. Good leaders create effective followers. Neither are supermen and women. They are normal, hard-working, honourable people whose mindset is tuned to a strong self-belief, who understand that power is a tool with which to achieve not to grandstand, and that the Sinhalese Buddhist vote can be used for the good of all. It is therefore to the mind that the leaders in Sri Lanka need to appeal first. It is in the mind that people achieve their great aims and ideals. Although they may fall short of their ideals, good leaders strive to keep their own mind and those of their followers on the far horizon. The pen is mightier than the sword because it captures the mind, whereas the sword scars the body.

A country is a human gearbox, a mass of intricately engineered gearwheels enmeshed in the great task of nation building. Human gearwheels have much more than teeth. They have minds and hearts that govern their actions. No process, however efficient, can substitute for the human will or sublimate it for ever. So, if the politicians start, others must follow. When the small cog in the gearbox first starts to move, it encounters enormous resistance from all the other bigger cogs. The inertia may be such that it has to exert much greater force than its little self can muster. But its determination, self-belief and perseverance will eventually turn the others and then they all contribute to the forward momentum. Of course, the bigger cog could be so inert that it breaks the small cogs. But the whole gearbox then becomes useless. And it is in the interests of all the people to prevent that from happening. There is another, more compelling reason. The cog that moves drives the gearbox; the other cogs simply follow. It is time that the honest, law-abiding citizen shakes off the inertia of indifference and starts to move so that the others will too. And the place to start is in their own backyard.

The duty of the good leader is to create the climate for change. Culture and climate are often spoken of as if they are interchangeable words. They are not. Cultures are very definitely about values and beliefs. Climates are the conditions in which cultures are expressed. A good climate will allow many cultures to coexist. It will enable people to value their own culture and respect those of others. It will encourage them to give them and others the space in which to practice their cultures. And a good climate will encourage people to take and use the best values and beliefs of their culture knowing that, in principle but perhaps not in practice, they deviate only marginally. A good climate will nurture and feed many different cultures, just as a clear pool will sustain a myriad of fish. It is when the pool stagnates and the water gets poisoned that the fish die or fight for survival. Good leaders make sure the pool is always more than fit for the fish. Then the fish will take care of themselves and the pool will benefit too. All that good leaders need to do is to remember the words in Charles Reade's *The Cloister and the Hearth*:

> Not a day passes over the earth, but men and women of no note do great deeds, speak great words, and suffer noble sorrows.

The role of the political leader is to hear the voices of their constituents, observe their deeds and gain inspiration from the great words they speak; to ennoble each voter by making each individual know that he or she matters. That is the true art of leadership. And last, but by no means least, is the view that all good leaders know that the quality of their leadership is judged by the behaviour of their *followers* and not by the size of their office, their ego or their bank balance.

Chapter 35

Recovering the Island for all the People

In a democracy, people get the leaders they deserve. The people of Sri Lanka have chosen leaders whose avowed objective is to protect the Sinhalese language and the Buddhist religion. But their purpose in espousing its cause is deeply suspect. It provided no advantage to the country. Time would have resolved the issue. By virtue of the disproportionate number of people who were Sinhalese and Buddhist, both causes would have arrived at centre stage in an evolutionary and non-confrontational way. By pushing it to the forefront and turning it into a test of loyalty and virility for political purposes, the politicians and the Buddhist clergy did a disservice both to their religion and their people.

Since 1956, this policy has brought the island and its people nothing but trouble. The most valuable resource of the island, its people, was and is continuing to be squandered on the altar of chauvinist ideology. And the future is bleak indeed.

As long as the statute books and the constitution give the Sinhalese Buddhist pre-eminent status by virtue of race and religion, and deny talent and merit its rightful place in the affairs of the country, the 'freedom wars' will continue. As long as there is a significant volume of unemployed youth among the Sinhalese Buddhists in the hinterland, the potential for insurgencies will always be there. As long as the economy limps along on the output of the plantation sector, low-cost manufacturing, inward remittances from domestic service and on the benevolence of the international aid programmes and loan agencies, the country will be a debtor to the world. That is an untenable state – even the *bhikkhu* has abandoned the mendicants bowl for a tax-free income. As long as the young are denied the fluent use of a universal language like English they will be denied the knowledge of the world, and with every passing day, their ignorance will grow – as will their isolation from the world community. The longer their isolation continues, the greater their frustration will be at lost opportunities for a gainful youth and prosperous old age. These are the underlying truths. Here is a country whose clouds do not have a silver lining because the sunshine of freedom, equality under the law, justice, tolerance and magnanimity, has been obliterated by prejudice, bigotry and selfishness. The villains are in charge and denying the heroes – a free and honourable people – their rightful place in a democratic society whose values must be tinged by the generosity and benevolence of the Lord Buddha's teachings.

If the people are to get the leaders they deserve, they, too, will have to change their focus and remove the huge impediments to achieving these changes.

Only the people can deny the dynastic ambitions of its leaders who treat their country as a personal fiefdom to be handed down (or sideways) from husband to wife, mother to daughter or father to son.

Only the people can relegate the feudal mentality of its leaders to history and prevent the arbitrary use of the democratic process to further their ends.

Only the people can call to account those whose disproportionate wealth epitomises the greed and venality of a debauched elite. The obscenity of the unproductive wealth of a few can be seen on the streets of Colombo as they travel in their shiny temples of newly acquired wealth – not wealth earned from wealth created and shared through a thriving productive nation, but the wealth of middlemen acting as intermediaries between suppliers and a monopoly government procurement process that pays for most of its capital purchases with borrowed money or aid funds. Their power to corrode the integrity of poorly paid public servants and their political masters so that they spend money on irrelevant and strategically wasteful enterprises for personal gain is a shameful tendency that must be totally eliminated. To them the situation of the country is irrelevant as is the poverty of their fellow countrymen and women. They invest their assets abroad rather than reinvest them to drive a productive economy and return benefits to the hungry mouths from which their wealth was created.

Only the people can halt the absurdity of an ever-rising population that demands more than the land can give. It takes a highly productive economy to sustain population growth from 7 million in 1947 to 20 million now without harming their standard of living. The stumbling economy of the country is accelerating the poverty of the people, and the juggernaut of poverty is travelling faster and faster down a steepening slope. This is exacerbated by the fact that what the country earns and gets in the form of international loans and grants is spent on paying interest on the loans and buying armaments after some of the money has been siphoned off by corrupt officials and their commercial intermediaries.

Only the people can demand that their offspring learn a language that has currency outside the island's shores. The only language that matters in the international arena is English, and yet it is only the children of the rich who can benefit from it. It is therefore only the children of a select few who, by keeping abreast of current thinking and events on a wide range of issues, can benefit from the phenomenal growth of knowledge and thereby be attractive to the international workplace. The language policy must be changed so that every child on the island is taught English to a very high level of competence. But in the current political climate this will not happen. Many in the Buddhist establishment know that once the eyes of the majority are opened to the obscenity of their patronising religious leaders they will lose their power to extort money from the poor and superstitious.

Only the people can become a nation. It is only they who can come together to become a cohesive whole that rids the island, once and for all, of sectarian differences and violence. Nationalism has raised its head from time to time, and the ancient heroes of a proud people brought them together to oust invaders occupying their capital cities of Anuradhapura and Polonnaruwa. Today, the unwelcome visitor to its shores is racial and in recent years persecution of Christians. In the absence of progressive leaders, the people themselves must lead the renaissance. In this they must be helped, not led astray, by the sangha who alone can inject the secular body politic with the civilising force of the teaching of the philosopher prince. Only then will the people get a government fit to rule a *dharmadipa*.[129]

[129] A land that accords with the laws and teachings of the Lord Buddha.

Chapter 36

Treat India as a Valued Neighbour

It would be wrong for the Sinhalese to label the Tamils of the north and east as expatriate Indians. The Tamils of Sri Lanka are Sri Lankans first and foremost and wish to be treated as such. They and their offspring are kept in bondage, as there is really no scope for them to break free from the captivity of Sinhalese racists and their own belligerent leaders and build new lives as free and equal citizens of Sri Lanka. The situation of the plantation Tamils is probably even bleaker as they have no one with adequate bargaining power to fight for them.

Neither the Sinhalese nor the Tamils can survive in isolation from the other and still share the same island. There are huge issues to do with fishing rights, territorial boundaries, the relationship with India, recognition by the wider world community and so on to be dealt with. The Sinhalese have found that genocide is an unlikely option as the Tamil Tigers have proved, time and again, that they can mount a strong and stubborn defence against malignant forces. Isolating the Tamils will only send them into the arms of the Tamil state of Tamil Nadu where people such as Mr Karunanithi, a one-time chief minister of the state, have expressed pan-Tamil sentiments in the hope of extending his influence more widely across the Tamil communities of India and Sri Lanka. The refugees from the conflict in the north form another bridge across which political alliances can be forged. But this is not a route that the Tamil separatist movement in Sri Lanka has sought. Since neither group can prosper without the constructive help of the other, it would be most sensible if both groups abandoned their tribal nature and combined their talents to form a single common nation as the first step to exploiting the opportunity that a global economy now offers.

But there are obstacles to overcome. The Sinhalese politicians and a smaller section of Buddhist clergy realise that there is considerable political mileage in keeping India and the Tamils in the north as bogeymen. These are levers of power and control that they will not give up easily. Their message to the Sinhalese people will be that Buddhism would be at risk if India were to play a greater role in the affairs of the islanders. If the fundamentalist Sinhalese Buddhist group persist in believing this nonsense, their suspicion of India will grow. This is at the crux of the argument and the basis of Sinhalese fears and as long as that fear persists there is no hope of peace between these two communities. However, if the Sinhalese disown their Tamil cousins they are likely to make this supposition a reality.

This fear of India and the fear that the Tamil allegiances lie with India has been reinforced by the fact that the Tamil Tigers have used South Indian bases, and the leaders of the state of Tamil Nadu have taken a benign view of their presence there. These fears were heightened even more when Mr Jayawardene invited an Indian peacekeeping force to the island. But the federal government of India had taken a harder line, and since the assassination of Rajiv Gandhi their indulgence has given way to anger and resentment that their good intentions were abused by those they tried to help.

The reality is that India does not need the help of the Tamils of the northern peninsula to occupy the island if it did so wish. In fact is it unlikely that such a huge country with ample resources of its own, racing to gain super-nation status, would wish to expend its goodwill with the global community, its people and or its resources annexing Sri Lanka. More importantly, China will not stand idly by if Sri Lanka is invaded by India because the strategic implications of such a move would send out the wrong signals to others who may have imperialist tendencies in the region. However, India and China would resist any other power attempting to camp out on the shores of Sri Lanka. India would prefer that Sri Lanka become a neutral and prosperous nation because it would not want China to befriend it and infiltrate Chinese ideology into the island by channelling it through its Buddhist establishment, even though Chinese Buddhism is based on the Mahayana tradition.

However, China may use generous gifts to win the heart of the people because they know that by compromising the neutrality of the island they could make it a 'dependency' and gain leverage over India by threatening its southern flank. But if the 'friendship' of China took on the nature of China's occupation of Tibet, it would be utterly unwelcome to the Sri Lankan people and will be resisted by them. And India would help them keep China at bay.

There are a whole series of similar scenarios that can be played out, but in the final analysis, an independent Sri Lanka that has strong trading links to India would more than please India at this present time, particularly as it is attempting to play a more significant role in world politics. This means, of course, that the fear of the Sinhalese nationalists that India would use the Tamils in the north to infiltrate and subjugate them should be debunked for the nonsense that it is. India would use more subtle means: the proposed ship canal and bridge between Sri Lanka and India and the proposal by the Indian Oil Corporation to use Trincomalee Harbour are more likely to increase Sri Lanka's dependence on India. At present, ships plying their trade between the east coast of India and the west coast of India, Africa and the Middle East and South Africa need to go round the southern tip of Sri Lanka. Many would dock in Galle to unload and load goods and to refuel and replenish food and water stocks. India's proposed Sethusamudram Ship Canal Project will divert this trade to the north of the island. By digging a canal through the twenty-two miles of water called the Palk Straits that divides the south of India from the north of Sri Lanka, ships could bypass Colombo and Galle completely. This would reduce ship traffic in the south of Sri Lanka but increase it in the north, because ships carrying goods to Sri Lanka and the east coast of India will prefer to dock and unload their Sri Lankan cargo in Trincomalee or Jaffna. If, at the same time, there was a road bridge between Talaimannar and Trichinopoli, like the rail link that existed until recently, Sri Lanka's commercial future will be securely tied to that of India. And those who would benefit most would be the Tamils in the north. It must, therefore, make sense for the Sinhalese in the south to keep their northern cousins happy.

However, India will always be wary of the political complexion of the island, and if it really felt that it was taking a turn that was unfriendly to it, India might act to annex Sri Lanka. Any suggestion that the Tamils in the north of the island are essential to such Indian intentions can be dismissed as irrelevant as they were a millennia or more ago. In fact the reverse is true. As long as there is an autonomous group of Tamils in the north, India is likely to leave things well alone. Besides, it knows from the experience of the peacekeeping forces sent to the island by Rajiv Gandhi that it will need a significant presence to contain the island people if they combined their efforts to resist any Indian incursion. One hopes that the modern Sri Lankan has learnt the lesson that his forebears failed to learn – that there is strength in unity.

There is, however, another fundamental reality. Size is important in the global economy of today. The cost of entry into new markets is beyond the reach of the Sri Lankan exchequer. Piggybacking on global businesses such as American and European multinationals has its attractions, but in the main it provides very low-value-added work and makes the government of the island at risk of blackmail from them. So, unless there is a plan to grow out of its current subsistence economy, the talented people of Sri Lanka will continue to earn labourers' wages.

What is needed now is high-value-added work, and India can make this a reality. Because Sri Lanka lacks industrial production and the cost of entry would be prohibitive, its best bet is to move to a knowledge-based economy. India, its closest neighbour, has a head start. So India should be treated as a source of strength and support rather than as an enemy if the people of Sri Lanka wish to exploit the huge potential of the giant next door.

Part Seven

Discussion Papers

Summary

In reviewing the recent history of Sri Lanka, I observed a series of governance issues there that seem to have parallels in other countries that gained independence from colonial powers during the later years of the twentieth century and became self-governing democracies. I have summarised these issues in the two discussion papers that follow. In the first, I raise a series of questions to do with the governance of a unitary multi-ethnic state in which one ethnic group dominates and where the electorate can be encouraged to vote according to sectarian rather than political or economic criteria to favour certain power groups. The second paper seeks to raise a discussion about whether terrorists and suicide bombers are the creation of bad governance or whether they are wicked people who seek any excuse to express their bloodlust.

Discussion Paper 1

The Governance of Unitary Multi-ethnic Democratic States

During the writing of this book, despite my strong criticism of the leaders of modern Sri Lanka, there is no doubt that they had to grapple with some rather thorny issues to do with the governance of a unitary multi-ethnic democratic state. This discussion paper details the issues that arose and I offer them to the student of politics as questions seeking answers. It seems clear that the political leaders of Sri Lanka have not been able to square the circle.

Sri Lanka started its new life on an optimistic note. It had gained independence without bloodshed. The transition had been smooth, but it ran into stormy waters soon after independence, and is floundering still.

The story of how that came about and how it affected the people of the island is charted in the preceding pages of this book. There has been a catastrophic failure of leadership among majority and minority groups. But that is not the whole story. It is tempting to lay the blame at the feet of human wickedness, the selfishness of sub-groups or the greed and lust for power of politicians and so on *ad infinitum* for the current troubles on the island. But human frailties dog political systems and sometimes they accentuate rather than moderate or nullify the negative. Dwelling on them rarely helps to shed light on the route to a better future. The disharmony, the petty bickering and the settling of old scores was an unavoidable human response of a people who had wanted but were not totally prepared for self-government. The leaders who chose the British model of parliamentary democracy believed that because it had worked so well for Britain, it would work in Ceylon. But it has not.

Although over the last fifty-six years Sri Lanka has had its share of governor generals, prime ministers and presidents and all the other paraphernalia of democracy, democracy in its true and widest sense has eluded the island people. What the world saw or wanted to see was an illusion. An electorate that voted on communal lines distorted the democratic process for communal advantage. The constitutional changes in 1972 and 1978 made matters worse. So, the story of democracy in Sri Lanka is that it has failed to deliver peace, prosperity, equality under the law, equality of opportunity, an independent judiciary or a meritocratic society.

Those who have lived in democratic societies that have been forged through argument and negotiation over centuries or who have, as one people, evolved their own democratic institutions to match their cultural values do not understand fully the burdens it places on a people new to it. They probably are even less able to understand the pressures and tension it brings to a state that is made up of a cultural, racial and religious amalgam and where all these three elements of the culture are as dear to the people as life itself that they would willingly die to sustain them. They may also not understand that new and emergent democracies depend more on personalities than on a sound party system. They may fail to see that lacking sound foundations democracy can be easily high jacked by pressure groups and that where a single communal group dominates the electoral process it can be used to legitimately oppress and disadvantage minority communities. Most of all, they cannot comprehend that in newer democracies the process is seen as a means to power and wealth. Niall Ferguson, writing in the *Telegraph*, makes this point when he refers to a conversation with a Tanzanian opposition leader's son:

> For most of his life, his father had been in jail. 'You see,' he explained to me, 'what African politicians find hard to understand about democracy is why, once they have got power, they should have to hand it over to someone else just because of an election.'[130]

Whilst Africa is poor, its leaders are wealthy. Ferguson also points out in the same article, referring to Gordon Brown's undertaking to use British Taxpayers money to pay off the debts of Tanzania and other similar countries: 'For power means, above all, money. It means being the guy to whom Brown hands the bulging envelope.' This is not just an African disease. The process of subversion of the democratic ideal in Sri Lanka was subtle and went unobserved by the international community because, in its early stages, there were no visible signs to alert the world that it is happening. It is only when war or civil unrest highlights the problem that the world takes notice. By then it is too late.

The current problems are not a carry-over from pre-colonial days. Nor are they the fault of Britain, the country's last colonial master. They are of recent making and have to do with the way democracy works in a multi-ethnic unitary state where people vote on communal lines and one community has an overwhelming majority. The problems highlight the fact that, like all human systems, the country's failure has more to do with the way democracy is operated than in the process. This chapter explores the issues that can waylay the democratic system in a multi-ethnic unitary state. We start with the architects of the current system and then go on to consider issues related to the key players and the process.

The Challenge faced by the Soulbury Commission

Lord Soulbury knew that behind the nice words and good manners displayed by the leaders of the Sinhalese, Tamils, Muslims and Dutch Burghers (the oligarchy that purported to represent the people of the island) there was tension among these different groups, particularly about how the majority

[130] Niall Ferguson, 'Africa doesn't need handouts: it needs honest governments', *Telegraph*, 5 February 2005.

community would use its powers. But the minorities did not make these concerns stumbling blocks to achieving independence. As Ludowyk points out 'Communal rifts were plastered over by the oligarchy in its anxiety to persuade the Soulbury Commissioners that it spoke for the whole country.' But there was an attempt to make the electoral system fair. The Delimitation Commission appointed in 1946 took great pains to ensure that the way the electoral boundaries were defined enabled minorities in sparsely populated areas to gain higher representation. They assumed that by so doing they could ameliorate the obvious advantage the electoral system would give the Sinhalese people, especially if voting was based on communal considerations. The findings of the Delimitation Commission attempted to, as far as possible, embed the long held tenets of Colonial Office policy – 'that no single community can impose its will upon the other communities'. But this attempt at fairness was soon reversed by the first multi-ethnic government appointed in 1948 and succeeding governments continued to pass laws that disadvantaged minority communities. The behaviour of the electorate and the actions of succeeding governments to match communal expectations of the majority further skewed the process and heightened differences between communities. Democracy was seen by the people not as a liberating influence but as a political mechanism with the potential to grasp and keep power so that they could get their own way. The mindset was feudal. The fallout was a natural extension of this thinking and affected the areas discussed here.

Electoral Integrity

Within months of gaining independence, the new government made up of multi-party representatives set out to clarify the position of the plantation workers who were Indian Tamils and Hindus. Independent India's definition of its citizens excluded the plantation workers in Sri Lanka, who were considered to be Indian citizens during British rule, but they were not formally citizens of Sri Lanka, so they ended up being stateless persons. However sincere the government's objectives were in trying to sort out the citizenship issues of these plantation workers, it is hard not to conclude that it was seen more as an attack on the minority community that was the weakest and the least able to defend itself. A more liberal and probably correct interpretation was that, although there were more pressing issues to deal with, the government chose this racially explosive issue to gain political advantage. By declaring the plantation workers stateless the government increased the Sinhalese majority in these areas and increased the number of Sinhalese parliamentarians. This piece of gerrymandering presaged many similar efforts by succeeding government to tilt the balance in their favour. The politicians and the people failed this first test of political integrity and personal magnanimity. The voices of protest, although loud, had no legislative weight and were therefore ineffectual. So the questions that come to mind are:

- What are the preconditions for democracy to work in the interests of all the people in a state particularly when the people living in it feel more strongly about their ethnicity, religion and language than other factors such as health provision, economic strength, safety and education for example?
- How can electoral integrity be preserved in a multi-ethnic unitary state if a government intent on keeping power redefines boundaries to increase its majority in Parliament?
- How can minority groups in Parliament stop the political parties that represent the majority community from barring them from Parliament on one pretext or another as was done to the TULF by the Jayawardene government?

Political Maturity of the Voters

The people of Sri Lanka had never before been asked to select and appoint its leaders. So they did not know how to go about such a process. Despite the constitution and the fine sentiments the integrity of the democratic system was placed in the hands of an unsophisticated electorate that was genuinely incapable of judging political programmes or the leadership qualities needed to secure their future prosperity and peace. The questions that relate are:

- How do those who make the use of the democratic process a condition of their freedom judge that the people they wish it on are able to carry its awesome responsibility?
- When should the democratic process be initiated?
- Could the people leapfrog from being ruled by kings or tyrants to ruling themselves, even if they have had a short period of self-governance under the supervision of experienced colonial masters?
- Can a people who have the democratic process willed on them by others really understand and use the true scope and capability of the process? This is not to imply that they are stupid or ignorant, far from it. But it is necessary to ask whether it is not very much like giving someone who has just passed their driving test a Formula One racing car. It could be argued that, without the rigorous mental and physical preparation necessary to change from a learner driver into a racing car driver, a successful tour of the circuit at racing speeds would be more one of luck than skill.
- Can a people who do not understand the process by which they elect their leaders, even though their leaders may understand the process and exploit it to their advantage, make judgements about it and those who operate it?

- In a country where Politics in Sri Lanka is personality rather than ideology or party based and the majority of people still choose their leader according to tradition and family background, community or racial bias, how do those voters who lack the training and understanding to make choices from the various political programmes offered to them avoid choosing on the grounds of personality rather than issues? How can they avoid voting for the individual they believe in most? Are they not placed in the position of a punter who, because he does not understand the intricacies of handicapping, bets on the name of the horse or the name of the jockey?
- How can voters learn to act rationally rather than sentimentally? It is generally accepted that Dudley Senanayake was voted into office in 1952 partially on his own merits but also because of the sympathy people felt for him at his father's untimely death. Similarly, Mrs Bandaranaike's victory over Dudley Senanayake in 1960 was due, in large part, to the sympathy people felt for her at the assassination of her husband the previous year.
- How can an unsophisticated electorate be prevented from falling back on communal rhetoric and racially motivated objectives when that is an issue that they understand best and can relate to most and find the easiest to judge?
- When does an electorate recognise that electing a leader who has a gathering of associates rather than the backing of an effective political party is unlikely to be able to deliver the promises they make? In personality-driven politics, those who tag along with the leader do so, not because they share the leader's vision, but because it will give them a handle on power and the benefits of office. In these situations expediency determines policy and the leader forms alliances that are detrimental to the leader's objectives purely to gain and keep power. This is illustrated by the alliances made by Mr and Mrs Bandaranaike and their daughter Mrs Kumaratunga whose current allies in government are from the party that viciously and brutally challenged the government headed by her mother and whose allegiance to her and her political objectives is deeply questionable. In other words, the party exists because the leader exists. This is very different to what happens in consolidated democracies such as those in Europe where the leader exists because the party exists. In consolidated democracies the leader may make the party electable but nonetheless the party is an important element in the political process and in the leader's ability to govern. It is also a brake on the leader and often the mechanism by which an unsatisfactory leader's political life is ended. In these democracies, leaders who cannot gain the support of the party they lead are unlikely to win

through because they will find it difficult to establish electoral credibility.

- How can a less experienced electorate manage their leaders so that democracy works for and not against them? A sophisticated electorate knows how to manipulate the democratic process to bring their politicians to heel. They use protest marches, the legal process, the media, and political lobbying to get their message across. This type of public behaviour is too much to expect in new democracies as the culture of peaceful protest has not been established and few know how to use it constructively. What often happens is that resentment against a perceived injustice is nursed until it explodes into violence. This is a national trait that was experienced by the Portuguese, the Dutch and the British on many occasions.
- How should the electorate deal with undemocratic leaders who maintain the process purely to gain acceptance in the wider world and benefit from its generosity? Or who change the rules to keep them in office longer? This is not an unfair question. As previous chapters have shown various prime ministers and presidents of Sri Lanka have used the democratic process to prolong their stay in office and to modify the rules of engagement to suit their own chances of winning. The democratic vote in these circumstances is nothing more than a robbers' charter. And the constitutions of 1972 and 1978 achieved nothing more than the legitimisation of vote winning opportunism that has left one segment of the population permanently disadvantaged, created a state of war that is destroying the country and has created a situation that is totally contrary to the basic principles that govern constitutions – that the people should be protected from the excesses of the state or the pressure groups that dictate its policies.
- How does the electorate deal with politicians who betray their trust or exploit their naivety? Scare mongering has been used to create situations and to use them to gain emergency powers and to then use these powers to subvert the democratic process.
- How can the people mobilise world opinion to protect them from their leaders when their leaders abuse their powers, the judicial system fails them and the world is not listening? This is a real problem because in recent years the judiciary in Sri Lanka has become complaint to government wishes. The answer must be that they should have access to an independent arbitrator who is outside the sphere of influence of the government or its external sponsors. Because, even if their findings cannot be enforced, their judgements will confirm injustices to the international community and the opprobrium of the international community would matter to the Sri Lankan people. But international

bodies have not, as a matter of principle, challenged those sections of the constitution that are contrary to good practice, preferring to ignore them provided the government in power is sympathetic to the political objectives of the superpower and its allies. Their silence has emboldened the majority community.

Governing for all the People

In a multi-ethnic unitary state, it is tempting for politicians to focus only on the community that can elect them to high office and keep them in power. That is the only certainty they have of protecting their careers, their lifestyle and their privileged status. But this proves, in the end, to be a beggar's charter as is evident from the recent history of Sri Lanka and other similar countries. They lose if the country loses, unless their main aim in seeking office is to enrich themselves. This is true of some but, one hopes, is not true of all. To avoid the energy and enterprise of the country being wasted on internecine strife, governments have to govern for the benefit of all the people and be seen to be bending over backwards to protect the most vulnerable. They have to move the agenda away from community issues to the wider platform of the economy, health, safety, justice and so on. The people must realise that their ethnicity is a given but that the others have to be worked for and that, if they wish to put a gloss on their ethnicity, they must achieve wider social and economic objectives. To achieve this governments need answers to the following questions:

- How can they secure the unitary state and protect it from those who wish to divide it? This will prove more critical as the growing literacy that will be a key characteristic of this new millennium will create educated people who will eventually wish to break away from the guardianship or dominance of others and seek to create an independent life in which they deal with others as adults rather than children or supplicants.
- How can they evolve and adjust the democratic process they have inherited to accommodate the wishes and desires of a multi-ethnic community, especially when one group dominates the electoral process and holds the key to who gets to sit on the president's and prime minister's chairs?
- How can they protect themselves and their people from the excessive demands of today's superpowers who, through threats and financial inducements, seek to encourage them to operate domestic policies that support the superpower's foreign and domestic objectives, when these are detrimental to their own people?
- How can they protect the democratic process and the people from the usurpation of government by military or rebel forces that seek to achieve narrow objectives?

- How can they draw on the skills and abilities of the most advanced countries whilst protecting their cultural integrity?
- How can they encourage individuals and groups who have genuine grievances to openly voice their displeasure rather than nurse their grievances and then to explode with destructive energy?
- How can they respond positively to stated grievances rather than brushing them under the carpet or suppressing dissent? Suppression has never prevented or stifled the human spirit. History also shows us that the hypocrisy of fine words will not mask an iron hand for ever nor will financial inducements contain the free spirit from breaking free from its shackles even if they are made of gold and lined with velvet. When a people reach out for freedom they will pay any price to reach their goal and through persistent effort erode the will of those who stubbornly stand in their way.

The Duty of the Majority Community

As Lord Soulbury pointed out, the majority community also has needs and expectations and they will hope to secure these using their electoral advantage. It would certainly be unfair to suggest that they should not. Neither should the majority community be expected to act altruistically. But what the global community expects of them is that they not abuse their power, act unfairly or use their electoral power to victimise minorities. If they do not act fairly out of goodwill they should because it makes economic and social sense to do so. The last fifty-six years have shown that, in reality, successive governments have knowingly tilted the balance in the favour of the majority community because it kept them in power. It would be different if the population discarded communal politics and voted on issues that would deliver social and economic benefits. Unfortunately, the politicians representing the majority community will not want them to change their voting criteria, because to stay in power they have to maintain communal tension at its current fever pitch. The questions facing the majority community are:

- What will it take for them to shed communal politics?
- Are they capable of showing the discipline and goodwill needed to persuade the electorate to grant the needs and aspirations of the minority groups?
- Will they, as a first step towards achieving a lasting peace, voluntarily subject themselves to an audit by an independent international judiciary and abide by its decisions so that all the people can feel fairly treated? By using the democratic process to legitimise unfair behaviour it has heaped burning coals on the people. If an independent process of overview and appeal exists as part of the process of governance the minorities can

challenge the government when they think it is acting undemocratically and outside the law and justice.

- Should the majority community believe that it is their right to ask for and get a disproportionate share of what the country has to offer?
- Should government-sponsored terror be used to victimise and disadvantage minority communities even before they had risen up in arms? (This question refers to the communal riots where the rioters were not made accountable.)
- Should the policies and aspirations of a nation be governed by the demands of a powerful pressure group – the Buddhist nationalists – to whom the government is subservient? Perhaps it is time for the majority community to take a good hard look at the way they are using their democratic rights given that they have succeeded in enshrining Sinhalese and Buddhism as the predominant language and religion of the country.
- Given that the majority have a natural advantage, why is it necessary for them to provoke confrontation with the minorities?
- What will it cost the majority community to act magnanimously and to even out some of the biases built into the legislature so that all the citizens of Sri Lanka can play on a level playing field since the democratic process gives them a natural advantage?
- How much more degradation must the people of minority ethnic groups endure before commonsense prevails?
- Why has the majority community not harnessed the influence of the Buddhist clergy and the moderates in the country to still the storm and to rebuild this ravaged country?
- Why do the Sinhalese politicians still play-act at wanting peace? Is it because they feel that they can defeat the Tamils and subjugate them. Otherwise would they not have begun talks long ago?

The Role of Minority Leaders

Minority leaders have a duty to their communities. Naturally, they have an obligation to protect them and to secure their interests. But they also have a duty to develop strong ties with the majority community so that, as friends, they can collectively reap greater benefits for both communities. This is not altruism, it is a higher form of self-interest in that it is not self-serving and therefore does not give rise to valid claims of selfishness. It improves the ability of both communities to survive in a wider world context and gains secure futures for both groups. This requires the minority leaders to recognise legitimate concerns and needs of the majority and to be willing to contribute to the majority community's own needs and aspirations. Should the leaders of the minority groups:

- Allow their community to disintegrate like the Burgher community in Sri Lanka did in the 1950s when families, using their European ancestry, migrated to new lives in Europe and Australia because they felt unwanted and unwelcome in the country of their birth?
- Connive with the majority groups to disadvantage other minority groups?
- Cope as best they can, like the leaders of the plantation workers had to do because they were unable to mobilise support from other groups?
- Try politics, like the Tamils, and then resort to revolt – even to the point where such belligerence reduces them to exploiting children in their 'freedom' struggle?
- Use force, like the Low-Country Sinhalese youth did, to gain political visibility and acceptance – even though they were beaten when they tried?
- Work closely with the political leaders of the majority community to achieve mutual gains for all?

The paramount question among the Muslims in Sri Lankan politics today is how their leaders should behave now to prevent any peace accord between the Sinhalese and Tamils from disadvantaging them or sacrificing their interests. If they emulate their Tamil and Sinhalese cousins in the hope that violence will win them a seat at the negotiating table and recognition as a legitimate group whose views matter in the country's affairs, it is likely that a new war will erupt and no one will benefit from it. Similarly, if the Sinhalese and Tamil communities ignore the needs of the Muslims, they may invite an influx of 'fighters for Islam' from the Middle East and elsewhere. Surely it makes sense for the Muslim community to work with the government of Sri Lanka and their Norwegian friends and the representatives of the Tamil community to stop any potential victimisation – not act as stumbling blocks to the achievement of peace in the country. At one time the different communities were fighting over the cake, now they are fighting for the crumbs – and what price is a crumb worth? Is it worth the sacrifice of the lives of the young caught up in the struggles and the lives of others who get hurt in the crossfire? The overriding issue is whether a system that drives people to such extreme behaviour in an attempt to get redress for their grievances and be branded as terrorists and criminals is worth sustaining. If not, what alternative is there?

Relationship between Minority Leaders and Majority Leaders

In multi-ethnic unitary states the relationship between the leaders of minority groups and the leaders of the majority groups is a key issue. Since, in a democracy, people have to be persuaded by argument, both groups of leaders need each other if the system is to work. If either or both groups denigrate or diminish the other, both will weaken their ability to influence their followers. In the final analysis, the credibility of a leader is enhanced by the leader's ability to deliver results. If leaders are unable to do this, they lose their influence and cease to be credible channels of communication. Once that happens, they will not be able to mediate and sell policies to their electorate. If the leaders of the majority groups make the leaders of minority groups impotent it opens the door to rebel leaders who claim that concession can only be obtained by the sword. Once rebel leaders have captured the hearts and minds of the minority communities they are able to mobilise them for acts of aggression on the grounds that their elected political leaders are ineffective or are stooges of the other political groups. The questions that come to mind therefore are these:

- How do all leaders maintain their credibility as effective operators for the good of their communities in a system that depends on persuasion and argument to achieve its aims?
- Does it ever make sense to place democratically elected leaders outside the political process so the people they represent feel unrepresented?
- During periods of war or rebellion does it make sense to break off communications with the belligerents?

Relationship between the Government and the Judiciary

When even the most benign and benevolent of governments are put under pressure they tend towards a disciplinarian approach to law and justice. They become progressively more dictatorial. As long as this is considered well meant they may earn the sobriquet of the 'nanny state'. But when things really hot up, they become overbearing and seek not to solve the causes of discontent, but to suppress or stifle it. A ploy that governments tend to use is to immediately declare that the dissenting group are troublemakers. If branding them and setting them apart fails, they attempt to pass laws that impinge on their civil liberties. In most consolidated and mature democracies, people who feel discriminated against in this way can seek redress through the legal system and, if that fails, appeal to international judicial processes such as the European Court of Justice to help them recover their lost ground. Sometimes, governments pandering to a majority viewpoint may be content to allow the judicial system to return a sense of proportion to the debate and be pleased that they can still hold their heads high for having tried. There is therefore a symbiotic relationship between governments and the judiciary that can be used for good rather than be seen as confrontational. In emergent democracies, this route is not available to the majority of citizens because they just do not have the means to invoke these super-judiciary processes to help them. So they may depend on their local judicial system but if that fails they have nowhere to go but get militant. The questions for the judiciary are:

- How do they avoid becoming instruments of the state, particularly a means of suppressing dissent or condoning government actions that breach the rule of law or the wider conventions of human rights?
- How do they maintain their personal integrity when under political pressure?
- How do they give the nation total confidence in the impartiality and integrity of the judicial process?
- How should they protect the people from bad laws and bad governments?

Managing Pressure Groups and Vested Interests

Since independence, the governments of Sri Lanka have been subject to powerful pressure groups. The Buddhist establishment sought redress for the wrongs it felt had been committed against it by various foreign powers over a period of 450 years. The others were the Low-Country youth and the Tamil liberation movements. The latter two have resorted to violence and terror to get redress for wrongs they felt had been committed against them. How should these pressure groups be dealt with by governments?

- Should they identify them, annihilate them, and forget the causes, hoping that the problem will not recur?
- Should they be managed to prevent them from waylaying the democratic process and taking the whole nation down a spiralling path to self-destruction?
- Should they pre-empt them? This is not easy to do even if the problems can be predicted. For example: The Soulbury Commission acknowledged it, the influential group of Ceylonese who won independence from Britain submerged it with an icing of good behaviour and the crop of leaders since 1956 realised that their actions were creating an underclass of disaffected minorities but none came up with an answer. Similarly, had the first UNP government addressed the genuine concerns and needs of the Sinhala Buddhist community perhaps things would have been different now.
- How can these pressure groups be co-opted by the state to help it return peace and stability to the country?

Harnessing Pressure Groups to gain Peace

During periods of communal unrest, civil war or rebel activity some pressure groups can be harnessed by legitimate governments to help them in their search for peace and reconciliation. The governments of Sri Lanka could have worked with the Buddhist establishment to bring a quick end to the current troubles. They could have worked closely with the Tamil political leadership and the Buddhist hierarchy to carve out a middle ground that they could all sell to their respective constituents. The most powerful of their conciliatory voices would have been the Buddhist clergy and with their support most solutions can be sold to the majority community. It could well be that this was done in Sri Lanka but the overwhelming evidence is that the Buddhist establishment, especially the younger members of it, argued for a position that demanded complete domination of minorities and the subjugation of their faith, their culture and their values. The questions that come to mind are:

- Why did the Buddhist establishment place successive governments under pressure to make concessions to the majority community, knowing that it would create hostility among the other communities?
- How could the governments have used the most powerful influencing group in the country – the Buddhist clergy – to help bring peace and reconciliation to the country?
- Should the Buddhist clergy allow itself to become an instrument of political manoeuvring and become a propagandist for political parties?

Timing of the Introduction of Democracy

Timing is everything. The right action at the wrong time produced the wrong results. Were the people of Sri Lanka, like those in many other countries that emerged from colonial rule, right to adopt a means of governance that was less than ideal for their requirements in their state of political development as at February 1948? Probably? But:

- When is a democracy a democracy?
- What value is a system that appears like democracy but is not?
- What alternatives did Britain and the leaders of the people have? They probably felt that a democratic process, however inadequately it is operated, was better than not having one at all. Choosing a king was impossible.
- Could another, more suitable form have been devised by or for them and if they had been given choices would they have know how to choose one that suited them best? Those leaders of the Sri Lankan people who collaborated in the drafting of the constitution were all educated in the leading English schools in the island and most of them had graduated from the premier universities in England. They admired the British way of life and lived it at home. The British form of parliamentary democracy seemed like the one to use and they did.
- Why were safeguards not built into the constitution to ensure that the minority communities were assured of greater autonomy before independence was won?

What is the best form of Government for a Multi-ethnic State?

Linked to the previous question of timing is one to do with appropriateness. Catapulting a people who had been ruled by kings and governed by colonial powers into mainstream democratic politics borrowed from a country that had honed democracy for centuries seems irresponsible. Perhaps a mild form of authoritarian rule under strict supervision whilst still under colonial rule may have proved a good starting point. Since this was not done it is necessary to ask whether:

- the country would have been better served if one of the two coup d'états had succeeded? Is Pakistan worse off for being ruled by Generals Zia ul-Haq or Musharraf rather than Benazir Bhuto or Nawaz Sharif?
- the country would not have benefited from a benevolent dictatorship/quasi democracy like that adopted by Lee Kuan Yew in Singapore and Dr Mahathir bin Mohamad in Malaysia?

In these cases, the international community, acting expediently, categorises these different leaders as good or bad depending on the circumstances leading one to the view that good governance depends, not on moral, ethical or ideological principles but on what is most convenient for its sponsors at any one time. Cynical, perhaps, but an unavoidable conclusion from the way the world community changes its view on good and bad regimes. If the world community acted with greater integrity, such sponsored dictatorships would not become tyrannies.

Are Separate States a Better Answer?

How can the tendency of unitary multi-ethnic states to deteriorate into internecine warfare or animosity be stopped? As we have discussed earlier, the different ethnic groups living in Sri Lanka are broadly concentrated in specific regions of the country – the Tamils in the north and north-east, the Muslims in the east and the Sinhalese in the rest of the island. At various times after independence, governments have tried to encourage internal migration, primarily from the Sinhalese areas to the north, central and eastern regions. But these attempts have not proved successful. Life in the south, south west and the hill country is much easier than in the rest of the country purely because the climate in better, it is easier to grow food and the job opportunities are greater. So there is a case for seriously considering dividing the country into three independent states or of creating a federated structure. The questions that come to mind are:

- Would the country be at peace if, as in Belgium and Switzerland, the ethnolinguistic differences are constitutionally recognised and the unitary state of Sri Lanka is restructured to give the Sinhalese, the Tamils and the Muslims greater autonomy?

- What is the likelihood of such pragmatism in the Sri Lanka of today, given all the bad blood that has flowed between the different communities?
- Is there any likelihood of peace within the unitary state and the current constitution?
- Or will the worst happen and the state abdicate its responsibilities to the people of the north and leave them to the mercy of the militant groups that are unaccountable to anyone?

The Wider Impact of the Sri Lankan Experiment in Democracy

When the international community wishes democracy on a people, or their leaders adopt it because it is the form of government that their sponsors wish them to have, they may be heading towards a future like that experienced by the Sri Lankan people. Lacking sophisticated electorates, the democratic process tends to be nothing more than a charade and a sop to international sensibilities, but inappropriate for the people who are governed by its outcomes. If, to this, strong communal feelings are added, the result could be explosive. This question bothered Lord Soulbury but he was unable to find a workable answer, so he left it unanswered and the people of Sri Lanka are still struggling to find the answers. He hoped goodwill and common sense would bridge the shortcomings he anticipated, but they have not. To ignore the Sri Lankan experience in the multi-cultural world of today would be folly. This is no longer the problem of a single country. It is a global issue. The same design considerations keep repeating themselves as is now happening in Iraq, where the questions are different but the impact could be the same. If any group feels ignored or disadvantaged, rebellion will certainly break out. The current issues facing those involved in Iraq are:

- How are the issues now troubling Sri Lanka going to be avoided in Iraq, where the intensity of feelings about religion and race are as acute?
- How long after conferring democracy on a people should the external powers that bring it about decide that the democratic institution it has created is mature enough to be left to manage itself?
- What is the risk that the state will be split three ways to meet the demands for self-government by the Shi'ites, Sunnis and Kurds?

Democracy must now evolve to meet the imbalance of power in a multi-ethnic world. What price if it fails? In the meantime, how are the problems of the island to be solved?

Discussion Paper 2

Terrorists and Suicide Bombers – Where do they come from?

The militancy and extreme brutality shown by the Sinhalese youth of the country in 1971 and again in 1987 took Mrs Bandaranaike's and Mr Jayawardene's governments by surprise. Similarly, Mr Bandaranaike had been caught unawares when, in 1958, Sinhalese thugs had roamed the streets of Colombo and the southern coastal belt, burning and looting Tamil homes and businesses and killing and maiming Tamils living amongst them. The ruling clique were too busy fighting each other for political supremacy to note the fact that the people were suffering and the youth of the country were restless or that the racists' message of hate had woven itself into society.

This shameless show of self-indulgence by the ruling clique had far-reaching consequences. The people, particularly the youth, had lost faith in the ability of their elders to create a world fit for them to live in. They had lost hope in ever living in an opportunity-filled future. Most of all, they felt vulnerable and politically powerless. Worse still, there were a large number of these young people all looking for a Moses to lead them to the Promised Land. Marx filled their minds but not their stomachs or their pockets.

> In 1969, 60 per cent of the total population of 12.5 million were under the age of 25. In the 14–25-year-old category, 45 per cent were out of school and unemployed. Approximately 74 per cent of the population were literate – the majority literate in only one language as a result of S.W.R.D. Bandaranaike's policy of vernacular education. Despite the high Sinhala literacy rate, English remained the language of status and the key to getting employment in higher paid jobs.[131]

Tamil and Sinhalese youth were trapped in this futureless world, and it was this that eventually drove them to use armed conflict – the last resort of the inarticulate and powerless person. Terrorism by the Tamils was resorted to only after almost thirty years of peaceful protest. The Tamils resorted to civil disobedience (*Satyagraha*) in the early 1960s and eventually to war in the early 1980s. The insurrection by the Low-Country Sinhalese youth also arose from a deep sense of frustration and powerlessness. A government focused on serving the people would have seen the warning signs and the cries for help that preceded these incidents and acted sooner. As Lindowyk points out:

---

[131] Bush, *The Intra-Group Dimensions of Ethnic Conflict in Sri Lanka.*

> No one who heard the crowds of young students in the provinces who had had an education in Sinhalese, and now having sat for their GCE or school-leaving examination had nothing to do, could doubt the vigour of their protest that they did not want two languages.[132]

By ignoring the voice of peaceful protest of the politically able and being unaware or dismissive of the resentment of the disaffected Sinhalese youth – something that was plain to see except to the wilfully blind – the ruling clique inadvertently encouraged violence as a negotiating tool. It is hard to determine whether the ruling clique saw the potential of youth militancy as a means of holding on to power but it certainly has helped the ruling clique to pass laws that would have raised howls of international protest if done in a peaceful nation. The troubles have helped them retain their right to rule, but whether they will solve them and risk the loss of power it may bring, is open to debate.

The parts of the country where insurgencies and 'war' have arisen are mostly the areas that are poorest or where government policy has reduced the people to poverty and a future without hope. In Sim's words they lack the 'universal preconditions for normal existence', which he describes in the concluding chapter to *Fundamentalist World* as:

> ...equality of opportunity, an end to cultural oppression and the tyranny of tradition; the eradication of discrimination on the grounds of gender, ethnic group, social position, or sexual preference.

He goes further and suggests that these conditions are harder to achieve '...where multiculturalism is replaced by an all too obviously Western monoculturalism'. For monoculturalism to work the people must shed their tribal attitudes. What happened in Sri Lanka was that multiculturalism was supposed to operate within a unitary democratic state. The ruling clique did nothing to bring about a multicultural nation. Instead, they used the inherent tendencies of territorial, caste and tribal allegiances to hold on to power. By this means they were able to pick off one group of challengers at a time. They appeased the Buddhist nationalists and the Low-Country Sinhalese activists and hoped to defeat the Tamil nationalists through force of arms. But, as the years went on the political awareness of the population grew and with it their demands. So, even if the Tamils had been subdued by force of arms, new pressure groups representing the same old or new causes would have, like the tide, kept returning. The problem was that universal suffrage had not delivered power to the people. What it did do was deliver power to some of the people so that they could rule the rest of the people all of the time. The ruling clique may have pulled this trick off if they had broadened their powerbase by appealing to a wider constituency and taking ethnicity out of party politics. This they did not do.

[132] Ludowyk, *The Story of Ceylon.*

Consequently, both the Sinhalese and Tamil youth separated tribe from nation. Asked to chose between their nation and their tribe they choose the tribe because the tribe was a safe haven from the nation that was their oppressor. The choice they had to make is like the hard choice children have to make when their parents divorce. Whose side do they take? Is it fair that they should have to take sides at all? The aptness of this analogy becomes apparent only when one accepts that to the Sri Lankan Tamil or, for that matter, the rural Sinhalese youth, their tribe and their nation are like parents. The nation gives them international identity and the tribe, reduced to their extended family, defines them as people and is the source of their safety and their strength. So when they feel that their nation is the enemy of their tribe, they are willing to sacrifice their life for their tribe even if it means hurting their nation. This is not to justify their actions but to explain that their actions are multidimensional and must be viewed in their total complexity. Furthermore, their actions are also a test of loyalty and love where relative values impinge on their strength of affection. Like Hamlet, they struggle with their consciences. The Sri Lankan government finds it easier to condemn them and ostracise them rather than attempt to remove this deep emotional dichotonomy by welcoming their tribe into the nation.

The Tamil and Sinhalese youth, who were least able to influence what was done in their name and for them, were the true victims of this rule by elites. They looked around for champions and found none. They hoped that the international community would help them but all it did was condemn the violence and the injustices perpetrated on the people by the government and organised vigilante groups. But the words of the international community had no effect because they were not accompanied by measures that would make the government stop and take note of what they were saying and mend its ways, or even punish the thugs who did the ruling clique's dirty work for it.

So the Sinhalese and Tamil youth felt that they had to fend for themselves and set out to find ways out of the cul-de-sac that the past and present policies of the governments of Sri Lanka had driven them into. So they organised themselves into a military force and decided that terror would be one of their weapons in the hope that it would make the ruling clique put pressure on the government to take note and act. Instead, they were rewarded for their impertinence – that's how the ruling clique saw their actions – by a greater show of force and terror. The greater the forces that they repulsed, vanquished or neutralised, the greater the reputation and status of the insurgent groups became. This was both ambrosial and addictive to the insurgents and freedom fighters. Sim points out that:

> Terrorism is a denial of debate, and thus of difference and dissent, those fundamentally fundamentalist characteristics. The case for terrorism in these areas is that the authorities don't always listen to dissenting opinions expressed through normal channels.

Due to government social and economic policies, this group of youths who had had little opportunity to gain money and status had, at long last, found the respect and recognition that they longed for and did not get before and had no hope of getting without the conflict or substantial concessions. Almost overnight they were people of consequence – warriors of freedom. They had money, power and international recognition. As Sim points out:

> The terrorists see advantages both for themselves and for their families in the sacrifice they make for the cause. They are guaranteed a place of honour in the history of their people, no small matter in such traditionalist cultures, and even promised a place in heaven. Their family generally also receive some form of financial compensation from the political organization in question.

But, after a time, the glamour dies out and they are left with the grim reality of living the lives of fugitives. In their frustration at not gaining a quick win and status as heroes, they resort to more horrendous means and get branded as terrorists. So, to speed up the resolution of the conflict, they demand greater and greater sacrifices from those involved in the fighting and from the communities among whom they have taken shelter. At this stage they are willing to make any sacrifice to retain their social standing. It is then that suicide bombers are deployed.

> If we want to understand suicide terrorism ... we have to look at the wider socio-political context in which it takes place. Cultural background is more important than psychological type in explaining why individuals can be willing to do such things ... *what* people believe is of greater importance than *why* they believe it.[133]

A Tamil suicide bomber is like a Hindu widow who commits suttee – the act of immolating herself on the funeral pyre of her husband – a custom that prevailed mostly in poorer communities and is now mercifully outlawed and extinct although the disadvantage she suffers still persists in very poor communities. Fitch had observed the custom in his travels and said '...when the husband dieth his wife is burned with him if she be alive; if she will not, her head is shaven and then is never any account made of her after.'[134] In other words, at the death of her husband the widow loses her identity as a person. In fact it is said that the widow often lost her identity, her status, her source of income and her dignity as a person and that the indignity and humiliation that befell her was, to some women, a worse fate than dying with their husbands in what was considered an act of honour.

Suicide bombers can be described as the widows of government policy –

[133] Sim, *Fundamentalist World.*

[134] Richard David, *Hakluyt's Voyages: A Selection.*

their actions are not the result of a chance happening or a deranged or unstable mind. The young, unemployed, futureless youth of the Tamil community are, in a sense, throwing themselves into the funeral pyre because they find purpose and respect in their militancy and self-sacrifice. It is important to understand that people who do such things are not 'crazy' or inherently wicked. As Sim points out, the choice to be a suicide bomber:

> ...is not to be considered an irrational choice for the individual to make. Instead, a range of social and economic factors combine to create a situation in which suicide terrorists emerge because there is a demand for their sacrifice, and the individual concerned can see the logic of that demand. Suicide bombing is part of a political campaign ... and it's rational in terms of the objectives sought: the destabilisation of the enemy such that they are forced to negotiate...

Some people may argue that Sim is 'soft' on the suicide bomber. But that is to ignore the reality of being a 'non-person'. People with careers, education, reasonable incomes, freedom of choice, roofs over their head, loving and caring families cannot empathise with the plight of those who have none of these things and feel they cannot achieve them by fair means. Their feeling of powerlessness is all-embracing and debilitating. This is a real issue and the frustration experienced by these people is released in various acts of violence from vandalism to suicide. When it happens to an individual, it may be possible to help that person. But when whole generations of youth and the communities they live in feel that way, help is harder to find and only radical social initiatives that return power to them will change the situation.

Instead, the world is quick to condemn them as evil and shun them even more. This, of course, makes the situation worse as they are forced into a corner by more powerful external forces such as laws that permanently disadvantage them because of their ethnicity, caste or tribe. In Sri Lanka, over forty years of government actions distanced the Tamil youth from the nation.

The Tamil youth are not the only people who have lost futures. The actions of the ruling clique distanced the rural Sinhalese youth from their better-off cousins, too. The Low-Country Sinhalese youth also felt powerless and betrayed by the governments that purported to care about them. Their sense of betrayal was even greater than that of the Tamil youth because they felt abandoned by those they considered 'family'. The Low-Country Sinhalese youth found that their purses were empty too, and that the promises of a future full of milk and honey, that their politicians had promised them, were also words empty of meaning or intent. They formed a militant group – called the JVP – and exploded on to the political scene, not as a political force, but as insurgents, twice in twenty years. In both instances they behaved with extreme barbarism. They may not have used suicide bombers, but they used the most vicious and unimaginable force on defenceless civilians. They mutilated and dismembered bodies, killed innocent men, women and children and raped and pillaged at will. The weapons they used were knives and axes and other objects that prolonged the agony of their victims. It offends the senses to write, hear or read about their actions and it was beyond the comprehension of many on the island. None could believe that any group could behave with such barbarity. Those who sought reasons for the bloodlust of the insurgents felt that these were the acts of a group of people whose anger and frustration had taken them to the extreme edge of madness.

Bribing some of its leaders – giving in to terror – with political office did no good either, as the JVP resurfaced in 1987 wearing the same clothes but voicing new slogans and making new demands. The ruling clique, having made whole communities powerless and valueless, joined in the blame game to hide their culpability and avoid being identified as the true culprits.

There are those who may argue that although there is no moral justification for buying terrorists off by giving them high office, it could be politic to do so as it removes one group of belligerents, thus allowing other groups to be dealt with. This may be true but unless there is a 'real' meeting of minds nothing really changes. Marriages of convenience lack the glue to bind them.

The established political leaders of Sri Lanka may argue that in taking the bold step to invite the JVP to move from being a terrorist organisation to participate in the political process they have shown great insight. Mr Dershowitz would disagree.[135] He has pointed out that giving in to one group only emboldens them and makes them raise the stakes even higher and that their success encourages others to follow. His solution is to annihilate them, and he may well be right. The JVP will raise the stakes. Now that it is part of the ruling clique, it will attempt to gain approval for its Marxist objectives by holding the government to ransom even whilst it is part of the government. But one supposes that it is better that they do this than start another bloody insurgency. Besides, Mr Dershowitz's solution will only work if it is possible to kill or jail the terrorists. This is extremely difficult to do because there is always another wave waiting to flow in unless the underlying causes are removed. Armies fighting according to the conventions of war find it hard to unearth and kill terrorists, particularly if the civilian population on whose behalf they are ostensibly fighting support the fighters or are terrorised by the fighters to give them sanctuary. Besides, as the Sri Lankan government has found, it is not a viable option as, eventually, government forces are goaded or forced to act in ways that bring dishonour to the country and enhance the terrorists' cause. So peaceful means have to be found to disarm terrorists, this means removing their excuses or reasons. Mr Dershowitz, like many of the Sinhalese community, interprets peace initiatives as giving in to terrorists. Sadly, such an attitude results in a catch-22 situation. The standoff does no one any good. The peace-loving may have to walk the extra mile to bring the belligerent to the negotiation table. And as long as they talk, everyone has a reason for suspending violence.

---

[135] Dershowitz, *Why Terrorism Works.*

Subsequent events appear to vindicate Mr Dershowitz's view that terrorists should be eradicated, not given in to. The marriage of convenience between the President and the JVP did not last. On 16 June 2005 the JVP left the alliance, as it disagreed with the policy of the President to form a joint mechanism with the LTTE to distribute the aid funds and facilitate tsunami rehabilitation work in the north and east. The JVP argued that the joint mechanism would be the first step in granting the Tamils territorial sovereignty, a claim hotly denied by the President. However, the JVP is resorting to political rather than physical means to pressure the government of Sri Lanka to break its ties with the LTTE, so perhaps making it a legitimate political party may have prevented another blood bath – thus proving that political means can work where force has failed. However, it is important to recognise that the government may have given in to the JVP's wish if the international community had not put pressure on it to enter into a joint arrangement with the LTTE to ensure that the aid funds were distributed fairly. Money, it seems, talks loudest, and the benefactors can and should define how their money is spent. However, the government received strong opposition to the joint mechanism to share out the Tsunami Aid funds from politicised Buddhist monks who marched to the president's house on 10 June 2005. The money remains unspent and the poor remain in makeshift shelters – their cries for help too faint to be heard by those who can help most.

Humanity has consistently failed to hear the faint cries of innocents for help when they are being unfairly treated, being marginalised and dumped on the refuse heap of life due to determined, calculated and premeditated acts of discrimination and bullying by the strong. It happens when children are bullied at school, or adults at their place of work, and no one hears the victim's muted cry for help. The signs of distress are visible, but the victims suffer in silence because they are ashamed to ask for help lest they be branded as sissies, or because they think that those whose job it is to love, cherish and protect them will not believe them or will laugh at their ineptitude at being unable to stave off a bunch of bullies. Eventually, the victims are so terrified and traumatised that they erupt and take horrible vengeance on their tormentors or take their own lives as the ultimate way out. And sometimes they do both. Bullies, on the other hand, have perfected the art of masking their behaviour. They usually get their message across first and by so doing make the victim appear oversensitive or mistaken. They portray a benign face to the world and by so doing they persuade others that they are the victims and disarm those who may feel inclined to stop them. The bully predisposes those who can help their victims to pass by on the other side and this makes it harder for the victim to convince a potential source of help to intervene.

The governments of Sri Lanka have learnt to emulate the bully. They use their power and access to rationalise their actions, damp down concerns and hide behind the respectable cloak of democracy and the democratic process. Provided that there is no overt tyranny or despotism or genocide, and if the bullying government maintains a benign face, the international community, its members wrapped up in their own domestic problems, too readily gives them the benefit of the doubt. Sometimes, the bullying government buys the silence of the international community by serving the foreign policy needs of its most powerful and influential members. The victim community feels abandoned and falls back on its own resources until, having nothing to lose, it erupts with devastating ferocity. It seems that the international community and institutions such as the UN will tolerate evil, and by their silence and inaction, allow evil to multiply until its inaction makes it complicit in the crimes of the bully. By the time evil is unmasked, the winds of discontent are blowing too hard and fast for them to be calmed without significant effort on all sides.

In a civilised world, someone, some state or institution, must pick up the faint early cries for help of the people who feel so abused, and act on their behalf to right the wrongs they suffer. And what is true for the individual must be doubly true for an abused and bullied people. Journalists and historians can alert the world to these wrongs, but both come to it too late. Despite umpteen prior examples of the abuse of individuals and communities from which the patterns of abuse can be anticipated and the abuser stopped, the world always asks for proof of malignity before it takes notice, let alone acts.

But in this tangled web that is the political and social climate of Sri Lanka, it is hard to separate the bully and the victim. Unfortunately, the causes and therefore the cures have been submerged by the publicity surrounding their excesses. For people to keep their sanity under the continuous pressure of insecurity and personal abuse, they have to desensitise their senses. They have to make sense of the horrors perpetrated in their name if they are to continue to lead 'normal' lives. They have to learn to live with fear, distrust and denial. And they have to suffer the guilt of condoning actions taken in their name but which they deplore.

Unless realism enters Sri Lankan politics and the stranglehold the ruling clique have on the island is released, every new generation of the 'reasonable man', frustrated by their parents' reluctance to use their vote to throw out the self-serving politicians who now rule them, will become 'unreasonable men' and use extra-electoral methods to change the status quo. These militant groups have failed so far because the immediately preceding generation of 'unreasonable men' have been won over by the ruling clique by the lure of personal wealth and status. But this method of defusing generational frustration will not succeed for ever.

The young see the helplessness of their guardians. They know only terror and believe it to be a way of life. Men lose their courage and their children see them as cowards, rather than compromisers bent on protecting them from even greater horror. Not even the warmongers know how or where it will all end, because they are no longer in control of their actions. To survive and remain free, they have to keep the belligerence going. To finance themselves, they have to keep the belligerence going. To make them feel 'manly' and indulge their ego, they have to keep the belligerence going. Belligerence becomes a way of life.

This is what the war between the Tamils and the Sinhalese has mostly achieved for those in the northern and eastern provinces. Those in the south are relieved that their life is only occasionally disrupted by a devastating bomb. Such is their conditioning that the notion of no bombs is unthinkable.

Unless power genuinely passes to the 'reasonable man' who is most likely to be drawn from among the village communities the country will continue to be in turmoil. The only option open to governments is to pay heed to the minority groups and act equitably to defuse their anger. This means removing or ameliorating the impact of the things that create militancy and to show that peaceful negotiations can achieve much more, more rapidly than the use of force. It also means building up the credibility of those who advocate peaceful approaches to righting wrongs by showing that they can access those who matter, gain their ear and win their cause.

This takes courage. It means winning support for policies that some pressure groups, which claim to be 'friends' of the government, may object to vehemently. But that is politics – the art of winning the support of your 'friends' and opponents for policies that may not help them directly but will help other people lead a better life. This takes exceptional skill. There is some evidence that Mrs Kumaratunga, after ten years in office, has at long last awoken to the fact that she should support the silent majority rather than give in to the belligerent and intractable minority. At long last it seems that she is willing to call a spade a spade and take the side of the peace-loving majority. One hopes that she keeps her resolve and holds out and that the LTTE help her. There is no doubt that through negotiation, communication and resoluteness, the President can win the hearts and minds of all the people so that collectively they can solve the problems of some of the people and rid the country of the scourge of war and the suicide bomber. One also hopes that the other political parties and the large group of peace-loving *bhikkhus* will condemn their warmongering brothers and join her or her successor and help bring peace to the island.

Much has changed in fifty years. The Sinhalese Buddhists nationalists have gained their prime objective of making Sinhalese and Buddhism the language and religion of the state. Tamil and Sinhalese are national languages. Hinduism and Buddhism have never been in conflict so there is no religious antagonism to feed the flames of war. The prime objective now is for the people to rebuild their country, right its economy and regain its reputation as an epitome of Buddhist rule and beliefs. The last real challenge to peace comes from the community of *bhikkhus* who wish to remain in the political arena because of the power and money it brings. The politicians cannot drum them off the field of battle but the Buddhist community led by the senior clergy can and ought to. Only they have the authority to demand and get equality of treatment for all those living on the island in accordance with Buddha's teachings that supersede and exceed the conditions in any human rights convention. If they are unwilling to do this, and they are not persuaded to do so, the island will always be in turmoil. But the ruling clique will go on until the tumbrels cart them off to oblivion and leave the political arena to the ordinary folks for whom the democratic system was created. It is only then that the colonial shadow will be lifted from the island for ever.

Select Bibliography and Recommended Reading

This supplementary bibliography lists books that shed further light on topics covered and opinions expressed in the text. Some of the books highlighted the weaknesses in the quality of governance in countries that seek to be exemplars of democracy and made me wonder whether my criticism of the post-colonial leaders of Sri Lanka was too harsh. Others raised questions on the use of democracy as a means of choosing leaders and as a system of governance. They highlighted the increasing tendency to create a cult of personality and by this means to distort the lens through which people see their leaders. They highlight the fact that the glossy image that money and a partisan media and publicity machine presents can result, very often, in populations electing egocentric but insubstantial leaders who become captives of manipulative and self-seeking advisors. Other books cover issues such as terrorism and suicide bombers and the quality of life of people serving the British Empire during its most successful period.

Abeyasekera, Henry, *Sri Lanka under a Brahamana Curse*, Vijitha Yapa Publications, 2002.

> More a series of essays about issues that are likely causes of the current troubles of an island that the author states is: 'Politically riven by the lack of statesmen-like patriotic leaders, religiously being torn apart by subtle and covert manoeuvring of local and foreign NGO groups with hidden agendas, socially its moral fibre torn asunder and foundering in a morass of lies and deceit and riddled by bribery and corruption and economically on the verge of collapse...' Sadly, he blames the problems on India, public servants who 'sabotaged the implementation' of the Sinhala Only Act by being overzealous and a host of others. I would have appreciated a chapter on the role of the Buddhist clergy and nationalists and the current batch of competing politicians. On this criterion he has failed the reader interested in an impartial discussion of the causes of the conflict.

Abley, Mark, *Spoken Here: Travels among threatened languages*, William Heinemann, London, 2003.

> A very interesting and informative book which, although it focuses on language, is really a commentary on the cultures and traditions of people whose self-identity is as much to do with language as it is to do with location. It certainly points out the challenges faced by people trying to retain their native language in a world that is increasingly being dominated by English, which, as he explains, is the natural language to over 400 million people and is spoken by at least another billion and a

half. It is becoming the *de facto* language of the planet. He believes that English itself is beginning to fragment through dilution with native languages and may reach a point where different groups speaking English will not understand each other. It seems that the Tower of Babel will always be with us.

Abram et al., *The Rough Guide to South India*, November 2003.

The guide provides an overview to the history of the peninsula region that forms South India. The quality of the content is every bit as good as the *Lonely Planet Guide to Sri Lanka*. A good place to start if you are interested in the Dravidian people, their language, religion and literature.

Anthonisz, R. G., *The Dutch in Ceylon: An account of their early visits to the island, their conquests, and their rule over the Maritime Regions during a century and a half*, CAC Press, Colombo, Ceylon 1929, reproduced by the Asian Educational Service, 2003.

This book presents a Dutch viewpoint of their time as rulers of the Maritime Provinces. The book makes very interesting reading and attempts to explain more fully some stories about the Dutch and their behaviour when first they arrived on the island and during the 156 years that followed.

Armitage, Richard L., *Sri Lanka: Prospects for Peace*, Presentation to the Center for Strategic and International Studies, Washington DC, 14 February 2003.

His remarks, published on the State Department website, were made in the presence of Ambassador Subasinghe, ambassador of Sri Lanka to the US and Tezi Schaffer, the director of the centre. His objective was to win support for US assistance in helping resolve the conflict on the island. Everything he says rings true because it is derived from first hand knowledge of the situation there, including visits to the war-torn north. Unfortunately, his remarks about human rights, particularly after Guantanamo Bay and Iraq, could as well apply to his country as to Sri Lanka. But what they do highlight is that when governments are under intense pressure and are at the end of their tether as regards resolving conflict (9/11 for the US, and conflict between the government and the Tamils in Sri Lanka) they can slip their civilised moorings and enter the rough waters of torture and ill-disciplined soldiery. Severe frustration eventually overcomes training. This does not, however, diminish the power of his message. The fact that the US has fallen short of its founding fathers' high principles does not make it the devil's disciple.

Balachandran, B. K., 'India's industrialization inspires Lanka', *Hindustan Times* 13 December 2004

An interesting article highlighting the fact that, unlike India, Sri Lanka has stubbornly clung on to a policy of importing the country's needs. What is of great importance in his article is his suggestion that this import led policy is the result of 'an entrenched import lobby'. He does not say this, but the import lobby gets rich recycling foreign aid. An insightful economist has suggested that foreign aid is the movement of money from the poor in rich countries to the rich in poor countries. How true this is in Sri Lanka's import-led economy.

Bancroft, Anne (ed), *The Dhammapada: An Essential Buddhist Text*, Grange Books PLC, 2002.

The *Dhammapada* is a collection of sayings and teachings of the Buddha that was accepted at the council of Asoka in 240 BC. It is very explicit about the path the *bhikkhu* should follow and it is a tragedy for Sri Lanka that it's Buddhist clergy have deviated so sharply from it.

Country profile: Sri Lanka, BBC News, 18 November 2005, http://news.bbc.co.uk/1/hi/world/south_asia/country_profiles/1168427.stm

A rich source of information about the island. The timeline of the island provides key dates starting from 1505. Strangely, the website fails to mention Mr J R Jayawardene, despite his long period of office (1977–1989) as prime minister and president, and a very long political life from about 1940.

Hardtalk interview by Tim Sebastian with the Hon. President Chandrika B Kumaratunga of Sri Lanka, BBC, 31 October 2001.

This was a difficult interview for the President. Tim Sebastian wrong-footed her early and from then on she was on the defensive. Her advisers should have made sure that she was better prepared as the questioning can be unrelenting and tough. The interviewers treat the interviewee with respect but do not pull their punches. Many Sri Lankans were disappointed by her performance and I am sure she was too. Allowing for this and accepting that she is well intentioned but cannot be everywhere at once, she is unable to ensure that the security forces do not abuse their powers. She also does have a point that in many cases the rule of law requires evidence, and in situations such as those discussed evidence is very hard to get. However, the judicial system and the rule of law in the country fail to live up to their billing. They are both subject to political pressure and influence. This aggravates the situation, as vulnerable people may find that their evidence will be distorted or ignored when the person or organisation they are complaining about has access to privileged treatment.

Black, Jeremy, *War and the World, Military power and the fate of continents 1450–2000*, Yale, 2000.

A fascinating study of military capability during the period of European expansion to recent times. It is an easy read and a book that would be of value to someone dipping into the subject for the first time.

Bremner, Rory, Bird, John and Fortune, John, with Atkinson, Geoff, *You Are Here: An Updated Dossier*, Phoenix, 2005

A devastating satirical commentary on the way Britain has been governed under the leadership of Tony Blair between 2 May 1997 and the time of publication. It provides an insight into how democracy can be practised more in name than in substance. It shows how a group of people, who shed the values of the founders of their movement to win power, subverted it for their personal gain. It shows how they walked all over a weak and insubstantial opposition and unashamedly used the skills and artifice of the public relations industry to serve their ends. The book shows how every area of life from health, education, transport, crime, border controls, pensions and so on have been mismanaged despite a huge increase in the costs associated with each.

Brendon, Vyvyen, *Children of the Raj*, Weidenfeld and Nicholson, 2005

This book takes you into the hitherto hidden world of the children of those British men and women who served, many with distinction, in the Indian subcontinent, Burma, and Ceylon. These children were sent to Britain when still no more than infants (two to four years of age) and destined to live in boarding schools and with uncles, aunts and grandparents. The plight of the Eurasian children of British men was greater than the mental anguish suffered by their white children. These children, whatever their colour, represent the true cost of the Britain's Empire. *See also David Gilmour,* The Ruling Caste.

Brohier, R. L., *Seeing Ceylon*, 1971.

Dr Brohier was a senior official at the Survey Department and has personally visited most of the sites he writes about in this book. His view of the quality of the irrigation engineering during the Anuradhapura period is an authoritative one.

Bush, Kenneth D., *The Intra-Group Dimensions of Ethnic Conflict in Sri Lanka*, International Political Economy Series, Palgrave Macmillan, 2003.

This is an exceptional book in the depth of its coverage of the conflicts in the island. I am indebted to Prof Tim Shaw, Professor of Commonwealth Governance and Development and Director of the Institute of Commonwealth Studies at the School of Advanced Study, University of London, for introducing me to this book. The author draws on a huge volume of contemporary literature about the island to show that the Sri Lankan people have the ability to fight among themselves whilst everything around them is going up in flames. He would have found this to be true even in the pre-colonial period. It is in the genes and a capability that has evolved to perfection over two thousand years. It seems beyond them to collaborate to put out common fires or to defeat a common enemy. As I have shown in Parts One and Two this ability to collectively self-destruct is also a feature of the history of the island during the time of the Portuguese, Dutch and British occupations. Then, when one king opposed the Europeans, the other collaborated with them and a third group, usually aspiring courtiers, connived in traitorous activity to usurp the power of the king they were pretending to serve: so true of the politics of the island today! Everyone is so busy plunging knives into everyone else's back in some sort of sadistic orgy that they do not stop to feel the pain they are inflicting on themselves – crazy.

Coates, Ken S., *A Global History of Indigenous Peoples, Struggle and Survival*, Palgrave Macmillan, 2004.

Interesting read. The book provides a short but informative paragraph on the Veddahs of Sri Lanka. They were the original inhabitants of the island. According to the authors they have lived there for between 14,000 and 16,000 years. He points out that 'Vedda lifestyles have been adversely affected by water-control projects and, in the 1980s, by a campaign launched by the World Wildlife Fund to create a local conservation area.'

Codrington, H. W., *A Short History of Ceylon*, Asian Education Series, 1994.

Codrington's history of the island formed the base on which the chapters about the Indian, Portuguese, Dutch and British occupations were written. It is comprehensive in its coverage and provides a huge volume of references to support his views.

Cowie, Ian, 'For £1 million, you too could retire in the style of an MP', *Telegraph*, 13 October 2004.

Cowie, Ian, 'Comment: Put not your faith in politicians - they do not share our problems', *Telegraph*, 16 October 2004.

This is a very thought provoking article that cuts to the chase. Mr Cowie is a very angry man indeed, but he is right to point out the selective nature of the report and the total silence on this disparity among the politicians as they lined up in various TV and radio studios to rubbish or defend the government. How do you defend the indefensible?

CIA, *The World Factbook,* 'Sri Lanka', of 11 May 2004.

Eleven A4 pages listing facts about the country. It provides a snapshot of its geography, people, government, economy, communications and transportation.

Crick, Bernard, *In Defence of Politics*, fifth edition, Continuum, 2000.

This is an excellent book. It debates the pros and cons between politics and: ideology, democracy, nationalism, technology and false friends. His prime argument is that politics, which he defines as 'the activity by which differing interests within a given unit of rule are conciliated by giving them a share in power in proportion to their importance to the welfare and the survival of the whole community', is preferable to other 'labels' by which groups of people are organised for mutual benefit. He defines political systems as 'that type of government where politics proves successful in ensuring reasonable stability and order'.

David, Richard, *Hakluyt's Voyages: A Selection*, Chatto & Windus, London, 1981

Hakluyt was an Elizabethan clergyman, diplomat, linguist and scholar who collected and published about 1600 eyewitness accounts by various seamen, courtiers, merchants, gentlemen adventurers, menservants and tourists. The account of Ceylon and India come from Master Ralph Fitch, Merchant of London who travelled in the Middle East and Near East from 1583 to 1591. His observations of the social habits and customs of the people he went among are very precise and make very interesting reading. It seems that he visited Colombo, a Portuguese fort and trading post, when it was under siege by Rajasinha

Davies A. J., *To Build a New Jerusalem: The Labour Movement from the 1880s to the 1990s*. Michael Joseph, London. 1992.

Highly readable history of the British Labour movement. In some senses it is the story of the courage and persistence of Keir Hardie and his valuable legacy to the working man and woman in Britain. In particular it helps the reader understand the strength of the movement.

Dershowitz, Alan M., *Why Terrorism Works*, Yale University Press, 2002.

Mr Dershowitz, a Harvard law professor, chooses to ignore the causes of terrorism. Instead, using his renowned skills as a criminal defence and civil liberties attorney, he makes the case that 'the real root cause of terrorism is that it is successful – terrorists have consistently benefited from their terrorist acts'. He argues his case by listing in great detail all the terrorist acts committed on behalf of the Palestinian cause from 22 July 1968 and the rewards these acts gained for them until 22 March 2000. His thesis is that if you don't reward them then terrorism will cease. One wonders what would take its place. He quotes Leila Khalid's interview in the *Guardian* to support his case. She says, "Until [we began hijacking airplanes], the world only dealt with us as refugees. We demonstrated and screamed and shouted to make the world listen, but the only answer we got was more tents and humanitarian aid.' Mr Dershowitz fails to explain how the Leila Khalids of this world get help from those with closed eyes and ears. Perhaps he thinks that she and her people have no right to anything better than 'humanitarian aid' or that as a people they are not entitled to natural justice. He also fails to answer the point that Ray and Schaap make in their book i.e. that the US must stop creating terrorist groups to further its foreign policy objectives if it wishes to rid the world of terrorism. Who will square this circle? There must be a way for the voice of the dispossessed peoples of this world to be heard and for them to receive positive help.

De Silva, P. H. D. H., *Illustrated Guide to the Colombo Museum. Part 1: Ground Floor Galleries*. National Museums of Sri Lanka 1976.

Mr de Silva was the director of the Department of National Museums, Sri Lanka when he wrote this highly readable overview of the island's history. He sees it through the lens of the country's art, architecture, jewellery, furniture and other cultural artefacts. He also discusses the different influences on the country's artistic traditions particularly the influence of Indian art and architecture.

Dunn, John, *Setting the People Free: The Story of Democracy*, Atlantic Books, 2005

The author traces the history of democracy to its origins in Athens and how it worked in those faraway times, why it lay dormant for nearly 2,000 years before its resurrection, first in its republican form in the United States and France and its spread throughout a large part of the world until it is seen, today, as the 'best' form of governance. He tries to explain why 'America and Britain set out to bury Baghdad in its own rubble'. He seeks also to answer whether it is 'a sustained exercise in fraud or an index of utter confusion'. More importantly, he tries to understand whether it is 'a huge moral and political advance'.

English, Richard, *Armed Struggle: The History of the IRA*, Oxford University Press, 2003

This book begins with the Irish Revolution (1916–1923) and ends with the cessation of violence (1994–2002). The author says 'this book has been written in the belief that, whether one supports the IRA or not, it is important to understand what they have done, why and with what consequences – and to do so in terms of serious, detailed explanation rather than simple stereotype.' If the world is to learn and build a future free of such strife, it is vitally important that those who govern it look at insurrections, civil wars, or uprisings (however you wish to name them) as symptoms of something wrong in the body politic rather than label them as acts of evil men and women.

Farmer, B.H., *Ceylon: A Divided Nation*, Institute of Race Relations, OUP, 1963.

An excellent review of the countyr's history and the events that shaped its current parlous state. Also contains a valuable preface by Lord Soulbury.

Fernandez-Armesto, Felipe, *Civilizations*, Macmillan, 2000.

The author provides a broad sweep of civilisation as opposed to history. It makes fascinating reading. He shows how civilising influences to unify peoples, places and times through the magic of civilisation as it matures and then is exported to other regions and peoples.

Ferguson, John, *Ceylon in the Jubilee Year*, Asian Education Services, 1994 (3rd edition)

The book was published in 1887. It narrates with pride British achievements in Ceylon during the first fifty years of Queen Victoria's reign. It provides a detailed and statistically supported record of how the infrastructure, income and social changes improved the lives of all those who lived on the island.

Ferguson, Niall, *Empire: How Britain Made the Modern World*, Penguin Books, 2003.

Mr Ferguson provides a comprehensive overview of how Britain achieved mastery of the seas and a vast part of the peoples and lands of the world during a period of about 350 years. It shows also how a nation that began its world adventure on the back of legitimised piracy and built its early fortunes on the back of slaves growing sugar in the Caribbean, transformed itself in the nineteenth century into a more liberal and moral-minded people who fought hard to abolish slavery and moderate abuse in its colonial possessions.

Finer, S. E., *The History of Government* particularly 'Book V: Pathway to the Modern State', Oxford, OUP, 1997.

This is a phenomenal work tracing the history of government right back to the beginnings of civilisation. His sections on the democratic form of governance informed many of the thoughts expressed in the chapter that covers this subject.

Field, John, *The Story of Parliament*

A fascinating history of the way the parliamentary system in Britain began and grew to its current state of maturity. The book also provides information about the buildings that have occupied that site and been home to 'parliament' during its centuries of evolution to its present form. It also enriches it with anecdotes about the people who have used it over the many centuries of British parliamentary history.

Country Profile: Sri Lanka, Foreign and Commonwealth Office of the British government, www.fco.gov.uk, 25 November 2005

Valuable source of information on the island. Its friend-of-the-family view, befitting the long association of the British with the country, is reflected in the small details such as the number of species of birds and fish. It covers roughly the same areas as the CIA *Factbook* and the US State Department's website.

Gambetta, Diego [ed.], *Making Sense of Suicide Missions*, Oxford University Press, 2005

An excellent study of the phenomenon, using the kamikaze pilots of Japan, the Tamil Tigers, the Palestinians and Al-Qaeda as case studies. Each of the eight chapters is written with the precision one would expect from contributors with impeccable academic credentials. They draw attention to the fact that suicide missions have a long history. They define suicide missions as 'a violent attack designed in such a way as to make death of the perpetrators strictly essential for its success'. The book suggests also that those who undertake suicide missions 'must be neither deceived about their prospect of survival nor blackmailed into carrying it out'. Gambetta points out that 'we [his fellow contributors] consider this matter without prejudice, comparing the SM perpetrators not only to peaceful self-immolators but also to war heroes.' They do not ask that their readers should view suicide missions in this light, just that their carefully researched case studies are read with an open mind.

Gilmour, David, *The Ruling Caste: Imperial Lives in the Victorian Raj*, John Murray, 2005

A fascinating insight into the way the British ruled India. It points out that not all those who went there were carpetbaggers. Rather, it points out that many generations of families lived and worked there and contributed to the development of the country and that they did make significant sacrifices during their stay in that country. The book gives the reader an insight into how the members of the Indian Civil Service administered the country and managed to keep a balance between those of different religions and cultures. On the whole, it paints a picture of a fine body of men and women. Of course British India also had businessmen, planters and others whose approach to India may not have been so benevolent. *See* Children of the Raj.

Gray, Albert, *IBN BATUTA in The Maldives and Ceylon*, Asian Educational Services, 1999

This book was originally published in *The Journal of Ceylon Branch of the Royal Asiatic Society* in 1883. Ibn Batuta's travels of twenty-four years from 1325-1349 covered almost the whole of the then known world. He used the extensive land and sea trading routes established by the Arabs and the authority of the Baghdad caliphate to make the rulers of the lands he went to to protect him. He arrived in Ceylon in 1344 from the Maldives and was the guest of the ruler of Jaffna who helped him visit Adam's Peak. He also describes the Sinhalese king at the time whose capital was at Gampola or Kurunegala.

Gray, John, *False Dawn*, London, Granta Books, 2002.

Gray's excellent study of the 'delusions of global capitalism' is especially interesting as it questions some of the arguments made by Huntington in *The Clash of Civilisations*. Gray makes the telling point that there are countries in the world where multicultural societies do exist in peace. He nominates the UK, Spain, Australia, New Zealand, Singapore and Malaysia as 'stable multicultural societies'.

Gray, John, *Al Qaeda and What it Means to be Modern*, London, Faber and Faber, 2003.

Another thought-provoking book by Gray in which he discusses the many facets of modern politics and terrorism. 'Unconventional warfare … has developed in the context of corroded or failed states … failed states have become the normal condition. In such semi-anarchy, the protagonists to armed conflict continuously shift and split, form new alliances and acquire new enemies. Peace cannot simply be declared. If it is achievable at all, it is only as a precarious balance of forces, liable to break down at any time.'

Hague, Rod, and Harrop, Martin, *Comparative Government and Politics: An Introduction*, fifth edition, Palgrave, 2001.

This book provides comprehensive coverage of the different forms of governance. A good foundation on which to build an understanding of governments and governance.

Harris, Richard, *Independence and After: Revolution in Undeveloped Countries*, Institute of Race Relations, OUP, 1962.

This is a very insightful book written by someone with a good understanding of the people and countries. For example, he says, 'the idea that the present leaders of these newly independent countries are a good guide to public opinion or to the outlook of their societies needs careful checking. Many of them are not.' Similarly, he points out the issues to do with territorial changes and the grouping together of different ethnicity into a single nation state. For example, referring to the Sinhala Only Act, he says, 'in Ceylon's case, it is not simply a matter of displacing an English-speaking upper class in favour of a national language, but using the language as an ingredient in a cultural self-assertion against the Tamils.' And finally, his comment that 'if political independence is handed over peacefully then the full sense of independence may take some time to work out' is so true of Ceylon.

Horner, I. B., 'Buddhism: The Theravada', in Zaehner, R C [ed.], *The Hutchinson Encyclopaedia of Living Faiths*, The Open University, 1998.

This is a thoroughly interesting and comprehensive summary of the form of Buddhism practiced in Sri Lanka.

Huntington, Samuel P., *The Clash of Civilizations and the Remaking of World Order*, Simon & Schuster, 1996.

The author explores the proposition, 'In this new world the most pervasive, important, and dangerous conflicts will not be between social classes, rich and poor, or other economically defined groups, but between peoples belonging to different cultural entities.' A great job he does of it too.

Jayawardena, Kumari, *Nobodies to Somebodies, The Rise of the Colonial Bourgeoisie in Sri Lanka*, Zed Books, 2000.

Thoroughly researched study of the English-educated Western-orientated Sri Lankans who, during the British period, benefited from the increased opportunities the plantation sector, the domestic liquor trade and the related import/export sectors offered them for personal enrichment. It is a fascinating social history of this group of people covering almost 120 or so years.

Jenkins, Palden, *Healing the Hurts of Nations*, Gothic Image Publications, 2003.

Jenkins takes a human-oriented view of world events and points up the 'soft' issues to do with colonialism past and present.

Katiresu, S., *A Handbook to the Jaffna Peninsula, and a Souvenir of the Opening of the Railway to the North*, Asian Educational Services, 2004.

The book is very much laid out as a guide to the Jaffna peninsula. However, it has interesting details about the work of the American missionaries who worked there and through whose good offices the Tamils of Sri Lanka gained a early introduction to Christianity and a English education. Some of his views and information of the history of Jaffna has been questioned by others. Nonetheless a valuable work.

Keay, John, *India*, Folio Society, 2003.

Keay's book, with its exceptional coverage of the history of India, was particularly helpful to me when looking at the spread of Buddhism during the reign of Asoka.

Knox, Robert, *An Historical Relation of the Island of Ceylon…*, Tisara Prakasakayo, 1966.

Knox recounts his twenty-year imprisonment – more like house arrest – among the villagers of Kandy. He, his father and some shipmates, had been captured by the King of Kandy's soldiers and held as 'guests' of the king but looked after by the villagers. His accounts of the people, the king, his methods of justice and the way of life of the people shed considerable light on the feudal society that existed probably since the inception of the island's history.

Koenigsberger, H. G., *Early Modern Europe 1500–1789*, The Silver Library, Longman, 1987.

The book provides a wider, European perspective of the first half of European occupation of Sri Lanka. In particular, it shows the rapid advances in a whole range of disciplines during this period and enables the reader who is looking at Asian affairs to appreciate the huge demands on Asian people trying to keep up during a period, in comparison to today, of very poor communications and information dissemination.

Kirk-Greene, Anthony, *On Crown Service. A History of HM Colonial and Overseas Services 1837–1997*, I B Tauris, 1999.

As the title explains, the book provides a good overview of how the overseas civil service of Britain selected and appointed people to serve in her colonies. There is no denying the quality of the people who went out there to administer the countries under British rule. These officers should not be confused with the commercial and other people who went out although, even among them, there were people of outstanding ability – as indeed there were black sheep.

Laqueur, Walter, 'Sri Lanka's Conflict: a General Overview', in Whittaker, David J, *The Terrorism Reader*, Routledge, London and New York, 2003.

This chapter on the Tamil Tigers and the way they organised and managed the movement aimed at gaining independence for the Tamils of Sri Lanka is instructive in many ways. It points out the fact that the motivation was economic not religious, that it was the young who joined and nurtured it and that suicide bombers were used more extensively by the Tamil Tigers (time of writing, 1999) than any other movement worldwide.

Lewis, Bernard, *From Babel to Dragomans: Interpreting the Middle East*, London, Weidenfeld and Nicholson, 2004.

A collection of essays written over a period of half a century and demonstrating a deep understanding of the region. Of special note are the essays 'In Defence of History' and 'Targeted by a History of Hatred'. The latter essay shows that ignoring minor acts of aggression can lead to major ones as the aggressor, thinking as a belligerent bully, regards indifference as acquiescence or timidity. To this extent there is congruence in his thinking with that of Dershowitz about how terrorism should be treated. However, the question needs to be asked, 'Who created the monsters of terrorism?' then the answer points to different approaches, as discussed in 'Covert Action'. This question is less relevant if the creators or sponsors of terrorist groups feel that they would suffer no backlash when the groups began to terrorise rather than act as surrogate warriors for their sponsors.

Lonely Planet Guide to Sri Lanka, eighth edition, Campbell and Niven [ed.], 2001; ninth edition, Plunkett and Ellmor, 2003

These guides are well researched, and the information they contain about the island goes well beyond a 'tourist guide'. All the authors seem to have taken great pains to include interesting facts that they have gleaned during their research for the guides.

Ludowyk, E. F. C., *The Story of Ceylon*, Faber and Faber, 1962.

A beautifully written account of the island's history covering the main periods. His personal knowledge of the many players in the early days of the newly independent Ceylon makes his book of special interest. I believe it must be read by anyone attempting to understand the period immediately following independence. Ludowyk knew many of those he writes about and observed them at close quarters.

Matthews, Bruce, 'Trouble in *Sri Kotha:* Strains and Perils of Democracy in Sri Lanka', *The Round Table,* 322, 1992, pp.215–27

Menand, Louis, The Metaphysical Club: A Story of Ideas in America, Flamingo, 2001.

An extremely interesting overview of how the ideas of people such as Oliver Wendell Holmes, William James, Charles S Peirce and John Dewey shaped modern America. The book shows how the interaction of the ideas of these people influenced their time and left a legacy for future generations of Americans that in the authors view 'changed the way Americans thought – and continue to think – about education, democracy, liberty, justice, and tolerance'. The chapters on pragmatism, pluralism and freedom were of very special interest to me.

Mendis, G. C., *Ceylon Under the British*, Asian Education Services, 2000.

This book first published in 1952 provides a comprehensive record of British Rule in Ceylon from it inception to when the British handed the island over to how it was transformed into a plantation economy with the attendant changes to its laws, infrastructure, and methods of governance and administration. It also shows how the social movement in the UK influenced policies in the Crown colony. A companion volume to this is Calvin R de Silva's *Ceylon Under British Occupation 1795-1833*, which he wrote to obtain his PhD from the University of London in 1932, but first published in 1941.

Mendis, G. C., *The Early History of Ceylon*, Asian Education Series, 1998.

Mr Mendis's book covers the very early history of the island, leaving out the period of European occupation. He, like Knox, provides information about the way of life of the people and dips into the engineering, trading and religious aspects of the island during the 1,500 years up to the arrival of the Portuguese. He writes with the authority of a historian and scholar. Ludowyk says 'The pioneer work in examining the ancient records from a scientific and critical point of view was G C Mendis's *The Early History of Ceylon*'.

Micklethwait, John, and Wooldridge, Adrian, The Company. A short history of a revolutionary idea. Weidenfeld and Nicolson, 2003.

Its coverage of the issues to do with the creation of the East India Companies and their role in imperialism make interesting reading and place the role of these companies in perspective.

Mukherjee, Andy, 'Sri Lanka is repeating past socialist follies'. Bloomberg.com, 14 October 2004

An excellent article that covers a series of critical issues that link the potential for unrest in the country to the lack of opportunity for the youth of the country. Those he quotes in the article seem to have taken a refreshingly new look at the issues of unrest and their causes.

Muttukumaru, Anton, *The Military History of Ceylon: An Outline*, New Delhi, Navrang, 1993

Major General Muttukumaru was the first Sri Lankan to head the Ceylon Army after independence. A question he poses in his book is why the Sinhalese kings did not maintain a strong independent army sourced by the people of the island rather than depend on mercenaries. The other issue he raises is to suggest that prior to the arrival of the Europeans, the island was overshadowed by India and that in many ways the period from 500 BC to AD 1500 was an 'Indian period'. His intimate knowledge of the early leaders of independent Sri Lanka provides useful insights into them. He is, as ever, discrete but it is possible to read approval and disapproval in his comments about them. His comments on the issues to do with the Tamil/Sinhalese issues are worth noting. As a Tamil it is easy to suggest that his views are biased but that would be unfair to him. He does suggest that 'The Tamils had negotiated peacefully with all governments which had governed Sri Lanka since independence but found that no finality had been reached on the issues outstanding.'

Obeyesekere, Gananath (1984). 'The Origins and institutionalization of Political Violence,' in James Manor [ed.] *Sri Lanka in Crisis and Change*. London and Sydney: Croom Helm, pp.153–174.

Palast, Greg, *The Best Democracy Money Can Buy*, Robinson, 2002, 2003

Palast highlights political shenanigans that would make the president of a banana republic blush. Since Palast has not been thrown in prison for libel, one has to take the contents of his book seriously. And if you do, then the picture you get is of democracy being in hock to powerful vested interests in the most powerful country in the world and, worse still, that the disease is spreading to other exemplars of democracy. *See, Bremner, Bird, Fortune and Atkinson 2005.*

Penguin Encylopaedia, Penguin, 2004.

A wonderful source of information on people, events, places, laws, and things scientific, medical and so on. Highly recommended as a first port of call in a long journey of discovery.

Piyadasa, L., *Sri Lanka: The Holocaust and After*. London, Marram Books, 1984.

Ponting, Clive, *World History*, Chatto & Windus, 2000.

The author's treatment of history is very refreshing. It lacks the pedantic element, thus making his book extremely readable and enjoyable. The layout also helps the reader get a comparative perspective of what was happening simultaneously in many countries during a specific period. The sections of particular interest are Parts Five and Six, which cover the period from 1500 to 1900.

Przeworski, A., *Democracy and the Market: Political and Economic Reforms in Eastern Europe and Latin America*, Cambridge University Press, Cambridge and NY, 1991.

Ramamurthy, Anandi, Imperial Persuaders, *Images of Africa and Asia by British Advertising*, Manchester University Press, 2003.

A fascinating insight into the way British colonial planters established brands for their products. Of particular interest was the way Indian and Sri Lankan planters used advertising to establish the superiority of their tea over that of Chinese tea producers.

Rasanayagam, Mudaliyar C, *Ancient Jaffna, being a research into the history of Jaffna from very early times to the Portuguese Period*. Asian Educational Services, 2003.

First published in 1926, it was the first attempt to record the history of Jaffna and its surrounds and to provide information about the kings of Jaffna, its trading links, its pre-history and the lifestyle of its inhabitants. It is a scholarly work that draws on a wide range of sources and was written with pride in his heritage.

Ray, Ellen, and Schaap, William H., [ed.], *Covert Action: The Roots of Terrorism*, Ocean Press, 2003.

The contributors to this book take a rather different view of terrorism, its causes and its proliferation to that taken by Dershowitz. The editors, in their introduction, say that materialism alone does not explain US foreign policy. In their view: "There are more metaphysical forces at play, undercurrents of the US psyche as old as the nation itself. One such theme is US exceptionalism, the notion that the United States is somehow unique, somehow beyond any need for international consensus, somehow entitled to do whatever it wants.' Followers of current world events can only agree, as the US persists in taking a unilateral stance on such issues as global warming, accountability to international law and war crimes obligations and so on.

Renfrew, Colin, and Bahn, Paul, *Archaeology*, Thames & Hudson, 2001.

The authors make specific reference to Sri Lanka in page 185: they refer to the Ramayana and suggest that the 'legend may have its origins in the southward movements of Hindu people after 800 BC. But – as always with oral tradition – the difficulty comes in disentangling history and myth.' They also record in page 363 that finds of Rouletted Ware in Bali, Sri Lanka and, Southern India suggest 'the presence of substantial trade networks linking the two areas by the first century AD.'

Roberts, J. M., *The Penguin History of the World*, third edition, Penguin Books, 1995.

The book provides a wealth of information on peoples, places and governance of nations. A wonderful but exhausting read, and a good starting point for delving into the past.

Reuter, Christoph, *My Life is a Weapon: A Modern History of Suicide Bombing*, Helena Ragg-Kirkby [trans.], Princeton University Press, 2004

The author, a reporter and international correspondent for the German magazine STERN, writes with the intimacy and authority of someone with first hand experience of suicide bombings. His interviews with members of the family, and the community of suicide bombers gives a human face to people whom the world labels as 'terrorists', as if they were individuals with no feelings. In fact, we see individuals who feel compelled to act out of a deep love for their own community, the sense of hurt they feel at the injustices they see perpetrated on them and their people, the helplessness they feel when faced by superior forces and the hopelessness of a long protracted struggle. We read of people who are not demons or psychopaths, but ordinary people driven to extraordinary actions. The author does not ask that we condone their actions but he does suggests that we cannot ignore the pleas of those so affected. The reality is that the developed world consistently ignores or condemns whole communities and races that are still struggling to find their feet, to be recognised as people with legitimate grievances or who attempt to counter the abuses heaped on them by their own governments with or without the help of superior foreign forces.

Senior, Walter Stanley, *The Call of Lanka: Ceylon in Prose and Verse*, Kandy, Trinity College Press, 1960.

A wonderful collection of poems and essays by a man who loved both his God and his 'Foster-Mother' Lanka and saw in the natural beauty of one the exquisite handiwork of the other.

Sim, Stuart, *Fundamentalist world*, Icon Books, 2004

His chapters on religious fundamentalism and nationalist fundamentalism especially his views of martyrdom are worth careful study. A world that is connected by technology is increasingly being fractured by cultural divergence and intolerance. It is as if, the more we see of each other, the more we want to separate from each other. Is familiarity breeding contempt, leading to dislike and distance rather than understanding and cohesion? Perhaps, the people of the world cannot handle the proximity that technology brings. Or, maybe, technology is sweeping away the patina of benevolence and exposing the hypocrisy of our age in a way that no previous age has experienced and this is causing trauma.

Smith, Bardwell L. [ed.], *Religion and the Legitimation of Power in Sri Lanka*, Chambersberg, PA, Anima Books, 1978

Sri Lankan government website, http://www.gov.lk/

This provides considerable information about the governance of the country including publishing the whole constitution and information on the progress of the peace process. Surprisingly devoid of pro-government bias and containing articles such as that about the resignation of Mark Fernando (3 September 2003), a senior judge, which is not at all complimentary about the impartiality of the judicial system of the country and the chief justice.

Strong, John S., *The Buddha: A Short Biography*, Oxford, OUP, 2001.

The book provides an excellent insight into the Lord Buddha, his teachings and their impact on a range of societies and cultures. The coverage is such that it gives the reader an understanding of why Buddhism is considered a way of life, a philosophy, rather than a religion, which enables the follower to absorb the values and truths of Buddhism into their own culture and beliefs. As Huntington points out Buddhism, unlike Islam, Christianity, Hinduism and Confucianism – has not been the base of a 'great civilisation'. Exclusivity was never its aim. This is why the conflict in Sri Lanka, which was instigated and sustained by the Buddhist clergy, is inexplicable to those who understand and value the teachings of Buddhism.

Tampoe, F. M. K., *Liberating Leadership*, The Industrial Society, 1998.

In the summer of 1997, in collaboration with the Industrial Society, I decided to take a bottom-up view of leadership. Unlike most studies in this area that ask leaders (however judged) how they became leaders; we asked followers whether they had experienced leadership in their lives and what form it took. 998 people participated in that study. We learnt that many had not experienced any form of leadership. Others pointed to their peers, family members and strangers as having demonstrated leadership qualities. In most instances leadership was associated with their own sense of powerlessness and the willingness of another to shoulder the burden of providing guidance and emotional, physical and material support.

Turner, Jack, *Spice: The history of a Temptation*, London, HarperCollins, 2004.

A highly readable book on the history of spices. He introduces the reader to spices as natural products, pointing out that their purpose was to protect the tree from insects and danger, and to spices as commodities that fuelled and fed the economies of Europe and, to some extent, triggered off the colonial period between the 1500s and 1940s.

Teeple, John B., *Timelines of World History*, Dorling Kindersley, 2002.

The book provides an invaluable list of what went on where. The list is broken up into four major territories – Asia, Africa, Europe and Americas and Australasia – and provides the year in which specific events took place. It enables corresponding events to be seen at a glance. Hugely valuable as a reference work when researching the past events in many countries across the five continents.

Vittachi, Tarzie, *Emergency '58: The Story Of The Ceylon Race Riots*, Andre Deutsch 1958.

Tarzie Vittachi was the editor of the *Ceylon Observer* and a well-known political commentator and lampoonist whose Sunday articles under the soubriquet 'Flybynight' told it as it was, much to the dismay of the politicians. He wrote the book in August 1958 immediately after the riots, and Collette (a distinguished Sri Lankan cartoonist) did the cartoon. I was fourteen at the time, my brother, Arun, who was studying law remembers, that 'His book was highly thought of as a realistic and faithful account of the 1958 riots. Due to severe press censorship he had to publish the book in the UK in Aug 1958. Considering that the 1958 riots was a Sunday school picnic when compared with the 1983 massacre, it does not have same impact today as it had when first published. It did not endear him to the establishment ... so he left the country for good – Malaysia, I think, and worked there until his death.'

Waites, Bernard, *Europe and the Third World. From Colonisation to Decolonisation, c. 1500–1998*, London, Macmillan, 1999

This interesting book studies the impact of colonialism on the economic and social structure of the indigenous people, especially the claim that Europe got rich at the expense of the 'third world'. It discusses the counter claim that in the round the colonies were a drain on the intellectual and financial capabilities of Europe and that Europe still suffers from, what is now, an ancient legacy.

Weight, Richard and Beach, Abigail, *The Right to Belong: Citizenship and National Identity in Britain, 1930–1960*, I B Taurus, 1998

This book charts how institutions like the Church, the BBC, the Women's Institute, the Ministry of Information and the production of Government Propaganda Films, research organisations like the Political and Economic Planning organisation, Urban Planning, Arts Centres, have helped 'Britain's elite forge a group of disparate peoples into a single powerful nation, using not only economic activity and political legislation, but also art, sport, religion, architecture, philosophy, science and music'.

Wickramasinghe, Nanda, 'Communal protests inflame tensions in eastern Sri Lanka.' World Socialist Web Site, 15 October 2004.

This is an article written from the heart, and the frustration and despair of the writer comes through. Nonetheless the writer does make some very telling points. As John Gray points out, in a twist of Gresham's Law, bad politics is pushing out good politics.

Sri Lanka, World Bank, http://www.worldbank.lk/

This website gives an independent assessment of the economy of the country and points up obstacles to successful economic growth. Generally speaking, it paints a favourable picture of the island, although it does point out that it lags behind Singapore, Korea and Malaysia judged by per capita income – even though it was on a par with these countries in the 1960s.

Worsthorne, Peregrine, *Democracy Needs Aristocracy,* Harper Perennial, 2004

An interesting book that argues not for the return of an aristocracy but that an effective democracy needs leaders who have a strong moral and ethical dimension that prevents them from abusing the power of their office for personal gain. In his view this becomes more important as the ranks of Parliament are filled by compromised career politicians who are subservient to the Whip lest it lose them ministerial opportunities. He also highlights that this compromised political group are complicit in condoning and, sometimes, fostering the erosion of the moral and ethical values of a nation and that eventually they will lose the respect of the electorate and undermine the democratic process.

Printed in the United Kingdom
by Lightning Source UK Ltd.
130248UK00001B/134/P